CAGED

CAGED

ELLISON COOPER

Minotaur Books
New York

CAGED. Copyright © 2018 by Ellison Cooper. All rights reserved. Printed in the United States of America. For information, address St. Martin's Press, 175 Fifth Avenue, New York, N.Y. 10010.

www.minotaurbooks.com

Library of Congress Cataloging-in-Publication Data

Names: Cooper, Ellison, author.
Title: Caged / Ellison Cooper.
Description: First edition. | New York : Minotaur Books, 2018.
Identifiers: LCCN 2018004438| ISBN 9781250173836 (hardcover) | ISBN
    9781250200518 (Canadian) | ISBN 9781250173850 (ebook)
Subjects: LCSH: Serial murder investigation—Fiction. | Women
    detectives—Fiction. | Criminal profilers—Fiction. | GSAFD: Suspense
    fiction. | Mystery fiction.
Classification: LCC PS3603.O582623 C34 2018 | DDC 813/.6—dc23
LC record available at https://lccn.loc.gov/2018004438

Our books may be purchased in bulk for promotional, educational, or business use. Please contact your local bookseller or the Macmillan Corporate and Premium Sales Department at 1-800-221-7945, extension 5442, or by email at MacmillanSpecialMarkets@macmillan.com.

First U.S. Edition: July 2018

First Canadian Edition: July 2018

10 9 8 7 6 5 4 3 2 1

CAGED

ANACOSTIA,
WASHINGTON, D.C.

The D.C. police cruiser idled on an empty residential street. Officer Wilson Tooby sipped his scalding coffee and squinted in the early-morning light. Blooming cherry blossoms arched over the road, casting long shadows along tended lawns and well-kept homes.

Unlike some corners of southeast Washington, this neighborhood was quiet. Idyllic even.

Wilson and his partner, Mike, sat directly out front of the only run-down place in sight.

Wilson leaned toward the passenger seat to get a better look at the abandoned town house. Boarded-up windows and a rotting front porch were common enough in D.C., but he was sure he recognized the rusty green-and-gold FOR SALE sign hanging out front.

"Isn't this the same damn house we checked last week?" he asked.

"What?" Mike slumped over his cell phone, still texting his new girl-friend.

"Remember, we came out for that 911 call. Girl all confused, sounded drugged out."

"Maybe." Mike shrugged.

Mike was the kind of guy who lifted weights obsessively but couldn't run half a mile. Not the best cop Wilson had ever worked with.

Wilson pulled up the file on the dash computer and read the note he'd written twelve days ago. "Yeah, this is it. Was all quiet when we came by."

"What's the call this time?" Mike leaned over to read the computer screen as well.

"Bad smell."

They both looked back up at the town house. Not a good sign.

Wilson tapped the screen and brought up the 911 call. God love newfangled technology. He hit play and a girl's voice filled the car.

"Hello?" in a tentative whisper.

"911, what's your emergency?" the dispatcher barked.

"H . . . hello? Someone please help me."

"What's your emergency, dear?" The dispatcher softened her own voice.

"I don't understand what's happening. There's . . ."

"Where are you, sweetheart?"

"I don't know." She began to cry. "I don't know . . ."

A loud sound shook the speakers in the car, and then the call disconnected.

"That a dog barking?"

"Dunno." Wilson read his own report. The call had come from an old landline that was supposed to be inactive, so they weren't sure where it originated. This address was as close as they could pinpoint, but they weren't sure.

Wilson and Mike had knocked repeatedly. Circled the property. Spoke with a neighbor who said the address was empty, no one coming and going. There was no sign of disturbance and the place was locked up tight. Since they weren't even sure this was the right location, they closed the file. Wilson remembered that had been his daughter's birthday and he'd wanted to get home to her party.

Now people reporting a smell.

"Well, damn," Wilson muttered as he hefted himself out of the car, desperately hoping they weren't about to find some dead addict. The two cops carefully made their way up the uneven stairs and Wilson banged hard on the door.

"Hello. Police. Open up."

As he knocked, the unmistakable stench of dead flesh oozed out around the door.

"Oh damn," he murmured again.

"That ain't good."

"You think?" Wilson was about done with his partner. "Call it in, I'm knocking it down."

While his partner spoke into his radio, Wilson kicked the old door right above the lock. It splintered under his first kick. Despite the circumstance, he couldn't help but let out a "Yeah!" Kicking down a door could be downright embarrassing when it didn't budge.

He stepped in and gagged. Though it was a cool spring day, the air trapped in the house felt thick and hot.

Mike stepped in and retched. "Jesus!"

"Don't puke, man. Step outside if you need to," Wilson said.

"No way I'm clearing this place. Just call in the wagon."

"Can't call it in until we've got a body. Could be a raccoon or something."

Mike cursed.

Wilson's entire body tingled with apprehension. Trusting his instincts, he slid his gun from its holster. Mike raised an eyebrow but did the same.

"Hello?" Wilson called out. He swallowed furiously, fighting the urge to gag again.

They fell into a natural rhythm clearing the house. Wilson moved down the dim hallway, head swiveling back and forth. The first floor was empty. The smell grew stronger and became more acidic in the kitchen. Wilson's eyes watered and he gestured toward a door. Most likely led down to the basement. A shiny new slide bolt stood out against the grimy walls of the town house.

With a nod, Mike slid the bolt. The door swung open and a wave of rancid air ballooned out, enveloping the cops. They both took an involuntary step back and flung their arms up over their noses, guns forgotten.

Through his shirtsleeve Mike called out, "Let's just get down there and find the damned body so we can get out of here!"

He stepped down onto the first stair, looked down as though he'd just stepped on something, and said, "What the—" at the same moment the shotgun hanging just inside the door went off.

Standing directly behind Mike, Wilson was shielded from the full blast. A few pellets hit his left arm and the left side of his face, but it hit Mike head-on.

His partner screamed in pain and instinctively jerked away. With flesh sloughing away from his face and chest, the muscle-bound cop backed into Wilson and both men toppled onto the floor.

COFFEEWOOD
CORRECTIONAL FACILITY, VA

FBI Special Agent Sayer Altair watched the killer through a narrow crack in the door. Dugald Tarlington sat out in the medical unit waiting room perched on a threadbare orange sofa with his head bowed over something in his lap. The man filled the space around him like a mountain forged from solid rock. Thick jowls hung like slabs of meat off his face. Matted blond hair sprung from his head like a bird's nest. Most terrifying were the killer's hands, with fingers like muscled eels.

Shuddering, Sayer took a small step back into the shadows of the exam room and glanced down at his file. It fell open to a photograph of one of Tarlington's victims. The woman's neck was mangled by repeated stranglings as he brought her to the edge of death over and over again. Sayer wrapped her fingers over the thick stack of photos, each one depicting a similar scene. Photos of the four young women Dugald Tarlington had murdered in an unthinkable way.

Under stark fluorescent lights the massive killer's body began to shake gently. The two uniformed guards in the room glanced up but then turned away, bored. Sayer leaned forward to see what Tarlington was looking at. When her weight shifted forward, the floor squeaked.

Tarlington turned toward the sound and Sayer could see tears rolling down his ruddy cheeks.

In his lap, an old JCPenney catalog lay open to a page depicting a cheerful family barbecue. Bile rode up the back of her throat. She had no sympathy for a killer as deranged as Dugald Tarlington.

Putting on a blank face, Sayer pushed through the door.

"Mr. Tarlington, thank you for agreeing to let us go forward with this. Do you understand everything that's about to happen?"

He rubbed away tears while looking back down at the catalog. "Barely even get to see my kids anymore. Eldest is twelve, needs his daddy," he said with a deep southern twang.

Sayer fought the urge to say that he probably shouldn't have killed four innocent people if he'd cared about his kids. Instead she said, "Mr. Tarlington, I need verbal confirmation that you understand what the functional magnetic resonance imaging will entail."

He finally shifted his full attention to her. "You the FBI gal that studies killer brains?"

"I am."

"But"—he paused, studying her—"you're a black lady."

"Thanks for noticing." Sayer bit back further comment. "Do I need to go over the procedure for you again?"

"No, ma'am, I got it. You want to see what the brain of a killer looks like. Am I allowed to ask what you wantin' to find?"

"According to my theory, the front of your brain, your prefrontal cortex, should be far less active than that of a typical male brain. I also theorize that your amygdalae, the glands that control empathy, will be smaller than average."

The killer contemplated this, then gave a short nod. "Good. So when you don't see that in my brain, will you know I'm innocent?"

"That's not how it works, Mr. Tarlington." He looked so sincere it was frightening, but Sayer had read his case file, DNA, fingerprints, the works. A forensic slam dunk. True psychopaths were frighteningly good at manipulating people's emotions, and she was clearly staring into the eyes of a true master.

He frowned in disappointment and ran his slithering fingers over the edge of the catalog. "I'll let you scan my brain if I can keep this."

Sayer's stomach did a flip-flop imagining that he would take some perverse pleasure in the images of young women, but the man was behind bars for the rest of his life, so she nodded. Let him have the damn thing.

"Thank you," he whispered with a crack in his voice. It was almost possible to believe that Dugald Tarlington had actual human emotions.

A few minutes later, the killer slid smoothly into the fMRI machine and Sayer watched on the small computer as it recorded his brain while he looked at a series of images. She pulled out her worry beads and slid the smooth amber pebbles between her fingers. The technician who had traveled from Georgetown University with the fMRI machine hovered over her shoulder, watching the image slowly forming.

"So, how's his brain look?" the technician finally asked.

Sayer frowned. She would obviously have to do a direct comparison, but she'd studied thousands of similar images and she could tell that Dugald Tarlington had been right, his brain looked perfectly normal. She was about to respond with a curt dismissal when her phone buzzed.

"Sayer Altair."

"Sayer, we've got a crime scene and I'm activating your unit. I've already sent an evidence response team and a hazardous-devices squad. I want you to hustle there." FBI Assistant Director Janice Holt sounded pissed. Her perpetual state of being.

"Assistant Director Holt, I'm in the middle of my scan on Tarlington. It should be done in less than an hour."

"Don't care. Research takes a backseat to a case. That's the deal."

Sayer fought the urge to disagree. "Fine." She squeezed the word out in almost-polite form. "What's up?"

"Murder site. At least one body found in the basement of a D.C. town house. Place was booby-trapped. Have two officers injured, one in critical condition."

"Oh no." Sayer's mouth went dry. She knew all too well what it would be like for the families of those cops.

"Yeah, shotgun set up with a trip wire. The scene is trashed. EMTs and DCPD all the hell over the place. But cooler heads eventually prevailed and they called us in."

"Why call us in?"

"They called it, and I quote, 'freaky.' I'm making you lead," Holt said.

Despite Sayer's frustration at being called away from her research, her heart beat faster.

"I want you front and center on this one. I'm sending Vik Devereaux from Crimes Against Children to be your partner since we don't know the age of the victim yet. Don't fuck up." Assistant Director Holt disconnected.

Sayer arranged for the technician to complete Dugald Tarlington's scan and stepped out in the crisp spring evening. She took a deep breath, enjoying the scent of honeysuckle wafting off the rolling hills to the southeast. Her phone rang. The screen said it was her grandmother calling, and Sayer decided she didn't have the energy to talk to the force of nature that was Sophia McDuff.

Ignoring the call, she let herself feel the potent mix of apprehension and excitement every murder case brought. With a quick look at her GPS, she pulled on her helmet, revved her motorcycle to life, and roared out of the parking lot.

CRIME SCENE, P STREET, WASHINGTON, D.C.

A cluster of gawkers gathered along the crime scene tape. In the fading daylight, the ring of curious faces strobed red and blue in the flashing lights.

FBI Special Agent Vik Devereaux stood on the porch. His pale skin looked like a white balloon floating on top of a rumpled dark suit. The man had perpetual bags under his eyes and slightly hunched shoulders but managed to pull off the scruffy-yet-handsome-detective thing despite his undertaker vibe.

Sayer ducked beneath the police tape and raised a hand in greeting. "Looks like you're my partner on this, eh, Vik?"

"Hey, hotshot." Vik nodded, grim-faced. His comment wasn't meant as a compliment. Like Sayer, Vik was a special agent with the FBI's Critical Incident Response Group. The units there coordinated all the agency's serial killer investigations and risk management for things like school shootings and random gunmen. Though Ph.D.s were common at the FBI, most academic types were psychologists and a lot of agents didn't see the need for a neuroscientist on staff. It didn't help her popularity that Sayer was moving up the ranks faster than most. But Vik had a good reputation, known around the office as totally unflappable in high-stress situations. Sayer hoped he would handle being second fiddle.

"What've we got?" Sayer asked as she peeled off her leather jacket and sat on a low chair to gear up.

"We've got a nightmare is what we've got," he said with his mild Cajun accent. "Bomb squad had to go in and clear it and they tramped all over the place. Plus the EMTs up here with the injured cops. Thinking maybe we should just call in a zydeco dance troupe to perform a step routine while we're at it." He ran fingers through floppy brown hair. "Anyway, body's still in place while we wait for Joan to finish up and give the go-ahead to move her."

"Her?"

"Yeah, victim looks like a female. Could be young."

"Oh shit," Sayer said, pulling her puff of curls into a tight head wrap.

"Yeah. Anyway, rest of the house is empty, real show's down in the basement. It's pretty bad; you got any tricks to keep from puking, I'd use 'em."

"Nah." Part of Sayer's degree included a lot of medical work and she'd seen plenty of gore. Like anyone working with dead bodies, she could pull that curtain in her mind between her humanity and what she was about to see. A terrible truth, but necessary for her sanity. She'd seen what happened to people whose mental curtains weren't as solid as they thought. No other way to do the job unless you were a psychopath yourself.

"So," Vik continued, flipping open his notebook, "911 call twelve days ago. Young girl saying she was confused but then the call cut off. They couldn't trace an exact location. Thought it might originate near here. Uniforms did a routine check, banged on some doors, assumed it was some tweaker calling in high as a kite. Place looked deserted so they left."

"Oh man." Sayer checked for loose objects on her person, then finally pulled on a pair of gloves.

"I know!" He drew out the *I* so it sounded more like *aaaah*. "So, call comes in today about a bad smell. Same two cops kick in the door. Smell's coming from the basement. Guy trips a wire on the stairs rigged up to a shotgun. Blasts the poor guy full on. His partner took some rock too, but he'll be fine. First guy not so much. He's listed as critical."

Sayer and Vik moved slowly along the hall toward the kitchen in back, where two evidence technicians knelt on the floor.

She paused at the top of the stairs looking down into the basement. The shotgun still hung in place, where it would be recovered later. Floodlights shone up the wooden staircase, casting a long shadow behind Sayer across the bloody floor. The scent of death hung in the air like ancient creosote.

"Why call us in? One of their guys down, thought the DCPD would want to handle it themselves."

"You'll see. Nothing's been removed yet. Not even the dog," Vik said.

"The dog?"

"I know, right? They found a goddamned puppy down there."

"A dog," Sayer repeated as she descended into the basement.

The stairs came out at one end of a large windowless room. Floodlights glared off the concrete floor and plain brick walls. Across the room, FBI Chief Medical Examiner Joan Warren stood in front of a massive iron cage that hung from the ceiling. The cage looked like something you would expect to find in a torture chamber beneath the Tower of London. Big enough for a large animal, the black iron gave the cage an old-world Gothic feel. It hung from an equally heavy-looking black chain bolted to the ceiling on a shiny new hook.

Joan leaned into the open cage, hunched over something at the bottom. Though Sayer couldn't see her face, she knew that the medical examiner's expression would be the same serene smile she wore at every crime scene. Of all the people at Quantico, Joan was the only one who didn't seem to need a mental curtain to work with the dead. She firmly believed that people passed on to a better place. At every autopsy, Joan's face radiated with the comfort of a person tending to the mortal remains of a someone whose spirit had departed to heaven or nirvana or wherever they went. Sayer sure wished she could have some faith in that idea; maybe it would blunt the horror.

Ignoring Joan and the cage for the moment, Sayer turned her focus back to the room. She liked to have the whole scene in mind before she went to see the victim. She stood perfectly still, her only motion her fingers sliding over the string of amber worry beads in her pocket. The rest of the room was empty.

Two evidence techs hunched together near the bottom of the stairs. They greeted Sayer with strained smiles and she recognized Ezra, a young man with blue hair and a few dozen piercings. He held a wriggling puppy wrapped up to its neck in a cloth collection bag while the other tech kept trying to roll a lint brush over the dog's face.

The puppy let out a series of yips, tail wagging wildly against the bag.

Ezra let out an exasperated groan. "Hi, Special Agent Altair. I can't process this dog here. I've bagged him, but we need to get him back to the lab to finish." Whimpering slightly, the dog stopped wiggling but kept trying to lick Ezra's hand.

"You're the expert, Ezra. One of you take the dog now; the rest of you can finish up here."

A third tech with a camera made a slow circuit of the basement, flash strobing as he took pictures.

With a deep breath, Sayer finally approached the cage. Back when Sayer started graduate school, she'd felt a dark thrill with every serial killer case she joined. The allure was impossible to resist, the brutality mesmerizing in its horror. Now she felt nothing but sick. Every victim tore another small hole in the curtain in her mind, making it harder and harder to cut off her feelings and objectively view the dead women and children that the monsters she hunted left behind.

"Unusual." She pointed at the cage.

Vik hung back, letting her move forward without him. "Yeah, maybe we can trace its origin."

This was their first scene together, and Sayer was grateful Vik wasn't a crowder or a chatter. Because of her research, Sayer wasn't assigned a full-time partner, and she never quite knew what to expect when she was stuck with someone new. Nothing worse than people who couldn't shut up over a dead body.

"Now you see why they called us in." Vik's voice sounded flat.

Without looking over at Vik, Sayer nodded and stepped next to the medical examiner.

"Hear you're heading up this one," Joan said over her shoulder. Joan always gave off a little bit of a Stepford Wife aura: a dirty-blond, perfectly coiffed, cardigans-and-knee-length-skirts kind of lady.

"Looks like."

The medical examiner glanced up from the body. "Good."

Sayer forced herself to stare at the victim. Though decomposition was well under way, her clothes and hair clearly suggested female. Simple sneakers that were once white, filthy jeans, and a purple T-shirt that said THIS PRINCESS SAVES HERSELF in green block letters. Slightly matted blond hair spread out from her head, a few strands curling down through the slats of the iron cage. Clumps of newspaper rotted in one corner, clearly where the girl had been forced to relieve herself.

"So, what've we got?"

"Well, caveat as usual . . ."

"I know, this isn't your final report."

"Right, so, keeping in mind this is just a preliminary take . . . I'm thinking she's between sixteen and twenty, general good health, probably died of dehydration." Joan worked with practiced motions, wrapping collection bags over each of the girl's hands.

Sayer said nothing, knowing Joan would continue if she had anything else.

"Note the bite marks along her arms and legs."

"Dog in there with her?"

"Yep, though unclear if they are dog bites."

Sayer's lips curled up into a grimace.

Joan continued, "I'd say she's been dead about six days."

Sayer calculated backward. "How long you think she could've gone without food or water?"

Joan shrugged. "Food, she could go for weeks; it's lack of water that would kill her. How long that takes would depend on a lot of things. How hot it got down here. What her health was like beforehand. Too many factors to guess. My—"

"I know, your preliminary assessment."

"Probably a little less than a week. Five to seven days tops."

Sayer rubbed her hand over her chin. Six days plus a week. "The cops got a call out to this address twelve days ago. Maybe they spooked the kidnapper and he just never risked coming back."

"Timing would work." Joan's frown creased her narrow face.

After processing the scene, Sayer and Vik emerged from the house and stood together on the porch. Her phone rang and Sayer glanced down, just another call from her nana. The woman would not stop pestering her about coming by for a family dinner. Rather than deal with the guilt trip, Sayer clicked off the ringer.

"We should head back to the office," Sayer said. "Holt wants an update and I suspect she's already throwing together a task force."

"Want me to get a statement from the cop?" He pointed to D.C. police officer Wilson Tooby, leaning against the bumper of his patrol car, still surrounded by an ambulance and half a dozen cop cars. Even from the porch, Sayer could see his hands trembling. His face pinched into a geography of sorrow like a man trying desperately not to cry.

"Nah, I'll go talk to him. Meet you at Quantico."

One of the things any good investigator understands is people. Wilson was clearly shaken and he was more likely to open up to her.

"Officer Tooby?"

He flashed an attempt at a greeting but his hand barely moved. "FBI?"

"Yes, sir. Special Agent Sayer Altair. I need to get a statement from you if you're up for talking."

"Sure. Sure." He seemed to be reassuring himself.

Sayer leaned against the car next to him so he wouldn't have to look at her while he spoke.

"So, you got a call twelve days ago," she prompted.

"We sure did. They're saying they found a dead kid in there." He stared up at the town house and said nothing more.

Sayer let the silence stretch for a minute, then answered, "That's right. One victim, appears to be female, late teens."

Tooby was unable to keep it together; tears squeezed out of the corners of his eyes. "That poor kid. She tried to call for help and it was my job to save her. She was right there, probably heard us pounding on the door. Maybe she thought it was all over. That we'd be right down to help her. Instead, I walked away. Left that poor girl to die because I was anxious to get home to my own kid." His shoulders collapsed. "And my partner. That asshole was the worst cop I've ever worked with, and he goes and accidentally saves my damned life." He let out a barking laugh. "Isn't that just the most assholish thing ever."

Sayer put a hand on his forearm. "You want me to say some platitudes here like it wasn't your fault? You couldn't have known? I can reassure you with some bullshit if you'd like."

He let out another short bark of laughter. "I can do without the pep talk."

They sat in silence until his tremors stopped. "I'm afraid I don't have much to share."

"The first time you came out, did anything look suspicious at all?"

"Nothing. We spoke with one neighbor and some buyer."

"Buyer?"

"Yeah, some guy trying to rabbit around us. Looked nervous as hell but was probably just here to score drugs."

Sayer contemplated. Drug sales weren't unusual in the area, but she'd follow up anyway. "Let's get a sketch of the guy you saw. I'll send over our artist tomorrow. Anything else?"

Wilson wrung his hands together twice before quieting them. "Sorry, Agent Altair, I've got nothing else. Just a sackload of guilt that I'll be lugging around for the rest of my days."

Sayer handed him a card. "All right, call if you think of anything."

"Agent Altair," he called out as she walked away.

She turned.

"Will you let me know? I mean, would you tell me when . . . how?" He gestured to the town house.

"I'll fill you in on the details if you're sure you want to know."

He closed his eyes but nodded. "I'm sure."

FBI HEADQUARTERS,
QUANTICO, VA

Sayer roared south on her motorcycle along I-95 toward Quantico, Virginia. The FBI headquarters housed the training academy for new agents next to the National Center for the Analysis of Violent Crime, which coordinates FBI involvement in counterterrorism, risk management, serial crimes, and crimes against children. At the Behavioral Research and Instruction Unit, Sayer conducted research on the neurology of violence. Her mind wandered to her research as she drove. She hoped to find clear neurological deficiencies in murderers' brains. So far she had scanned twelve men, and two of them didn't support her theory. Or maybe three after Dugald Tarlington. That meant that three out of twelve didn't fit her hypothesis. Which probably meant that her theory was utter bullshit.

But her research didn't matter right now. Sayer refocused her attention on the girl. Righteous fury flamed like a wildfire in her gut.

At Quantico, she passed the security checkpoint and parked in the half-empty lot. Sayer made her way up to Holt's office on the top floor of the Behavioral Analysis Unit. Holt's assistant was gone, so Sayer poked her head through the assistant director's door.

"Finally." Janice Holt didn't bother with small talk. Her demeanor, coupled with her cropped gray hair, hatchet face, and severe power suits straight out of the eighties were why people often referred to her as an old battle-ax. A nickname she welcomed.

"So?"

"One dead body, late-teens girl probably killed by dehydration. Left to die in a cage with an animal."

"Animal?"

"A puppy."

"Your gut says this is a serial."

"I'd say so. Ritualistic elements for sure." Sayer paused. "I think there's a good chance our guy got spooked after the cops came to check out a 911 call."

"Call?"

"Yeah, the girl must've gotten hold of a phone somehow. She called for help but got cut off. Uniforms found nothing amiss and didn't follow up."

"Shit."

"Yeah. We think he never went back after that. Killing might not be his primary goal."

"Well, that's not exactly comforting," Holt said. "Not much you can do tonight. I'll pull the task force together, meeting set for six A.M. tomorrow. Check in with Joan and the evidence lab, let them know I want them to have something for us by morning. Then you go get some sleep. It'll be the last you get for a while." Holt smiled. Her wrinkled jowls made the smile look more like a predator baring its teeth.

Making her way through the complex, Sayer punched her personal code into the security door and strode to the lab, the massive, mirrored building that housed the most advanced crime lab in the world.

First stop, the medical examiner's block. Multiple autopsy rooms lined the narrow yellowish hall that branched off to the left. Sayer peeked into the first room and found Joan and two assistants bustling around a sealed body bag at the center of the sterile room.

"Anything new?" Sayer asked from the doorway.

Joan dismissively waved a gloved hand at her. "Nope, just got here."

"Holt says to work through the night. We've got a task force meeting at six A.M."

Joan let out a huff. "Like she had to tell me to work through on this one."

Sayer chuckled and moved on toward crime scene analysis. She wound through the warren of labs until she found Ezra organizing a series of plastic bags on a large stainless steel table. His row of eyebrow piercings and cobalt hair made him look more like a hipster malingering around Adams Morgan in downtown D.C. than an evidence recovery tech with the FBI. Though Sayer knew well enough that plenty of people didn't think thirty-something brown-skinned women looked like FBI agents either.

"Hey, Ezra. Anything new?" Sayer called out.

"Agent Altair." The tech greeted her with a broad smile. "I just started processing the stuff we got off the dog. The rest of the team's in the next room if you want to follow up with them, but so far we've got nothing."

"All right, just let them know that Holt wants you to work through the night. Task force meeting at six A.M., so write up whatever you've got before then."

"Will do."

Sayer turned to go.

"Oh hey," Ezra said, "what should I do with the dog?" He pointed to his feet, where the puppy was curled up on a towel leaning against the tech's ankles. "He's slightly dehydrated but otherwise seems fine. We'll need to keep him until trial, just in case. There's an impound for animals up in D.C., but I can't go now and there's no way I can let him stay here all night. While I was processing him it was fine, but now that I've got everything I need, he's a potential source of con-tamination. You've got to get him out of here."

"Me?"

"Unless you want to ask Holt?" He gave her a wink.

Sayer gave him a fake grimace. "Fine, smart-ass. I'll take the thing home and drop him at the impound tomorrow, I guess."

She approached the puppy. "Uh, it's friendly?"

"Totally."

"Do I need to say something to it or . . ."

Ezra stopped what he was doing and looked up. "Never had a dog before, eh?"

"This is true."

"He definitely needs a lot of water, probably needs something more to eat. I gave him some of my sandwich but he's way underfed. Prob-ably needs a bath too."

"All right. Oh, did you make an impression of its teeth? Joan found bites on the victim. Might need to compare bite marks."

"I sure did, but I doubt that dog did the biting. I found hair in his mouth; looks like rat hair to me, though I still need to process it. I'd bet the farm that the dog was protecting the girl from rats. Probably what kept him alive so long. Yummy rat nutrients."

Sayer rolled her eyes at Ezra, then awkwardly lifted the sleep-ing puppy in her arms. He stirred and settled in against her body. His gangly limbs and oversized paws made him look like a snoring muppet.

Out in the parking lot she lowered the sleeping dog into her motor-cycle's sidecar, hoping he would stay put.

"Hey, dog, this is a fancy vintage Silver Hawk, so let's keep the slobber to a minimum."

The puppy woke, gave her a groggy yip of excitement, and sat up in the seat, eyes forward like he'd ridden there his entire life. A thin whip of drool slowly fell from his mouth onto the deep-blue leather seat. With a sigh, Sayer revved the bike and made her way to the highway. The wind blew back the puppy's floppy ears and his tongue lolled out. Sayer would've sworn that the dog smiled as they took off toward home.

ALEXANDRIA, VA

The moon shone on the mountains as Sayer wound her way toward Alexandria. Sayer preferred taking the single-lane highways through the Virginia countryside. Towering trees choked with kudzu and honeysuckle vines blanketed the landscape in shades of smoky blue. The rumble of the old bike and the whistling wind around her helmet drowned out all other sound, quieting her mind.

She hated this point in an investigation—the urgent need to do something tempered by the fact that there wasn't anything she *could* do. Real investigations were rarely like TV shows where they pop something into a machine and get useful forensics ten seconds later. Or the neighbor has that perfect memory of the unknown subject knocking on the victim's door. Or even the video surveillance camera catching the perfect image of the doer. Most investigations took a day or two to ramp up. Until then she had no forensics to analyze, no witnesses to interview in the middle of the night, nothing to do but sit on her hands and wait for the ball to get rolling. Drove her crazy.

Eyes burning with fatigue, Sayer finally pulled into her driveway. Her apartment took up the top floor of a historic row house on one of the few cobbled streets still remaining in Alexandria. The dog paused to pee in the small garden, then cheerfully followed on her heels up the staircase to her private entrance on the second floor.

Inside, Sayer threw a whole package of hot dogs in the microwave in her otherwise bare kitchen. She took a quick shower while the dog explored the apartment, sniffing around half-unpacked boxes and the single, threadbare futon in the living room. The dog eventually stuck his nose into the shower and, after cocking his head to the side to assess the situation, enthusiastically jumped in.

"Dammit, dog! Get out." But the puppy frolicked around her feet, almost knocking her over. Giving up, Sayer decided the dog could use a good washing, so she lathered him with shampoo and let the caked-on gore wash away, revealing silvery fur under the muck.

They toweled off; she ate one hot dog and tossed the rest to the dog. After he scarfed the food, she closed him in the bathroom with a bowl of water for the night.

The dog immediately began whining and scratching as she settled into bed and clicked off the light.

Scratch, scratch. Whine, whine.

Sayer glanced over at the framed photo on the box next to her bed. She couldn't see the image in the dark, but she knew it was of her and Jake hiking at Yosemite what felt like a million years ago. For just a moment she let herself remember how it felt to be so connected to another person.

That was before the night she got the call that every family member of every law enforcement officer dreaded—agent down. Jake killed in the line of duty.

She shoved those agonizing feelings back behind the wall she had created in her heart after her parents died, the wall that protected her from dangerous feelings like love and trust.

Sayer closed her eyes, willing sleep to come.

Whine. Scratch.

She listened to the pathetic dog for ten minutes before throwing off the blanket with frustration. She sat up and put her head in her hands. "All right, Sayer, your research is going to crap. A young girl was murdered. An officer almost killed. You watched not one but two adult men cry today. You now have an annoying dog keeping you awake. Truly the perfect life you've built for yourself."

She stalked to the bathroom and flung open the door.

"Fine, you win, you foul beast."

With a yip of excitement the puppy scrambled onto her small mattress. After a few turns, he settled with a rumble of contentment.

Sayer curled herself around his warm body and fell into a deep sleep.

Still stuck in the Evidence Analysis Lab, Ezra swigged acrid coffee and flipped through the crime scene photos on the computer. Over a hundred images of the cage, the barren basement, the dead girl. He glanced up at the clock. Almost 4:00 A.M. and he still had to write everything up before 6:00. He clacked his tongue stud along his teeth to keep himself awake as he stared at the screen.

On autopilot, his brain took a second to register something strange. Shaking his head, he went back to the previous image and squinted, trying to figure out what he was seeing. The cage took up half the frame, but along the wall behind it, a flare shone from the grout between two bricks. Ezra enlarged the image. Sure enough, something was reflecting the flash, creating a glint of light.

"Hey, Cindy, come here and look at this," Ezra called loud enough for the techs in the next room to hear him.

Cindy peeked around the corner. "What's up?"

"Come look at this photo. I think the flash might be reflecting off something in the wall."

She bent over him at the table to take a closer look, and Ezra thought about last night. They had just started sleeping together, and he wondered if it might be something more than sex. She smelled of stale coffee and chemicals, which made him smile.

He reached up and tucked a strand of thin blond hair behind her ear. She swatted him away. "Not at work!" She focused on the photo. "I think you're right. Let's go check it out."

"Now?"

"Yeah, we're going to have to go back today anyway. Let's go now so we can write it up before the task force meeting. It could be important."

After leaving a quick message on Sayer's voice mail, the evidence techs drove the van back up to D.C.

The residential street was deep in slumber when they arrived. The barest hint of sunrise glowed on the horizon.

A single D.C. police officer sat outside in his car keeping an eye on the scene. He recognized them and gave a nod as they made their way into the town house.

Ezra pulled aside the door propped against the entry. A rat scurried across the floor. The smell of death lingered in the air.

With a flashlight they descended the creaking stairs and clicked on the floodlights still in the basement. Ezra held up the printed image so they could figure out exactly where it was taken. They circled the room until the image lined up. Cindy hurried to the wall and found a small hole.

"There really is something here," she whispered, even though they were alone.

"What do you think? A camera lens or something? But where would it lead?" Ezra looked around. "I looked at the floor plans and there's no basement next door, so where would the camera be? Maybe it's wireless, but there would have to be some kind of receiver nearby."

"A false wall? Or maybe an entry somewhere else in the house?"

Cindy's voice cracked with excitement. This was every evidence tech's dream, the big find everyone else missed.

They circled the room in opposite directions.

Cindy walked over and squatted next to a plywood wall that covered the back of the stairs.

"Hey, check this out." She slid her fingers along a seam between two boards.

Ezra looked up just as she pushed.

"No, don't!" he shouted.

The panel swung inward.

Ezra held his breath.

Nothing.

He let out a puff of air. "God, Cindy, didn't you see that the guy rigged a shotgun on the stairs? Be careful."

"Yeah, sorry." Cindy didn't look sorry at all. Her eyes glowed with the thrill of discovery. "Come check this out."

Ezra squeezed next to her and looked into the crawl space underneath the stairs. Just inside, a metal hatch sat in the concrete floor.

They stared for a moment, contemplating their next move.

"We've got to call Holt and Sayer," Ezra said.

As he pulled out his phone, three staccato clangs echoed up from the hatch, then three slow clangs, and three fast again. Over and over.

"What is that?" Cindy cocked her head.

"Someone down there hitting a metal pipe or something? Too regular to be old pipes."

They listened, ears buzzing, and it struck Ezra like lightning. "That's SOS in Morse code!"

"What?"

"Yeah, SOS, someone's down there calling for help!"

Cindy stepped forward into the crawl space and thumped her foot hard on the hatch. The reverberation sounded like a huge drum being struck.

A faint young girl's voice echoed up from the floor. "Is someone there? Please help me!"

Cindy looked up, wide-eyed. "You call it in while I go down."

Before he could even shout for her to stop, Cindy yanked open the hatch.

The world exploded.

Bang bang bang!

Sayer bolted up in bed. The dog flew toward the front door, growling all the way.

Bang bang!

"Sayer?" Vik called through the door.

She stalked to the door and yanked it open. The puppy stood at her side, hackles up.

"What?" she barked.

Vik paused for a moment, looking up at her wild hair, then down at her red flannel pajamas and the snarling puppy pressed to her leg.

"Uh"—he fought a smile—"the task force meeting is in forty minutes and you weren't answering your phone. Thought I'd swing by on my way to make sure you're up. See if you want a ride."

Wide awake with adrenaline coursing through her system, she blinked a few times. "Settle down, boy." She rested her hand on the puppy's head. "What time is it?"

"It's five twenty."

"What?" Sayer hadn't slept past 4:00 since Jake was killed. She didn't even own an alarm. Her phone displayed seven missed calls and two messages, one from Ezra the evidence tech and one from Nana. Even though the ringer was off, it was set to vibrate and she couldn't remember the last time she slept through a call.

"Guess I slept in." She moved aside and gestured him in. "I'll take a ride. No need to both drive. You want some coffee?"

"Sure." He cautiously stepped inside.

"Great, you can make it while I get dressed."

Sayer shut her bedroom door, and Vik stared after her in disbelief. Grumbling, he rifled through her kitchen and started the coffee.

"When did you move in?" he asked, eyeing the half-unpacked boxes and barren living room.

From her room Sayer shouted, "I've been here almost three years."

"Three years?"

Sayer came out dressed in black boots, slim jeans, white cotton button-up, and burgundy leather jacket.

"Sayer, you know this isn't how adults live, right?" He gestured to her apartment. "I'm a confirmed bachelor and I have more furniture than you."

"Whatever, get yourself some coffee and let's go."

"You gonna let the dog out to pee at least?"

"Oh damn, what am I going to do with this thing? I'm sure the impound isn't open yet." She yanked the door, and the dog ran down to the garden to relieve himself.

"Good morning!" a voice called from below. Sayer went to the balcony and waved at her downstairs neighbor. A stout, middle-aged man, Antonio de la Vega sat at their shared patio table, wire-frame glasses perched on his nose, black coffee and a book in one hand, puppy pressed against the other.

"Since when do you have a dog?" Tino playfully ruffled the dog's ears.

"He's not mine, from a case I'm working on. I'm taking him to the FBI impound later today."

Her neighbor gasped. "Oh no, no, you can't take this adorable little creature to the pound!"

"We have to keep him somewhere for a case. You want him?"

"No, sorry, I'm not . . . I mean, my life right now won't accommodate . . ."

"Neither will mine." Sayer whistled and the dog completely ignored her.

"Why don't you let him stay down here with me. I can at least keep an eye on him for you today," Tino said.

Relieved, Sayer forced a smile. "That would be great. I'll owe you one. I'll try to send someone by to take him away later today."

Her neighbor sniffed with displeasure. "I've got him; go save the world, Dr. FBI."

Sayer and Vik took off in his old Nissan toward Quantico. They rode in silence until both their phones rang at once.

CRIME SCENE, P STREET, WASHINGTON, D.C.

Sayer stood among the charred ruins of the basement, barely listening to the hazardous-devices tech talking to her. Sayer and Vik had rushed up to the crime scene. Ezra and Cindy were both already in ambulances pulling away as they drove up. Her eyes kept wandering to the blood smears along the concrete floor and she pictured Ezra. She really liked that damned kid.

"The bomb was set up to go off when someone opened the hatch. A small but powerful charge," the tech said.

"And you've cleared below?" Sayer leaned forward and stared down into the hole blackened with soot from the hot fire that burned after the explosion.

Before he could answer, the audio recording began to play again. First an SOS banged out on a metal pipe, then a girl's voice crying, "Is someone there? Please help me!"

"And that just keeps playing over and over?" Sayer asked.

"Yeah, was rigged to start playing as soon as the plywood door to the crawl space was opened. Now it just goes off every twenty minutes."

"Which is why Ezra and Cindy must've opened the hatch." Sayer looked at the blood one more time. "So what should I expect down there?"

"Single room, looks like it was probably someone's bomb shelter from the cold war. Also has a sealable door that drops into the sewer. We've got two guys down in the sewers now, but it looks like our guy could've come and gone that way without being seen."

Vik appeared next to her. "Let's check it out."

He climbed down the stairs, his face in a tight frown. Sayer followed reluctantly, not particularly fond of tight underground spaces.

At the bottom, the cramped room barely gave them enough space to stand side by side. Only about ten feet long, it wasn't much. Concrete walls and floor, single exhaust fan along one side, and an open hatch in the floor where the sewer ran. A folding table sat at the end stacked with electronics.

A photograph hung from the wall above the equipment. From across the room, Sayer could tell it was of a young woman in a cage.

"I talked to the tech guy; he says this is recording equipment, video and audio," Vik said. "Far enough from the fire that it wasn't damaged. Stuff's fairly high-end but not fancy enough to be traceable. The main room was video-recorded here and the data stored on the hard drive here, but the perp could have downloaded the video stream remotely."

Sayer stepped up to the wall and leaned in to see the photo better. It wasn't of the girl they had found in the basement above them. Different room, different girl. A second victim.

A teen in black T-shirt and jeans looked clean in the photo. She had her face turned slightly away from the camera, but Sayer could just make out the tears staining her coppery skin. In her hands she clutched a tabby kitten.

Her collapsed body language made Sayer's stomach clench.

"Dammit," Sayer said again. "We've got at least one more victim."

Underneath the photograph, a series of symbols marred the wall in dark brown. Runes or Japanese kanji or something? Maybe painted in dried blood?

"What is this, some kind of cult thing?" She gestured to the symbols.

"No clue," Vik said, furiously chewing on his bottom lip.

Sayer nodded slowly, still staring at the photo and symbols.

"Let's let the evidence team get in here. I want to find out how Ezra and Cindy are doing, and then we need to get our task force going so we can nail this guy to the wall. With real nails."

Vik grunted with approval. "One other thing. The tech guy said there was a single file uploaded remotely to the hard drive. Looks like our friend left us a video to watch."

Sayer strongly suspected that she did not want to see what was on that video.

UNKNOWN LOCATION

The girl tried to open her eyes. The tang of metal filled her mouth. The sound of the kitten mewling was all she could hear.

One of her eyes finally cracked open.

The thick smoke was long gone and the monster hadn't been back in so long that thirst constricted her throat. Made it hard to think about anything but water. Water flowing across her cracked lips, wetting her dry mouth, filling her sour stomach. Her body ached and craved and shuddered, like it was collapsing from the inside out.

At least there were no more nightmare pictures. Gaping monsters and fanged cats clawing at her flesh. They felt so real.

But now the monster was gone. Called her a failure, left her to die of thirst in this cage.

The other eye opened and she leaned forward to cry, though no tears fell.

In the darkness all she felt was the weakening heartbeat of the kitten under her fingers. Bast hadn't had food or water either. She would die first. Bast's dry sandpaper tongue licked her peeling skin as she gratefully faded away.

FBI HEADQUARTERS, QUANTICO, VA

Sayer and Vik parted ways back at the offices in Quantico. Sayer made her way to Assistant Director Holt's office for a quick one-on-one before the task force meeting.

She peeked into Holt's office and momentarily wondered if the woman slept sitting up at her desk.

"Morning."

"Come in." Holt looked haggard, her body wound tight with emotion.

"Have you heard from the hospital yet?"

Holt's face was grim, and Sayer's stomach fell.

"Cindy Fields was killed immediately in the blast. Ezra is . . ." Holt paused. "Ezra lost both his legs. He's still in surgery but it looks like he'll pull through."

Sayer blew out a shaky breath and sagged against a chair. She could barely picture Cindy, slender, always serious, but that was all she could really remember. And Ezra, goofy young kid, great evidence tech, endless smart-ass.

"Shit." Sayer struggled to not react. It dredged up feelings that she worked every day to keep in check. Her mind flitted to Jake.

She'd been home working on paperwork at their kitchen table among the joyful detritus of everyday life. Dirty dishes and empty wineglasses in the sink from a shared meal the night before. Photos of their happy courtship hung on the wall behind her.

When the phone rang, Sayer hoped it was Jake calling. She knew he was almost done with his deep-cover operation.

She'd known as soon as she heard the soft sorrow in Holt's voice. Jake was never coming home, killed in action, an honor to the FBI and his country. Sayer hadn't cried. Not during the funeral. Not as they hung his name in the FBI Hall of Honor. Not as she packed their joyful photos and drove all of Jake's clothes to Goodwill. In fact, Sayer hadn't cried a single tear since that phone call three years before.

But now, an agent killed on her case felt like someone tearing open an almost-healed scab from her heart. A gasp threatened to escape her lips.

Holt cleared her throat. "Anyway, looks like Cindy and Ezra found us a break. Now we use it to find the bastard that killed one of my agents." Holt squinted one eye, thinking. Coming to a conclusion, she continued, "You've shown me that you're up to the task. In fact, you've done nothing but exemplary work, which is why I think it's time for a promotion. As of right now you're officially Senior Special Agent Altair."

A promotion on the wave of anger and sorrow Sayer felt made no sense.

Holt gave her the squinty-eyed look again. "Don't make me regret it. I've given you the best team we've got. Vik will be your second. You've got a full analysis and data team. I've assigned Andy to be your profiler."

Her tempest of emotion promptly crashed into dismay. "Andy Wagner?"

"Yeah."

Sayer groaned. Andy Wagner believed he was God's gift to the FBI. He also believed that any woman who didn't love his distasteful jokes was just a sour-grapes feminist with no sense of humor. His arrogance had exponentially increased recently after he landed a book deal.

Andy was not going to like the fact that Sayer was now equal to him.

"You'll work with whoever I tell you to," Holt continued.

"Yes, ma'am." Sayer swallowed her annoyance. Despite being hard to work with, Andy was a rock star in the world of profiling and he was on a streak, cracking cases left and right. Hell, Sayer would work with the devil himself if she thought good ole Beelzebub could help her find that missing girl before she starved to death . . . if she hadn't already.

Slurping the dregs of coffee from her massive travel mug, Sayer strode down to the conference room.

Vik and a data analyst had already started the murder board. The analyst was arranging photos of the crime scene along the whiteboard, including a blowup of the image of their second victim, a girl trapped in another cage at a crime scene they hadn't found yet. Sayer wondered who she was and if she was still alive in some dark basement, afraid. Or was she already dead too?

Joan sat at the far end of the table. The medical examiner looked tired but she held a stack of paper, a good sign.

All the other agents from Sayer's unit and the few DCPD officers in the room wore tight grimaces of tension and anger. Cindy and Ezra were on everyone's mind.

Andy wasn't there. Profiling rock star though he might be, he was late for the meeting.

"All right, let's get started. You've all read the basics?" Sayer asked. Everyone nodded.

"This has gone from a standard murder investigation to something way more personal. Our perp has injured and killed multiple officers, so everyone be on high alert. Holt's throwing resources at us, so let's be strategic. We'll meet at the start and finish of every day to make sure we're on the same page until this case is closed. Right now the secondary scene at the town house in D.C. is still being processed. They'll send someone here as soon as they get anything and will be updating us as they analyze everything they found in the bunker."

Sayer took a deep breath. "I've got one of our artists over with Officer Tooby getting a sketch of the guy he saw at the scene twelve days ago, though that's looking like a long shot since the perp probably came and went through the sewer. Let's get an update from everyone and then strategize next moves. Joan, let's start with you. You had a chance to complete the autopsy?"

"Sure did. Short version—victim is a young girl, Caucasian, approximately seventeen. Based on her size and extensive dental work, I would say she was a healthy, well-cared-for young woman before she was kidnapped."

"Any ID yet?"

"Not yet, which is confusing. She should be in the system if she was well cared for, though she might've been old enough to be on her own. Still looking."

Joan continued, "She was dead approximately six days, give or take a day. Cause of death, dehydration complicated by starvation and . . ." Joan paused. Her eyes fluttered once. The sight sent a jolt to Sayer's gut. It was the first time she had ever seen signs of disgust on Joan's face.

After a slow breath, Joan continued, "Starvation complicated by fear."

"Fear as cause of death?" Vik asked.

"Partially. She had evidence of extremely high cortisol levels, a stress hormone. All her systems showed stress beyond what you would expect, even from captivity. The only thing I've ever seen cause that kind of systemic response is chronic fear." Joan cleared her throat and smoothed the sleeve on her pale-blue sweater. "No signs of sexual assault or any other physical abuse. A small amount of atrophy in her muscles and sores along her legs and buttocks suggest that she was held in that cage for at least three months."

People around the table groaned.

"Only other injuries, other than some muscle atrophy and the beginning stages of vitamin D deficiency, were a few bite marks on her body. I'm still waiting for lab results, but they look like rat bites. I'm comfortable attributing them to rats, postmortem. Just snacking after the girl was dead."

Joan flipped through her report.

"Is that all?" Sayer asked.

"No, just making sure I get this right. One clearly unusual thing." Joan read through her notes. "Though well fed and hydrated until very recently, the victim was subjected to regular, large doses of *N,N*-Dimethyltryptamine, better known as DMT. I almost missed it because that particular drug isn't included in the routine tox screen. But I had a gut feeling and followed up."

"That's why you're the best, Joan. So what's DMT?" Sayer asked.

"It's a plant-based hallucinogen. It's actually found in the human body in small amounts and in about sixty plants around the world, the most famous being the ayahuasca plant in the Amazon. Shamans there use it for vision quests and religious rituals. It is a fairly unusual drug, so hopefully that helps. I found no injection sites but she had high doses in her system; maybe the unsub force-fed it to her, though I found nothing in her stomach to support that."

"Great, so we've got some drugged-out tweaker kidnapping kids and what, turning 'em into addicts?" Vik said.

Joan shook her head. "DMT is not some street drug. According to everything I read, it's actually considered sacred by many people. It's used in coming-of-age ceremonies and vision quests."

Sayer nodded. "Yeah, I read about this back in school. Lots of cultures use hallucinogens in culturally important rites of passage. If

I remember right, in the Sierra Madre, people use peyote, but DMT is similar."

Joan licked her finger and paged through more of her notes. "That's correct. DMT is actually called the *spirit molecule* by scientists because it can alter your perspective so much it can, and I quote, 'change your life.'"

"So maybe the religious aspect of the drug means something here." Sayer wrote on the murder board in a scrawling hand: *Drug: DMT, high doses, spirit molecule, ritual?*

Joan finished, "That's all I've got for now. Victim's DNA results are in the works and I expect word any minute now."

"Thanks, Joan. Uh, we don't have anyone here from evidence, because they're all working on the stuff we just got, but Vik's got Ezra's notes that he wrote before they went back for a second look."

Vik scanned the single-page report. "Looks like the scene was so trashed by the EMTs and bomb squad that they're still trying to sort out the forensics. One definite hit from the house—a tissue with human semen was found upstairs but it's unclear if it's even tied to the scene."

Sayer wrote *Tissue, semen* on the board.

"Otherwise they have a ton of contamination and are sorting through all the damn hair and footprints. There's no clearly unusual fiber or other evidence that stands out from what we expect to be there. Let's see, one more note here. It says, 'Ask the bomb squad guys if they set up some kind of machine in the center of the basement. There were impressions that looked like some kind of tripod. Bigger than you'd expect for a camera. Might not be anything, it was faint and people stepped all over it.'" Vik looked up from the notes. "All right, that might be something."

Sayer wrote *Tripod, center of room, machine?* on the board.

"Anything on the cages or symbols?"

The lead data tech scrunched her face. "I've got nothing on either. I just got them an hour ago and I've been focused on IDing the girl in the photo first. Only problem is we've got no time frame. For all I know this girl died ten years ago and he just kept her photograph."

"True. All right, you stay on IDing the girl for now, but pull in someone to help you chase down the symbols." Sayer paced in front of the mostly empty murder board. "Well, not much. Thoughts?"

Vik spoke up. "Timeline looks right for the unknown subject getting spooked after the 911 call."

"Yeah, which means our unsub might be jumpy. We better tread lightly, don't want to trigger another freak-out. If he's feeding the other girl, we want our unsub to keep doing so until we're banging down his front door."

Sayer stopped pacing and stood at the head of the table. She looked each of them in the eye. She saw the same anger, determination, and focus that she felt. "Let's figure out next steps."

Sayer paced again. "Data team, stay on the IDs and get some help sourcing the cages and symbols painted on the wall."

"I'll search through ViCAP and see if I can find anything similar," the data tech said. Searchable by modus operandi and victim type, the Violent Criminal Apprehension Program database would help find any similar crimes.

Sayer paced slowly in front of the murder board. "Vik and I will track down the owner of the property and see if there's any leads in that direction. See if we can figure out who would've even known about that bomb shelter."

As Sayer paused, Andy breezed through the door. His ruddy cheeks matched his deep burgundy suit that probably cost more than Sayer's apartment. His lidded eyes, blocky jaw, and thin lips gave him a perpetually smug look. "Sorry I'm late. I was working up my report."

No one responded as the stocky profiler sat across from Joan.

"Andy, we're almost done, you want to give us your thoughts?"

"Of course." He stood back up and went to the front of the room next to Sayer, standing just a little bit too close. She took a half step back, annoyed at his physical imposition.

"This is just what I could throw together on short notice, but I'm very excited by this case. I just recently began looking into serial killers that don't sexually assault their victims. It's far more rare than you'd expect. Most serials have some sexual component, but we've had a few cases now that I'm analyzing. This case is also unusual because of the differing races of the victims."

"And your profile?"

"Based on the gentle treatment, the inclusion of young animals, and the lack of sexual assault, coupled with the clear level of planning involved, I think our unknown subject believes he is protecting these kids from something. Maybe even providing them with a safe happy place of refuge. Our victim is white, but the other victim looks darker skinned, maybe Latina or Middle Eastern. Cross-race killing is highly unusual, so I'm not as confident about our unsub's race, but I expect him to be white, high IQ, between twenty-five and thirty-five years old, a loner, single, perhaps he once longed for his own children but was denied them for some reason. He'll probably seem sort of sad or pitiable to those around him, but he won't seem dangerous. Look for solitary jobs, things where he can work on his own."

Andy finished and flashed a winning smile.

"Great, thanks," Sayer said as she wrote, *Loner, 25–35. Maybe white.* "So that's two unusual things about this case. No sexual assault and cross-race victims. Andy, you keep working on two things, victimology and pathology. Why these victims? What similarities do they have? And what's the pathology playing out here? This kind of behavior is playing out the same fantasy over and over. See if you can come up with some ideas."

Andy nodded, clearly not happy being told what to do by Sayer. "Actually, I'll just focus on victimology first. It's most important," he said with authority.

Before Sayer could respond, Joan's phone pinged. She glanced at her screen. "Oh, DNA results came in. I think we have an ID."

Her eyes scanned the message while the whole room anxiously watched.

"Uh-oh."

"What is it?"

"The DNA is a match to a missing-person case reported last spring. Or should I say *the* missing-person case last spring."

"Last spring? A year ago. Wait . . . not . . ."

"Yeah, the DNA matches Gwendolyn Van Hurst."

Another collective groan went up around the room. Everyone knew about the missing senator's kid. Charles Van Hurst was a beloved senator from Georgia. His wife died in a freak accident, and then his teen daughter went missing a few weeks later. Now there was talk about him running for president. Nothing messed with a murder investigation like a media bomb, and this was going to be a nuke.

Sayer contemplated, rolling her worry beads between her fingers. "All right, I'll go talk to Holt. We're going to need a media liaison on this one. Then Vik and I'll go talk to the senator right away.

"Andy, while you're working up a more in-depth profile, can you also head down to the canvass tomorrow and coach the DCPD officers there on what to look for? Get some uniforms out and cover the whole area around the sewer exits as well. Maybe someone saw something. Oh, also pull the local security cameras so we can look through them. And follow up on the sewer access."

Andy looked sullen but nodded. "I'm on it, Special Agent Altair."

Joan raised a finger. "That's actually Senior Special Agent now. Hadn't you heard?"

Andy's face fell into a blank mask, but color rose on his already red cheeks. He blinked for a long while, a vein throbbing on his forehead.

"Congrats, Altair," he grunted.

"Thanks." Sayer smiled at him broadly. "Hopefully overseeing the canvass will give you access to some good witness interviews until we've got more for you to profile from.

"All right." Sayer refocused on the room. "Last thing to talk about—Ezra . . . he's in surgery but the doctors think he'll pull through. He's . . . lost his legs. We're collecting for a gift and encouraging everyone to send him a card. He's got no family nearby, so Holt set up a volunteer system to make sure he's being taken care of. If you want to take a shift at the hospital, signup's in the coffee room. Evidence lab already has the first week and a half covered." Sayer's voice cracked.

The room sat in silence, faces grim.

"Listen." Sayer didn't let them dwell. "We're going to be under the microscope even more than usual on this one. Let's do it right. I've flagged everything as priority with all the labs. We're keeping everything in-house for continuity. This is officially the clearinghouse; make sure Vik and I see everything you get. Keep everything in Rapid Start, so upload anything you've got there." Rapid Start was a computerized case management system that allowed everyone to upload their investigative material. "You all know, without access to all the data, we'll miss connections, so be diligent. Here's hoping we'll break this today and have that girl back home by bedtime. Let's do it for Cindy and Ezra."

"Hear, hear," Joan cheered.

Another tech poked his head in the doorway. "Agent Altair, we've got the video from the bunker cued up. You want me to play it in here?"

Sayer swallowed but gave a curt nod. Time to see what the killer wanted her to watch.

Everyone sat down. The lights dimmed and the tech puttered for a minute warming up the projector. The bulb clicked on and the first still from the video appeared on the screen. Sayer squinted, trying to understand what she was seeing.

The cage took up most of the view. Gwendolyn Van Hurst lay sprawled on the bottom of the cage, eyes shut. The puppy had curled up next to her, head resting on her stomach, eyes wide open. The room itself was a confusing swirl of light and shadow blurred by the paused video.

"Have you already watched it?" Sayer asked the tech.

He nodded grimly.

"What are we looking at?"

"Far as I can tell, the black-and-white stuff you see is being projected on the walls. See there." He pointed to the edge of the screen. "I think that's a projector, a big one, looks like it's sending out a three-hundred-sixty-degree image so the whole room is lit up. Like a video in the round or something."

As he spoke, Sayer could see it.

"The projector, bet that's what was in the room on a tripod," Vik said.

"That sounds right." Sayer got up and wrote *360-degree projector* on the whiteboard. "These can't be too common. Let's put someone on tracking that along with the cage?"

"All right, all set. You ready?" the tech asked.

"Go."

The video began.

The girl didn't move.

Smoke swirled around the room like a dry-ice machine ran in the background.

"Smoke?" Sayer asked for theories.

"DMT smoke," Joan said. "I bet that's how she was dosed; a vaporizer filled the room with DMT."

Through the haze, the images projected on the wall became clear, and the hair rose on Sayer's arms.

A strange patchwork of human figures floated against a black background connected by undulating white lines like umbilical cords. An arch of symbols framed the central figure, a stylized man kneeling on the ground before a tree. He held a long, thorny rope that looped up to his mouth, piercing directly through the center of his tongue. On the tree, human heads grew like fruit. In another image, two men sat holding baskets of scrolled paper. A snake loomed above them. In the final panel, two men stood facing away from each other, bound together by a single white cloth.

Beneath the figures, a white doorlike opening led into the underworld and a dog waited just inside the doorway.

"I recognize this . . ." Sayer searched her memory banks trying to place the images. "These are Maya."

"Like the ancient Maya? From Mexico?" Vik asked.

"Exactly! Those are Maya glyphs."

In the video, the puppy in the cage nudged the girl and licked her face. Conversation stopped as they watched the video, all irrationally hoping the girl would somehow get up.

Her fingers fluttered. Her chest rose and fell. Rose and fell.

"She's still alive here," Sayer whispered, not trusting her voice.

"Watch," a robotic voice boomed from the speaker, making them all jump. "The moment she moves beyond the veil."

Sayer watched, unable to look away. The girl's hand lifted slightly, up then down. Her chest rose and fell, rose and fell. A barely perceptible tremor shook her body. Then nothing.

The image cut off, leaving the room dark.

They sat temporarily in silence processing the horrific scene.

Finally the tech flicked on the lights and Sayer took a loud breath. "All right, that was . . ." She trailed off, bile filling her throat. She had investigated many murders, but she had never before witnessed the exact moment of a victim's death. That it was relatively peaceful made it no less terrible to watch.

"All right," she said again, gathering herself. "Andy, figure out why he wanted us to see this. Why did he leave just this one video? Data team, see if you can track the projector. Andy's on the neighborhood canvass, and stay on top of the evidence analysis. Vik and I will go see Senator Van Hurst and follow up on that angle. Maybe our perp is someone she knew. After that I'll run down those Maya images. I want to know everything there is to know about what we just saw.

Anything else?" She looked at the table of grim faces. "If there's nothing more, let's get going." Shuffling papers was the only sound as people filed out.

Only Sayer and Andy remained behind.

Andy stared up at the murder board, an excited gleam in his blue eyes. "This is a really unusual case."

"Yeah, hopefully you'll get to write it up once we catch the guy. That'll be a feather in your cap."

Andy ignored Sayer's sarcasm.

"Yes, it would be a good addition. Assuming we clear this." He glanced over at Sayer. "You know this should be my case, right?"

Sayer turned to face him. "Think what you want, Holt gave it to me."

Andy rolled his eyes. "Sure, I know how it works. You women are all the same."

"Us women?" Sayer flushed with anger.

"I see what Holt's doing here, building her little empire."

"Empire? Are you serious?" Sayer didn't know whether to be pissed off or laugh in his face.

Andy smiled, clearly happy to get a rise. He turned to leave the room and as he strolled away, he said back over his shoulder, "Oh hey, how's your research going?"

Sayer bit the inside of her cheek until it bled. Once Andy was gone, she gathered her things and stalked out of the room.

Vik drove toward Senator Van Hurst's house in D.C., his baggy eyes tight with tension. Sayer practically rubbed the surface off her worry beads thinking about Ezra, Cindy, and the poor girl possibly still being held somewhere in a cage. A girl whose life hung in the balance, Sayer's hand holding the scales.

After a few minutes of silence Vik asked, "So, you religious?"

"What? Why?"

"That's a rosary, right?" He gestured to the string of worry beads.

"Oh." Sayer laughed. "No, these are worry beads. Just gives me something to do with my hands. Helps me think. My . . . dad brought them back from Greece just before he died."

Vik nodded, acknowledging the personal meaning of the beads. "If you're not religious, then why so interested in curing killers?"

"Curing?"

"Yeah, that's what you're after with your research, right?"

"No, that's not what my research is about." Sayer watched him clenching the steering wheel, flexing his hands. "You have a problem with me, Vik?"

"Not a problem with you as an investigator or anything; guess I'm still trying to understand why Holt's so hot on you."

Sayer rolled that over in her mind. "You pissed that you aren't lead on this?"

"Nah, I don't care about that. I'm moving up the ladder slow 'n' steady. I'm happy with that. Mostly I think your research is all academic, no application. Doesn't help us actually find killers. You're not DNA matching or even profiling. Doesn't mean you're not a good field agent, I just feel like you're wasting our resources with brain scans and theoretical musings."

Vik maneuvered the car expertly through perpetually heavy traffic along I-95.

"Well, thanks for your brutal honesty."

"We work together, think we should be honest."

Sayer took a long deep breath. Little fiery strands of stress ran along her shoulders and between her shoulder blades. A vague headache throbbed behind her eyes.

"You want to hear what my research's actually about?"

"I do," Vik said.

"I want to understand how killers are made and how we can find them early in life. Maybe if we can figure out why they do it, we can prevent it from happening in the first place. Say you've got two kids in the same family, abusive situation. One grows up just fine, the other shows up at school with a gun and murders ten other children. Why? How did one kid turn out fine and the other kid shoot up a school?"

"Guess I don't care. Nothing could ever excuse what that kid did."

"Right, not an excuse, but what if I could find something wrong with his brain?"

"Like what?" Vik asked, turning off Rock Creek Parkway into an upscale neighborhood in northwest D.C.

"You really want to hear all this right now?"

"Yeah, I do. Distracting me from thinking about a girl stuck somewhere in a cage."

"All right, each part of the brain does something different. You've got the cerebrum with four lobes. That's the main wrinkly part we think of as our brain." She tapped her forehead. "It's responsible for things like impulse control, emotion, reason, all the complex things our brains control."

"Like math word problems," Vik said.

Sayer laughed. "Sure, exactly. Under that, you've got this tiny part called the cerebellum that mostly regulates movement, balance, that kind of stuff. And finally you've got the brain stem, which controls automatic functions, breathing, heart rate, body temperature. When the brain stem stops working, you die."

"All right, so we've got complex brains."

"We do." Sayer's eyes shone with the excitement of someone who loves what they study. "You really have no idea. For example, there's something called developmental agnosia. Say you stopped using your left leg. Just stopped using it at all. Eventually you would lose the ability to control that limb. But even more interesting, you would become convinced it didn't belong to you. I met one woman who kept trying to throw her own leg out of bed, convinced someone had put a severed limb in bed with her!"

"Whoa." Vik cringed at the thought.

"I'm interested in two specific parts. The orbital cortex, which controls empathetic decision making, caregiving, that kind of thing. Second, I'm interested in the amygdalae, two little bundles of nuclei in our temporal lobes."

"Amigda-what?"

"Amygdalae; they're directly linked to empathy. If you've got big amygdalae, then you're super empathetic. People with oversized amygdalae are the ones who donate kidneys to strangers or go into war zones with Doctors without Borders. But, if you've got little pea-sized amygdalae, then you're probably a psychopath. So I'm looking for brain markers like those."

"But so what? I'm not just some meat puppet doing what my brain tells me. I have free will, I make decisions. So what if every serial killer out there has the exact same kind of brain damage?"

"It's way more complicated than that. Our brains are shaped by the way we live our lives." Sayer desperately rubbed her right shoulder, trying to release the growing knot. The last thing she wanted to be thinking about was her floundering research.

"So something makes their brains shrivel up?"

"Sort of. We know that some people have a biological predisposition to violence. There are genes, like one called the warrior gene, that are clearly linked to violent behavior. If you have that specific gene, you're much more likely to be a violent person. But plenty of people with the warrior gene are never violent. It hasn't been triggered. Brains are the same. Some kid might have small amygdalae and a skimpy prefrontal cortex, but if he grows up in a loving household, his brain will develop ways to encourage empathy. But if that kid is thrown into an abusive home, he turns into a violent killer. It's a complex interaction between nature and nurture."

"Still, so what?" Vik glanced over at her, his face full of curiosity but no malice.

"If we can understand how it works, then maybe we can catch them before they turn into killers."

"But how would you ever measure that? It's not like you can just jail someone because their brains are messed up."

"No, I mean figure out how to intervene. I'm talking about kids. Catch a kid in elementary school, put him in social programs. After-school programs. Put his family in parenting classes. Help the kid before he grows up to murder someone."

Vik drove in silence for almost ten minutes. Sayer let him think.

"Well, that's a little more reasonable," he finally said. "Though I think you forgot one key element."

"What's that?"

"Evil. *Mamere* used to call them *possede* kids, possessed. Some people are just born evil, and no amount of love or attention would make them good. That seemingly normal kid raised in a loving household that kills kittens and sets fires and eventually kills someone."

Sayer sighed. "I agree. Those are the ones I'm most interested in. Was there something we could've done? Or were they destined to be a killer from the day they were born?"

On that cheery note, Sayer and Vik turned onto the long driveway leading to a massive colonial mansion.

"And now to tell a father we found his daughter dead," Sayer muttered under her breath.

A man in pressed khakis and navy-blue polo shirt stood out front, holstered gun strapped to his side.

"Private-security welcome wagon?"

"Yeah," Vik answered. "Think Senator Van Hurst hired his own security detail after his daughter went missing."

The bodyguard watched them approach but didn't greet them, just raised his chin in acknowledgment as they passed.

They rang the doorbell. As they waited, Sayer could feel a slight shift in Vik. He turned his body toward her, shoulders down. She hoped that meant the air between them was clear.

A frizzy-haired woman in a formal maid uniform pulled open the door. "Have you found Gwen?" she demanded.

"I'm sorry, Ms. . . ."

The pale woman seemed to realize she was blocking the entry. She stepped aside and gave a half bow. "I'm sorry. I just . . . I'm Maxine. I keep house for Mr. Van Hurst. Was Gwen's nanny . . ."

"Maxine, would you offer the agents a drink and bring them to the sitting room?" a deep voice called from above.

At the top of a grand staircase stood Charles Van Hurst, bright-eyed, perfectly coiffed, shoulders back. Sayer could immediately see why people compared him to Kennedy.

"Please excuse Maxine," he said as he descended. "She loved Gwen as much as we all did."

Maxine didn't manage to hide her frown but mumbled, "Would you like anything to drink?"

"No, thank you. We would like to talk to you after we speak with Mr. Van Hurst, if you're willing."

"Of course!" Maxine opened a mahogany door and gestured for them to enter before bustling away.

Van Hurst strode into the room first, and Vik and Sayer followed. He stood before a towering marble fireplace and gestured to a nearby sofa like a man about to hold forth for an audience.

"I've already spoken to your boss."

Sayer's eyebrows rose.

"Assistant Director Janice Holt and I go way back, same class at Georgetown Law." He flashed a white-toothed smile. "Janice says that you've found my daughter, and I want to hear what you plan to do to catch the bastard that did this." He spoke directly to Vik.

Sayer opened her mouth once, shut it, then opened it again, letting herself think before speaking.

"Well, Senator, as I'm sure Assistant Director Holt told you, our investigation is still in the early stages but we will be following up on every lead."

Van Hurst seemed momentarily surprised that Vik wasn't the one answering, but he recovered quickly. "Yes, yes, spare me the assurances. I've already made sure you have as much manpower as you need. The FBI knows well enough to listen when I make a request. The man who did this to my poor Gwennie won't get away with it. Imagine, drugging my little angel! Keeping her in a cage!"

"Yes, sir," Sayer said calmly, though she was genuinely shocked that Holt had told Van Hurst so many details. Normally such things would have been kept quiet, at least at first. "We have your statement from last year when Gwendolyn first went missing, but we would like to start over from the beginning to make sure we don't miss anything."

"Very good. I'm happy to have my typed statement sent on to your office."

"We would rather get it from you directly, right now."

Van Hurst waved them away. "Sorry, I don't have time right now, don't want to miss my own press conference, after all. If you insist on getting it from me, I'll have to arrange to meet you another time. In the meantime, feel free to look over Gwen's room and interview my staff. They all have instructions to cooperate in any way possible."

"Uh, press conference, sir?"

Van Hurst looked Sayer hard in the eyes, like a dog testing the aggression of his new playmate. "Yes, I'll be talking to the press about Gwen right away. That you've found her is a huge step for me."

"Sir, we would request that you hold off on that until we can—"

Van Hurst interrupted her. "Too late. I've already sent out the press release and I plan to leverage the media to our advantage. I've asked for help tracking the cage, the weird drug he forced on her, even the dog. Someone out there will know something. No reason not to move things along."

Sayer struggled not to let her anger seep into her voice. "With all due respect, Senator Van Hurst, not only might releasing those details compromise our investigation, but it has also just put the life of another young woman in grave danger. By telling the killer that we are on his trail, there is a very good chance that he might not return to the other girl he may have in captivity."

"Other girl?" Van Hurst's brows knitted momentarily. "Damn, Janice neglected to mention that there was another victim." He turned with an accusatory look at Sayer. "That will teach all of you to withhold anything. I need to know everything or I can't help you." Van Hurst paused to contemplate. "Well, I didn't know about the other girl, so no one can hold that against me."

He moved on with no real concern in his face, and Sayer had the sickening realization that this press conference was as much about his own upcoming presidential campaign as it was about finding Gwen's killer. The elections were approaching and this would boost his visibility.

"Sir, you have no right—" Sayer began.

"I have every right," Van Hurst snapped. "Gwen has been gone a very long time and I've done my grieving. I won't let her death go to waste."

Sayer stood up, fury blinding her. "You would exploit your own daughter's death for a press conference? You would risk the life of an innocent child to promote your own agenda?"

Van Hurst's face transformed from aloof patrician to a red mask of rage. "How dare you!"

Sayer and Van Hurst faced off, both panting with emotion.

Vik leaned back against the sofa, eyes slowly shifting back and forth between the two.

"I will be talking to Janice about this," Van Hurst growled. "I won't listen to these kinds of accusations when I am the one who's lost everything. Everything! Now get out of my house. When the FBI replaces you as lead on my daughter's investigation, the new agents are welcome to come speak to my staff. Now . . . Get. Out." As he spoke, he managed to rein in his anger and was calm once again.

He straightened his crisp shirt and walked briskly out of the room, pushing past Maxine, who was hovering just outside.

She rushed forward. "I'm so sorry! Mr. Van Hurst, he isn't handling any of this very well. Doesn't know how to express his emotions, so he does what he's always done. But he really did love his daughter," Maxine babbled as she bustled Vik and Sayer out the front door. "Please don't let that display stop you from finding whoever did this."

Vik stood next to Sayer on the front porch as the door shut behind them. "Well, that probably could've gone better. You really went toe to toe with that guy," he said with a lopsided grin.

"Shit" was all Sayer said as she stalked to the car, yanked open the door, slid in, and slammed the door behind her.

Vik slid in calmly, and they sat in silence for a minute.

Sayer fought her raging emotions. She knew she should have handled that differently, but she had gone on autopilot. Damn, she had to stop doing that. Would Holt pull her off the case? No matter; for now she should just keep doing her job.

She read through her e-mails. "Looks like the owners of the house on P Street live in Europe somewhere and know nothing about the property. The owners haven't ever even been there and suggested we talk to the local real estate agent trying to sell the place if we have any questions. Let's head over and interview this real estate agent before I get fired."

CAPITOL HILL, WASHINGTON, D.C.

Only a few miles from Van Hurst's mansion, the back side of Capitol Hill might as well have been on another planet. Empty lots, run-down apartment buildings, abandoned brownstones. Real Star Real Estate opened onto a narrow alley behind a Kwik Konvenience store. Sayer and Vik followed the green sign with the yellow shooting star until they found a locked wire security door. Sayer banged hard, causing a deep metal reverb to echo along the damp concrete alleyway.

They waited in the musty air until the inner door cracked open. Suspicious green eyes peered out.

"I help you?"

"Yes, sir, Special Agents Altair and Devereaux with the FBI. We're investigating a murder on one of the properties you have listed for sale, and we would like to speak to you."

Another long pause.

"Can you show me your ID, please?"

Sayer flipped open her wallet and held up her badge to the darkened doorway.

Pause. Then finally the sharp click of a lock opening. And another. And another.

The door swung open to reveal a slender man with movie-star looks, green eyes behind hipster glasses, thick black hair, sparkling smile. "Please come in."

Sayer and Vik entered the small office cluttered with old brown furniture and a Formica desk.

"A murder at one of my listings?"

"Yes, Mr. . . . ?"

"Oh, my apologies!" He awkwardly bowed. "Franklin Winters, Real Star Real Estate."

"A property on P Street Southeast." Sayer vaguely pointed in the direction of the town house. D.C. is laid out on a grid, letter streets running east–west, number streets running north–south, all radiating out from the Capitol Building in a diamond shape. While Northwest is home to the most upscale neighborhoods, Southeast is home to some of the most impoverished, including a few that could pass as third-world ghettos. Real Star Real Estate clearly specialized in less prestigious addresses.

"Ah yes, that one's been empty for a long time. How can I help you, Agent Altair?"

Sayer settled on the pleather sofa, which squeaked beneath her. "First, we need more information on the owner."

Franklin Winters nodded enthusiastically. "I'm happy to look up their info, but I can tell you that ownership on that place's a mess. Was owned by an elderly European gentleman, lived up north, Boston maybe. He inherited it from someone else. He passed away about two years ago and his children can't agree on what should be done with it. One brother hired a contractor recently to fix the place up; guess some of the kids are hoping to sell it for a profit or some such nonsense."

"How many siblings inherited?"

"Seven, I believe. Would have to double-check."

Vik groaned.

Franklin continued, "But none of them are here. They live in Europe. All over, like Luxembourg and Monaco, places I can't even find on a map."

"We'll still need all their information, please. Next question, when was the last time you visited the property?"

"Me?" He seemed genuinely taken aback by the question. "Am I a suspect?"

"No, sir. We just need to ask. Plus it might give us a timeline."

Franklin's eyes shifted back and forth, and Sayer felt a little tingle of interest. She recognized the intent to deceive on his face.

"I . . . I haven't been there in forever. Couldn't tell you exactly when. Maybe been more than a year." Franklin paused, green eyes darting again. "I've only been there three times total. It's been empty for a long time."

Giving him no time to think, Sayer pressed on. "Did you go to the basement when you visited?"

"What? No! You couldn't pay me to go into a basement in one of my places. Never know who or what is lingering there. Wait, is that where someone was killed?"

"And who would have known about the bomb shelter in the basement?" She watched his reaction closely.

Franklin's eyes widened. "A bomb shelter? Well, that's not on any of the specs I've seen. But . . . but as I said, I've never even been to the basement."

His surprise seemed genuine, and Sayer let him slip slightly down her nonexistent list of suspects. She knew well enough that anyone got nervous under questioning. His darting eyes might just mean he was feeling the scrutiny of the FBI, never a comfortable place to be.

He hurried over to his filing cabinet and pulled out a thin file. "Yeah, nothing about a shelter on the paperwork I've got. Didn't know it had such a thing."

Sayer glanced at the paper he held out and waved it away. "So, as far as you know, no one knew about the shelter?"

"Right. I wonder if the original owner even knew. Don't think he had ever even set foot in the place."

Sayer frowned. This damned investigation just couldn't gain any momentum. She knew how investigations went; either they picked up steam fairly quickly or they fizzled fast. And this one was fizzling like a flat soda.

"Is there anything else you can think of, Mr. Winters?"

The man tilted his head and genuinely seemed to be thinking something over.

"Anything at all," Sayer prompted. "You never know what might be important."

Franklin smiled uncomfortably. "Well, there is one thing, but it seems unfair."

"Unfair?"

"The contractor. He just felt off to me."

"Off?"

"That's the best word I can come up with. He was . . . meaty . . . and shifty." Franklin let out a small laugh. "That sounds silly, but it's true. He felt shifty."

"Thank you for sharing." Sayer turned to Vik and said with a tinge of excitement in her voice, "A contractor working the property might know about the bomb shelter."

He grunted agreement.

"We'll need his name as well as the owners' names. Plus the names of anyone who showed an interest in the property."

Franklin snorted. "Not a nibble on that place. They've got it listed at twice what it's worth," he said as he printed a list for them. "Don't think I ever got the contractor's name, but I'll call the brother who hired him as soon as it's morning there."

Sayer and Vik thanked Franklin and headed back out to the car. Her phone pinged and Sayer glanced at the screen. Nana. She rolled the call to voice mail.

"Let's track down our new contractor friend and see what's what there."

Less than a minute later, Sayer's phone pinged with a text from Holt that said, *Quantico. Now.*

"Shit," Sayer muttered. "Looks like the good senator finally spoke with Holt. She wants us back to the office ASAP. Here's hoping that after she pulls me off the case, she puts you in charge."

Vik snorted and gunned the old Nissan toward Virginia.

ASSISTANT DIRECTOR HOLT'S OFFICE,
FBI HEADQUARTERS, QUANTICO, VA

"He's demanding that I pull you off the case," Holt barked.

The FBI assistant director sat at her desk, midday light shining from behind giving her head silvery wings. Her eyes flashed and Sayer imagined just for a moment that Holt was a Valkyrie—granted, a Valkyrie with thick jowls and a 1980s red power suit.

"Moron just couldn't keep his trap shut."

Sayer let out her breath. Holt was mad at Van Hurst, not her.

"And you." Holt stood. "You couldn't keep yourself in check. You should know better. Always play nice with the goddamned politicians that run this godforsaken city."

Holt paced, shaking her head.

"I . . . ," Sayer began.

"No, don't say a word. I know perfectly well why you got in Van Hurst's face. He always was a self-serving jerk, and this is his most despicable stunt yet. But that doesn't negate the fact that he's the head of the Senate Select Committee on Intelligence. That just happens to be the committee that determines the FBI budget. He. Determines.

Our. Budget." Holt stopped pacing and pointed a finger at Sayer. "Do you have any idea how much power that gives him? I gave him a huge bone, let him know exactly where we stood in this investigation. Never in a million years imagined he would call a press conference. That was my mistake. But you . . . you basically poked a stick into the beehive."

"I . . ."

"No, stop talking. Let me tell you what is going to happen next. We are going to his press conference."

"But . . ."

"Shut it. What I mean is that you are going to his press conference and you are going to make nice. You are going to talk to the press as though this conference is a joint project. I want everyone to think that we are cooperating with the good senator. If you say one word about Van Hurst being a campaign-grubbing asshole, you are off this case before the words reach the microphones in front of you. If you can't manage this, you're out."

Sayer stood, silent. Holt finally dropped her pointing finger.

"Can you handle it?"

"I . . . uh, you know media relations aren't my strong suit."

Holt cringed, remembering Sayer's last foray in front of the cameras. She went from media darling to pariah in less than ten seconds. Turns out that when you punch a reporter, the press corps turns on you.

Holt contemplated for a moment, then continued her tirade. "Tough nuggets, Sayer. I don't care what happened in the past, it's time to woman up and work it out. I'm trying to help your career here. You need to work out a truce with the press or you're stalled at senior special agent. This is the perfect time to fix the damage you did back then. Just keep it simple . . . we're following all leads with lots of manpower. We're on top of it. Give them confidence, reassurance, and absolutely no information at all. Senator Van Hurst has already given them too much of that. I told him I couldn't pull you yet, so he's expecting you. Better hurry, conference begins soon."

Sayer and Vik raced to the community center where Van Hurst was already holding forth in front of a room of reporters. The Gwendolyn Van Hurst story was huge news, as was the powerful but distraught father vowing revenge upon those who hurt his darling daughter. More than a hundred reporters jammed into the hall, straining to get the right shot. Hungry for the right sound bite.

They stepped onto the stage just as Van Hurst broke into tears at the lectern, a huge image of Gwendolyn projected behind him. "He held her in a cage. Let her starve to death. I'm offering a hundred thousand dollars to anyone with information that leads to the arrest of the man who did this." His voice broke with emotion, and Sayer had to stop herself from rolling her eyes. She'd seen him mere hours ago calm as a cucumber and here he was sobbing. Plus that kind of reward would add yet another layer of nightmare to the already ridiculous case. Rather than chasing leads and pursuing the killer, Sayer would be stuck dealing with the fallout from Senator Van Hurst.

"Ah, the FBI have arrived to update us all on the latest." Wiping a tear aside, he held out his arm, welcoming Sayer to the lectern. "This is Special Agent Altair; she will be running the investigation." He flashed her a smile.

Sayer tried to smile back, though it felt like she had lead balloons in her cheeks, dragging them into a frown. She successfully fought the urge to correct him and say, *Senior Special Agent.*

Van Hurst leaned toward the mic with a sniff. "Agent Altair, please fill us all in on the latest."

He stepped away with a flourish, letting Sayer step up. She cleared her throat awkwardly.

"Thank you, Senator Van Hurst." She turned to the reporters. "We will be working closely together to make sure we catch whoever is responsible for this. The investigation has just begun, but we will be following every lead. We are throwing everything we have at this."

"Do you have any suspects?" a reporter called out.

"We have no suspects at this time. As I said, the investigation has literally just begun."

A few voices called out at the same time.

"Is the FBI taking this seriously?"

"What leads do you have?"

"What condition was Gwendolyn in when you found her?"

Sayer held up a hand to quiet them. "As I said, we have just begun investigating. We are following every lead. . . ."

"But you just said you had no leads."

Sayer bit her lip. "We do have leads including a person of interest, but we are at the very early stages of investigation. . . ."

"So you do have a suspect! Who? What can you tell us about the killer?"

A reporter from the back called out, "What about the contractor? Is he the person of interest?"

Sayer's mouth pressed into a flat line to keep it from falling open with shock. She tried to see which reporter had clearly gotten leaked information but couldn't single him out. As far as she knew, no one had heard anything about a contractor.

"As I said, there are no suspects at this time," Sayer finally said, but she could already hear the murmur of excitement as reporters frantically typed on their phones. She knew a hundred media researchers were already being tasked with finding the contractor working at that address. It would be an information frenzy—who could find the contractor's name first? Who could get to his house? Maybe get an interview before he realized he was a suspect? The media machine kicked into high gear and Sayer knew someone had royally fucked up.

"No more questions!" she insisted as she shuffled backward off the stage, digging her nails into her palms with frustration.

Vik stood just offstage, eyebrows up. "That went well."

"Oh, shut up." Sayer stalked past him.

Van Hurst stepped in her way as she tried to leave through the back door.

"Agent Altair, I appreciate you coming. Holt assures me you will cooperate with me during this investigation. Now, who is this suspect?"

Sayer poked her finger into Van Hurst's chest. "He could be a viable suspect, but now there's a very good chance he will be tipped off and flee before we can track him down, all thanks to your insistence on a press conference."

Calm-faced, Van Hurst answered, "I'm not the one whose people leaked information about the contractor. That was the fault of your people, Agent Altair. Now go catch the man who killed my Gwennie."

He stepped aside.

As Sayer stalked off, her phone buzzed.

"What the hell was that?" Holt shouted.

"Well, we've clearly got a leak somewhere." Sayer stopped at the car, relieved that no reporters seemed to be swarming her from the conference hall.

Holt spoke low and soft, which freaked Sayer out. "That was unacceptable. You get a handle on the leak or you're off the case. Got it?"

Sayer swallowed past her tight throat and managed to squeeze out, "Got it," before she hung up.

She looked over at Vik standing at the driver's-side door, eyebrows still up. He gave her a wide smile. "Where to next, tiger?"

Grumbling, Sayer slid into the car. "Guess we'd better track down our contractor. Let's hope he doesn't watch the news or he might be halfway to Mexico by now."

CONTRACTOR'S HOME,
BLUE RIDGE MOUNTAINS, VA

Sayer stared out the kitchen window, avoiding eye contact with Hal Dillinger, the already infamous "contractor." It had taken the data team less than an hour to track him down, and Sayer just barely managed to get to his rural cottage before the media.

Dillinger, a scruffy Irishman missing two fingers on his left hand, slid a manila folder across the table. "I sure did go up and check out that property in the city, but I turned the job down without stepping past the foyer. Could tell the job was too big for me and my boys." He flipped open the folder, revealing a pile of receipts. "Like I said, I've been doing wilderness training for the past few months with my boys. All my records are here. We've been out in Colorado since March."

Sayer took a deep breath and looked down at the crinkling stack of paper documenting the fact that Dillinger could not possibly be the man who murdered Gwendolyn Van Hurst. She looked back out the window. Beyond Dillinger's lovely garden, another media van pulled up, antenna rising to the sky like a hungry proboscis. A row of breathless reporters lined the rural street, staring into cameras with the solemn frowns they reserved for reporting on murder.

Despite looking like a biker, Dillinger was a do-gooder; he ran a school for at-risk kids who needed to get out of the city. He was even known to law enforcement, helped train dogs that worked with the police, all-around good guy. Sayer rubbed the throbbing headache radiating from her temples to her shoulders.

Vik took the folder. "Mind if we hold on to these for a bit?"

Hal Dillinger spread out his hands. "You do what you need to, man. Want to swab my cheek or something?" He looked slightly bemused at the furor outside his window.

Sayer stood up. "That won't be necessary, Mr. Dillinger. I'm truly sorry the media got wind of you before we even had a chance to talk to you. Mea culpa." She gestured to the folder in Vik's hands. "This should be enough for us to verify your alibi. Once we've cleared you, we will release a statement to that effect, which should make the media lose interest."

Dillinger chuckled. "Sounds lovely, Agent Altair. To be honest, this is the most excitement I've seen in years. I might go out and growl at them a bit while they still think I'm a killer." He winked.

Sayer tried to smile. "We'll be in touch."

Sayer and Vik walked the gauntlet of reporters waiting for them out front.

"Did Dillinger kill Gwendolyn Van Hurst?"

"What evidence links Dillinger to the murder?"

They no-commented their way to the car.

Back at Quantico, after crossing every infernal *t* and dotting every evil *i*, Sayer was fully convinced Dillinger was innocent.

"What a cluster." Vik grimaced as he plopped into the chair next to her desk.

"You said it." Sayer stared down at the thin case file.

Vik reached over and lifted the handwritten statement signed by Hal Dillinger. "He's not our guy."

"Nope."

"So what now?"

Sayer snorted. "Hell if I know. Follow up on the owners. Pound the pavement around the town house and hope someone saw something. Figure out who the hell knew about that bomb shelter. Figure out what the hell those symbols meant. Where the cage came from. Who knew how to build that bomb. Who has access to DMT. Figure out why we haven't ID'd the missing girl yet and then fucking ID her. This damned case, I swear." Sayer let herself imagine that lone girl in a cage, scared, maybe slowly starving to death. It was an image she consciously let invade her mind. It stoked the rage and horror in her belly. A surefire way to keep her on top of her game.

"Yeah . . ." Vik nodded, chewing his lip.

"Task force meeting in an hour. Then I guess we see where we're at."

"Hey, I asked around about Van Hurst," Vik said.

"Oh yeah?"

"Yeah."

"And?" Sayer prompted, her temper slightly short.

"And nothing interesting. Reports say that the good senator really loved his daughter. That they were a happy family before his wife died and Gwen disappeared."

"You've got a source close enough to the Van Hursts to have info about their personal relationships?"

Vik chuckled. "You're not the only one with insider info in this city."

"Yeah, but I grew up here. You've been in D.C. what, ten years?"

"Not even. Six years here. Before that I was at the New Orleans office."

"Your hometown, right?"

"*Bien sûr, mon amie.* I'm Cajun through and through. Lived in New Orleans till I was fourteen. The Devereaux clan is . . . not small." He chuckled again. "Which means I've got extended family everywhere."

"You have family nearby? Your parents or . . . ?" Sayer trailed off, genuinely curious about her new partner. Endlessly mellow, Vik wasn't cut from the same cloth as most FBI agents.

He looked thoughtful for a moment before answering. "I was raised by my mom and *mamere,* my grandmother, but they're both gone. My sister and I moved to Houston when I was fourteen after some . . . trouble in New Orleans. My sister's down in central Virginia now. My connections up here are all third cousins or something. Not close family, but we Devereauxs stick together."

Something about Vik's story triggered a memory. "Oh my God, you're the kid in New Orleans that saved that cashier?" Sayer said.

She had been seventeen when it happened. The whole country fell in love with the teenage boy caught on camera during a convenience store robbery. The kid stepped between the robber and the cashier and talked the robber into fleeing. Cashier said that the robber was about to shoot him and the kid intervened, saving the man's life. The kid's name was Devereaux.

Vik grimaced. "Yep, that's me."

"Damn, Vik. I remember that whole thing. What a brave thing you did! That guy was about to shoot." Sayer couldn't believe she hadn't known about Vik's history. Most agents would've never shut up about something so heroic.

"Yeah, it's complicated. . . ." Vik waved his hand dismissively. "Anyway, we went to live with our aunt and uncle in Houston after that. . . ."

Sayer's phone chirped in her hand and Vik looked more than happy to stop talking about his past.

She realized she'd missed three calls while questioning Dillinger. Two messages from Joan and one from Nana. The sight of two calls from the medical examiner made her sit up straight. She put the phone on speaker and pushed play.

"Sayer, I've got something. Come on to the lab when you've got a chance."

The second message played: "Sayer, where are you? I've got something . . . just come see me."

Sayer could hear a tightness in Joan's voice. With a mix of excitement and a flutter of apprehension, Sayer and Vik hurried to the lab.

As Sayer and Vik rushed along the long hallway to Joan's lab, Andy Wagner emerged from a door and almost collided with Sayer.

"Oh, sorry!"

"Watch it, Andy!"

The two briefly stood face-to-face. Andy's eyes darted between Sayer and the ceiling.

"Sorry . . . I was just . . . I mean, I was in the wrong place. . . . I'm off to finish my report for the task force meeting." Andy fled back toward the offices.

Sayer and Vik looked at each other.

"The hell was that?"

"Dunno." Vik shrugged.

As they pushed open the thick metal door to the lab, Joan leaped from her chair.

"Finally!" Joan stood at her desk. Her normally perfect hair was pulled back in a mussed ponytail. Dark smudges of stress circled her eyes.

"Sorry, Joan. What'd you find?"

"First, that tissue with DNA we found upstairs was a dead end. Was a match to a drug addict who OD'd three months ago." Seeing Sayer's disappointment, Joan gave a tight smile. "We also found this."

She led them over to one of the long metal tables. On top, a series of photos were laid out in perfect rows. All of them showed close-ups of Gwendolyn Van Hurst's corpse. Pale bloated skin, close-ups of split fingernails, desiccated lips.

Joan lifted a photo and handed it to Sayer, then took a step back as though she wanted to be as far away as possible from the image.

A smear of something glowed a strange purplish blue.

Sayer blinked a few times, trying to orient the image properly. Only after turning the photo did she realize that she could make out the curve of flesh, a sprinkling of freckles.

Vik strained to look over her shoulder.

"What is this?" he asked.

"Something I just found this morning."

"Is this on her skin?" Sayer's tongue felt thick in her mouth.

"It is. Here is a better shot of the location."

Joan handed them another photo, this one showing the victim's entire head and shoulders. Barely visible just under the hairline, the blue smudge stood out against paler blue skin.

"It was up on the back of her neck. I processed the rape kit when we first brought her in, but I didn't run the black light on her entire body after finding no signs of sexual assault. Wasn't until this morning I thought to check her head to toe. Even then, I could have easily missed this . . . it's so small."

"So this is . . ."

"Human semen. I've confirmed. Plenty for a sample. I've sent it over for DNA analysis. The works."

Sayer's heart kicked up a notch. DNA found directly on the body was as good as forensic evidence got. "But when was this even deposited? If he was spooked by the DCPD when they came around, then this had to be left before that."

"That is a fine, fine question, Sayer. It hasn't degraded as much as I would expect for two weeks. Possible we were wrong."

"Damn" was all Vik muttered.

Sayer was about to reply when her phone buzzed. Two messages popped up at once, one more from Nana, and one from Dr. James Batra from the Smithsonian. She listened to the second.

"All right, the art historian guy over at the Smithsonian is willing to meet with me as soon as I can get there. I'm going to run up to the city and see if I can get any info about the Maya stuff we saw in the video." Sayer put her hand on Vik's shoulder. "You up for checking in with the data team before the meeting?"

He groaned but nodded. "I drove, take my car." He tossed her the keys. Sayer made a face at the thought of driving the old sedan.

SMITHSONIAN MUSEUM
SUPPORT CENTER, SUITLAND, MD

An elderly security guard let Sayer into one of the massive warehouses of the Smithsonian Museum Support Center. Two bright fluorescent bulbs hung from the high ceiling, casting sharp shadows across the huge room. The scent of dust blended with a heavy chemical odor that followed Sayer like a loping beast. Burnished wooden drawers lined the walls, floor to ceiling. Stainless steel tables filled the center of the room. Some of them were ominously covered by lumpy cloths.

Sayer contemplated lifting the corner of a cloth to see what was underneath but then realized it could be a table full of human remains rather than ancient artifacts. Despite her work, she was still never comfortable around dead bodies, even if they were nothing but bones. Sometimes she wondered if the curtain in her brain was as impermeable as she hoped.

While she waited for Dr. James Batra, ancient-art expert and head of the Smithsonian's Anthropology Collection, Sayer muttered her to-do list. "Review the Gwendolyn Van Hurst case file, ID the girl, ID the origin of the cage, ID the symbols painted in blood, ID the Maya images from the video . . ."

"Agent Altair?" A man strode toward her. Somewhere in his early forties, wearing a rumpled but clearly expensive shirt, his long face was handsome in a good old-fashioned way but with the rugged edges of someone who spends a lot of time outside, wind-bitten way beyond a few trips to the beach.

"Dr. Batra?"

"Special Agent Altair." He bowed his head. "Call me James, please."

They shook firmly and he gestured for her to follow him to a small office that opened off the main room.

Inside the windowless space, towering stacks of paper covered every surface. Leather-bound books lined the walls. A phalanx of wooden masks from around the world hung behind his desk. Intimidating but also magnetic.

"Please, sit. Can I get you coffee or something?"

Sayer sat in the worn leather chair that melted like butter around her. "No, thanks. I have to get back for a meeting. So, what can you tell me about the images I sent you?"

James sat behind his mahogany desk and smiled warmly. "Long version or short version?"

"Let's start with the short version and I'll ask questions."

He steepled his callused hands like a stereotypical academic. "The photos you sent me all depict parts of an ancient Maya legend about the Hero Twins, Hun Ahpu and Xbalanque."

"Hero Twins?" Sayer asked as she typed notes on her phone.

"Yes." James continued, "The twins were a duo of demigod brothers that had all kinds of adventures in ancient Maya cosmology. They were hunters, magicians, and scribes, but these images all depict a very specific myth."

"Can you summarize it for me?"

"Of course; this story is really their most important. Basically, Hun Ahpu and Xbalanque descended into the underworld and defeated the lords of death."

The hair stood up on Sayer's neck. "Okay. Go on, please."

James got up from his chair and pulled a leather-bound volume from a shelf. He pulled his chair around next to Sayer and opened the book to the image of two men sitting before a god.

"Oh, that's one of the images we found."

"Exactly. So the story says that the twins' father was tricked and killed by the lords of Xibalba, what the Maya called the underworld. The gods of death hung their father's head in a tree and a young maiden found it. The head spit in her hand and she soon gave birth to the Hero Twins."

"A dead head spit in her hand . . ." Sayer trailed off.

James's eyes crinkled with a smile. "And she got pregnant. Exactly. And so, when the two boys were older, they sought revenge for their father's death." He tapped the book in his hand. It let off a puff of dust that made Sayer cough.

"What you see here is a picture of the twins meeting the lord of the underworld. It's hard to see, but this is their father's skull next to the god."

"So they met with the god that killed their father." Sayer typed as fast as she could.

"Precisely right. And they challenged all the lords of Xibalba to a ball game, just as their father had. The lords of the underworld were cocky and accepted, with the agreement that the twins would pass a series of trials."

"Sort of like Hercules in ancient Greek mythology?" Sayer asked.

James's face lit up, making him look twenty years younger. "Exactly right!"

Sayer smiled at James's simple joy, trying to ignore how much more handsome he suddenly looked. She wished she had a job that made her feel that way instead of the burning pitch that lived perpetually in her gut.

"So," James said, "the Hero Twins descended into the underworld, where they faced trials in the House of Cold, House of Blades, House of Scorpions, House of Pus, and so on. Everything went well until the House of Bats. The brothers were hiding out from deadly bats, killing them one at a time with their blowguns."

He flipped to another page in the book, showing the next image.

"See, this is Hun Ahpu with his blowgun. But before they could kill all the bats, Hun Ahpu stuck his head out of their hiding place and a bat with bladed wings cut off his head."

"Okay . . ."

"So, the twin Xbalanque is alone when the ball game begins. With horror, he realizes that the gods of death are using his brother's head as the ball!"

"Whoa. Maya mythology is even more gruesome than I thought. So one of the brothers died," Sayer said.

"Yes! But wait! Xbalanque grabbed his brother's head and shoved it back onto his body. Which is how he discovered that they had the ability to resurrect dead things. Together, the brothers won the ball game, denying the lords of the underworld the right to their heads. The gods were furious but also amazed at the Hero Twins' ability."

"Resurrection?" Sayer asked. Something about twins and resurrection might play into the pathology of their killer.

"Exactly. The twins could bring anything back to life. The lords of Xibalba asked to see this miraculous magic. So the twins killed numerous animals and brought them back to life. They even sacrificed each other, taking turns lying down and carving each other to pieces, then springing back to life. Caught in a frenzy of delight, the lords of Xibalba cried out, 'Now do us!' And so the twins sacrificed the two leaders of Xibalba, only they didn't bring them back to life. The rest of the Xibalba lords knew they were defeated."

James snapped the book shut, sending up more dust that made Sayer's eyes water.

"And that, Agent Altair, is how they beat the gods of death."

"Very interesting." Sayer let her mind spin on this new information. "Mind if I ask a few more questions about the Maya?"

"Of course." James leaned back in his chair, an easy smile on his face. He ran his hands through his hair, and the faint scent of sandalwood wafted toward Sayer.

"Would the use of drugs mean anything to the Maya?"

"Drugs?"

"Yes, like DMT or other hallucinogens."

"Yes! Very much so!" James jumped up again to retrieve another book.

"See here?" He pointed to a photo of a figure reclining on his side, liquid running along his back, a funnel-shaped jar in his hand. "This is an enema."

"Enema . . . ," Sayer repeated.

"Yes, they did drug enemas before rituals. Though they did drugs in many ways. But hallucinogens and other ways to achieve altered states of consciousness played a big part in Maya ritual."

"Can you explain that?"

"Of course! The primary goal of most Maya ritual was to open portals to other worlds so the priests could communicate with gods or dead ancestors."

Sayer contemplated for a moment. "So how do drugs play into that?"

"When you alter your state of consciousness . . ."

"Wait, I'm coming at this from a neurology perspective. . . ."

"You're a neurologist?" James seemed genuinely shocked.

"A neuroscientist. I specialize in the interconnections between neurology and aberrant behavior."

His smile widened, a feat Sayer wouldn't have thought possible. "So I should really be calling you Dr. Altair rather than Agent Altair."

"Either will do. So, when you say altered state of consciousness, you mean . . . ?"

"I mean anything that alters your consciousness; that would include hallucinogens, but you can alter yourself with rhythmic dancing, drumming, or even chanting. Imagine a monk chanting; he is altering his consciousness dramatically."

"So why was that important to Maya ritual?"

"Let me ask you, as a neuroscientist, what happens when a monk meditates or a nun prays?"

Sayer thought back to her neurology of religion class. "Well, parts of their prefrontal cortex go quiet."

"Exactly; the parts of their brain that distinguish self from other stop working. They have the very real experience of becoming one with the universe."

"Right. So that's what the Maya were doing?"

James shrugged. "An oversimplification of their ritual, but yes. They were inducing experiences of the sacred. Just talk to any old hippie eating a bunch of mushrooms. They'll tell you they see portals opening, they experience union with the universe, they talk to ancestors and commune with the dead. The bands weren't called the Doors and the Grateful Dead for nothing." He chuckled at his own joke.

Sayer thought about human hallucinations, a key part of many religious rituals. Even simple meditation can induce a strong sense of something numinous beyond ourselves. When people alter their states of consciousness with heavy drugs or even with intense pain, they begin to see geometric visuals—flashing diamonds, grids, repeating lines, the kind of imagery found in ancient rock art around the world. When a person proceeds into heavy hallucination, reality fades and they begin to experience portals, doorways; they feel as though they are entering alternate realities. Could this be what the killer was trying to create?

She reluctantly left James's cheerful company and hurried to report everything she had learned. This was one messed-up case.

Sayer's head spun as she made her way up to the conference room for the evening task force meeting. She paused at the door, needing to collect herself before talking to a room full of people.

Inside, almost twenty people were gathered, the manpower being pulled in by the various teams as they tried to find the missing girl.

Sayer strode in to find Vik and Joan at the table covered by a thin layer of notes, photos, and case reports. Behind them, numerous agents, crime scene and data techs, and two uniformed D.C. police officers stood waiting for Sayer to begin.

She glanced at her phone. "It's late, so let's get right down to it. Dillinger's alibi checks out, so the contractor's not our guy." Sayer looked down at the report from the DCPD. "Looks like nothing from the canvass of the neighborhood."

She looked around for Andy, but he was late yet again.

She grabbed up another thin file. "An agent from the London office is doing phone interviews with the owners of the property on P Street, but so far no leads there. None of them seem to even remember that they own this property. None have traveled to the States in the past year, and none have made phone contact with people in the D.C. area."

Next she lifted a thick folder and was surprised to see that it was from the evidence team. "Uh . . ." She flipped through the file, not sure where to begin.

One of the evidence techs spoke up. "All of us have come in and are working around the clock. It's the first time an evidence tech has ever been injured in the line of duty. We're . . . upset."

"And this is your work so far?" Sayer waved the stack of at least a hundred pages.

"Yeah, we're analyzing every single item found there. So far no joy from it, but none of us will go home until every last piece of evidence has been logged, analyzed, and filed in the system."

"All right, well . . . damn."

Silence fell. Sayer let it ride out for a minute while they all thought about Cindy and Ezra.

Grim-faced, she finally broke the reverie. "Okay, it's late, let's move on to the symbols beneath Jane Doe's photo."

A young data tech scooted her chair closer to the table and nervously cleared her throat. "Still haven't found any source for the symbol painted below the picture. We do have a lead on the cages, but it hasn't panned out yet. Possible they are from a group of similar cages imported four years ago from Russia. We're still tracking paperwork and tracing out the destination of those." The analyst gestured to the phalanx of people clustered behind her.

Sayer reflected on how much some aspects of police work had changed. Used to be, to figure out where unusual cages came from, they would need dozens of uniforms pounding the pavement, knocking on doors of specialty shops until they made a connection. Now it was a room full of tech wizards hunched over their computers tracking that info down in less than half the time.

The data tech continued, "We've found no similar crimes anywhere. We're searching the whole U.S. but nothing even remotely with the same signature came up. We also still haven't ID'd the girl."

Another murmur spread.

"One thing we do have, we've worked out the date that the photo was taken."

"How? I thought there was no digital tagging on it," Sayer said.

"Nope, not digital. I zoomed in on the image. See right here." The young woman went up to the photo tacked to the whiteboard and pointed to a blur in the corner. "That's a newspaper. Using an algorithm I was able to match the vague images here to actual pages of the *Washington Post*. This photograph was taken October nineteenth, approximately six months ago."

Everyone groaned.

"Any idea why she isn't in the system? Surely someone is missing this girl?" Sayer asked.

"Possibly not. Maybe sex trade, might be from out of the country. Lots of reasons she wouldn't be reported. We're on it. Looking for links to our first victim."

"All right, thanks. Hey, one quick note for everyone on the task force. I'll ask that we call our victims by their first names when we can."

The room fell uncomfortably silent.

Sayer continued, "I know it's a distancing mechanism we all use. Calling them the vic, or victim, or even by their last name helps us keep them at arm's length, but I think that's dangerous. I want us to remember them. I want us to say their names over and over. So, from now on, let's call her Gwendolyn or Gwen."

Sayer tried not to let the lack of progress and her admonition bring down the room. "All right, moving on, the one thing I have to report is more about the Maya images we found."

She clicked on the overhead projector.

"I consulted with an expert over at the Smithsonian. He said that these all depict the Hero Twins, a duo of demigod brothers that had all kinds of mythological adventures in ancient Maya cosmology. The images we saw on the video of Gwen all depicted the twins descending into the underworld and defeating the lords of death."

"Whoa," Vik muttered.

Sayer summarized everything she had learned about Maya mythology and ritual.

"So." Sayer refocused. "I'm thinking that twins might be an important part of our unsub's pathology. With that in mind, let's pull out the themes of the Maya Hero Twins legend."

Sayer went up to the whiteboard and wrote *Defeating death. Twins. Portals to the underworld.*

"What else?"

"Using intelligence to defeat a more powerful enemy," Vik called out.

"Could tie into our booby traps; maybe he thinks he is tricky and can outwit us," one of the DCPD uniforms offered.

"Great, anything else?"

"The twins' love for each other?" Joan offered.

"Love?" Sayer asked.

"I remember this myth from a class I took in college. They always came back for the other one. They eventually became the sun and moon together. They were partners."

"All right, *partnership and love.*"

"Anything else?"

Silence.

"All right, so twins might play a role here. The use of hallucinogenic drugs ties this pretty clearly together with the Maya ritual. What is our unsub after here? Is this some kind of cult activity trying to become a modern Maya shaman or something? Should we be talking to the Maya community here in D.C.? Let's keep pondering." Sayer pulled out another glossy photo and pinned it to the whiteboard. "Last but not least, we need to talk about this." Sayer tacked the luminol photo on the whiteboard.

The image of a semen smear glowed in the dim conference room.

"The DNA is being processed as I speak. This adds a new element. It seems possible that this was deposited after Gwen passed away, which means that our original theory was wrong. Maybe he wasn't spooked by the cops, or at least not so spooked that he was too scared to return to the scene."

Silence.

As the entire room looked at the photo, Andy breezed in.

"Sorry, I was taking a look at the contractor but I've concluded he can't be our guy."

Sayer didn't manage to contain her eye roll. "Well, thank goodness for that."

With a scowl, Andy came right up and stood next to Sayer at the front of the room. He straightened the blazer that strained across his midsection and pushed back his thick auburn hair.

Sayer flourished her hand. "Please, share your latest."

"I've spent some more time working on my profile, bringing together everything we know so far. This guy is scary smart. The kind of person who can make these traps needs to have some level of intelligence but really, the bomb squad says everything here could've come right off the Internet. So our guy doesn't need to be a bomb expert or anything. But the level of planning and brutality tells me we are after someone seriously organized."

Andy walked slowly across the front of the room like a professor holding forth. He passed close enough to Sayer that it forced her to take a half step back.

"Most killers are disorganized and impulsive. We're all familiar with the guy who flies into a rage and shoots his wife, or the road rage incident that ends when one guy runs over the other. Even the guy who drives home, gets his gun, and goes all the way back to shoot someone ultimately has an impulse-control, anger-management issue. That's ninety-nine percent of murders we see. Rather than from impulsive anger, most serial killers kill to fulfill some deeper psychological need. They are re-creating a scenario or targeting a specific kind of person, usually tied to their own history and their own delusional needs and desires. These individuals can have incredibly high IQs but are rarely good at hiding their pathology."

Andy stepped in front of Sayer, facing the room. "Last but not least, you have the truly rare serial killers that are so intelligent they can maintain a front to manipulate everyone around them. They often seem sincere, likable, attractive; they generally fit in and can even have families and steady jobs. These are the Ted Bundys of the world. I'd bet my career that this case is going to turn out to be someone even more intelligent than Bundy was."

"So . . . the addition to your existing profile is . . . ," Sayer said.

"High intelligence. Very, very high. But no matter how smart or rational he is, we shouldn't forget that there is also a deep pathology there. Something profoundly influencing his behavior. Once we can figure out what the narrative is here, that's how we'll understand the pathology."

"Right." Sayer scrawled *Intelligent* and *Deep Pathology* on the whiteboard under their list of perp attributes.

"This is definitely a serial doer with experience under his belt," Andy said. "There's no way this is his first kill."

Still standing at the head of the room, Andy turned to the data team. "If you haven't already, I would definitely be looking for similar crimes. Maybe not with the exact same MO, but with some similar elements—animals, cages, girls held for long periods of time, drug administration, ancient symbology, that kind of thing."

With a completely flat expression, Sayer responded, "Gee, Andy, that never occurred to any of us. Thank you so much for the advice. They will get right on it."

He smiled.

"Oh, Andy." Sayer smiled back. "What about the discovery of semen on Gwen's body? Doesn't that change things now that there seems to be some evidence of a sexual component?"

His smile faded as he looked over at the new photograph. "I . . . I hadn't heard about that." He glanced around the room. "Let me look at what Joan found and I'll get back to you."

Sayer tried not to take some small pleasure at the sight of overconfident Andy stammering, clearly thrown by the new information.

Andy's momentary embarrassment faded directly into animosity. He glared at Sayer as though she were responsible.

"All right, day's done." She purposefully ignored him, glancing down at her phone. Almost midnight. "Get a few hours of sleep. Tomorrow Vik and I will focus on Gwen's disappearance. We need to reinterview everyone, piece together everyone's timelines, double-check everyone's alibis. The original investigation never figured out exactly where she was taken. Let's see if we can figure out how and when she was grabbed; maybe that will give us something to build on. Spend your time figuring out what I'm forgetting. What other leads should we be running down? You come up with an idea how to ID this other girl and I'll pay for a vacation to Hawaii when this case is over. Reconvene here at 8 A.M. sharp."

Vik dropped Sayer off at home. As she mounted the stairs her body buzzed with exhaustion. Focused on food and a few hours of sleep, Sayer almost ignored the phone buzzing in her pocket, but the display said DCPD; no way she could miss a call about the case. Maybe a break would finally hit.

"Agent Altair," she barked.

"Ms. Altair?"

"Who is this?"

"My name's Officer Berry with the Washington, D.C., police department. I'm calling about one Sophia McDuff."

Fear jolted her body. Nana. "What's happened?"

"Uh, we've got Mrs. McDuff here in our holding cell. She said that we should call you even though it is late."

"You've got my nana in jail? Sophia McDuff, seventy-two years old? Wife of a former senator? That Sophia McDuff?" Sayer was already rushing toward her motorcycle.

"Yes, ma'am, she's being charged with assault. Between you and me, the charges'll be dropped, but in the meantime I can't imagine you want her to stay here overnight."

"Oh, for fuck's sake, that's clearly ridiculous. I'll be there soon. Which station?"

Less than thirty minutes later Sayer rolled up next to the cinder-block building. So much for sleep.

The young cop at the front desk raised her eyebrows when Sayer introduced herself.

"Sophia McDuff is your grandmother?"

Sayer was used to the strange looks. The McDuffs were her maternal grandparents and were white as could be. Sayer's father was Senegalese, and she had inherited his lean build and rich brown skin. After her parents died, Sayer and her sister went to live with their grandparents, and they were all used to people asking why the conservative white senator had two black kids hanging around all the time.

Sayer just gave the cop a hard stare. "Yeah, she's my nana. What happened?"

The cop moved on from her skepticism and seemed more than happy to fill Sayer in. She leaned in conspiratorially. "Your nana was caught by a security guard beating the holy hell out of some guy. She claims he's been mugging elderly folks around Dupont Circle." The cop barely seemed to need a breath as she gushed. "Guess there's a few retirement homes nearby and some jerk's been targeting the elderly, blackjacking them and picking them clean. Hurt quite a few people pretty badly. Anyway, your grandma apparently caught him in the act and beat the crap outta him. Like, he's in the hospital." She smiled and kept spewing words. "Ain't that the most hilarious thing you've ever heard? Bet that guy won't mess with no old ladies ever again." The cop chuckled, but Sayer was too busy chewing on her anger to be amused. This was not what she needed right now.

All her anger dissolved the second she saw Nana. The elderly woman was normally vital, giving off that inner glow some people carry with them. But Nana looked disheveled and worn. Most of the time it was possible to forget that Sophia McDuff was over seventy, but tonight she looked every bit her age. Sallow skin practically translucent, sunken eyes, wearing an old housecoat. Wait, what? Nana, widow of former senator Charles McDuff, would not be caught dead in the floral orange-and-yellow muumuu that she currently wore.

"Nana?" Sayer jumped up, suddenly worried.

The elderly woman met her eyes and the glint of glee relieved all her fear.

"What the hell, Nana?"

Sophia McDuff strode past Sayer, head held high despite her clear exhaustion. "Well, I certainly tried to tell you that I needed your help but you were too busy, so I took care of it myself."

"You . . . took . . . ," Sayer sputtered, and followed her out to her bike.

Nana climbed into the sidecar, tucked the muumuu daintily around her legs, and pulled on her helmet without a word.

Sayer yanked on her helmet, swallowing her mix of worry and anger. She clicked on the mic and said, "So, you were arrested . . . want to explain what happened?" as she revved the engine.

"I guess you didn't get my messages last week? Two of my friends at Vintage Gardens were mugged; one of them is still in the hospital with a head injury. They aren't sure if she'll recover."

"And so you decided to take a mugger on yourself?"

"Well, I did ask you to look into it. Pull a few strings with your friends."

"Nana, I'm on a case right now. I've got things on my mind."

"Exactly, and when I didn't hear back from you, I decided to go undercover."

Sayer stopped at a red light and looked over at her grandmother. "The muumuu . . ."

"God yes, you don't think I'd wear this thing on purpose." Through the face guard a broad smile erased her age again, making Nana look like an excited, silver-haired twenty-five-year-old. "Candace and I devised a plan. I dressed in this thing so I'd look nice and old. I borrowed Stanley's walker and spent the last few nights tottering around the neighborhood where that criminal was attacking people."

"You made yourself the bait?" Sayer yelled into the mic. "Nana, he could have really hurt you. What if he had a gun?"

"Oh pish, he's been using a blackjack on people, not a gun. But don't worry, Candace was in the bushes with a pistol just in case."

"I . . . you had a friend staked out in the bushes with a gun?" Sayer's voice rose further. "I have no words for how stupid that was."

"Then you should've helped. I told you someone was targeting my friends. What am I going to do, just sit back and let them get sent to the hospital?"

Sayer tried to take a deep breath. "So why exactly were you arrested?"

"The official charges are for assault, though the very nice policeman said they will drop the charges. They all thought it was funny."

"You assaulted the guy?"

"I did." She winked. "With Stanley's walker. Used it like a baseball bat on the kid."

Sayer's mouth fell open. "Are you serious?"

"They said I broke his nose and two ribs."

Sayer stared, mouth agape. The light turned green and she didn't notice until someone behind her honked.

Nana continued. "The cop said I shouldn't have hit him again once he was down, but the bastard hit Vicki Henderson so hard her brain is swelling. Anyway, I had to make sure he was down for good. I've seen the movies where the bad guy gets up."

"You took a mugger out with a walker?" Sayer's mouth twitched.

"I sure as hell did." Nana chuckled. "You should've seen the kid's face. Didn't expect Granny to come out swinging."

A laugh gurgled in Sayer's stomach. Bubbled up to her mouth.

"That'll teach him to mess with an old librarian," Nana continued.

The manic laugh escaped Sayer's lips in an explosion. Her pent-up stress came out in a wild cackle.

"Well, it's true," Nana said defensively.

Sayer laughed until she coughed, took a long breath in, and kept going. Eventually Nana joined in.

"Librarian . . ."

"I beat the ever-loving hell outta him. . . ."

"You . . . beat him . . ."

The two women dissolved into laughter. Not a joyous laughter, but laughter born of relief and fatigue.

Finally, as they drove, their laughter faded into a gentle silence, yellow streetlights sliding across their faces.

"Hey, do you know Senator Van Hurst?"

"Of course. He was elected during your grandfather's last election cycle. Poor man."

"Did you give any credence to the rumors that he had something to do with his daughter's disappearance?"

Nana tilted her head. "You found her? Is that the case you're on?"

Sayer nodded but didn't add anything more.

"Well, no," she finally answered. "I really didn't. She was their miracle baby. You know, we knew Charles and his wife when they had Gwen."

"Oh yeah?"

"Yeah . . . I probably shouldn't share this, but they were pregnant with twins."

"Twins?" Sayer swerved the bike, snapping her head to look at Nana.

"Careful!" Nana grasped the sidecar with both hands.

"She was pregnant with twins?" Sayer's heart did a foxtrot of excitement as she got them back on course.

Nana looked reluctant but nodded. "No one knew. But we were at a dinner together when she started bleeding. I ended up going with her to the ER." She let out a gruff harrumph. "The Van Hursts were old-school; men didn't go into hospital rooms with women having lady trouble."

"What happened, Nana?"

"What happened was the twins were somehow hurting each other. I can't remember the details. But they had to make a choice: save one, or lose them both."

"Oh my God," Sayer murmured.

"Yes, it was terrible. But that's no choice at all. They sacrificed the one twin to save Gwen's life. Now, whenever I hear Charles Van Hurst go off on pro-choice politicians . . . well, there's a reason I'm out of politics now that my husband is dead."

"Nana, that is more helpful than you can know."

"Well then, maybe something good can come from all that awfulness."

Twenty minutes later, Sayer dropped Sophia McDuff off in front of her Georgetown brownstone.

"Sorry I didn't help you, Nana. I didn't understand what was up."

Sophia climbed out of the sidecar, pulled off her helmet, and reached out for Sayer's cold hand. "I know you're busy with work. I know what you do is important. But you need to remember that we're important too. You should call your sister. Macey needs you too."

Sayer nodded vaguely.

Nana's voice turned sharp. "I feel like we're losing you again."

"Again?"

"After the car accident, you were so angry. You just shut down, and who wouldn't after their parents died?" Nana's eyes crinkled with a smile. "By God, you were such a terror, fierce and so driven. But also angry and distant. Then Jake came along . . ."

She squeezed Sayer's hand. "I know losing Jake was devastating, but don't lose us too, okay?"

Nana gave Sayer a kiss on the cheek and bounded up the steps.

Sayer waited until she was inside, then swung back around toward Alexandria, her heart in her throat.

Sayer dragged herself up the stairs, gratefully pushed open her door, and froze in the doorway. Her neighbor and the dog sat on her thread-bare futon. She had completely forgotten about the dog.

"Tino. How did you get in here?"

At the sight of Sayer, the puppy bounded toward her, tripping over his feet while barreling into her.

Tino plucked off his wire-rim glasses, closed his book, and hefted himself off the futon. "I picked the lock. Though *picked* is a polite word for it. I could have sneezed on that thing and it would have sprung open beneath my deft fingers. Seriously, darling, for an FBI agent, you should have a better dead bolt. Vesper has been fed and pottied and is ready for bed."

"Picked my lock? . . . Vesper?"

"All of God's creatures need a name." Tino patted her shoulder as he slid his broad belly past her out the door.

"How do you know how to pick a lock?" she shouted after him.

"A story for another time, calida. Happy to watch Vesper again tomorrow," he called back up as he trotted down to his apartment.

Sayer crouched down and let the slobbering beast nuzzle her. He licked her ear and then rolled over, begging for a belly rub. Barely conscious, she ruffled his fur, then stumbled to the kitchen, where she pulled a cold hot dog from the fridge and popped the cap off a nice stout. She dropped her bag onto her kitchen table and collapsed into a seat. Vesper curled against her legs and promptly fell asleep, vibrating her feet with puppy snores.

Sayer contemplated the pile of papers on the far end of the table.

Her research. Her life's work.

She stretched across the table and lifted the final scan of Dugald Tarlington's brain. The convicted serial killer's brain was perfect. Not a single anomaly. Underneath that scan sat copies of the twelve scans she had completed.

Sayer finished the hot dog, wiped her fingers on her pants, and picked up the familiar black-and-white brain images.

She plucked out the three perfect scans and lined them up on the table—a little monument to her failure. Three serial killers with three perfectly normal brains. Three scans that basically proved her theory wrong.

With a sigh, she pushed the pages aside. No time to deal with that right now.

"All right . . . Vesper. Bedtime. We've got a girl to save."

In the darkness, Sayer curled around Vesper on her lone mattress and fell sound asleep.

The girl's legs cramped. Her tongue was so swollen her cries sounded like throaty gurgling.

Her heart pounded so fast against the inside of her skull that she almost didn't hear the shuffling footsteps in the darkness.

A figure approached the cage.

The girl struggled to sit up, to call for help, but she couldn't control her limbs.

Please, she tried to say, but she could no longer speak, the words swallowed by her wheezing breath.

"Please," she exhaled before she realized it was the monster.

The monster with goggle eyes and snaking nose. She knew it was a face mask but the sight made her scream. She howled with incomprehensible need.

The monster calmly lifted a camera. The flash blinded the girl.

Unable to see anything, she collapsed, shaking, empty.

A jolt to the head woke Sayer with a start. She bolted up, reaching for her gun.

Her hand brushed against fur. A whimper and another jerky body movement. Vesper was having a nightmare.

"Hey, hey, you're safe, little guy." Sayer wondered if he was back in the cage with Gwen dying beneath him. She stroked his ears and the dog lifted his head, licking his floppy lips.

She breathed in the strange corn chip scent of the paws jutting into her face.

Vesper half yawned, half groaned as he stretched, then leaped up like they were late for something very exciting.

Groggy, Sayer checked her phone. Almost 6:00 A.M. At least she wouldn't be asleep when Vik got there in a few minutes.

Watching Vesper's goofy excitement, Sayer actually smiled as she shuffled out to her kitchen. The expression felt strange on her lips.

She let Vesper out to the garden, then turned on the small TV in the living room on her way to the sink. The sound of CNN filled the background while she got her coffee going.

"That's all for traffic. Now on to the latest development in the on-going saga of Gwendolyn Van Hurst. Senator Van Hurst released a statement early this morning claiming that the FBI have arrested a man in connection with the disappearance and murder of his daughter, the so-called Cage Killer."

Sayer dropped her mug of coffee onto the counter, sloshing burning fluid on her hand. She stepped back into the living room to stare at the perky reporter smiling through coral lipstick.

"The senator says the man they arrested is Hal Dillinger, the contractor mentioned as a person of interest in their joint press conference just yesterday. This latest development gives us all hope that this case will finally have some closure. The FBI has not yet confirmed the arrest, but our team interviewed the residents of the facility where Dillinger works and they confirmed a visit from the FBI."

Disbelief slowly boiled over into rage as Sayer stalked into her room. She threw on her clothes and stalked outside. Tino sat over a coffee out in the garden, Vesper at his side enjoying an ear rubbing. Tino raised his hand, about to offer a cheerful greeting.

"Don't," she managed to say. "I have to head in."

"All right, my dear. I've got the pooch."

Avoiding any further interaction, she jumped on her bike and roared off toward Quantico.

She seethed all the way there and stormed up to Holt's office.

At the sight of Holt, every drop of Sayer's rage drained straight into fear for her own life.

Holt stood behind her desk, leaning forward, phone against her ear. Sayer would have sworn she could see an actual tempest of dark emotion swirling around her. The assistant director's face glowered with murder.

Holt held up a finger, telling Sayer to wait.

"Yes, please connect me to the good senator." The contrast between Holt's murderous face and calm voice was frightening.

Both women waited in silence.

"Yes, good morning, Charles." Holt spoke into the phone with a low voice. "Would you like to explain this to me? . . . I don't care if you think you're helping. . . . Yes, I'm aware that it's your daughter we found. I don't know where you got your information, but I am calling to inform you that you got it wrong. Dillinger isn't our guy. Well, yes, I know you released a press release." Holt's teeth began to grind, but she maintained a soft voice. "That's why I'm calling. You've got to stop. Yes, fine. Thank you."

Holt ever so slowly hung up the phone.

"Guess you saw the news," Sayer said.

Nose flaring, Holt calmly walked past Sayer to the far side of the room.

With a suddenness that made Sayer jump, Holt shouted, "Fuck!" and punched a hole in the wall.

Sayer took a half step toward the door.

Breathing hard, Holt turned back to Sayer, cradling her hand. "I have got to stop doing that."

Sayer studied the hole in the wallboard and realized that the entire wall was uneven with slightly mismatched paint in at least six other spots.

Holt went back to her desk and sat down. "Bad habit. Let's keep the momentum rolling in our investigation. Let the PR people take care of Van Hurst and this nightmare."

Sayer nodded.

"Wasn't me, by the way. I gave Van Hurst nothing, but apparently he has other sources here." Holt's mouth became so tight it almost disappeared right into her face.

"But that's—"

Holt held up her hand, cutting Sayer off.

Unsure what to say next, Sayer was relieved when her phone buzzed. She glanced down at the text from Joan. *DNA results from the semen found on Gwendolyn Van Hurst's body came in. No match in system.*

Sayer sighed and showed the text to Holt, who grunted in response.

Forget that they hadn't actually arrested Dillinger; it was going to look like the FBI had just made a massive mistake to the media.

She did not point that out to Holt as she left, deciding that she wanted to live to see another day.

CONSTITUTION AVENUE,

WASHINGTON, D.C.

D.C. police officer Wilson Tooby walked slowly along Constitution Avenue. His hands shook and he wanted a shot of whiskey more than he had in almost twelve years.

He'd put off the visit to his partner in the hospital as long as he could, but now he wished he hadn't gone at all.

Mike had looked bad, his face all wrapped and swollen; the shotgun blast had shredded his whole upper body. Doctors said that he'd never eat without assistance, never lift anything with his hands, maybe never talk clearly again. They said he was lucky to be alive, but Wilson wasn't so sure.

It wasn't the drool soaking the gauze packed around Mike's mouth, or the lopsided way his whole body hung beneath the weird hammock thing, it was the look in Mike's eyes that Wilson couldn't shake. Poor bastard was crying while Wilson stood there trying to chat away like nothing was wrong.

He'd planned to ride the bus from the hospital to the crime scene on P Street, but he decided to walk to clear his head before meeting up with the FBI. He had the sketch of the drug buyer he'd seen the first day, and he wanted to hand-deliver it to the FBI, mostly just to feel like he was doing anything but sitting at his desk.

In good news, if his sobriety survived this week, it would survive anything. The guilt of not finding that poor girl piled on top of his partner almost getting killed was about as much guilt as one man could take.

Wiping sweat from his upper lip, he rounded the corner to the old town house on P Street. Out front, half a dozen DCPD uniforms listened to a guy in a suit giving them directions. Damn. He'd been hoping Agent Altair would be there, not some slightly stocky L.L.Bean-model-looking guy. He waited until the rest of his D.C. buddies headed in for another day in the sewers looking for clues or maybe an entry point.

He could tell from their body language that the uniforms were antsy; one of their own was injured and they weren't running the investigation.

A few of them noticed Wilson lingering and nodded in his direction. When your partner gets shot, everyone expresses sympathy, but there's also an undercurrent. An unspoken question. *Why didn't you have his back? Why didn't you protect him?* He could see it in their eyes.

Wilson'd been asking himself the same damn questions.

When L.L.Bean was finally alone, Wilson pulled the sketch from his bag and approached.

"Uh, Special Agent?"

"Yes?"

"I'm D.C. police officer Wilson Tooby; my partner and I found the DB here."

"Hi. Special Agent Wagner." They formally shook. "Your partner the one that was shot? Hope he's doing all right."

Wilson didn't answer, just pursed his lips and shook his head.

"Sorry to hear it." Agent Wagner sounded about as sincere as a used-car salesman. "How can I help you, Officer Tooby?"

"I wanted to hand-deliver this. It's the sketch of the guy we saw here the first day we came out. Agent Altair asked me to send it along."

"Ah right, thanks."

"Um, hey, you mind if I head in and help the guys in the sewer? I'm not on leave or anything since I didn't fire any shots. Just on desk duty until they can assign me a new partner. I'd like to help . . ." Though he didn't say it, Wilson was going down there no matter what Agent Wagner said.

"Sure, sure." Agent Wagner waved his hand dismissively. "Check in with your guys in there; they can assign you a quadrant to search. We're meeting back here in four hours."

Wilson nodded thanks and trudged into the crime scene. He paused at the top of the stairs where Mike was shot, then again where the cage had once hung, before descending into the bomb shelter and dropping into the sewer below.

The D.C. sewer system is nothing like the iconic tunnels of New York. There are no walkways above the draining water, no warren of beautiful brickwork to see. Instead, the sewers are nothing more than tubes that can easily fill to the top, a dangerous place to be in the rain. Especially considering the fact that if they did overflow, the D.C. Water and Sewer folks would release them directly into the Anacostia River, raw sewage and all.

Flashlights danced on the low ceiling of the sewer ahead. Wilson decided to head in the opposite direction. He might be doubling up, looking where they had already covered, but he couldn't bring himself to face the guys and their sympathy, genuine or not.

Instead he pulled his headlamp from his bag and strapped it on. He stepped down into ankle-deep water and ducked through a narrow concrete arch. It smelled better than he expected, like damp earth and mushrooms.

He wandered for a few minutes before he came to a four-way junction and realized that he should keep track of his path. Without a better plan, he pulled a Sharpie from his bag and, at the very edge of the tunnel, drew a small arrow pointing him back the way he came.

He quickly glazed over, eyes scanning nothing but concrete and trickling water with occasional flotsam and jetsam clotting pipe junctions. Water slowly wicked up his pants, soaking him to the waist. He trudged on in penance for his mistakes, replaying everything he could have done differently.

Why didn't he follow up on the first 911 call? He should've heard the genuine fear in that poor girl's voice.

Wilson made another turn and marked another arrow.

Why didn't he listen to his gut when they entered the house? He could tell something was wrong. Maybe if he'd gone first he would have been more cautious.

Wilson drew another arrow.

Maybe if he'd been in front, he would've seen the trip wire on the stairs.

Wilson leaned down to draw another arrow and froze. An X was scratched into the concrete tunnel, so small he would never have seen it if he hadn't leaned in to draw his own arrow.

The perfect X stood out pale and clean against the water-stained concrete.

He hurried back to the last junction and inspected the edges until, sure enough, he found another perfect X. He hurried down the marked tunnel, breathing fast with excitement.

Wilson fumbled with his cell phone out but no reception. Damn.

Three more junctions, each one marked with an X. At the end of the third turn, the tunnel dead-ended at a circular iron door. He approached slowly, remembering the traps back at P Street. Wilson paused for a long time, thinking about that dead girl in the cage. Someone else's daughter might still be alive if he hadn't been in such a hurry to get home to his own daughter. Deciding that he might deserve it if the damn hatch blew up in his face, he climbed the short ladder and turned the wheel to swing open the hatch.

With shaking hands, he pushed aside a thick piece of fabric, and cool air flooded the humid sewer. Wilson cautiously stepped through.

"What the hell?" he whispered.

Back at her desk, Sayer gathered her thoughts before the morning meeting. She lifted the photo of the girl.

"Who are you?"

"Let me know if she answers." Vik plopped into the chair next to her. "I went by your place. . . . Neighbor told me you roared off on your motorcycle like the devil was on your heels. Guessing you saw Van Hurst's latest?"

"Yeah, Holt isn't happy."

Vik snorted. "I know!"

They walked together toward the task force meeting, faces drawn.

Sayer's phone chirped. "Agent Altair."

"Agent Altair, this is Officer Wilson Tooby. . . ."

"Of course. How is your partner doing, Officer Tooby?"

"Not great, I'll tell ya." He breathed heavily. "Thanks for asking. Listen, I'm calling because I was down here in the sewers beneath the scene. Found something."

"The girl?" Sayer couldn't keep the excitement out of her voice.

"No. But it's definitely connected to our guy. You need to come see this."

CATACOMBS BELOW MOUNT
ST. SEPULCHER, WASHINGTON, D.C.

A long-faced priest pulled open the heavy iron gate and led Sayer and Vik down an arched staircase. Over the entry was a single word: NAZARENE.

"So the church maintains actual catacombs?" Sayer tried to understand what the hell was going on. After Wilson's call, they had raced to the Franciscan Monastery of Mount St. Sepulcher on Quincy Street. Something about an altar with symbols in an underground burial chamber. She'd grown up in the city and never heard of catacombs below D.C.

The young priest paused on the staircase so he could face Sayer. "Yes, the founder of our church actually went to Rome and took exact measurements of the catacombs there. These are a perfect reproduction, minus the bodies, of course." A smile flitted across his full lips. It was a practiced joke and Sayer realized he was probably the regular tour guide.

"Of course." Sayer's voice sounded slightly unsteady. They descended into a narrow, dimly lit hallway. The scent of stale air with just a touch of mold signaled that they were far belowground. The bare lightbulbs exposed gaping black recesses on either side of the hall. The empty maws felt hungry for human bodies.

Just inside the entry, a sepia-tiled mosaic of a skeletal Grim Reaper smiled at Sayer. Across the top it read, *From Death*.

"That's not true, I suppose." The priest stopped again as though he were unable to walk and speak at the same time. "We do maintain two sacred remains here, both kept in the saints' crypts."

"I noticed the padlock on the gate. Is there another way to access the catacombs?"

"Well, if you'd asked me that question yesterday I would have said no. I've been here for almost three years and had no idea that hatch into the sewers was there."

"Who would have known about it?"

"Not sure, the cleaning crew maybe."

"Who would know the combination to that lock?"

The priest paused in the shadows. "We've never had any trouble before . . . all of us living here, plus the cleaning crew, plus many of the volunteers have access. Oh, and the entire choir."

"Come up with a list, please."

"Of names? But that will be a hundred people, maybe more." The priest seemed flabbergasted by the request.

"With names."

Wilson Tooby stepped into the light at the very end of the hall, wringing his hands. Sayer pushed past the priest.

"Officer Tooby, so glad to see you."

He bowed his head.

"You found us something?"

"I sure did."

They entered a small side room. Fake candles flickered above a low altar. A tapestry hung to their right, so faded Sayer couldn't even make out the image. Behind the tapestry, a small metal hatch hung open. Muggy air leaked from the sewer into the cool room, fighting with the stale, overcooled air of the catacombs.

"You followed marks in the sewer?" Sayer asked, gesturing to the hatch.

"Yeah, little Xs scratched in the concrete. Ran straight here from the P Street scene."

Sayer grunted and turned her full attention to the altar. A low terra-cotta table ran along the back wall. Beneath the table, a glass crypt displayed the velvet-wrapped bones of what Sayer presumed was one of the saints.

On the stone wall behind the altar, two symbols were painted in blood. Each about the size of her palm, they were hastily drawn. Dried rivulets of blood ran in streaks down the wall, pooling around two large books at the center of the altar.

"No sign of any traps, I assume?" she asked Wilson.

He shrugged, neglecting to mention that he'd consciously decided to risk tripping one earlier. "Figure I would've set it off already if there was one."

Sayer's gaze roved around the small room, making one last sweep for traps, before she approached the altar. She focused first on the two symbols painted in blood. "Definitely our guy. These are the same symbols we found beneath the photo of the girl."

Vik looked down at his phone. "Evidence techs and hazardous-devices teams are here. On their way down now."

Sayer nodded.

"So what the hell are these?" Sayer leaned in to examine the symbols. "What do you think? A crescent and a cross? Religious symbology of some kind?"

Vik snorted. "Or a rabbit and a spear? These don't look like anything to me."

"Well, we are beneath a church, gotta mean something . . ."

Sayer leaned even closer to the symbols, holding her breath. When she finally stood up, she bared her teeth in an excited smile. "Whatever they mean, I'd bet my pension that this"—she pointed—"is a partial fingerprint!"

"Well, I'll be damned," Wilson Tooby said from across the room.

Finished assessing the symbols, she turned her attention to the most interesting thing in the room, two books stacked on top of the altar. They looked very out of place, a bright-blue plastic rectangle on top of a bright-red one.

She called to the priest over her shoulder, "Father, I assume these books don't belong here?"

"Definitely don't belong."

Unwilling to disturb anything before the evidence team got there, Sayer pulled out her worry beads to keep her hands occupied. The books were an unusual shape, tall slender rectangles with rings instead of a binding. A gold floral design circled the edges of the top book. She crouched to inspect the sides. The pages were thick and looked like they had plastic inserts.

"They're photo albums." She turned to Vik, a mixture of excitement and dread in her voice.

Voices echoed down the hallway.

"Evidence collection team," Vik said. "Let's back out and give them space to get started so we can see what kinds of photos our friend wanted us to see."

"I'll reschedule the task force meeting. I want to get a look at these as soon as we can."

With her shoulders practically knotted up around her ears, Sayer backed away from the altar, knowing for certain that she did not want to see what the photo albums contained.

It took almost thirty minutes for evidence techs to document and photograph the site enough that Sayer could touch the photo albums.

When they finally gave her the go-ahead, she hesitated for just a moment.

Vik stood next to her, working gum in his mouth like a punishment. "Don't want to open it, do you?"

"Not even a little bit."

"I know! Sometimes I wonder why I didn't become a journalist or something."

Sayer snorted at the image of Vik doggedly interviewing celebrities.

"We'll take a cursory look now just to make sure there's nothing actionable inside. If not, we bring it back to the lab for analysis."

With a gloved hand she gently opened the book. The first page contained two photos, both of Gwendolyn Van Hurst. In the first one, Gwen held a newspaper, terrified eyes, different puppy clutched to her side. Next to the photo was a scrawled note: *Day 1*.

"Not Vesper." She pointed at the puppy.

"Wonder what happened to the first dog?"

The second photo looked similar but lacked a newspaper. Next to it, *Day 2*.

Sayer flipped a few pages ahead. Then a few more. Each page contained four photos, each with a notation about the day. Occasionally the photographs would skip a day or two. Sometimes additional notes were written next to the day. *Unsuccessful attempt* or *Increase DMT*. Eventually the first dog disappeared and Vesper showed up, a silver bundle of gangly limbs.

Sayer stopped at one photo. In it, Gwen held Vesper and the two stared at each other. The young girl was purposefully, defiantly ignoring the photographer. It showed a strength that made Sayer's throat tighten with emotion. Next to the picture it said, *Day 262. Failed experiment.*

"Experiment!" Sayer pointed to the writing. "This is some kind of experiment!"

"Ho-leee shit," Vik said.

Not really wanting to, Sayer flipped to the very end of the book. The last photo showed Gwen like a flesh-covered skeleton collapsed on the floor of the cage. Next to it the scrawling script said, *Beyond the veil, Day 312.*

"Good God," Sayer muttered. "Three hundred twelve days."

"And now we know he came back after she died. So much for being spooked by the cops. He left her to starve on purpose and came back to take a photo of it."

She flipped back a week to when Wilson and his partner came by the first time based on the 911 call. No note on that day. But two days before that, a long note ran along the margin next to a photo of Gwen looking blank but fairly well nourished. *Experiment 9.1 deemed a complete failure. Subject's support terminated.*

"My God. It wasn't ever the phone call that spooked the perp. He decided to stop feeding her two days before the call, then came back right up until she died, taking photos every day."

Sayer closed the album.

"He documented her death." Vik swayed with disgust.

"Yeah, looks like he deemed her a failed experiment, whatever that means." Sayer swallowed hard. "I really don't want to see what's in this one."

Despite what she said, Sayer flipped open the second album.

The first photo was missing but the second photo showed a frightened girl holding a tabby kitten.

"It's our Jane Doe," she whispered. Vik peered over her shoulder. "9.2, see."

Together they flipped through page after page.

"Same stuff," Vik said as they read about Jane Doe's experiment.

When they got to Day 180, Sayer let out a soft gasp. It read, *Experiment 9.2 deemed a complete failure. Subject's support terminated.*

She did some quick calculations in her head. "This was only five days ago. She could still be alive!"

They got to the last photo and stared.

The girl looked up into the camera with feral eyes, mouth open in a scream of terror.

"This was yesterday," Vik growled. "That bastard set it up for us to find this, didn't he?"

Sayer looked away from the image, sour bile gathering at the back of her throat. "Let's get these back. We need to go through all the notes and see if there's anything more we can figure out."

As they left, a gaggle of reporters jostled outside shouting, "Any news on the Cage Killer?"

"Any new leads, Agent Altair?"

"Any luck finding the missing girl?"

Sayer ignored the mics and cameras, gritting her teeth as she passed them. The Cage Killer. She hoped the bastard didn't know that the media had given him a name. She would ask him when she caught him.

Sayer's phone buzzed just as she entered the task force meeting. She answered, holding up a finger so the full room would quiet down.

"Special Agent Altair."

"Hi, Agent Altair, I'm calling from the evidence team in the catacombs." His breathless voice kicked Sayer's heart up a notch. "We're still here processing but wanted to update you. We lifted that print! Not a full one, but it'll be plenty to make a comparison."

"Yes!" Sayer pumped her fist and the entire task force perked up.

"We're estimating the blood isn't more than a day old," the tech said. "No explosives found. Will keep you up to date."

Sayer grunted a thanks and turned to the room.

"All right! We've got DNA and now a partial fingerprint from the catacomb scene. Now we just need someone to compare them to!"

Smiles transferred round the room. Vik held up a hand to Joan for a high five, and she looked at him like he was crazy but then relented with a half smile. Even Andy was there on time and smiled. Sayer tried to smile, but the image of Jane Doe burned her mouth into a taut line.

This was the first break since they found Gwendolyn Van Hurst's dead body, and Sayer let the team have a moment to enjoy. None of the task force had seen the photos yet.

"All right, all right, it's almost lunchtime. Let's focus so we can all go get something to eat. This is a good step, but it doesn't mean a thing unless we find our guy. Let's do a quick once around the room, share what we've got, then get back out there. I'll start.

"I've done a once-over of the photo albums we found in the catacombs. There isn't much, just a few notes about experiments and a record of the girls' days. Gwen's last photo was from day three hundred twelve. And we now know for sure he went back to watch her die."

The room groaned.

"Yeah, it's a long time. The photos really drive home how long that poor girl was there. The second album . . ." Sayer trailed off, willing her voice not to crack. "Jane Doe has also been deemed a failure, but she was alive as of yesterday."

"How long ago did the unsub stop providing water?" Joan asked.

"Five days."

Joan put her hands to her mouth with horror.

"Yeah, so she won't have long. Maybe one or two more days before dehydration kills her."

The cheerful mood drained from the room.

"So we've got to focus. Based on what we found, we now know that the perp views this captivity as some kind of experiment."

"Experiment?" one of the DCPD uniforms asked.

"Yeah, we're not sure what yet, but clearly something related to the administration of the drug DMT and probably related to the video. I've handed the albums back over to evidence. They're going to do a full collection, check for trace and fingerprints, and do a close look at each photo for any clues. Maybe our guy missed something in the photos he left behind. I've also sent copies of the handwriting for analysis just to see if we can get anything there."

Sayer wrote *Experiment* on the whiteboard.

"All right, data team, where are you on everything?"

The mousy blonde shuffled papers. "Well, we tried to track the DMT, but apparently you can order that online no problem. We located the origin of the cages. Unfortunately we tracked them to a sort of warehouse that sells . . . used oddities. I just got off the phone with the owner. The bad news, they sold three cages."

Sayer groaned. Three cages meant there could be a third victim out there.

"The worse news," the data tech continued, "is they sold the cages over a year ago and have no record of anything. No exact date, no credit cards, nothing. The employees there turn over a lot, so we're trying to track down whoever sold them, see if they can remember anything."

"Sounds good," Sayer said, trying to keep the fatigue from her voice. "How hard are the cages to move around? They look massive."

"Not that hard considering how formidable they look. They actually break down at the joints and could be moved by one person with a dolly. They were originally designed as bear cages for traveling circuses, so they needed to break down flat, and the sides even fold." The tech shuffled pages, reading off her notes. "One thing, the guy said they got them cheap because the cages were defective."

"Oh?" Sayer asked.

"Apparently the corner bolts that supported the weight of the animals were really weak. Said bears kept falling out the bottom."

The room chuckled, imagining bears suddenly crashing to the ground, free from their cages.

"All right, what else?" Sayer asked.

"Nothing new on the girl's ID. We've expanded out beyond missing-person reports." The data tech took a long breath. "The Smithsonian people think the symbol beneath the photo in the bomb shelter might just be designed by the unsub."

"What does that mean?" Sayer paced at the front of the room. "I can think of two possibilities," she said, answering her own question. "Either he's creating his own symbology as part of his pathology, or he's messing with us." She paused her pacing. "I'm inclined to believe the second. We've wasted tons of time on them.

"A diversion would fit with the traps. Our unsub is showing off. Messing with us. Trying to show us he's smarter than us. It's also a good delay tactic. He has us looking up all kinds of stuff: symbols, bombs, cages. It's brilliant because it means we can't figure out which of these clues are misdirection and which are genuinely essential to his pathology. We need to weed that stuff out, focus on the things we know are part of the murder modus operandi."

"I disagree." Andy stood up to address the room.

"Okay, Andy, why?"

"I think we need to drill down on those symbols. They've clearly got meaning to our unsub. We need to know why he's sending us these messages."

Sayer was briefly stunned at the blatant challenge from Andy. "Your opinion is noted, but this investigation will continue in the direction I believe is most important. You have a problem with my leadership, take it up with Assistant Director Holt."

Andy muttered soft enough so only she could hear, "Sure, know how that'll go," as he stepped aside.

"Sit down, Andy," Joan said from the table, eyes squinting with genuine anger.

Sayer's heart pounded. Purposefully ignoring Andy, Sayer turned to the data team. "Did we ever figure out how Gwen got a phone to make that call to 911? No phone found near the cage."

A tech shook her head. "No clue."

Sayer grunted and paced at the head of the table. "Okay, I've got one more key piece of information to share. From a private source, I found out that Gwen was actually a twin in vitro. The twin was aborted to save Gwen's life, but she was originally a twin."

Vik whistled. "So we've got another thing that points to twins. They've got to be important."

"Important to our unsub, but also gives us another lead. Who could have possibly known that Gwen was a twin? Seems like something only people close to the family would know."

The room perked up.

"All right. Andy, you've still got a bunch of DCPD uniforms helping you. Shift your canvass to the area around the church. Talk to parishioners, interview neighbors, see if we can knock something loose there."

"Sure," Andy grumbled, furious at being shunted to canvass duty again.

"Vik and I will keep combing through the original Van Hurst file." She held up a hand. "Just a reminder that Gwen's funeral is tomorrow morning. It's going to be a media circus. I've compiled a list of agents who should attend. Your assignments will be handed out in the morning. I'll be there as well. I doubt the unsub will show up, but be on watch.

"Last but not least, Cindy's family is having a private service for her on Sunday. They've requested family only, but feel free to send flowers or make a donation in her name."

Sayer paused. "Anything I'm missing?"

The room remained silent.

"All right, we've got DNA and a fingerprint. Things are moving slow but steady. Time to dig in. Let's go get him!"

Sayer sat down at her desk and spread the old Van Hurst case file out in front of her. She shuffled the pieces, moving them around, hoping to connect the dots somehow.

Her phone rang and she jumped to answer it, edgy with frustration.

"Agent Altair," she barked.

"It's Wilson again. Officer Wilson Tooby. Listen, in all the excitement in the catacombs I forgot to follow up. See if that suspect sketch panned out."

"Which sketch is that?"

"Of the drug buyer I saw that first day we went out to the house. Hinky white guy. I wondered if it turned into anything."

"Oh, I haven't seen a sketch yet. When did you send it over?"

"I gave it to the agent running the sewer search this morning."

Sayer sat up. A sketch of a possible suspect, no matter how unlikely, should've been immediately filed and flagged. She flipped through the docs and images submitted to Rapid Start. Nothing about a sketch.

"Well, I'll have to track that down. You remember the name of the agent you gave it to?"

"Sure, fellow named Andy."

"Agent Wagner?"

"That's the guy."

Sayer barely managed to mutter a thanks and hang up before marching to Andy's office.

No one was there, so Sayer made her way to the break room.

Vik sat at the small table sipping a coffee, looking over his own copy of the Van Hurst file.

"You seen Andy?"

Vik glanced up. "Whoa, what did he do? You look like Holt right now."

"Apparently Officer Tooby gave him a sketch of the guy they saw near the scene. Handed it to him early this morning, but it's not in the system and he didn't mention it at the meeting just now."

"What?" Vik looked mystified. Not much worse than withholding data during an investigation. There was a damned good reason Rapid Start was implemented. Studies found that a key factor in solving rates for felony crimes was communication and sharing data between investigators.

Sayer dialed her phone, muttering, "Goddammit, Andy. What are you up to?"

She hung up when she got his voice mail.

"Maybe he's down in the cafeteria?" Vik offered.

Sayer spun and stalked all the way across the Quantico grounds to the cafeteria. Vik gathered his files and followed at a safe distance, clearly wanting to see what would happen next.

Inside she spotted Andy at a table with three other agents.

"Andy!" she shouted as she approached.

He looked up, confused.

"Did you get a possible-suspect sketch from Officer Tooby this morning?"

Andy shrugged. "Yeah, I got his sketch of a drug buyer or something."

"Is there a reason it's not in the system?"

Andy rolled his eyes. "Listen, Sayer. It looks like a movie star. Clearly Tooby's idea of a drug buyer scoring a hit."

Sayer stood there breathing hard, trying to calm her temper.

Andy raised both hands in mock surrender. "Fine, fine, I've got it right here. You want it?" He gestured to his file folder on the table.

"Yes, Andy. I want the sketch. Even if it's nothing, that's not how you run an investigation. You know that."

Andy's face darkened at being scolded. He thrust a page at Sayer.

She looked at it and sucked the air through her teeth.

Vik cautiously approached, looked over her shoulder, and let out a low moan.

Andy's eyes darted between them. "What?"

Sayer stepped so close to Andy her nose almost touched his.

"Andy, we know this guy. If you'd done your job, we could've brought him in hours ago. There's a girl dying out there and it's possible we could have her home by now. This one's on you." Sayer poked his chest, hard, then stormed up to Holt's office to coordinate a raid.

"The real estate agent?" Holt leaned on her desk, face gleaming with the thrill of the chase.

"Yeah, Franklin Winters. He was there, just outside the town house on P Street when the D.C. cops came the first time. There at the scene! We questioned him and he pinged a suspicious bell with me, but he cooperated." Sayer paced, connecting a few dots as she spoke.

"Pointed us to the contractor, in fact," Vik added.

"Exactly. He lied flat out about the last time he went to the house, then gave us Hal Dillinger. Obviously trying to throw us off. Said he hadn't been to the house in months. Here's proof he was there that morning."

"I'll be damned." Holt grinned.

"I've got the data team info-gathering. They're doing basic recon, but we already have his home and office address. I called him to casually ask some follow-up questions. He said he'll be in his office for the next few hours. I want to go in now and I want a team to come in with me."

"You've got it, Sayer. With potential booby traps and the possibility that the girl is there, I'm sending SWAT and Hostage Rescue with you."

"Perfect." Sayer headed to the locker room to gear up. As she walked she imagined the wrath of the gods about to descend on Franklin Winters, and she smiled.

CAPITOL HILL, WASHINGTON, D.C.

An hour later, Sayer stood with a small group making the final preparations a few blocks from Franklin Winters's office. She shifted from foot to foot to let off some energy.

The gruff SWAT lead gestured her and Vik over. "All right, the team's in place. Winters has been spotted through a window, so we know he's still there. Here's the plan: Agent Altair, you and Agent Devereaux go to his door. You get him to open the door, make sure there are no possible hostages nearby, and take him down right away. I'll be listening in. If there's a possible hostage situation, just say, 'No go,' and I'll understand. If he's got a weapon or there's a problem, the SWAT team will be there before he can twitch a pinky finger. Your job is to get the hell out of our way."

Sayer nodded. "Got it. Say 'no go' if possible hostage situation. Otherwise try to take him quickly. Any problem and we will skedaddle out of your way and let you do your thing."

The burly man nodded and grunted. Vik also grunted understanding. Sayer almost grunted as well, then had the intense urge to laugh at the Neanderthal communication. The visceral electricity of the impending hunt must be how human ancestors felt before a mammoth hunt.

Shoulder to shoulder, Vik and Sayer set off down the short alley to Winters's real estate office.

She knocked on the metal door. "Mr. Winters? It's Special Agent Altair. We've come to ask you a few follow-up questions."

Franklin Winters pulled open the inner door and squinted at Sayer.

Sayer casually scanned for any possible weapon.

"Afternoon, Mr. Winters. Thanks for agreeing to see us again. We just have a few follow-up questions."

"Heard you arrested that contractor fellow." He made no move to open the security door.

"May we come in, Mr. Winters?"

The real estate agent seemed to be thinking something over. Sayer's body buzzed with anticipation. She was ready for him to slam the door and run. His hand hovered at the lock for a few moments longer than it should have.

He leaned forward and looked down the alley behind Vik. Nothing but damp concrete and a few overflowing Dumpsters.

Winters unlocked the last bolt and swung the door inward. He turned to lead them down the short hallway into his office.

They made their move.

Vik slammed into him from behind, taking him facedown while Sayer swiftly wrenched his arms back and slipped the zip tie over his hands.

"Hey! What the . . . !" Winters shouted.

Sayer cinched the ties.

"What the hell are you doing?" Winters struggled against Vik, who was hoisting him up.

"We got him." Sayer spoke into the small mic. "Winters is secure."

"Aw, no fun . . . ," the SWAT leader joked in her earbud. "I'll send in the hazardous-devices crew to clear the scene."

Vik dragged Winters out into the alley, reading him his rights as a phalanx of vehicles screeched to a stop around them. The bomb squad began to suit up to make sure nothing at Winters's office was rigged to blow.

"You want to tell us where the girl is?" Sayer demanded.

"What girl? What the hell is going on here? I demand someone tell me what's happening!" Winters sputtered.

Ignoring him, Vik pushed Winters into the back of the transport van and clicked a cuff over one wrist.

"I demand—"

Sayer slammed the door in the face of his protests.

Vik and Sayer smiled widely at each other.

While Winters was processed, Sayer and Vik went by Franklin Winters's Capitol Hill town house. The outside was as bland as a building could be: tan shutters, dark brown trim accenting light brown brick. Inside, the hazmat team had already cleared the entire place and the evidence team swarmed every room.

"No hidden rooms. No raving journals of a murderous madman . . ." The lead evidence tech wiped sweat off his brow. "Nothing at all, really. This feels like one of those model homes. No mementos, no photo albums, nothing personal at all except a photo of Winters and what we're assuming is a girlfriend on his desk."

Sayer and Vik stalked the place top to bottom.

"This's the most average place I've ever seen," Sayer said. "It's got to be a front. Where he sleeps at night but nothing more."

Vik agreed.

"All right, we're not going to find anything here." Sayer smiled, feeling slightly giddy about the arrest. "Let's head back and see what our new friend has to say for himself."

Sayer met with the mousy data tech in her cubicle overflowing with stacks of paper teetering around four separate computer monitors. "He's got no record. But there's something strange with his background. I'm not finding anything before 2009. Like nada."

"No birth records?"

"Literally nothing. No social security number, no birth record, no credit history, no evidence of prior residence. Either he moved here from the moon or he miraculously appeared fully formed."

"Or he's got something to hide . . ."

"You said it."

Sayer spent a minute contemplating. Where would Winters keep his second victim?

"Hey, can you cross-reference Franklin Winters's real estate listings with the bomb shelter registry?"

The data tech grunted an affirmative. "Can do, though it might take a while. The bomb shelter registry is kept at the courthouse, which is closed for the weekend. I'll make sure someone is there

Monday morning, but then we'll have to manually compare the lists. It's not digital." She sniffed with disdain at the thought of paper records.

"All right. Let me know as soon as you find anything."

Sayer met up with Vik in the hall heading down to interrogation. Even though it wasn't either of their expertise, Holt decided that they should do the initial interrogation since he already knew them. Sayer reviewed interrogation basics in her head. Despite all the good-cop/bad-cop nonsense on TV, the science of interrogation is clear—rapport and connection are key to gathering accurate information. Sayer and Vik would both try to connect with Winters, and then whomever he responded to would run with it. Once a connection was established, they would begin to tell a long, rambling but friendly account of the events that happened on P Street. The more long-winded they were, the less Winters would be able to keep everything straight. Especially if he had rehearsed answers planned. Hard to believe, but more often than not criminals would interject corrections when the interrogator telling the story got facts wrong.

As they made their way through winding hallways, Sayer could feel the entire office building humming with excitement. The unit had been on edge after Cindy and Ezra, and this felt like a reason to celebrate. The pieces were finally falling into place.

"Our friend has a past. Or should I say no past." She explained to Vik that Winters had no records before 2009.

Joan ran to catch up with them, waving a piece of paper.

"Good news. I pulled a print from Winters's office. Don't ask me to testify in court yet, but I did a quick comparison and I'd say his print matches the one we got in the catacombs."

"Yes." Sayer pumped her fist. "Now we've just got to get him to give up the location of the other girl."

"I hope for his sake she's still alive," Vik growled.

.   .   .

"I absolutely refuse to say anything to any of you. This is an absolute miscarriage of justice and I plan to sue you into the ground. I did not hurt that girl and I'm confident the facts will prove it."

"I understand, Mr. Winters. Can I call you Franklin?" Sayer smiled and sat across from Winters. She held out a cup of coffee, since research shows that people with a warm drink in their hands are inclined to relax and chat more.

He ignored it.

"No, none of this good-cop bullshit. I know how this goes, and I refuse to talk to you until my lawyer gets here."

"Franklin." Vik spoke up. "Listen, we don't know what happened. That's why we want you to explain it to us. Maybe this is all just a misunderstanding. Maybe you were protecting Gwendolyn from something?"

Slightly wild-eyed, Winters stared at Vik for a moment. Sayer couldn't tell if he was close to violence or tears.

"Not a word without a lawyer. I did not kill that girl!" Winters spat out, then turned away in his chair.

As Sayer watched his combination of indignation and fear, her gut twinged with concern. His reaction seemed pretty damned genuine, but she knew better than to trust her gut with a killer like this. A high-IQ sociopath is dangerous exactly because he knows how to manipulate your gut instincts.

But the interrogation was over. Asking for a lawyer meant they had to wait. Sayer gritted her teeth so hard they verged on cracking. For a moment she let herself picture the last photo of Jane Doe. Rage welled in her chest and she fought the urge to slam Winters's face into the table.

When lives are on the line, do the ends ever justify the means? Could justice ever be served through violence? Sayer didn't know the answer to that one.

She shook off the anger and stood up.

"All right, Franklin. Your lawyer is on his way. Things would be better for you in the long run if you'd just talk to us."

As they walked through the door he spoke up again. "You're wrong about this."

"That's not what the fingerprint data says. Nor the cops who saw you there on P Street last week."

Sayer felt some satisfaction at the look of shock on his face as they left the room. Let him stew on that.

Sayer, Joan, and Vik sat together in the cafeteria as it shut down around them. Sayer chowed on a cheeseburger and french fries while Joan picked at her salad. Despite the knot in her gut about the missing girl, Sayer was hopeful that they had their man. Now to either get him to talk or to tear apart his life until they found her.

"We got DNA from his house. The lab is using the new three-hour analysis machine. Won't be long now before we can compare our guy here to the DNA found on Gwendolyn," Joan said.

Sayer grunted, "Good," with her mouth full.

Vik read over a printout. "Winters's got no family here."

Sayer grunted again. All she could think about was Franklin Winters sitting in the interrogation room while that girl rotted in a cage somewhere. Given the fact that he had bought three cages, maybe two girls. Possibly terrified, clearly starving. If he sat on his hands long enough and Sayer couldn't find that girl, she would die.

"Looks like good ole Franklin wasn't doing all that well in the world of real estate. Looks like he sold low-end stuff, not a shock seeing the place on P Street."

Sayer nodded and thought about the neighborhood. Not terrible but not great either depending on the block, sort of half gangs and half underpaid interns from Capitol Hill. "Well, nothing we can do here tonight. Let's all go get some rest. Start fresh first thing."

They patted each other on the back, and Sayer felt a moment of closeness to Vik and Joan that she hadn't felt in a long while. Camaraderie, friendship, the sense that someone else out there understood the nightmare she waded through every day.

That feeling carried through to her arrival home. Tino's placid warmth, Vesper's enthusiastic greeting full of adoration.

As Sayer drifted off to sleep, she vowed to herself that she would find that girl if it was the last thing she did.

UNKNOWN LOCATION

The girl could barely move. The sharp pains in her stomach had faded into a longing that consumed everything. Longing for food, water, anything.

Her body felt dull, collapsed. Her arms and legs like insect limbs, slender and brittle.

The kitten was barely breathing, limp in her hands like a pile of tiny bones held together by matted fur.

The girl felt thirsty. So thirsty that she thought she was imagining the sound of water dripping nearby. But it persisted: *drip . . . drip . . . drip*.

Water hitting plastic.

She opened gritty eyes and pulled herself toward the sound. A drop hit her arm and she froze, body quaking. Another fell. The girl remembered the old pipe above the cage that had occasionally leaked water.

With a cry, she licked her arm, then turned her mouth upward to catch more. A drop hit her cheek and she keened with frustration at missing the fluid.

Another drop hit one of the old food wrappers next to her. Then another and another. She probed with a trembling hand and found a small pool of water on the crumpled plastic.

The dripping stopped.

The girl imagined the water sliding down her throat, how good it would feel, but then Bast shifted by her side, breath raspy and shallow. The kitten was on the verge of death.

She paused for only a moment before sliding Bast next to the wrapper and guiding the kitten's mouth to the little pool.

Bast greedily lapped up the water with little mewling grunts of joy.

As the girl faded yet again into blessed unconsciousness, she felt the rumble of the kitten purring next to her chest.

NATIONAL SHRINE OF THE IMMACULATE CONCEPTION, WASHINGTON, D.C.

Sayer rumbled up to the Basilica of the National Shrine of the Immaculate Conception and, as usual, the sight of the massive church took her breath away. The Romanesque-Byzantine fanciness didn't do much for her, but it was where she went to church with her mom and dad before they died. She had refused to return afterward, no matter how much Nana pushed. To Sayer, God had died with her parents.

The golden glow of early morning cast long shadows across the ground as somber people filed through the trio of arches into the main sanctuary. Around them in an obscene semicircle, the media jostled and called for attention, begging for a comment. The media circus made her stomach churn for the poor people who were here to mourn the loss of someone they loved. Senator Van Hurst worked his way down the line of reporters, flashing a bereaved pout for each camera as he gave a brief interview. Sayer felt the bile of fury rise in the back of her throat.

Trying not to punch Van Hurst on camera, she refocused her attention on the crowd. An entire Behavioral Analysis Unit team was strategically placed to observe everyone here, and she identified at least three agents. Sayer had arranged the observation herself even though they had Winters in custody. Something just didn't feel right about him and she didn't want to miss anything important.

She spotted Andy, no doubt leading the BAU team observing the funeral. Then Sayer noticed her nana arriving alone. Sayer hurried to catch up.

"Nana!"

Sophia McDuff turned in her classic black dress and veiled hat. As Sayer got closer she realized that Nana was crying.

She hurried to her side. "Nana, are you okay?"

Nana slowed slightly and stared into Sayer's face, seeking something.

"I mean . . . you've been crying," Sayer added.

"Of course I'm crying. I'm walking into the funeral of a child who was murdered by some kind of monster. The question is, why aren't you crying as well?"

Sayer let the comment roll off her back, but it still stung.

"I'm sorry." Nana shook her head and took Sayer's arm. Sayer noticed how thin her wrists looked.

Nana continued, "I know things are different for you. Have to be different. You know I'm so proud . . ." Her voice cracked and Sayer wrapped an arm around Nana's bony shoulders. "You know I'm proud of you, I just don't have the ability to distance myself from the images of that poor girl before she died. She was just so full of life. Had so much ahead of her."

Heads bowed, they made their way inside. The National Shrine's interior gleamed, ceilings glowing with rich red and blue mosaics.

The two women took a seat on a burnished pew. Sayer marveled at her nana. The woman was the toughest person she knew, and that was including Janice Holt. Nana was fierce and aggressive, and she never backed down from a fight for something she knew was right, but the most amazing part was that, despite all of her awesome ferocity, she never relinquished her humanity. Nana just seemed to feel love and compassion as much as righteous fury, a balance Sayer longed for.

The crowd settled into their seats and the D.C. Boys Choir began a high, piercing song of mourning. Their clear voices echoed along the cavernous sanctuary, raising goose bumps on Sayer's arms with the beauty of it. The casket arrived with no additional fanfare, just a grim-faced circle of men carrying a heartbreakingly small coffin up the aisle.

As they approached, a video began to play, projected at the front of the sanctuary.

Accompanied by the sweet, soaring song, Gwen's face appeared, a single tooth akimbo in her mouth as she took her first steps. Gwen as a little girl twirling with a sparkler on the Fourth of July. Senator Van Hurst running behind her bike, releasing it and watching as she pedaled away. Her climbing into a limo for prom wearing a poufy concoction of taffeta and lace.

This was a theatrical production meant to throttle the attendees with emotion. And it was working too. Even Sayer felt her eyes water at the images of Gwendolyn Van Hurst so full of life.

Sayer felt herself emotionally pulling away. Shutting down the empathy that squeezed her heart. Realizing what she was doing, Sayer forced herself to watch more of the slide show. The child's face full of pure joy, eyes crinkled with the genuine pleasure of being safe and cared for. Gwen carving a pumpkin last Halloween. She and Senator Van Hurst wrapping Christmas presents at some local shelter. A gaggle of teenage girls wearing Santa hats, arms thrown over each other's shoulders.

Wait. The girl next to Gwen . . .

Sayer's heart spiked into her throat. Heart-shaped cheeks, copper skin, just enough for Sayer to feel an electric jolt of recognition. Jane Doe!

She stood up abruptly, gathering scowls from those around her. With a pat of apology on Nana's hand, Sayer began to crawl over the people blocking her from the aisle, not letting herself look at Nana, who was no doubt reacting to her sudden departure with horror.

She rushed to the front of the church. Murmurs began to spread among the mourners at the strange woman storming toward the front of the church in the middle of the funeral. A private-security agent stepped in front of Sayer.

She hissed, "FBI, I need to ask the senator a question."

"Right now?"

Sayer answered by shoving her badge in his face.

The agent's eyebrows rose, but he stepped aside.

Van Hurst watched her approach with an incredulous mask. His nostrils flared with fury, eyes blinking with the need to remain fairly calm as he sat to the side of the dais.

Sayer ignored the murmurs and Van Hurst's rage. "The girl in the Santa hat with Gwen?" she tried to whisper, but the urgency in her voice made it come out as a gruff demand.

"What?" Van Hurst was equal parts shocked and furious.

"The girl with Gwen in the Santa hat?" Sayer repeated.

"I've no idea . . ."

"Where was it taken? The photo?"

Van Hurst looked directly into Sayer's eyes, realizing that this had something to do with the case. "Sanctuary House. Downtown." He leaned forward, eyes blazing.

Without another word, Sayer fled the church, frantically texting an update to the entire task force. *Sanctuary House downtown DC, Jane Doe and Gwen both there! Could be the connection! Forward address and info asap.*

Outside, Sayer made her way down the line of cameras pointed at the reporters all performing solemn faces as they reported the funeral. She managed to tune them out until she heard one particularly lantern-jawed reporter say the words "Sanctuary House" into the camera. Sayer froze.

Her phone buzzed with an address and phone number for Sanctuary House.

The reporter held his hand to his ear, listening to something. "We've just gotten an update. It appears that the killer might have found the victims at the downtown shelter for immigrant children. Is this shelter his hunting ground? More as our reporters arrive on the scene."

Sayer strode over to the lantern-jawed fellow.

"Hey, we're live!" the cameraman shouted.

"Where did you get that information?" she demanded.

"Uh, Special Agent Sayer Altair"—the reporter looked over her shoulder into the camera—"lead of the Cage Killer investigation. Do you care to comment? What's next now that you've linked the victims to Sanctuary House?"

Sayer leaned dangerously close to the reporter and poked him in the chest. "No, I will not comment. Instead, you will tell me where you heard about Sanctuary House."

He paled slightly but put on a winning smile for the camera. "As a reporter, I'm unable to reveal my sources."

Sayer stalked away, knowing she'd better leave before she punched him on camera. The FBI forgave her for the first time she socked a reporter, but she would not get a second chance.

Far enough from the media, she furiously dialed the number for Sanctuary House to warn them that reporters were about to descend on their facility. The shelter director seemed annoyed but clearly had no qualms about locking the press out.

Sayer stalked back over to the lantern-jawed reporter. The camera was off and he looked furious, about to light into her.

"A source is one thing. Illegally accessing FBI communications is another," Sayer said, interrupting his impending tirade.

"What?"

"I have reason to believe that someone is illegally accessing FBI communications. A felony."

Lantern Jaw's smooth forehead would have shown anger except for the Botox. Finally he shrugged. "Whatever, it's anonymous anyway. We just get updates as they come in. Texts straight to our producer."

The reporter showed Sayer his phone. The text on his phone was a verbatim copy of the text Sayer had sent the task force not five minutes before.

She dialed Holt.

"Did you just see that?" Sayer practically yelled.

"You almost punching Brock Tanner on live TV. Yes, I saw that."

"You know what I meant."

Holt sighed. "Yes, I saw."

"I texted the task force less than five minutes ago and it's already out to reporters! Either someone hacked us or we've got someone inside forwarding our communication to God knows who."

Holt's breath grew slightly labored, and for a brief second Sayer wondered if Holt was going to have a heart attack. Instead she finally growled, "I'm on it. We'll track who accessed those communications and when. No one inside my org leaks like this and gets away with it."

As Sayer threw a leg over her bike and pulled on her helmet, she thought, *Thank God we at least caught the monster that did this terrible thing. Now to find Jane Doe before it's time to attend her funeral as well.*

SANCTUARY HOUSE, WASHINGTON, D.C.

Sayer pulled up in front of the Sanctuary House shelter for orphaned immigrant children. The rambling, one-story older building was covered with a rainbow of murals. Sayer could identify art from around the world and wondered if the kids themselves contributed. A few picnic benches sat out front and a diverse mix of teenagers lounged, laughed together, and hunched over their phones. At first they looked like any group of teens, but the longer Sayer watched, the more she noticed a scarred arm here, a forced smile there. Though they laughed and chatted, these kids had none of the easy body language of American teens hanging out. These were kids who had survived wars and refugee camps, and lost their families in the process.

The kids all turned to watch Sayer, clearly aware she was an official of some kind despite showing up on a motorcycle. One girl with purple hair and kohl-darkened eyes rolled an unlit cigarette between her fingers. The others sat upright and looked forward, faces tight.

"Hey." Sayer tried for casual. "I'm an FBI agent looking for a missing kid. I was wondering if I could talk to you?"

As she approached the table, a petite woman in a flowing plum dress hurried from the building wagging a finger at Sayer.

"Excuse me, this is private property and these children are under my care. You reporters can just move along with your interviews or drugs or whatever you want to get these kids into."

A young boy no more than twelve let out a small laugh. "She's FBI, Mrs. Calavera."

The tiny woman continued her furious approach, squinting at Sayer with unbridled suspicion. "Ah, are you the FBI agent that called me? I've been swatting away reporters for the last twenty minutes."

Sayer shifted gears, realizing she wasn't going to get anywhere without Mrs. Calavera's support. "Hello, ma'am. I'm sorry about the media, but we are desperately trying to find a kidnapped girl and think there's the possibility she might have come through here."

The woman pressed her deeply pink lips together and straightened her low bun. "Kidnapped girl?"

"Yes. Is there somewhere private we could talk?" Sayer eyed the kids, realizing the last thing she wanted to do was scare them.

Noticing her concern, Mrs. Calavera's face softened. "Yes, yes, come on into my office."

Sayer followed her inside through a small kitchen, where another group of teens bustled around massive pots bubbling with something that reminded Sayer of her father's cooking. The familiar scent of Senegalese fish and couscous filled her nose and she smiled. "Yum, thiéboudienne. My father used to cook that for us when we were kids."

Mrs. Calavera stopped and looked at Sayer more closely. "Your father was from West Africa?"

Sayer nodded. She would soften the woman up yet. "Senegal. He came to the States for college, met my mom right here in D.C."

They passed a rec room where younger kids sat around a board game, giggling.

The entire place felt warm and happy. Not what Sayer came in expecting.

"You've created a place for them to feel safe," Sayer commented.

Mrs. Calavera gave her a curt nod. "The least we can do for these children. The things they've seen. For some of them, the things they've done to survive. It's inhuman. Here they know no one will hurt them."

They entered the small office.

"So, you think someone who lived here was kidnapped?"

Sayer contemplated how much to share with the fiery defender of these children. She decided honesty was probably the best policy with Mrs. Calavera.

"I'm investigating the Gwendolyn Van Hurst case."

Mrs Calavera sighed. "That poor, poor girl. Gwen was such a beautiful child."

Sayer's heart beat a little faster. "So you did know Gwendolyn Van Hurst?"

"Of course! She volunteered here. That's not why you came?"

"Well yes, I saw a photograph of her here in a Santa hat. She was with another girl. . . . Did she spend a lot of time here?"

"Yes, she was a regular. She often even came without her father."

"Senator Van Hurst spent time here?" Sayer's eyes narrowed, unable to keep the suspicion from her face.

"Yes." Mrs. Calavera gave her a rueful smile. "Hate to tell you, but half of Congress, hell, half of D.C. spends time here. It's a politically safe charity. You can be . . . anti-immigrant and still come help these kids. They're alone and need help. I've turned Sanctuary House into the political philanthropist's place to be seen. It's disgusting, PR grubbing, but it brings us tons of resources so I don't complain."

Sayer paused, disappointed, not even sure why she was still looking for a reason to link Van Hurst to all this. Probably just because he was such a raging jerk, which wasn't exactly a good reason. "Listen, what I'm about to say is confidential, all right? Can you keep anything I share with you to yourself?"

"Yes, of course," Mrs. Calavera said.

Sayer believed her.

"When we found Gwen's body, there was a photograph of one other girl being held in similar circumstances. Maybe you saw the press conference?"

"No, no." She waved her hand dismissively. "I see enough horrors here. No need to watch the news, but I did hear chatter about a cage. The other girl was also in a cage?"

Sayer was momentarily shocked by her matter-of-factness, but then she remembered that Mrs. Calavera had probably heard things from her wards that would make Sayer's curly hair straighten.

Sayer continued, "Exactly. And the photo I saw of Gwen and this second girl . . . was taken here, I believe."

Mrs. Calavera's hand flew to her chest. "Here?"

Sayer removed the photograph of Jane Doe and handed it to Mrs. Calavera.

"Oh no. Leila!" The woman grasped the crucifix around her neck.

"Leila?"

"Leila Farouk." Mrs. Calavera stared at the horrific image of the girl. "That explains it," she said under her breath, eyes watering.

"Explains what, please?"

Mrs. Calavera looked stricken. "I was shocked that Leila left without saying good-bye. That she hadn't gotten in touch with us in so long."

"She just left and you didn't look for her?" Sayer was slightly shocked.

"No! Of course not. I received notice from child services that she had been placed with a foster family. I just thought it was strange that she didn't say good-bye, but with these kids . . . it's hard to know what to expect. They're not always emotionally . . . coherent. You're telling me that she wasn't placed with a family . . ." The elderly woman's hands began to quiver.

"She wasn't placed with a family, no. Would you mind showing me the notification from child services?"

"Of course!" She hustled to an ancient filing cabinet. After wrestling open a rusted drawer, she rifled through files until she exclaimed, "Here it is!"

Sayer pulled on a glove and gently took the paper. "Could I see another one like this from another child? Side by side."

Mrs. Calavera pulled another paper from the cabinet and placed it next to Leila's on the desk.

The two women looked back and forth between the pieces of paper.

"My dear Lord. It's not the same," Mrs. Calavera said.

Sayer pointed back and forth. "Yeah, look here, the official seals are slightly different. And the header looks like a photocopy of a photocopy or something."

Sayer felt sick staring at the forged note. The level of planning and foresight this took was mind-boggling. This was the most organized killer she had ever heard of. She said a silent prayer to the universe that Winters was actually their man, because they needed to catch this unsub before he could kill again.

Sayer lifted the forged notice. "I'm going to need to bring this in with me," she said as she slid it into an evidence envelope.

Mrs. Calavera sat down hard in her chair, tears gathering in the corners of her eyes. "How could I be so stupid?"

"Hey, no. Why would you ever suspect that someone would forge something like that? We're dealing with a very deranged, very organized person who excels at fooling people. Speaking of which, have you ever heard the name Franklin Winters before?"

Mrs. Calavera's eyes widened. "Franklin? The real estate agent? Why, he helps with our fund-raising!" She raised a shaking hand to cover her mouth, head lolling slightly as though she might faint. "Is he the one who did these terrible things? How could I have missed it?"

"We aren't sure we've got the right man . . . but psychopathic killers can fool just about anyone. I've met Mr. Winters and I would've sworn on a stack of Bibles that he was innocent, so you can't blame yourself for missing it."

The woman let out a bitter laugh. "Of course I can blame myself. I spend so much time trying to make them feel safe . . ." Her voice broke.

Sayer put on her no-nonsense voice. "Mrs. Calavera, I need you to focus. I need you to tell me everything you can remember about Leila."

"I can tell you that she is sixteen, from Egypt, quiet but no pushover. You should talk to Leila's best friend, she's sitting out front. Adrestia Stephanopolous will be able to tell you much more."

Sayer sat down at the picnic table across from the teen who looked much less nonchalant than she had an hour before.

"I knew she wouldn't have taken off like that!" The young girl with purple hair and black clothes still held an unlit cigarette, rolling it between her nervous fingers like a talisman.

"You're right, Adrestia, she didn't take off. We believe Leila was kidnapped." Sayer kept it honest but vague.

"Adi."

"I'm sorry, what?" Sayer said.

"Adi," the girl said softly. "I hate being called Adrestia, some overblown Greek name my dad gave me before he died."

"Of course. Adi, then."

"Was it the Cage Killer?" Adi continued to whisper as if speaking up would call forth the killer himself. Her gold-flecked brown eyes reflected a dark well of suffering. "I heard about Gwen. . . . Is Leila in some bomb shelter too?"

"We don't know for sure." Sayer answered with a half-truth, knowing that one lie would shut this kid down for good. "Right now I'm trying to figure out exactly when Leila left and anything else you can tell me about her. So you thought something was wrong when she left?"

"Yeah."

"But you didn't say anything?"

"Who would I tell? Mrs. Calavera loves us, but she . . . she always thinks the best of people. It's sweet, but when I asked about Leila she went on and on about how great it was that she got placed with a loving family." The girl rolled her kohl-lined eyes.

"So, what can you tell me about Leila? Did she have any family?"

"She did . . . I mean, of course she did. We all did, once." The girl nervously rolled the unlit cigarette between her fingers. "But they all died."

"Do you know how?"

"Yeah." Adi momentarily put the unlit cigarette in her mouth and then removed it. "Some men in Egypt. Her dad worked for the old government there." Adi waved her hand. "I don't know the politics. We all avoid politics here." She gave a rueful laugh that made her look far older than her seventeen years.

Sayer remained silent, fighting the urge to hug this girl who reminded her an awful lot of herself as a child.

"Leila lost her whole family. Her uncle thought it would be a good idea to send her here to live with some distant relatives, but when she got off the plane, there was no one to meet her. No one to take her in. She wasn't exactly sure what happened, and now she can't get in touch with her uncle. Mrs. Calavera picked her up from the immigration detention place."

"Do you know if she had a twin?"

Adi's eyes flew up to Sayer's.

The girl nodded, pretending to take a drag again. "Yeah, Tarik. Why do you care about that?"

Sayer probed the girl's face, realizing she saw wild suspicion and maybe even a little fear. "Why are you so worried that I care about her twin?"

Adi realized she was revealing her emotions, and her face closed down again. "It's why we were so close."

"You and Leila?"

Adi looked up toward the treetops, fighting for emotional control, but a tear fell down her cheek. "We both lost twins. Leila lost Tarik and I lost my sister, Clem. No one understands what it's like to lose your other half. But Leila got it." Her voice trailed into a husky whisper.

Sayer took a deep breath. God, she hated this part of the job, because no matter how much she just wanted to hug Adi, she had to keep pressing. "So she lost her twin. Was that common knowledge around here?"

"Sure, we didn't hide it. I think most of the other kids knew." Adi wiped her eyes. "Clementia." The girl smiled for the first time, and it made her sad eyes even more obvious. "Can you believe it?"

"Clementia?"

"Just, ya know, Adrestia and Clementia, me and my twin. The Greek goddesses of vengeance and forgiveness. Who does that to their kid?" She laughed again, letting out the sorrow in a harsh bark.

"I thought Adrestia was the goddess of justice." Sayer dragged up a memory from her ancient-religions class.

Adi shrugged. "Justice, vengeance, what's the difference?"

Sayer nodded. "Fair question. I'll let you know if I ever figure it out."

The girl sighed and gave Sayer a half smile, trying to cover her emotions. "Thing is . . . I mean, I can't believe that this happened to Leila." Adi's bottom lip trembled. "I mean, we've all got tough histories, ya know? She was quiet, but she never gave up on anything. Leila was a survivor. For her to make it all the way here and then this happens . . . how is that even fair?"

Sayer wanted to agree; she wanted to punch the universe right in the nuts. Instead she wrapped up the interview and drove away, her own twisting emotions settling in her heart like stone.

ROAD BACK TO

QUANTICO, VA

Sayer rode back toward Quantico. Something about talking to Adi made this feel way more personal than usual. The girl was tough as nails, but Sayer saw right through her exterior. With all her posturing and nonchalant attitude, Adi was the spitting image of Sayer at that age. And young Sayer was furious at the world for taking her happy family away. She built a cocoon of aloof disdain to protect herself. So much so that Sayer wondered if anyone would have ever adopted such a broken, angry girl. After their parents died, Sayer and Macey had been lucky that Sophia McDuff insisted that she and Charles adopt their grandchildren. What a lifeline Nana had been. Would Adi have a lifeline like that?

Angry in Adi's behalf, Sayer was ready to have a long talk with Winters. A very long, perhaps violent talk. Which she knew wasn't productive and she still wasn't convinced he was their unsub, but she felt irrational rage toward him. Winters's refusal to talk only made it worse.

"Reel in it, Sayer," she said to herself. She'd seen agents get lost in that kind of anger, and it was a one-way ticket to a hell she didn't want. She tried deep breathing, but that just made her head swim and her gut churn. She had to find some way to release her frustration or she was going to explode.

As Sayer tried to calm down, her phone buzzed.

"Sayer Altair."

"It's Vik."

Sayer could hear the excitement in his voice. "You've got something?"

"Remember we asked the data team to cross-reference Winters's real estate properties with the bomb shelter registry?"

"Yeah, but she said they wouldn't be able to get to the files until Monday."

"Yeah, well, that girl might not have until Monday," Vik said. "I know someone who works at the archives. I called in a favor and got her to let me in. Just spent the afternoon combing through the bomb registry."

"And?"

"I got a hit! Another one of Winters's properties has a bomb shelter." Vik's voice echoed loudly into Sayer's helmet. "I'm texting you the address. I'll meet you there in twenty."

Sayer clicked off and sped up, praying to every sacred power in the universe that Leila Farouk would be there, still alive.

HUNTER STREET,
WASHINGTON, D.C.

The address led Sayer to a run-down ranch house just east of the Anacostia River. The now-familiar yellow-and-green Real Star Real Estate sign hung out front, though this one was so rusted it was barely legible. A clot of FBI agents gathered out front.

She jumped off her bike and hurried to confer with Vik and the hazardous-devices team, already suiting up.

Vik nodded a greeting. "According to the listing, this place's been empty for years."

It showed. The windows were boarded up and graffiti covered every inch of visible space. Crew signs from dueling D.C. gangs overlapped in exuberant color. The house must've been right on the border of contested territory.

The tall bomb squad agent shook Sayer's hand. "Agent Kennelwith, ma'am. We'll go in and clear the scene. I'm gonna need you all to wait outside."

Rather than sit on the curb, Sayer and Vik retreated to his car.

Vik stared up at the house. "Damn, hate sitting on our hands out here. What if that girl is inside dying right now, ya know?"

"Yeah. But she's been gone six months. An extra hour won't matter."

Vik grunted unhappy agreement.

While they waited, Sayer filled Vik in on her interview with Adi Stephanopolous.

The minutes ticked by. Thirty minutes. Then an hour. Then almost two hours.

"Your city is kind of a shit hole," Vik said, just to fill the long quiet. He gestured to the run-down neighborhood, half the buildings boarded up.

Sayer nodded. "Yeah, though this isn't where I grew up. I grew up in a mansion in Northwest with my rich grandparents. You knew my grandfather was a senator, right?"

Vik raised his eyebrows. "Nope, didn't know that. You do lack . . . street cred."

Sayer snorted. "I went to Sidwell Friends, the private school where presidents and Supreme Court justices send their kids. This is part of my city, but I'm definitely not from *here* here."

They sat up, attention snapping to the two bomb techs in full gear who emerged carrying a metallic box. The lead of the squad came out and gestured *not yet*.

They both collapsed back into their seats.

"Hey," Vik said without taking his eyes off the front door, "you think Winters is really our guy?"

Sayer shifted her gaze to Vik. "You don't? We're sitting out front of his property where they just found a bomb." She gestured to the bomb squad guys.

"I don't know. Something just doesn't feel right to me. Plus, I checked my sources. . . ."

"Your local Devereaux sources?"

"Exactly." Vik gave a half smile. "This time from my third cousin, Lucinda. She runs a cleaning service and knows a hell of a lot of women. Women who have keys to places like state archives." Vik chuckled.

"Ah . . . so that's how you got in to the archives on a weekend."

"Yeah, don't tell Holt. She probably wouldn't approve."

"Mum's the word," Sayer said. "So, your cousin had insight into Winters?"

"She didn't, but a friend of hers did. You'd be amazed what people are willing to say and do around the help. Winters's cleaning ladies say he was genuinely nice when their paths crossed. Normal, if there is such a thing. Slightly messy, worked regular hours, no sick porn stashed in the closet."

"You know that doesn't mean a thing." Sayer let her eyes travel back to the front of the house. "It's always the guy everyone thought was so nice."

"Yeah . . . I guess so. Just . . . I don't know."

"Well, let's follow the evidence. Evidence doesn't lie."

Vik grunted. "If you say so."

Sayer called to check on Winters, but the man still refused to talk to anyone. Another twenty minutes had passed when Sayer's radio crackled to life.

"Agent Altair?"

"Here."

"Kennelwith here, we're almost done. We have one more device to clear but we just opened the bomb shelter door. We've got a scene and possible live victim."

"There's a live girl inside?"

"Possibly. We can't get to her yet. Need to clear the room. But it's small, won't take long, we'll hurry. We've called in an ambulance and full evidence recovery team from the D.C. office, so they should be here in five minutes tops." The radio squealed off.

Sayer and Vik got out of the car. Sayer pulled out her worry beads, rubbing them so vigorously she could feel the heat radiating down her fingers. Her breath felt shallow. "Damn, I hope they hurry. I hope she's still alive."

Vik chewed his lip.

Finally the entire bomb squad emerged delicately, carrying three more boxes.

Kennelwith waved Sayer over. Face pale, the man was clearly shaken. "All right, Agent Altair. Scene is cleared. We found four separate devices. All pretty basic but plenty deadly."

Sayer waved her hand, not caring at all about the bombs. "What about the girl?"

"One cage in the bomb shelter. Entrance is on the north side of the kitchen. Girl appears alive, but . . . barely. One of my guys is down there now with bolt cutters working to get her out of the cage so medical can grab her ASAP."

Sayer and Vik yanked on gloves and booties. Sayer tucked up her hair and checked that her gun and cuffs were secure, and they hurried into the decrepit house. The acrid burn of urine stung Sayer's nose as they made their way through the cramped living room. In the dusty kitchen a hatch stood open in the floor, cracked linoleum curling around the dark entry.

"Once more into the breach," Sayer muttered, staring into the black hole. She clicked on her flashlight and shined it onto the rickety ladder that led down into the earth. "Let's go get that girl out of there."

Vik grunted. "Hope they get here with lamps soon."

"Ask and ye shall receive." An evidence tech came into the kitchen holding an industrial lamp and a bag of photography gear. "Rest of the team is suiting up and gathering their gear."

"Great. Vik and I will head down first," Sayer said. "Can you come photo the scene while we check on the girl? Medical team is less than a minute out, so we want to document everything as best we can before the EMTs come in."

The tech nodded and pulled out a massive camera from one of his bags.

Sayer swallowed hard and stepped onto the ladder. It swayed beneath her feet, wood creaking like an old boat. "Watch the ladder." She looked up at Vik and wondered about his much larger frame.

Sayer's boots hit bare dirt and she swept her light around the room. In the far corner, a cage hung from the low ceiling, its bottom only a few inches above the ground. A bomb scene tech worked with a bolt cutter, straining to remove the industrial padlock hanging on the iron door.

"No luck on the lock yet," he called to Sayer.

Soft whimpering drew Sayer to the cage, her heart in her throat. At the sight of the girl her eyes watered involuntarily. "Oh no," Sayer whispered in horror. In the corner of the cage, an impossibly emaciated girl lay curled into a ball. How was she still alive? Next to her, an equally emaciated kitten stirred, tried to stand but collapsed on its side.

Dull, glossy brown eyes blinked open, and Leila Farouk stared into the flashlight. Through lips so cracked they bled, the girl tried to speak. Nothing but husky whispers came from her mouth.

"Forget the camera!" Sayer shouted up. "We need something to get this cage open. Now!"

"Right, I'll grab the metal saw," he called down.

Sayer approached the girl. "Hey, Leila . . . hey, we're here. You're going to be okay now. You're safe." She slid her hand through the bars of the cage and took the girl's limp hand. The girl let out a low moan but did not respond.

"We've got you," Sayer said, hoping to hell it was true.

"Medical's here," Vik called down.

Two EMTs climbed carefully down the ladder, medical bags swinging off their shoulders.

"Still working on access." Sayer kept her voice low, trying not to frighten Leila.

The EMTs unpacked their gear and Sayer reluctantly stepped aside, untangling her slender fingers from the girl's overcool hand. Time slowed as nothing seemed to work. The bomb tech still snipping at the lock with his bolt cutters. The evidence techs fumbling to set up the industrial lamps. The metal saw, where was it? She wanted something, anything to get this girl out of this cage right now.

The medics worked silently as a team, running an IV through the bars. The thread-thin needle poked the girl's arm once, twice, three times as an EMT failed to find her vein. "She's so dehydrated. Won't be able to get a vein here."

Vik and three more crime scene technicians climbed down and began doing their jobs, photographing the scene with strobing flashes. Gathering and tagging trace evidence.

Finally Sayer snapped. "Where the fuck is the saw!"

"Coming as fast as we can," a voice echoed down.

Trying to control her temper, her need to do something, Sayer tore her eyes from the girl and refocused on the room. Bare dirt floors. Brick walls. The walls! There had to be a camera somewhere. Focus on finding the camera. Nothing she could do for the girl.

Sayer began a slow circuit of the room. On one wall hung an old tool rack, the faint outline of tools that once hung there still visible. On the other wall was nothing but an ancient dial thermostat. She crouched and made a second circuit of the room, eyes scanning the cracks in the plaster. Problem was, there were so many she couldn't narrow it down.

Finally another crime scene tech climbed down and someone lowered a metal saw on a rope. He rushed over to the lock and revved it up.

The sharp buzz of grinding metal sent a shudder along Sayer's teeth.

She looked back up at the wall. Wait . . . a thermostat? Who put their thermostat down in the basement?

Something was wrong.

She leaned in for a better look at the old temperature dial. A small red bar was set at 75 degrees. The slender golden needle said the current temp was 72 but, as Sayer watched, the needle slid slowly upward toward 73. The body heat of everyone in the basement was raising the room's temperature.

"Hey, bomb squad." She waved over the remaining bomb tech holding the useless bolt cutters. "No one puts their thermostat in the basement, right? Take a look."

His eyebrows rose and he gently probed the thermostat. With delicate fingers, he found a narrow wire covered by a thin layer of plaster running between two bricks. "Looks like this wire goes back into the wall here." His voice cracked with tension. He pulled out a flashlight and shined it into the growing crack between the bricks. He pressed his eye close to the wall, peering at something, then stood bolt upright, eyes wide. "We need to clear the room!"

Sayer's entire body snapped to full attention. "Bomb! Everyone out!" she barked. The crime scene techs and EMTs didn't hesitate. They calmly but quickly left their gear behind and made their way up the ladder.

Sayer's heart practically throbbed out of her chest as she watched their feet disappear through the hatch.

"I'll grab my gear and get the team back in here," the bomb squad guy said as he followed them up.

Vik hesitated. "Come on, Sayer, you next."

"Nope, I'm last, get up there and hurry the bomb squad back. I'm right behind you."

Vik squinted at her and Sayer grunted, "Hey, take the damn cat."

He plucked the half-dead kitten from the cage and tucked it into his jacket before clambering up. Sayer turned to the crime scene tech still sawing the bolt.

"Almost done here."

Sayer glanced back at the thermostat. The needle approached 74.

The lock snapped and she let out a huff of relief.

"Get out now, I'll grab the girl." Sayer took the saw from him. He hesitated, so she shouted in his face, "Now!"

He jumped at her voice and hurried away.

She yanked off the broken padlock and tried to slide the bolt. It held fast.

"Sayer?" Vik called down. "Get out of there. We're bringing in an AC unit to lower the temp so the bomb squad can do their thing."

The needle slid just past 74. Her entire body shifted into fight-or-flight mode. Her eyes began to jump and her hands shook from the jolt of adrenaline.

"They won't get here in time. Temp is still going up. Got to get her out of here but the lock mechanism is jammed." Sayer's voice remained strangely calm, almost monotone, despite her jittering body.

Blocking the sounds of protest from above, Sayer focused laser attention on the slide bolt. Damn thing was corroded, hopelessly stuck. The corner bolts, what had the tech said? They were faulty?

Sayer pulled her pistol and pressed her head to the cage. Just inside the corner she spotted a raised bolt. Sweat sprang up across her forehead, stinging her eyes. A drop rolled down her spine, making her shiver. Panting, she pulled the trigger.

The bolt shattered. She swung the gun around and aimed at the second bolt. It exploded and the floor of the cage bowed down, creating a small opening.

Sayer let out a cry as she pressed her weight onto the cage floor. It tilted farther and Leila slid toward her. Sayer pulled the girl out and tossed her over her shoulder. Staggered slightly by the weight, Sayer rushed to the ladder. In her panic, her foot landed hard on the first rung and it snapped. "Dammit!"

She wrapped an arm around Leila and jumped to the second rung, frantically grasping with her free hand.

Her damp palm slipped and she landed hard on the ground with an *oof.* Sayer made another wild leap and her hand clamped firmly down.

The ladder groaned beneath her but held. Trying to pull up with one arm while controlling the limp weight swinging dangerously from her shoulder, she yanked them both upward again. Up one more rung. Her hand slipped again but she managed to hold on with her fingertips. Almost there, she gave one last pull, feeling the muscles in her back and shoulders tear as her fingers curled over the edge of the opening above.

Below her she heard a faint click. A hand clamped down onto hers and yanked upward. She looked up to see Vik's wide eyes.

A boom thudded her body. The concussion jerked her upward so hard her arms and legs snapped back.

Her body flew through the hatch, slammed into the ceiling.

Then falling.

Fire. Heat and screaming.

A second boom. And another. Someone called her name a thousand miles away.

For just a moment Sayer was back in the car crash that killed her parents. The sound of metal screaming as it slammed into concrete. Fire and death.

Then nothing but darkness and a terrible roar of sound in her ears.

Sayer woke in the ambulance, her entire body twisting in pain. Vik leaned over her, his face blackened with soot, bleeding from a cut across his forehead.

"Hey, she's awake! Sayer, you all right?"

His voice sounded like it was underwater, garbled and distant.

She blinked, her eyes like sandpaper. "Leila?" Her voice faltered and she breathed out the word without really saying it.

"She's alive. In the ambulance just ahead of us."

Sayer tried to sit up. "You grabbed my hand?"

Vik nodded.

"Thanks."

Vik nodded curtly again, his bottom lip trapped between his teeth, bleeding slightly. "You saved that girl's life."

"Nah, you found the address. We saved her together."

The EMT next to Vik put a firm hand on Sayer's shoulder. "You might be fine, but we need to check and make sure." He pushed her back onto the gurney.

Though his eyes pinched with tension, Vik smiled. "I think you might just be a badass, Sayer Altair."

"I think you might be too." Sayer managed a smile before closing her eyes and letting whatever the EMT injected into her arm work its magic.

GEORGETOWN HOSPITAL,

WASHINGTON, D.C.

"Good thing you're as lucky as you are stupid." Assistant Director Holt stood in the door of the hospital room.

Sayer finished pulling on the hospital shirt and flashed Holt a pained smile. Her singed puff of curly hair reeked of smoke.

"Staying down there was a fool thing to do and you know it." Holt remained in the doorway. "And it broke protocol." She paused. "Still, the doctor tells me you're fine. No signs of head trauma. No serious injuries. Lots of soft-tissue trauma. Like I said, stupid but at least you're lucky too."

"Yeah, lucky. I'll just feel like I was in a boxing match with a freight train for a few weeks." Sayer winced as she bent to pull on the hospital slippers.

"Either way, you go home and rest for a few days. We'll keep things rolling with Winters."

"Bullshit." Sayer stood up straight, ignoring the spikes of pain along her back.

"Not negotiable, Sayer."

Sayer ignored Holt's comment. "How's the girl?"

Holt put her hands on her hips and silently stared at Sayer for a very long time. "You sure you're okay to stay lead on this one? You owe it to those girls, and to Cindy and Ezra, not to fuck around. If you're not in peak form, you have no right to run the case."

Sayer swallowed; her spit felt like acid going down, but she pictured Leila curled up into a ball inside that cage. She reached for her worry beads and realized they were probably blown up somewhere back on Hunter Street.

"Doctors gave me the go-ahead. I'm good."

Holt gave her a curt nod. "Then you'd better get down to the ICU and find out the latest on the girl you saved."

As Sayer squeezed by Holt in the doorway, Holt reached out and gently put a hand on Sayer's shoulder. "You did save her, you know. Good job."

Sayer gave her a half smile and limped away, slightly unnerved by any kindness from Holt.

She found Vik and Andy in the hallway outside the ICU.

"You gave me one hell of a scare." Vik smoothed the bandage along his forehead and fidgeted with his sooty clothes.

"Gave myself one, but doctors say I'm good to go. No signs of a concussion, no broken bones, so I'm back on the job."

Vik clapped her on the back and then snorted at her wince. "Yeah, you're totally not hurt, I can tell."

"So, what's the deal with Leila? She going to be okay?"

"We're just waiting for the doctor now. They rushed in and basically locked us out here. Said they would have word soon."

As he spoke the doctor emerged, reedy and hunched. Based on the pinched look on the doctor's face, Sayer thought for sure that Leila was dead.

"Is she okay?"

The doctor held up her hand. "Yes. The explosion did only minor damage, scrapes and bruises thanks to your body in the way." The doctor smiled grimly at Sayer. "She was very close to dying of severe dehydration. She has some damage to her kidneys and will need to stay here under observation for at least the next few days. I ran a rape kit that's already on the way to your lab, full swabs but no sign of sexual assault. I believe she will eventually be okay . . . physically."

The doctor's face pinched, nose crinkling. Sayer realized she was fighting tears.

"This girl . . . first thing she asked about when she came to was the kitten. She was dying of thirst and gave her last water to the cat, can you believe it?"

Sayer looked over at Vik. "Did it survive?"

"We don't know. Someone dropped the cat with a vet but we haven't heard anything."

They stood in a silent circle, contemplating what kind of nightmare the poor girl must have experienced.

Needing to do something to release some tension, Sayer fidgeted with the hem of the pale-blue hospital shirt, rolling it back and forth. She forced herself to refocus on the case.

"Wow, okay. Is there any chance we can talk to her?"

The doctor shook her head. "Social services is in with her now." She looked at Sayer and their eyes locked together in shared assessment. She seemed to approve of something she saw in Sayer, making a decision. "Listen, I'll allow a child psychologist to go in. No one else, sorry. She's too fragile, and she has to be my first priority."

"I understand." Sayer reached for her worry beads again and silently cursed their absence.

"We've got a child psychologist on the way already; she should be here soon," Vik said.

While they got vending machine coffee, the psychologist arrived and went into the girl's hospital room.

The TV in the corner of the waiting room blasted the news.

Sayer, Vik, and Andy watched talking heads tearing them apart on national TV, reacting to the widespread news that the contractor, Hal Dillinger, was not the Cage Killer.

"FBI got it wrong yet again."

"Arrested the wrong man. The contractor a false start. Are they taking the Van Hurst case seriously?"

"After years of scandal, the FBI still can't get it right."

Ugh. Sayer wondered if this case would be her last. Even though Assistant Director Holt knew she hadn't wrongfully arrested the contractor, Holt couldn't ignore the fact that her team was leaking like a sieve.

Andy watched, a smug grin on his face. "Looks like this is going well for you."

Sayer ignored him and endured her crucifixion on national television in silence until the child psychologist finally emerged.

"She's barely able to talk. All I could get is that she's sixteen, a refugee from Egypt. Came here alone about a year ago. She was unwilling or unable to say anything about her time in captivity other than that she never saw her captor but did watch what she called terror movies. She keeps asking for the kitten that was with her." The seasoned FBI psychologist looked stricken. "No way to get anything more without really pushing it."

"Then push it," Andy said. "We need more."

"No," Sayer said, and shot Andy a sharp glance. "We won't traumatize her again."

He pressed his lips in a line but didn't respond.

The psychologist nodded her approval. "Give it time. She might open up, but it could be a while."

Sayer let out a long, painful sigh. "All right. Well, let's see if the evidence found us any clues leading directly to Winters."

Vik and Andy headed off down the hall. Sayer paused. "Hey, while we're here, I'm going to swing in and say hello to Ezra. Catch up back at Quantico in an hour."

Vik stopped. "I'll wait for you out front, can drive you down."

Sayer grunted a thanks and steeled herself. She had no idea what to say to Ezra. What do you say to a young man who just lost both his legs?

Sayer stood in the doorway, watching Ezra in the hospital bed. His legs hung from spindly metal scaffolding, thick bandages swaddling both stumps. His arms, mottled with purple and blue bruises, jutted from his pale-green hospital gown. Two swollen black eyes made him look like a cartoon bandit wearing a mask. His normally brilliant blue hair had already faded into grayish blue, making him look like an old man.

Ezra sat propped against a mountain of pillows, a stack of papers on his lap. With shaking hands, he turned the pages one at a time. Slowly, intensely, he scrutinized each page.

"Ezra?"

He looked up and smiled, though not the same quick smile he'd had before. This one stopped at his cheeks, haunted eyes negating the rest.

"Agent Altair!"

"So sorry I didn't come see you sooner." Sayer lowered herself gently into the chair beside his bed.

"No way! You're chasing the asshole who did this. I'd much rather you be out there trying to catch him. Word on the street is that you just joined the honorable 'been bombed by this asshole' club."

Sayer grimaced and slid up the cuff of one of her pant legs, revealing her own bruised leg.

Ezra grimaced. "Well . . . shit. Sorry, Sayer. Didn't want any more members."

"Yeah."

They sat in silence for a few moments, both of them thinking about Cindy, the third member of their small club.

Ezra tried a smile again. "On the upside, I pestered Holt so much she's letting me look at the case files as they come in." He patted the stack of papers on his lap. Sayer noticed more file boxes on the floor.

"Paper files? That bomb turn you into a Luddite or something?"

Ezra snorted. "Not likely." He tapped the side of his head. "Concussed brain. Every time I try to look at a computer screen, I get a headache, starts to look like little wavy lines. The other techs are making sure they copy everything as it comes in so I can read on good old-fashioned paper."

Another slightly awkward silence fell.

Ezra finally held up a page that said ARREST RECORD across the top. "So, sounds like our guy. What's Winters like? I mean . . . is he . . . did he mean to do this to us? Do we know why?"

Sayer awkwardly patted his hand, wanting to comfort Ezra a bit but not exactly sure how.

"I don't know, Ezra. He's lawyered up and won't talk to anyone. There's definitely something going on with him, and the fact that both girls were found on properties he was selling . . . it's pretty convincing."

"Yeah, heard he has no past, like it's been wiped clean."

"Yeah. It's him," Sayer said, ignoring the twinge in her gut that they were still missing something.

"So now we just need to prove it, huh?"

"That's why we've got you combing the files."

"Damn straight." A real smile flashed on Ezra's face. "Hey, hear you saved that girl's life."

Suddenly the sensation of the bomb thudding her entire body returned like a ghost, faint but the same. Sayer's stomach quailed and for a horrible second she thought she was going to vomit all over the floor.

Ezra watched her face closely. "Hey, as someone who was also just blown up and managed to live, cut yourself some slack. . . . I'm here to talk if you need it."

Sayer waved her hand, dismissing his concern. "Nah, just hungry."

He raised his now unadorned eyebrows. "Okay, boss, whatever you say." He looked out the window, frowning. "Good luck out there, Agent Altair."

FBI HEADQUARTERS,
QUANTICO, VA

Back at Quantico, Sayer changed into the extra clothes she kept in her locker and sat at her desk chugging a water before she felt ready to enter the conference room.

When she walked through the door, the entire task force stood, applauding and hooting.

"Way to go, Sayer!"

The room buzzed with feral excitement. They'd caught the guy. Saved the girl. Every person in that room, FBI or DCPD, spent their days thinking about killers and rapists. They faced corpse after corpse. They lived and breathed the worst of humanity, which was why they celebrated these moments with fervor. This was the feeling that kept them going despite the darkness they waded through.

Ignoring the pain, Sayer held up both hands, accepting the praise. Letting them get it out. This was a part of the job she hated, but she knew it was necessary. For just a few minutes she had to be their coach and cheerleader rolled into one.

When things quieted down, she shook her head. "I didn't save that girl. We all did. We're a team!"

She pumped a fist in the air, ignoring the pain that radiated across her back. The task force rumbled with approval.

"All right. All right. Let's get back to it."

She walked to the whiteboard. "Okay, two big questions. Data team, what's the latest on Winters's properties? How many are we talking about? Any other matches to the bomb shelter database? We know Winters bought three cages, so we need to be completely sure he doesn't have another victim out there somewhere."

The mousy data tech stood so everyone could hear her soft voice. "He's got almost a hundred listings, some unsold for three or four years. None of the remaining listings are on the bomb shelter registry, but a lot of people didn't register their shelters, so we're cross-referencing survivalist forums and other places people might have mentioned their address."

"All right. We need to canvass every last one of them. Andy." Sayer scowled at Andy, who still hadn't recovered from the dressing-down he got from her for not entering the sketch of Winters into the system.

"What can I do?" he asked grudgingly.

"You take the uniforms and canvass every one of Winters's properties. Pay special attention to basements and look for possible subterranean rooms of any kind." Sayer turned to the data tech. "Can you look for blueprints of his properties? See if there's a way to track possible hidey-holes that way?"

"Already on it," the data tech said.

"Fantastic, thanks. Okay, other big question, crime scene, any word on the DNA or fingerprint?"

An older evidence tech held up a paper and waved it like a victory flag.

"We do, got both results back about two minutes ago."

"And?"

"Both a match for Franklin Winters."

"Yes!" Sayer pumped her fist again and immediately regretted it.

An assistant hurried in. "We got the list of people who had access to the catacombs. Guess who's on it!"

"Franklin Winters," Sayer practically shouted.

He nodded and handed the list to Sayer.

She put it on the pile and went to the whiteboard.

Beneath Winters's name Sayer wrote, *DNA Match, Fingerprint Match, access to scene.*

"Well, that's it. We've got our guy. Let's go tear this bastard's life apart," she growled.

Sayer and Vik headed to interrogation to talk to Winters again.

"We've got his connection to both crime scenes, his DNA, and his fingerprints. If this doesn't make him talk, nothing will," Sayer said as they wound their way through the maze of the Quantico holding cells.

"His lawyer just arrived. Maybe he can talk some sense into him?" Vik sounded skeptical.

They both stepped into the observation room and briefly watched through the one-way mirror as Winters conferred with his lawyer.

"Wish we could listen in." Vik looked longingly at the intercom button.

Sayer grunted agreement. "But we don't need to. At this point Winters is going away. I vote we make sure we don't do anything to screw up the legal case."

Vik smiled at the thought of putting Winters away. "You want to go in alone?"

Sayer nodded. "Yeah, I'm fairly certain playing nice won't work at this stage, so I'm going in hard. Let's keep you out of it so you can be good cop later if need be."

Vik held up his hand.

"Really, a high five?" Sayer snorted.

"Trust me, it's good luck."

Sayer slapped Vik's hand and tried to stride into the interrogation room. Instead, she half limped, her entire body throbbing in agony.

"Ah, Mr. Winters, I see your lawyer has arrived despite the late hour."

The lawyer stood to greet her.

"I've advised my client not to say anything to you."

"Fine, fine." Sayer turned a chair and straddled it, slowly lowering herself. "You can listen to me while I fill you in on the latest."

Winters looked over at his lawyer, who said, "Just listen."

"I'm listening." Winters leaned forward onto the table and looked away.

Sayer read distress in his hunched posture, but not fear. She hoped she was about to change that.

"Yes, just listen. We found the girl you were keeping on Hunter Street. You know, the one at your property listing there."

"But I—" Winters began.

"Quiet!" His lawyer put a firm hand on his shoulder. "They're trying to get a rise out of you."

Winters folded his hands in his lap and closed his eyes, clearly trying to rein in the need to speak.

"Yes, listen, because not only have we directly connected you to both scenes, we also found the trail of little Xs you left in the sewers. It led us right to your little ritual offering at the Mount St. Sepulcher catacombs."

Winters sat up, eyes wide. "Mount St. Sepulcher? But that's my church—"

Winters's lawyer raised a hand again, silencing Winters.

Winters huffed, his face turning red.

"But wait, there's more!" Since they were well beyond forming a bond with him, Sayer put on a fake late-night commercial voice, hoping to taunt Winters into a reaction. "We found the fingerprint you left in blood in the catacombs. A perfect match to yours."

Winters's brilliant green eyes opened wide.

His lawyer's eyes grew wide as well. He knew perfectly well that connections to crime scene sites could be coincidence, but a fingerprint was physical evidence pointing directly at his new client.

Sayer smirked. "Aw, you didn't know you left one?"

Winters's lawyer glanced over at his client, not looking entirely comfortable. It's not often a public defender is assigned a serial killer, but Sayer watched the lawyer realize what he'd just gotten into.

Sayer waited a moment in silence, hoping she'd said enough. When Winters sat silent, eyes closed, hands knotted in his lap, she figured there was no need to hold back. Might as well hit him with everything, see if it would knock something loose. "But wait, there's even more! In addition to the connections to multiple scenes and a fingerprint match, we matched your DNA to the semen sample we found on the dead body of Gwendolyn Van Hurst."

Sayer leaned across the table, pressing her face close to Winters's. "You smell the smoke on me. You see these bruises just starting to form?" She rolled up her sleeves. "That's from the bomb you set. But you missed." She sucked air between her teeth, purposefully letting some of the fury she felt leak out into the world.

Winters blanched before her display of anger.

"You, Franklin Winters, murdered an innocent child. You kidnapped another child, traumatizing her beyond imagination. You killed a federal officer. You detonated explosives on American soil in a deadly attack. You almost killed me!" She leaned back in her chair. "You qualify for the death penalty in so many ways it will be hard for the federal prosecutor to decide which charges to file. The only way to avoid the needle is to admit what you've done and tell us if you've got anyone else stuck in a cage somewhere. Tell us the truth and I promise we'll work out a deal."

Winters opened and closed his mouth a few times before his lawyer firmly shook his head.

"Thank you for apprising us of this new development in the case. I'd like some time to discuss this information with my client." The lawyer frowned at Winters.

Sayer stood up and smiled. "Happy to give you a little bit of time. But you tell your client that this offer is on the table for exactly one hour. After that, no one can save him."

She strode out of the room. Once the door shut, Sayer let out a shaky breath. She'd wanted to throttle Winters. Maybe even rough him up. His wide-eyed innocent act was infuriating.

Vik came out of the observation room. "Dammit, I don't think he's gonna talk."

"So much for high fives being good luck. But it's not over yet," Sayer said. "Let's wait out the hour. If he still won't talk . . ."

"Yeah?"

"Fuck, I don't know." Sayer eyed the wall and thought about Holt punching hers. She wondered if it would be worth the inevitable psychological eval that would follow.

Sayer spent the hour writing up her report on the bombing. When Winters's hour was finally up, she entered the interrogation room and could tell it wasn't good news.

"Mr. Winters, did you think about our offer?"

The lawyer shook his head. "I'm sorry to say that, despite my urgings, Mr. Winters will not be sharing anything with you, now or in the future." He let out an exasperated sigh. "My client maintains his total and complete innocence and is confident that a trial will prove it."

Franklin Winters gave her an indecipherable look, halfway between smug and arrogant. Sayer had to bite her cheek to prevent herself from punching him right in his smug face.

"Please keep us apprised of the latest developments," the lawyer said.

"I'll keep you apprised of nothing." Sayer slammed the chair back and left the room.

She stood panting in the hallway when Vik put a gentle hand on her shoulder.

"It's almost midnight. I'm heading back up toward the city. An agent's already dropped your bike off at your place. You want a ride? You did get blown up today, probably not a bad idea to get some rest."

Sayer looked around the empty office and realized the ringing in her ears was getting worse. A shower and a few hours' sleep would do her good.

"Thanks, yeah. Though I'm not sure I'll be able to sleep."

"I know! I can't stop worrying that there might be a Jane Doe Three in some cage out there, on the verge of death, and there's not a thing we can do about it."

"Well, when you put it like that, now I know I won't be sleeping." She looked at the list of tasks for tomorrow morning. "Everyone's in the field tomorrow. I'm canceling the morning task force meeting. More important to get boots on the ground out there. I wish I could shake the feeling that we're missing something."

They drove to Alexandria in companionable silence. Sayer wished like hell she had her worry beads. Instead worry pervaded her aching body.

SAYER'S APARTMENT, ALEXANDRIA, VA

Sayer's body screamed in pain as she climbed the stairs into her quiet apartment, and she wondered where Vesper was. Probably asleep downstairs with Tino. She sat down at the kitchen table and scarfed a slice of cheese and two cold hot dogs washed down by a beer. While she ate, she stared at her research. For a moment she contemplated looking back through the brain scans, hoping to find that something new had materialized while she was away, but instead she decided to head to her room. She smelled her shirt and realized that she still reeked of smoke and soot.

Too tired to even take a shower, she stumbled to bed only to find Vesper sprawled across her pillows.

"Some watchdog you are. You didn't even hear me come in, did you?"

He lifted his head, tail thumping the mattress as she climbed in next to him. She yanked a pillow free and collapsed. The puppy scooted against her body, sniffed her twice with interest, and immediately fell back to sleep with a contented sigh.

Sayer wrapped her arms around his warm body and let the shudders she'd held at bay all day rock her body. With her eyes closed, she felt the bomb tossing her. That moment of insignificance with no power, just her body at the mercy of the explosion.

She descended into a nightmare full of crying girls and thunder.

EZRA'S ROOM, GEORGETOWN HOSPITAL, WASHINGTON, D.C.

Ezra watched the clock illuminated only by the faint glow of hospital machines. The minute hand crept so slowly he occasionally wondered if time had completely stopped: 3:42 . . . 3:43 . . . 3:44 . . .

He'd tried to watch TV but his headache came raging back. He tried reading, listening to music, and he definitely couldn't sleep. Nothing could distract him from the burning agony radiating up his legs. His ankles felt like they were contorted sideways, calf muscles cramping into fiery knots.

Ankles and calves that were no longer there.

The doctors told him that phantom limb pain was common after amputation and would hopefully fade quickly. That they used the word *hopefully* was terrifying. He couldn't imagine this pain lasting for the rest of his life.

The only answer was to get back to work. With shaky hands Ezra clicked on the light and picked up the calendar he had been working on. Using the photo albums that Officer Tooby found in the catacombs, Ezra backtracked the dates of each photograph in the album. He figured that knowing the exact date each photo was taken would help build the case against Winters, though that was hardly necessary now that they had a DNA match.

No matter, he needed something to occupy himself and he'd done all the work on the calendar; might as well compare Winters's records to the dates. First he would cross-reference Winters's financial and phone records. Maybe Winters had stopped for gas near one of the crime scenes on a day a photo was taken. That would put him in the area, making the case even more of a slam dunk.

He rifled through the stack of papers looking for Winters's credit card receipts and began comparing charges to the dates the photos were taken. As he compared date after date, Ezra frowned.

Sayer woke to the phone in her back pocket buzzing.

She fumbled the phone from her jeans and almost screamed in pain at her knotted muscles. "Agent Altair," she answered, muffling her misery.

"Hi, Agent Altair, this is Dr. Martinez from the hospital yesterday."

Sayer sat up, realizing the sun was up. "Uuuh." She let out a grunt of pain at the sudden motion. Her phone said it was eight forty-five. How the hell had she slept so late?

"I'm sorry to bother you on a Sunday morning."

"It's Sunday?" Sayer realized she had no clue what the date was. Was it still even April?

The doctor laughed. "Yes, of course, your job probably doesn't respect weekends, just like mine. Anyway, I called because Leila Farouk wants to speak to you."

Vesper rolled over trying to get onto Sayer's lap for a belly rub. Sayer had to fight him off while crawling painfully out of bed. "She wants to talk?"

"She said she would only talk to you. The one who saved her. She found out somehow that there could be another girl missing." Dr. Martinez sounded extremely annoyed. "She said she wants to help."

"I'll be right there." Sayer hopped toward the bathroom, pulling off her filthy jeans.

"Can you come in a few hours? She's being seen by the neurologist soon. She'll be done by noon."

"Of course. I'll see you then. Thanks for the call."

"I just hope it helps. She's doing fine physically, but she is suffering severe emotional trauma. Be sure you don't make it worse."

Sayer hung up. She realized that with Leila saved and Winters caught, she felt some of the tension of the case bleed off. Her shoulders were almost down in their normal position rather than hunched around her ears with stress.

Vesper playfully jumped over to the front door, clearly needing out.

"Right, sorry, boy." She pulled on her robe and flung open the door. Vesper sprinted down to the garden. Sayer checked for Tino but he wasn't in his normal breakfast spot. She shuffled down and knocked on his door, wanting to make sure he had Vesper. No answer so she dialed his cell.

"Tino, it's Sayer. I'm going to head out soon, just wanted to make sure you've got Vesper if I leave him in the garden for now."

"Oh no, didn't you see the note I left on your fridge?"

Sayer shuffled back up and found the folded page held on by her single ALOHA magnet. "Uh-oh, yeah, I found it."

"Good, then you see that I had to leave town just for today. I'm helping out with my kids all day."

"You have kids?"

Tino let loose a deep belly laugh. "For neighbors who share custody of a dog, we should get to know each other better sometime. Listen, I can be back on Vesper duty first thing tomorrow. You'll need to find someone else to watch him until then. Talk soon, calida."

Sayer looked out at the puppy down in the garden, joyfully sniffing and peeing on everything. "What am I going to do with you all day?"

Sayer stared at Vesper until an idea hit. Her nephew, Jackson, had been asking for a dog; surely her sister would love a visit from a puppy for the kid to play with. Sayer pulled out her phone again and texted her sister. *Macey, I'm in a tight spot. Have a puppy that needs to be taken care of today. Mind if I head over now and bring the puppy to play with Jackson?*

Her phone pinged moments later. *What a great idea! Can't wait to see you. So glad you'll make it.*

"So glad I'll make it?" Sayer asked out loud, then shrugged.

While Vesper inhaled the dog food Tino had left, Sayer made a few quick phone calls. Uniforms were canvassing Winters's properties. The evidence team was tearing apart his boring house, still finding nothing. Andy was there as well, studying the new killer he got to write up for his profiling textbook. Winters confirmed through his lawyer that he still refused to cooperate. Last but not least, Sayer called Vik to let him know that the girl in the hospital wanted to talk.

Finally she decided to jump in the shower for a quick rinse.

Her sore body screamed as she removed the last of her clothes. Naked, she stared in the mirror. The bruises along her torso and muscled legs were already turning deep purple, formless blots of dark ink marring her body. The ringing in her ears had faded overnight, but she could still conjure up the whomping bang of the blast beneath her.

She looked herself in the eye. "All right, Sayer, this is PTSD material. You were blown up yesterday. Don't be the stereotypical cop and let it fester until you freak out. Process the pain. Let yourself feel the fear and the helplessness. Talk to someone if you need to."

She nodded, satisfied that she wasn't repressing anything. Sayer already knew she had anger management issues; no need to add more fuel to that fire.

After a longer-than-necessary shower, she was ready to drive Vesper over to her sister's place and resume tearing apart the life of Franklin Winters.

Vesper happily trotted with her to the motorcycle and jumped into the sidecar like an old pro. Sayer smiled at the sight of the puppy, silvery hair glowing in the sun, goofy grin on his face, pink tongue hanging out at a jaunty angle. He just needed some leather goggles and he would be a perfect bike companion.

"I promise we'll spend more time together when this case is over, okay, boy?"

His tail thumped the vintage leather and Sayer didn't even mind.

As they rode into the genteel Northern Virginia countryside, for a brief moment, Sayer let her mind wander away from the case. Away from her disastrous research. Away from the pain of the bike vibrating all 206 sore bones in her body. Away from everything but the warm air, the rumble of her bike, the adorable puppy riding alongside her. The sensation reached far down inside her to a place she could almost remember. A place where she once used to feel contentment; hell, she had once felt joy.

The brief moment of peace crashed into a brick wall when she turned onto the long driveway curving up to her sister's McMansion. Blue balloons bobbed on the mailbox. A stream of soccer moms and five-year-olds carrying presents headed across the perfectly manicured lawn toward Macey's house. On the front porch, Macey and Jackson greeted guests, ushering them inside. Above them a massive banner said, HAPPY BIRTHDAY!

"Oh shit! Jackson's birthday." Sayer vaguely remembered the e-mail, the phone message from her sister—Jackson would be so happy if Aunt Sayer, his favorite person in the whole would, could make it. *Shit shit shit.*

At the sight of all the children heading inside, Vesper didn't wait. He leaped from the sidecar and barreled up the stairs. At the top, Sayer watched Jackson throw his arms open. Vesper careened into him and they both toppled to the ground. For half a second Sayer held her breath hoping she didn't just kill her nephew on his fifth birthday, but his laughter rang across the grassy lawn and Sayer smiled yet again. That had to be a record, two real smiles in one day.

As she gingerly approached the house, Macey actually smiled at her rather than giving her usual scowl. "Sayer, I honestly didn't think you would come."

"And miss Jackson's birthday, no way!" Sayer said, feeling like the worst human being in the history of human beings.

Jackson tore himself away from the wild puppy licks to give Sayer a huge hug. Despite the fact that it hurt like hell, she breathed in the little-kid grassy scent and felt a momentary pang.

"Thanks, Aunt Sayer! A dog for my party!" he called out, and ran off, Vesper bounding after him.

Nana came out and gave Sayer a gentle hug and an approving smile. It was like goddamned smile central here.

"So glad you made it."

"Everyone keeps saying," Sayer grumbled. "I, uh, I can only stay for a little bit."

Macey gave her hand a squeeze. "At least stay to see the big surprise."

Sayer looked at her phone. "I've got thirty or forty minutes."

"Sure, all right." Her sister gave her yet another genuine smile, then hurried off to hostess. Sayer drifted over to the food table and got a heaping plate of potato chips.

Nana followed. "Sayer, I'll admit, I didn't expect you to make it today. I'm so proud of you for remembering. I'm also glad you're all right. Heard there was an explosion yesterday."

Sayer decided not to tell Nana that she had in fact been in that explosion.

They stood in companionable silence for a few minutes. Sayer realized that Jackson's father was conspicuously absent. Like Nana, Macey had married a senator.

"Guessing Tim isn't going to make it today?" Sayer asked.

A storm cloud formed over Nana's face. "That man, I swear."

"Yeah, fuck him," Sayer muttered. "Oh, sorry, Nana."

"Honey, fucking would be too good for him," Nana muttered back.

"Nana!" Sayer never expected such language from her very proper grandmother.

"What? I've done my time as a proper lady. I'm old and over that bullshit. Now my grandkids are grown, my husband is dead, I'm going to do whatever I want, and if that involves cursing sometimes, well then so be it."

Sayer let out a full laugh. "You're fierce, Nana."

"Darn tootin' I am. And so are you."

As Sayer and Nana laughed together, a trio of perfectly coiffed soccer moms approached. "You must be Macey's sister." The tallest of them held out her hand.

Sayer shook awkwardly and tried for a welcoming smile.

"We hear you're an FBI agent!" the one in expensive yoga pants and a stylishly tattered sweater exclaimed. All three women smiled and nodded like they were meeting a celebrity.

"I do in fact work for the FBI." Sayer aimed for polite but detached.

"Wow, are you, like a profiler or a special agent? Do you hunt serial killers?"

Sayer tried not to roll her eyes. "I'm not a profiler but yes, I do hunt serial killers."

Nana added with great pride, "She's actually in charge of the Gwendolyn Van Hurst case."

"Wooooow," the tall one cooed with pleasure. "That is so amazing! It must feel so wonderful to know you're making such a difference in the world. Putting away the bad guys like that."

The skinniest one piped up. "Have you . . . have you ever shot any-one?"

Sayer couldn't resist. She nodded vigorously. "Yeah, just once. Man, he was so close he exploded all over me."

The three women stared in horrified silence.

Sayer managed not to snort at their saucer eyes. She knew her re-sponse was unkind and she understood rubbernecking, but being forced to shoot anyone, no matter how clear-cut the circumstances, was always difficult for law enforcement. Or most law enforcement . . . there were assholes everywhere and she certainly knew some who en-joyed the violence.

"Anyway . . ." She was about to walk away when her phone rang. The screen said *Wendy Kritzer,* the analyst who reviewed the fMRIs from Sayer's research. She'd almost pushed her failing research from her mind, but Wendy had probably completed her analysis of Dugald Tarlington's brain scan.

Sayer pressed answer and turned her back to the women. "Wendy! Did you take a look at the latest fMRI?"

"I did." Sayer could hear Wendy shuffling papers. "Scan number twelve . . ."

"Was it as normal as it looked to me?" Sayer asked, slightly hold-ing her breath. She knew the brain scan of Dugald Tarlington was normal, but she sent all her fMRIs for a second opinion. Some small part of her hoped that Wendy saw some kind of anomaly that Sayer had missed.

"Not sure what you were hoping for, but I see literally no evidence of any systematic deficiencies or deformities in this brain. In fact, it could've been the textbook image of an average male brain in virtu-ally every way. This brain didn't even have scattered light spots. Healthy as can be."

Sayer closed her eyes, trying not to overreact to Wendy's bad news. "Thanks, Wendy. I'll let you know when we scan the next one . . . if there is a next one." She was due for a check-in with the regional director who allocated funding. It was possible that Sayer was about to lose her research funding since the data wasn't supporting her theory.

With a deep breath she opened her eyes to find the three women still hovering, all watching her with anxious eyes. Perhaps they hoped to catch some tidbit from a murder investigation. Sayer looked out into the backyard at Jackson's birthday party in full swing. Kids played tag on the vast expanse of grass, wheeling and turning like a flock of birds. Inside above the snack table, a massive TV played a slide show of photos of Jackson. His birth, his wide brown eyes staring at the camera. His toothy grin as he took his first steps. His long hair flying behind him as little-boy legs pumped, running across a grassy field.

It was eerily reminiscent of the slide show at Gwen's funeral, and Sayer shuddered.

The trio of women finally seemed to realize Sayer wasn't going to regale them with daring tales of FBI adventure, and they drifted away.

Nana noticed her scowl. "Bad news about the case?"

Nana's question knocked some sense into Sayer. Her research might be collapsing in on itself, but she had something much more important to deal with. Leila Farouk awaited.

"Nah, just my research stuff. No big deal." Sayer contemplated her nephew and sister preparing a piñata. Sayer didn't have the heart to interrupt their joy. "Can you tell Macey I had to go?"

Nana's forehead creased with disapproval, but she nodded. "And Jackson? Will you leave without saying good-bye to the birthday boy?"

Sayer looked away from her nephew. "Yeah, I don't want to interrupt. I'll make it up to him when I come grab Vesper later."

"Hey," Nana said softly. "What's wrong?"

Sayer realized that her entire face scrunched with stress. She searched for the right words. "I'm about to go interview a girl who was held in a cage for months."

Nana's hands flew to her mouth. "Oh no."

"Then I've got to try to figure out a way to get some asshole to tell us if he's got another girl just like her." For just a moment, Sayer's internal emotional wall cracked.

Nana wrapped an arm around her shoulder. Her Chanel No. 5 tickled Sayer's nose, the scent of security. Sayer let herself feel a moment of comfort from the gentle love flowing from Nana before stepping back.

She looked into Nana's blue eyes, seeking understanding. "To be good at my job, I can't be like them." She gestured at Macey and Jackson. "The only thing that keeps me sane is to pull the curtain shut between my humanity and my job. I . . . can't be normal like you."

Nana's eyes crinkled into a genuine smile. "Sayer, you know I understand. I just don't like to see you so shut off from everything. Since Jake died you've shut yourself off from life. But this is your choice and I know you're amazing at what you do. You save lives, Sayer, and I am nothing but proud of you, no matter how much of a hard time I give you."

The approval almost snapped Sayer's ability to hold back the tide of emotions she felt. Rather than cry, she squeezed Nana's hand.

As Sayer reached the door, Jackson called out, ran up, and grabbed her hand. Vesper joined them, winding between their legs, almost knocking Sayer over.

"You're leaving?" The young boy thrust out his bottom lip with genuine sorrow.

"Oh man, Jackson," Sayer croaked through thick emotion, "I've got to go. You know how much I love you, right?"

"Yeah." His eyes stayed down under a mop of kid hair.

"I promise we will do a Sayer–Jackson day as soon as I can work a day out with your mom. Okay?"

"Yeah." He seemed unconvinced, and Sayer realized she hadn't spent a day with the kid in more than a year. Guilt stabbed a knife right into her gut, and then it wiggled around a little.

"You take good care of Vesper. I'll see you soon." She gave him a gentle squeeze and practically sprinted down the stairs to her bike, guilt wrapping its foul fingers around her like a ghost.

GEORGETOWN HOSPITAL,
WASHINGTON, D.C.

On her way to the hospital, Sayer called the vet that had the kitten and let out a long sigh of relief to hear that the animal would survive. She vowed to bring the kitten to Leila as soon as it could be moved.

The hospital felt quiet compared to the chaos after the bombing. Sayer lowered her aching body into a chair outside Leila Farouk's hospital room to wait until the doctors finished up with her.

Ubiquitous TVs murmured from every hallway and waiting room. They were all still rambling on about the latest developments. A bomb, a live girl. Sayer could clearly see the glint of excitement in the eyes of the pert blond reporter. Nothing more exciting than a terrible series of kidnappings and murders. Sometimes Sayer just felt sick. Maybe she should get the hell out of this line of work. Start a bed-and-breakfast or something.

Dr. Martinez interrupted the ridiculous thought when she stepped out into the hall. "Leila can talk to you now."

"How's she doing?"

"Well, we're waiting to see if her kidneys will recover. Otherwise she's fully rehydrated and on the mend. The good news is we've gotten in touch with her mother's sister back in Egypt. They thought Leila was dead and are flying here now to bring her home. She seems very excited to go home to Egypt." The doctor paused. "Go easy on her, okay?"

"Of course." Sayer meant it. She highly doubted the poor girl had any clue where Winters's lair was or if there was another girl missing, and she certainly didn't want to traumatize her any further than she already was. She eased into the room.

The girl in the hospital bed made Sayer's heart twist in her chest. Surrounded by tubes and machines, Leila sat upright wrapped in a bundle of hospital blankets. Her wide brown eyes stared unseeing at the TV flickering a cartoon, muted on the wall. Though she was well hydrated now, her slightly swollen lips still cracked and peeled.

"Leila?" Sayer spoke softly.

The girl jumped like a gunshot had gone off next to her.

"Hey, sorry. I'm Agent Altair with the FBI. Dr. Martinez said you wanted to talk to me?"

The girl jutted out her trembling bottom lip and nodded. Sayer slowly approached and eased herself down into the chair beside her bed. She smiled encouragingly but gave Leila time to gather herself.

Finally the girl swallowed with effort and spoke. "I don't know much, but I want to help." Her voice was raspy with disuse, her accent thick. Tears squeezed from the corners of her eyes.

"Thank you so much, Leila. I know you've been through a terrible thing."

"He called me 9.2. Never Leila. I wasn't sure I'd ever hear my own name said out loud again."

"9.2? Did you know what that meant?"

"No, but I thought there were other numbers. Like he was counting us in some way."

"Can you tell me what else you remember? Do you want to tell me from the beginning?"

Leila nodded. "I was just a few blocks from the shelter where I lived. I felt a prick on my neck and then I blacked out. I woke up in that cage." As she spoke, her voice grew slightly stronger.

Sayer hoped the telling would unburden her from some of her pain.

"In the cage . . . I screamed for help until I lost my voice. I knew . . ." Leila's voice faltered.

"Take your time," Sayer said.

"I knew . . . the kind of man that had me. I thought I knew what would happen next." She paused for a very long time. "But I was wrong. What happened was much worse."

Sayer bit her cheek to avoid showing emotion. She wanted to ball her fists and flare her nose in anger at what Winters did to her, but if this girl was strong enough to talk, Sayer needed the strength to listen calmly.

"I was in the dark most of the time. Pitch-black. I was alone except for the kittens. Two of them. The first was a little tabby that died. Then Bast."

"Bast?"

"My second kitten." Leila's composure broke. She collapsed forward and sobbed into the blanket.

Sayer reached out and rubbed small circles on her back while she cried.

Tears streaming down her face, Leila looked up at Sayer with so much pain that her face contorted. "She's dead, isn't she?"

"Hey, no! I just got off the phone with the vet. Bast will pull through. She's a fighter, just like you."

Leila's eyes widened. "Bast will be okay?"

Sayer nodded. Tears flooded the girl's eyes.

"Thank you. Oh . . . thank you. You don't know . . ." She trailed off and shuddered one more time, then sniffed, gathering herself. "As I said . . . it was very dark. Always smelled of lavender cleaner. The lights only came on when the projector began to play."

"So you never really saw him?"

Leila shook her head. "No, I think he wore a mask and goggles.

The kind you use to see in the dark. He would come in and set up the machines."

"The smoke machine?"

"Yes, the machine with the smoke, and the projector. But sometimes, when the projector turned on, I could see him in the shadows." Her face set into a trembling frown. "It looked like an alien. His face all covered and the big green eyes of the goggles. Something over his mouth too so he wouldn't breathe in the smoke."

"Anything else you can tell me about him? Impressions? Thoughts? Anything?"

"I could see he was a small man. He seemed frail. Weak. It's why he had to keep me in a cage or I would have killed him." Leila's eyes flashed, and Sayer wanted to cheer. Anger could be useful for those trying to recover from something terrible.

Sayer let her keep talking.

"The smoke would fill the room and then the projectors would turn on. The images, they would come alive. I knew there must be something in the smoke, but they seemed so real. Sometimes he would talk to me. His voice sounded strange, electronic, and was muffled through the mask. He would ask me what I saw. Ask me if I . . ." Leila fell silent.

Sayer waited.

"He asked if I could see my brother. If I could talk to him. I miss Tarik so much. How did he know?"

"The man asked about your brother specifically?"

Through her tears she nodded. "Yes, he would say, 'Find your twin. Tarik is so close by. Go to him.'"

"So he asked about . . . traveling to see him?"

"Yes, like, when I was out of it, seeing things, watching the terror movies he showed me. That's all that happened, the whole time. I didn't know how long I was there. There was no day or night."

"Why do you think he was doing those things to you?" Sayer left the question as open as possible, letting Leila say whatever came to mind.

"I think it was an experiment. He said things about the experiment. He seemed most excited when I lost consciousness. The smoke would get so thick . . . it would choke me, then I would see impossible things. Then I would black out and, when I woke up, sometimes he would be there moving faster than usual. Excitement in his shoulders."

Leila let out a long, quivering breath and seemed done. Sayer let her sit for a moment while they both processed everything. She wanted to know more, but Sayer didn't have the heart to push much more.

Finally Sayer said, "Do you want me to tell you more about what we know? You have the right to know, but only if it will help you."

"I want to know. I think . . . I heard there was another girl too. A girl who is dead."

Sayer figured total honesty might not be appropriate but didn't want to lie either. "Yes. She's the reason we found you."

"So you figured something out from her . . . her body?"

"No, she was kept in a place just like you were and we used that connection to find you."

"That poor girl." Leila gathered the blankets into her fists and pulled them around her.

"The smoke had a drug called DMT in it," Sayer continued. "DMT causes intense, very realistic hallucinations. Some cultures use it for spirit quests."

"I figured there was something in the smoke. The way the movies . . . I guess they were hallucinations, looked . . . they felt too real."

Sayer scooted her chair up, and it made a loud scraping sound. Leila gasped in fear. Sayer put a gentle hand onto her chilled arm. "Sorry."

Leila tried to smile. "It's okay."

Sayer pulled a folder from her bag. "Would you be willing to look at some photographs? It is of the images the first girl looked at. We want to know if you were shown the same images."

"Of the movies I saw? Of my hallucinations?"

"I'm not sure. Are you able to look at them? If you're not comfortable I totally understand. If not, maybe you could just describe them to me."

Leila paused for a very long time. Her brown eyes looked so lost, like she could see something in the distance that no one else could see.

Sayer was about to put the photos away, unwilling to add to the trauma in those young eyes, when Leila whispered, "Yes, I'd like to see the photos. I want to."

Sayer handed her a single photo of the Maya Hero Twins, the main image that Gwen was shown. They both held their breath.

Leila exhaled sharply with relief. "No, this is not what I saw." A tear rolled from the corner of her eye. Looking at the photo had cost her something. "The images I saw, they were Egyptian."

"Egyptian? Like ancient Egyptian?"

"Yes, I remember them from school. We had to take an ancient history class."

"Did you recognize the specific images?"

"No, but I think they were of Osiris . . ."

"Like the ancient Egyptian god?"

"Yes. Maybe him and the god with the jackal head. Looks like . . . Osiris's brother, I think. I'm sorry, I can't remember."

"That's incredibly helpful, Leila. Thank you."

"Good." Her voice wobbled and Sayer knew it was time to be done. She spent a few minutes with Leila talking about the hospital and the food and mundane things that had nothing to do with cages or death.

As Sayer got up to leave, Leila slid her thin hand out from the blankets and curled her chilled fingers over Sayer's hand. She gripped hard. Her breath caught as she inhaled. "Thank you for saving me and Bast."

"Of course." Sayer gave her hand a squeeze back and then fled the room before Leila could see the tears in her own eyes.

EZRA'S ROOM, GEORGETOWN
HOSPITAL, WASHINGTON, D.C.

Emotions still swirling, Sayer decided to peek into Ezra's room just to say hello. As she approached, she heard low muttering.

"No, no, no . . ."

Sayer hurried to make sure Ezra was okay. She found him hunched over a stack of paper. He underlined something so hard the pen pushed through the paper, tearing it a little.

"Fucking hell." Ezra groaned.

"Hey, you okay?" Sayer approached the bed.

Ezra looked up, his face pinched into a mixture of frustration and fear. "Hey, Agent Altair. Not really. My damn brain won't work." Tears welled in his eyes and he shook the calendar he held in one hand. "I thought I was going to help, but clearly I can't." He gestured at his legs. "I thought . . . if I'm stuck here I could at least do something to put Winters away, and I can't figure out where I went wrong."

"Whoa, slow down. What do you mean?"

With a shaky sigh, Ezra pointed to copies of the photo albums from the catacombs. "I went back through these. We know the exact date of the last photograph from each album, so I used that to back-track and recorded the dates each photo was taken. So, see here, this photo of Gwen in the cage was taken on"—he flipped through the calendar—"February nineteenth."

"Okay, that makes sense." Sayer nodded encouragingly.

"Right, so then I got Winters's records. So, I go to February nineteenth for his credit card, and I see he got groceries that day at some bodega in D.C. If the address was near where he held Gwen, I figured it would put him near the scene, help put him away."

"Ezra, that's a brilliant idea!"

"Sure, it seemed like it at three this morning, but . . . I made a mistake somewhere."

"How so?" Sayer scooted a chair next to Ezra so he could show her his notes. They were written in a scrawling, wild hand. She realized he was having trouble with fine motor control. Sayer imagined Ezra painstakingly writing out each note, obsessed with doing something, anything to help their case despite his shaking hands and terrible headache.

"Well, check this out." Ezra flipped back and forth between two photos in the album.

Sayer squinted at the dates he pointed to on the calendar.

"They're over a week apart. Winters didn't go see either Gwen or Leila for seven days in March. Where was he?" Sayer said.

"Exactly! So I was excited when I found credit card charges in Hawaii. I thought maybe Winters went on vacation. And sure enough, looks like he and his girlfriend went to Hawaii for a week."

"Ezra, that's great!"

"Yeah, it would be . . . if the dates matched."

"What?" Sayer leaned forward to read Ezra's notes.

"See, he went to Hawaii from the fourth to the eleventh of January. Now look in the calendar."

Sayer flipped it open to January. "It looks like Gwen and Leila were photographed on January fourth, seventh, and ninth . . ."

"Yeah, so if Winters was in Hawaii, who took those photographs?"

Sayer and Ezra sat in silence, letting the weight of the question hang between them.

Finally, Sayer leaned back in her chair and said, "Well, shit."

Ezra fumbled through all his notes and held them up, crumpling some in his fist. "But we've got DNA on the bastard. We know he did it. So where did I make a mistake? I've gone over this fifty times and I can't figure out what I did wrong." Ezra's voice cracked. "I'm just not thinking straight."

He threw his notes toward the wall and they fluttered to the floor.

"I just wanted to help and I can't." His last bit of composure crumbled and tears rolled down his cheeks.

"Whoa! This is a great idea, Ezra. No one else thought of this. I'll have the data team double-check your dates, but I'm willing to bet you got it right. Hell, I think you just found us something new. What if Winters has a partner?"

Sayer arrived at Quantico fifty minutes later. Her body felt empty, like a husk incapable of emotion after her interview with Leila and her talk with Ezra. Unlike the drive to her sister's house, the entire ride down seemed bumpier than usual. Her bruised body felt battered by the time she pulled into the mostly empty parking lot.

She texted Joan and the data team, letting them know about the date mismatches that Ezra found so they could double-check his work. Vik appeared at her desk as she gingerly sat down.

"So?" he asked, eyebrows up.

"So, Leila Farouk is emotionally destroyed but desperate to help. Sanctuary House has to be where he found both victims. More importantly, I stopped in to talk to Ezra and I think he found something important."

"Uh-oh, you don't look happy about it."

"I'm not. He backtracked the dates of the photos in the albums, then cross-checked them to Winters's financials."

"And . . . ?" Vik asked.

"And, while Winters was in Hawaii for a week, someone took photos of Gwen and Leila."

Vik whistled.

"Yeah, so did he arrange for someone else to use his card all over Hawaii for a week, which seems pretty unlikely, or does he have a goddamned partner? I'm going to head down to interrogation and take a pass at Winters, see if I can shake anything loose."

Vik held up his hand for a high five and Sayer was thankful for something that made her smile, even if it was only a momentary reprieve from the emptiness in her chest.

Sayer entered the empty interrogation room. She wanted to be waiting for Winters when he arrived.

The real estate agent shuffled in moments later, lawyer on his heels. The man looked like he was about to jump out of his skin. His two days in the holding cell had not treated him well. Disheveled, with raccoon eyes, he had none of the smug swagger of the night before. He now wore the look a man has right before he confesses to something big.

The lawyer, on the other hand, was clearly nervous about something. Sayer tried not to feel the little bit of hope that danced around the edges of her heart. She realized that she needed to be careful; this case was poking holes in her mental curtain faster than she could mend them.

"Mr. Winters." Sayer tried to keep the vitriol out of her interrogation, but her interview with Leila had knocked away the last vestiges of her objectivity. Despite all her training, her voice had a clear edge to it. "We know you found Gwen and Leila Farouk at Sanctuary House and we know you forged Leila's release document."

"But—"

She held up a hand. "Just listen."

Franklin Winters looked down at the table like he was about to cry.

Sayer enjoyed the moment. "I've spoken to Ms. Farouk, who barely survived. We've found your photo albums. We know all about your experiments. We even know you have a partner. It's now or never. Talk to me, Franklin. Tell me where you planned all this. Tell me who your partner is. Tell me if there's another victim. Tell me if you have a third girl somewhere and we can work out a deal, a better cell, more privileges, no death penalty . . ."

Genuine tears streamed down Franklin Winters's face, dripping off his chin onto the table like raindrops. He had to lean forward to wipe his nose with his hands shackled tightly together.

The words *death penalty* hung in the air while Winters wept. He glanced over at his lawyer, and Sayer could practically watch him struggling with the decision: talk or not. He wrung his hands together, blinked rapidly, clearing the rest of his tears, and finally looked up at Sayer.

"I'll tell you everything."

Sayer kept her face blank, hiding the crescendo of excitement clanging in her chest. Rather than jump from her seat and pump her fist in the air, she gave a placid nod encouraging him to continue.

Winters's lawyer cleared his throat. "Franklin, I strongly suggest you discuss this with me first so I can properly advise you on the legal aspects of anything you plan to reveal to Agent Altair."

Winters dismissed the lawyer with a wave.

Sayer held her breath. This might be it.

"I can prove the DNA you found wasn't mine," Winters blurted out.

Sayer's calm façade fell. Rage flooded her, clouding her vision. How dare he play the innocent victim.

"You're seriously going to pull more of this 'I'm innocent' bullshit with me?" Her voice rose to a shout. Sayer stopped and took a deep breath, starting over. "Mr. Winters, the DNA we found on the body of a dead girl was a perfect match to you. There is no question it's yours. If you aren't going to tell me if there are any more victims, then, well, I'll see you in court, where I will strenuously support that they jab a needle in your arm."

She stood and moved to leave, but Winters frantically shouted, "Semen!"

"What?"

"You said you found my DNA in a sample of semen that you took off that girl's body."

"That's right." Sayer leaned forward over the table, glaring at Winters. "What of it?"

Winters's tears began again. "That is literally impossible." His body shook and his face flushed with emotion. "I'm transgender. A trans man. My body does not produce semen."

"What?" was all Sayer managed to grunt out, her brain unable to make sense of what he was saying.

"I was born without testicles. I was assigned female at birth and, when I transitioned, I took on a new identity. There is no physical way you could have found my DNA in a sample of semen!"

Sayer flopped down across from Winters, frantically processing this new information. "And that's why you have no history? A new identity."

"Yes!" His voice quivered. "I thought this was all a mistake and I wouldn't have to tell anyone. I'm begging you, Agent Altair, get me out of here! I need my medication!"

Next to Winters, his lawyer beamed at this news.

"You were seen at the murder site by the D.C. police when they came out to the original 911 call. You were there, Mr. Winters, and then you lied to us about it."

"I know!" Winters's entire body shook with emotion. "Someone called me on the phone. Said it was my ex . . . that she was in trouble."

"Someone called you?"

"Yeah, knew stuff about my ex, said that she was sick, needed to talk to me." Winters put his head down into his hands. "So stupid." After a moment he looked back up, eyes full of tears. "I knew how it looked. I knew I didn't do it, so I figured I would just lie and you would never know. But it was a setup. This is all a setup!"

Sayer thought about Ezra's calendar with the impossible dates and felt absolutely sick. There was a third possibility she hadn't even considered given the DNA evidence, but if what Winters said was true, the dates didn't match because he wasn't the killer.

Winters's whole body trembled. Damn, either he was a fantastic actor or Franklin Winters was telling the truth.

"You are telling me that you are transgender." Sayer said it out loud to let it sink in.

"Yes! I'm being framed or something. I don't even know what is going on. All I know is that I did not hurt those girls and there is no way you found my DNA in semen!" Winters looked almost manic with a combination of fear and excitement.

"Don't celebrate just yet, Mr. Winters. We still have your fingerprint at the catacomb scene, your DNA on the victim, and you were spotted at the scene by a police officer, plus you clearly had access to all three scenes."

"Can't you see someone is framing me!" He stood up and the chains holding his handcuffs clanged against the table. His lawyer put a firm hand on his arm to calm him down.

"Franklin," the lawyer said, "if it turns out that your DNA was planted, that means that their evidence is out the window. It will take a few days to clarify everything, but let the agents confirm. When they do, they will see that they have no case against you. The wheels of justice are slow, but they work."

Winters snorted, eyes wide with emotions out of control. "Yeah, I've seen how people like me are treated by the justice system. For all I know they'll put me in the wrong prison."

Sayer stood up. "Mr. Winters, I'm going to follow up on all of this and I promise, if you aren't responsible for this, you will be released. But until I can figure out what exactly is going on, there is still plenty of evidence to keep you here."

Winters nodded curtly and folded his hands in a ball.

Taking a deep breath, Sayer fled the interrogation room and made a beeline for the medical examiner's lab.

She flubbed her entry code a few times, her hands were shaking so hard. She finally slammed open the door and was disappointed to find a junior ME there instead of Joan.

"Is Joan in?" Sayer demanded.

The young man with white-blond hair glanced up from his paperwork. "No, she hasn't been in today. It *is* Sunday. . . ."

Sayer contemplated calling Joan in but decided the junior ME could probably answer her questions just as easily.

"I need help on a case."

"You mean *the* case. The Van Hurst murder."

"Yeah. What I'm about to tell you cannot be shared with anyone until I have it sorted out, do you understand?"

"Of course, Agent Altair." He looked slightly scared, and Sayer realized she wore a mask of fury as the foundations of her case shook beneath her.

Sayer headed over to the evidence refrigerator. "There is some confusion over the DNA sample from the Van Hurst case."

He joined her at the massive door. "What kind of confusion?"

"The DNA was a match for Franklin Winters. However, the report said that the medium of the DNA was semen, and Mr. Winters claims to be a transgender man designated female at birth. He could not have produced semen. Could the medium of the DNA sample be incorrect?"

"Whoa, that's pretty serious!" The ME pulled out a drawer from the refrigeration unit. Glass test tubes clinked together and a strange chemical scent filled the room. He slid a single tube out and held it up. "There's an easy way for me to tell. Give me a minute."

The ME created a series of slides. He slid them one at a time into various machines, taking brief notes.

"Goodness," he muttered.

"Yeah?" Sayer asked, impatient for him to tell her what he was seeing.

"Hang on, I want to do one more test."

While she waited, Sayer texted Joan to fill her in. She wanted to hear Joan's opinion on the possibility of a frame-up.

The ME took a small sample from a dish and transferred it to a new machine. When he looked at the computer screen, he let out a low moan.

"All right, start talking." Sayer couldn't wait any longer.

The medical examiner looked stricken. "We've all talked about the possibility, but I didn't ever expect it to show up in our lab."

"What? What is it?" Sayer practically shouted.

"Manufactured DNA," the ME said, incredulous.

"What? Manufactured? As in, man-made?"

"Yeah, it's possible to make DNA from scratch. Literally build it in a lab. Because it's such a new technology with no known medical application yet, none of the DNA sequencing machines would notice the difference between real and fake DNA. And checking for fake DNA isn't part of our standard protocol. So unless you had a reason to look directly at the sample to check, you would never notice."

"So the DNA is fake? Literally, someone made it?"

The ME nodded, too stunned to talk further.

Sayer sank into a chair and put her head in her hands. "So you're telling me that this is not a contamination problem? This is not a mistake? This is literally evidence someone must have planted to frame this man?"

The ME sat down next to her. "That is exactly what I'm saying. It's not hard to manufacture DNA. All you need is a sample to match; you could get that off a discarded soda can or anything really. But it's not easy either. This was something someone did on purpose."

"Goddammit." Sayer watched her case crumble before her. They were going to have to start over from scratch. Everything pointed directly at Winters, including finding Leila at one of his properties. At least they had saved Leila. After a few moments of silent churning, Sayer gathered herself.

"All right, tell me how it works. Can you give me the lowdown in the next few minutes?"

The ME looked vaguely nervous. "I mean, yeah, I can tell you what I know. Manufactured DNA has been possible for a while now, maybe almost ten years. We, I mean those of us in the medical examiner's office, we've talked about the possibility before, but no one has seen a real case of fake DNA in the wild."

"Would you know? I mean, we have state-of-the-art equipment here and you guys missed it."

He grimaced. "Yeah. The machines we use weren't made to detect it. The DNA sequencers we use just look at the DNA strands. Manufactured DNA is basically designed to fool our machines. Checking to see if it's man-made is fairly easy, but we just don't do it. I guess we will now. . . ."

"So, how hard is this? Can I find out on the Internet how to manufacture DNA, or do I need a university lab and a biochemistry degree or something?" Sayer asked.

"Well, somewhere in between. You need the right equipment, but I'm pretty sure I could make DNA here in our lab. I think you'd need some basic biology, but nothing you couldn't learn from the right book or two." He scrunched his face up to think. "How easy it would be to figure out? I think it wouldn't be too hard. I doubt it's common knowledge, but it's also not super secret."

Sayer's mind reeled. The DNA had been their slam-dunk forensic evidence. Fingerprints are easy to plant, and the connection between Winters and the crime scene locations was circumstantial. If he really was in Hawaii when those photos were taken, their case against him was shaky at best. If someone planted DNA evidence, there was no way the rest of the evidence wouldn't look like a frame job too.

"Goddammit." Sayer slammed her fist on the table and the junior ME jumped at the sudden outburst.

"Well, this certainly changes things with the Cage Killer case," he muttered.

"You think?" she said to him as she left. At the door, she looked back over her shoulder. "I need you to keep this quiet until I talk to Holt. You're the only person who knows, and we've got leaks in this case. If word gets out, I'll know it's you."

The ME nodded vigorously.

"Good. The last thing we need is a media circus. Which is exactly what this is eventually going to be."

As Sayer strode toward Holt's office, her phone buzzed from a D.C. number.

"Agent Altair."

"Hello, Agent Altair, this is Mrs. Calavera, from Sanctuary House." Her voice trembled.

"Yes, of course. Is everything all right?"

"I don't know . . . no one has seen Adi in a while. Normally I wouldn't worry, but she had plans with her friends this afternoon and she didn't show up, which is very unlike her. . . ."

"Oh no . . . ," Sayer groaned, picturing the purple-haired girl.

"I think that Adi's been taken."

Sayer sprinted to Assistant Director Holt's office with a lead ball in her gut. She turned over the implications of what she'd just learned. Someone had made and then planted DNA evidence on Gwendolyn Van Hurst, and now Adi was possibly missing. If Winters wasn't their unsub, the killer was still out there and might have just kidnapped Adi Stephanopolous.

Sayer paused outside Holt's door. Holt's assistant wasn't in, but, as usual, she could hear Holt on the phone in her office despite the fact that it was Sunday afternoon. This might be even worse than the time she had to explain to Holt why she punched a reporter. The future of this whole case played out in Sayer's mind. There would be scandal, questions, accusations, and recriminations. None of which she really cared about, but this was going to be ugly.

Taking a deep breath, Sayer knocked.

"Enter," Holt barked.

Sayer hadn't crossed herself in twenty years, but some childhood habit surfaced and she touched her forehead, chest, and shoulders before she pushed open the door.

"Assistant Director Holt," Sayer began.

"Holy shit, what's wrong?"

Sayer's eyebrows rose. "How . . . ?"

"Really? I'm an assistant director of the FBI. You think I can't tell when something horrible has happened?" Holt stood up and was next to Sayer in a flash. "Is an agent hurt?"

Sayer had never seen such emotion on Holt's face. "No, no. Nothing like that."

"Oh, thank God." Holt put a beefy hand on Sayer's shoulder and leaned forward with intense relief.

"Yeah, it's not quite that bad," Sayer said, "but close."

Holt straightened her power suit and smoothed her gray helmet of hair. "Nothing comes close to an agent of mine hurt on the job." The look in her eyes made Sayer's stomach quail. "So what is it?"

For a brief moment, Sayer contemplated not saying a word, but she knew that silence would be even worse in the long run.

"The DNA evidence on Winters was manufactured and Adi Stephanopolous might have been kidnapped." She blurted it out as quickly as possible.

Holt blinked rapidly a few times and a strange color rose on her cheek. "One at a time. DNA manufactured. Explain what that means."

"It's literally man-made. Someone went to a lab and made a DNA sample."

"A sample that's a perfect match to Franklin Winters?"

"Exactly."

"And we know this because . . ."

"Because Franklin Winters is a transgender man and is, therefore, physically incapable of producing semen." Sayer tumbled over her own words.

Holt began to clench and unclench her fists. "So what does that mean? We're sure it isn't contaminated evidence?"

"We're sure. The ME confirmed that it's man-made."

"So, he's been framed? That makes this one hell of a different kind of case. Fingerprints are a thousand times easier to plant, so that blows the fingerprint out of the water too. We're back to square one."

"Uh-huh." Sayer nodded in vague agreement. "If it's a frame-up . . ."

"Then we have yet again fingered the wrong guy, and this time we arrested the poor bastard. And now we've got another girl missing? Explain."

"Adi Stephanopolous, another girl from Sanctuary House, also a twin. She's been missing all day, which is apparently quite unusual."

Holt eyed the mottled wall, clearly contemplating a good punch. Seeming to decide against it, she resumed clenching her fists. "So we're not sure she's connected?"

Sayer shifted from foot to foot, wanting to get on with her investigation. "No . . . we don't know for sure, but I can feel it in my gut. She's been taken by our guy."

Holt took a labored breath and nodded slowly. "We can't tell anyone yet."

"What?" Sayer couldn't keep the shock out of her voice.

"We say nothing to anyone yet."

"You're saying we cover up the possible kidnapping of another girl?"

"No. What I'm saying is that you button this up for now. You figure out what the hell is going on before we admit we made another mistake."

"We didn't make a mistake," Sayer protested.

"It'll look like we did." Holt turned to look out the wall of windows over the rolling Virginia hills.

"Since when do we care about public perception?"

"Do you understand what we do, Sayer?" Holt spoke with her back to Sayer, voice scary calm.

"Catch the bad guy, save the innocent?"

"Our job is to protect and serve." Holt folded her hands behind her back. "Ridiculous platitude, I know, but if the public doesn't trust us, then they don't listen to us. They don't call us when something horrible happens. Not just the public. I'm talking about police forces, other law enforcement."

Sayer sighed; it was the part of the job she hated the most. But she knew Holt was right. "All right, I'll tell the task force to keep it quiet."

"You misunderstand me. You tell no one. Not even the task force." Holt spoke just above a whisper.

Sayer's mouth made a shocked O. "What? We need the manpower—"

Holt turned and glared at Sayer, eyes glinting like fire. "You just don't see the big picture. We have a leak on our team. I haven't given Van Hurst or the press anything in days, but they know exactly what's going on in those task force meetings. Hell, the press is getting up-to-the-minute copies of all our communication, including your texts to the team. What do you think Van Hurst'll do when he finds out that we've got the wrong guy again?"

Sayer's stomach fell. "Call a press conference."

"Exactly, right off the bat he's on TV sharing this with the world. Not only that, Van Hurst controls our budget. I'm worried that prick will lobby against us, yank our budget, do something to literally destroy the FBI if he thinks we aren't doing a good job of this."

Holt was right. Van Hurst seemed just petty enough to do something that could harm the entire FBI if they didn't play the game his way.

"And Van Hurst won't pull any punches. If we want to protect our reputation, we can't have him out there bad-mouthing us. Bad-mouthing you. We need to keep our attention on the big picture."

"I thought the big picture was the girl that our unsub probably just kidnapped." Sayer couldn't keep the comment in. To hell with politics.

"No, we don't know the deal there yet, and she's one of the many things that matter here." Holt's intense glare made Sayer's gut clench with discomfort. But then Holt's rage seemed to collapse and she suddenly looked like a harried, overtired woman rather than a Valkyrie about to strike.

"Listen, I'm not saying we prosecute Winters. I'm not saying we don't move heaven and earth to find this missing girl. But I am saying we kill two birds with one stone. We prevent another media circus and we use the opportunity Winters's arrest gives us."

Sayer nodded with understanding. "We know it's a frame job, but the unsub doesn't know that we know."

"Exactly. So we need to be strategic. Use the advantage we have to find the unsub and find that girl before the shit hits the fan."

"All right, but I need some kind of team. No way I can investigate on my own."

"You could."

Sayer shook her head. "No, that's not fair to that girl. She's stuck in some dark cage being drugged, or worse. If Adi's been kidnapped, we owe her our best effort, and to do that, I need a team." Sayer took a deep breath. Standing up to Holt wasn't easy, but she plowed on. "I'll pull together an inner task force. Just a few people I know would never leak. See what we can do."

Holt contemplated for a moment, then nodded. "Fine. Who're you thinking?"

"Vik, Joan, Ezra . . ."

"Yeah, that sounds right. Ezra can help from the hospital. You and Vik on point and Joan on physical evidence."

"I hate to leave out crime scene. They've been working so hard," Sayer said.

Holt scowled. "We just don't know who to trust there. They can keep doing analysis of anything you find; you would still be investigating Winters, so it won't seem strange that you're still out there. You get the work from them but keep them out of the loop. Maybe meet off grounds."

"We can set up in my apartment," Sayer said.

"That'll work. Won't be long before we have to let this cat out of the bag, but might as well work it as long as we can."

"What about Winters?"

"I'll talk to his lawyer. We'll get the process moving, but we still have plenty to charge him so I'm not feeling particularly worried about moving too fast there."

"Can we at least get him transferred somewhere more comfortable? Poor guy is miserable."

"You're really sure he didn't do it?" Holt looked deep into Sayer's eyes, searching. "You sure we aren't being fooled yet again?"

Sayer thought about the look on Winters's face when he told her why he couldn't be the unsub. Probably not that far from how anyone falsely accused and arrested for murder would react. "Yeah, I'm sure. We've got an innocent guy in lockup. Oh, and he needs some kind of medication."

Holt grunted. "Fine. Forgot you've got that goody-two-shoes 'justice is all about truth' thing," Holt said without any humor. "I'll make sure he gets what he needs."

Sayer turned to go.

"Good work so far, Agent Altair. Now go find out if that girl is really missing."

SANCTUARY HOUSE,
WASHINGTON, D.C.

Sayer leaped off her bike in front of Sanctuary House. Mrs. Calavera stood outside the cheerful mural-covered building, wringing her hands together.

"No word from Adi?" Sayer demanded.

The elderly woman shook her head. She wore no makeup and her hair sprang from her bun in a halo of loose strands.

"She would never do this to us. She knows . . . with Leila . . . something has happened."

"Take me to her room."

Mrs. Calavera nodded.

"You checked hospitals and the morgue?" Sayer asked as they made their way into a long hall lined with doors. Young faces peeked out, shell-shocked and wide-eyed. Sayer felt a moment of fury at the unsub. This place had been these kids' only safe haven and now they were all afraid.

"I have. No sign of Adi."

With shaking hands, Mrs. Calavera unlocked a door and stepped aside.

Sayer stepped into a stereotypical teen girl's room. Photos of Adi's family sat prominently displayed on a corkboard crisscrossed with purple ribbon. The girl's mother was beautiful, a slightly older version of Adi, eyes crinkled with a true smile. Next to her mother, Adi and her carbon copy held hands.

"Clem and Adi." Sayer traced her finger over the image.

She resumed scanning the room and picked up the open but still-full pack of cigarettes.

"Adi never smoked them?" she asked Mrs. Calavera.

The woman shook her head. "She never smoked a one that I saw. I believe her father smoked when she was back in Greece. I think the smell reminded her of him."

"You know the story of her family?"

Mrs. Calavera grimaced. "I don't know why they fled Greece, but they were all on a boat that capsized during a storm off the coast not too far from here. The Coast Guard managed to pull some of them out. They found Adi and her twin sister clinging together. Both dead. They were able to revive Adi, but not Clem."

Sayer sat on the bed to think.

As she let her eyes rove around the room, a young man poked his head in.

"Daour, this isn't the time," Mrs. Calavera said gently.

"I know, Mrs. C. But this just came and I think it's important."

He handed her an envelope.

"I was sorting the mail and found it in the stack. No stamp, see. Someone must've put it directly in the mailbox."

Sayer was already pulling on gloves.

"May I?" She plucked the envelope from Mrs. Calavera's hand.

The envelope flap fell open in her hand, barely sealed.

Sayer gingerly plucked out a notecard.

On the thick white card, printed type said, *You take one of mine. I take one of yours.*

"No," Sayer whispered. She quickly slid everything into an evidence envelope and sent a frantic text to Vik.

Mobilize evidence team over to Sanctuary House asap. ADI KID-NAPPED.

"Your mailbox on a surveillance camera?"

"What? No, sorry." Mrs. Calavera looked like she was about to collapse into tears.

"Any cameras?"

"No, sorry. I don't want the kids to feel . . . monitored." Her voice barely cracked above a whisper.

As the evidence team descended on the shelter, Sayer raced back to Quantico to have the note analyzed.

It came back clean. No prints. No evidence at all.

Sayer made sure Nana could bring Vesper home, then sat at her desk until almost two in the morning poring over file after file. Desperate to find any direction to go. In the quiet office, the moon shining through the dark-tinted windows, Sayer let herself momentarily give up. She had no clues to follow. No idea where to start. She needed a little sleep to think clearly. Exhausted, she headed home to bed.

UNKNOWN LOCATION

A metal door clanged open. Adi Stephanopolous's head still ached from the drug injected into her neck, but she was ready to fight back if her captor tried to stick a needle in her again.

In the semidarkness she heard footsteps. Then the *click click click* of some kind of machine. Brightness flooded the room. Adi tried to make sense of what she was seeing.

She sat in a large cage that hung from a chain. A projector cast harsh light across a massive room. Teetering stacks of boxes, a sagging piano, an old wardrobe, piles of paper. Some kind of old estate basement or something? The detritus surrounded the cage, casting towering shapes on the walls behind them.

A hunched creature labored over the projector. The person looked up and Adi realized he was wearing night vision goggles and a smoke mask with a tube that snaked down to an oxygen tank.

A dove flapped its wings in the corner of the cage with her and Adi wondered if she was hallucinating. A bird?

The projector clicked loudly and images appeared on the boxes and walls. Adi blinked rapidly, confused.

She recognized the images from back home. They were all of the Dioscuri—Castor and Pollux, ancient Greek gods.

Adi could picture her mother telling the tale of the ancient Greek twins to her and her twin sister when they were young. How their souls were intertwined forever, just like Adi and Clem's, even beyond death. How Pollux sacrificed his immortality so that Castor could return from the dead. Adi desperately tried to cling to the sound of her mother's voice. To the image of Mami gathering Adi and Clem in her arms and kissing them on the brown curls that fell across their foreheads. She tried to picture Mami laughing in the sun, her golden eyes full of joy.

Adi did not want to think about what would happen next. She knew the Cage Killer had her now.

The hunched creature went over to another machine and shook clumps of powder into a funnel.

With a *whir,* the machine turned on and began pumping smoke into the air.

"Usually I have time to prime my subjects, but time has run out," a muffled, electronically altered voice said. "But I've finally figured it all out. It's the mind; our brains open the gates to the afterlife. I need to open the gates before I kill you and bring you back. So simple!"

The acrid smoke quickly reached Adi, replacing the air with its foul scent.

Adi tried not to inhale but she couldn't hold her breath forever. The smoke burned her lungs. Then dizziness. The world slowly began to undulate beneath her. Bursts of light and color appeared behind her closed eyelids. For a moment she fought opening her eyes, but she couldn't resist. The drug buzzed through her body, the world shifting and tilting like a fun-house mirror.

Her eyes flew open and images on all four walls surrounded her. Castor and Pollux riding horses. Abducting the Leucippides sisters. And a sculpture of Pollux descending into Hades, the underworld, to rescue his brother.

For a brief moment, Adi's blurry eyes saw the masked monster. Logically, she knew it was a person wearing a gas mask and night vision goggles, but all logic fled as the masked creature transformed into a true monster before her. Claws sprouted from its hands. Horns from its head.

The thick voice behind the mask whispered, "Go to her. . . . Go. . . . Find your sister in the afterlife. Clementia is waiting for you."

The monster circled the cage, husky voice droning, "Let the dove guide you. The dove is the symbol of rebirth, avatar of Hermes. The dove can guide you safely to Hades and back. Go save your sister just as Pollux saved Castor."

Thick-mouthed, Adi managed to say, "The dove isn't the avatar of Hermes. The snake is, you moron."

The monster let out a growl of rage and slammed a clawed fist into the cage. The entire cage rocked gently as the horizon of Adi's universe collapsed. A loud humming sound replaced the raspy breath of the monster. At first the sensation was pleasant. The thrumming sound expanded until her entire body vibrated with the pulsing. She rocked back, head landing on the floor of the cage. Adi descended into a world where time and space became one, the universe flowing around her like a kaleidoscope of beauty. Small angels circled above her, dancing and laughing.

But then the imagery changed. The angels swirled together with the heavens and Zeus looked down upon her with furious eyes. Castor and Pollux rode in circles around her on their steeds that huffed and snorted fire. Pollux stopped in front of her and opened his mouth wide in a scream. From the hollows of his black mouth, a snake emerged, slithering toward Adi, hissing, "You let Clem diiiiiiiiiiiiiie. Yooooou did thisssssssss."

Adi tried to scream but her body was frozen. A dove beat its wings, battering her face. The entire scene began to waver, the snake curling around her throat until she could no longer breathe. She felt water surging around her, cold and angry. Her body convulsed, Castor and

Pollux watching her from the murky depths with eyes like smoldering coals.

A sharp pain stabbed into her arm and she felt burning liquid enter her veins.

I'm going to die was her last thought as everything went dark. Rather than terror, she felt a profound peace.

Then, a flickering light appeared like a small candle in the distance. Adi knew in her heart that the light would lead her to heaven. Beautiful, shining, glorious.

That's right. Go further. Further. Find her, a voice whispered.

She floated forward as if already a ghost. Maybe she could be with Mami and Clem. Escape this nightmare. The last sense of her own body faded away until she was nothing but air and she became one with the light.

In the overbrightness, Clem stood before her. Her twin sister held out her hand, brown hair flowing behind her like a water nymph. Her golden eyes, so much like Mami's, so much like her own, glowed with peace. Adi let out a cry of joy at the sight of her twin, and she reached out her hand. For a brief moment, their fingers connected and a radiant love warmed her skin, along her arm, running to her heart.

"Wake up!"

The voice slammed her like an assault. Clem's hand yanked away. Her body jerked and twitched as the agony of pins and needles poked her flesh.

"That's right, come back," the monster whispered. Adi's eyes rolled around the room, the projector still shining against the walls. The monstrous face hovering over her.

"No," she croaked. "Clem."

"You reached your sister?"

The monster grabbed Adi's shoulders, fingers digging into skin.

"I had her. We were together," Adi sobbed.

"Finally. The last piece." The monster let go and Adi realized that the cage was open. Despite the tremors shuddering through her arms and legs, she prepared to attack. She might not be able to hurt him, but she was sure as hell going to try.

With an anguished cry, Adi lunged toward the monster. But her arm caught on something and she realized that an IV needle snaked into her vein. The line slowed her down even more than her weakened body and she collapsed, not even reaching the monster's face.

The monster let out a long, slow laugh. "Oh, 9.3, nice try." The masked monster pulled the needle from her arm and swung the cage door shut.

Adi sank to the bottom of the cage to cry.

Sayer sat on her threadbare sofa with Vesper snoring at her feet. She tossed back the last dregs of cold coffee and grimaced at the mouthful of grinds that sloshed into her mouth. She crunched them absent-mindedly, letting the bitter grit scrape between her teeth.

With a brief glance up at her stack of research gathering dust on the kitchen table, Sayer looked back down at her notes about Adi Stephanopolous. According to Mrs. Calavera, Adi was sorrowful but also full of fire, angry about what happened to her family. She had been popular but relatively withdrawn. She was studying to get her GED, hoping to attend college. She wanted to become a pediatrician so she could save other children like her.

The doorbell rang and Vesper leaped up at full attention.

Vik stood in Sayer's doorway, his pallor even more pronounced than usual in the wan morning light.

"Can I just say, holeeee shit this is insane," Vik said as he gave Vesper an enthusiastic ear scratch. The puppy dissolved into full-body wiggles. With a genuine smile for Vesper's antics, Vik pushed past Sayer and walked straight to her kitchen, where he started making a fresh pot of coffee. "So Winters was framed, another girl's been kidnapped, and we're just going to keep those massive facts on the down low, lie to our fellow FBI agents, and try to solve this case on our own with a four-man team?"

Sayer followed Vik into the kitchen. "Well, when you put it like that, yeah, a little insane. But Holt's orders . . . and I think she's right." Sayer pulled a coffee mug from her cabinet, realizing that was all she had.

"I know! It's just, whew. That's a hell of a lot to put on us," Vik said.

"It'll only be for a few days. And we're the best at what we do."

After a long moment of silence, Vik sighed. "Yeah, well, for the sake of Adi Stephanopolous, I sure hope we're the best." Vesper licked his hand, hoping for more petting. Vik smiled again. "I see you still have the mutt."

Sayer didn't respond.

"And really, we're gonna meet here in your crappy apartment? You barely have furniture."

Sayer continued to ignore him and pointed to one of the mismatched chairs around her pockmarked dinner table. "Sit. Let me move these files." She reached for her research and fumbled. The folders tumbled to the ground, glossy murder scene photos fanning across the floor.

Vik came to help gather the files. "You looking at old murder cases in your spare time?"

"Nah, this is my neuro research. These are the murder cases of the serial killers whose brains I'm scanning," Sayer said.

"Right. Almost forgot about that." Vik flipped open the top folder and grimaced. "Wowza, this is some shit." He held up one of the Tarlington murder scene photos in glossy black and white. The close-up image showed a woman's head and bare shoulders, her skin mottled bluish gray, dead eyes blazing red with broken blood vessels, bands of bruises around her lifeless neck.

"Yeah, Dugald Tarlington's last victim. He strangled her over and over."

The bell rang again and Sayer pulled the door open to find Joan juggling two whiteboards and a bag of office supplies. She wore a pale-blue cotton cardigan and knee-length silver skirt, her thick hair pushed back in an ivory headband. Her eyes squinted with exhaustion.

Vesper bounded up to greet the newcomer.

"You have a dog?" Joan couldn't hide her displeasure.

"You don't like dogs . . ." Sayer tried not to laugh as Joan stood frozen, hands held high, while Vesper sniffed her with intense interest.

"I . . . I think I must smell like death and chemicals." Joan's nose wrinkled. "Dogs don't seem to like me because of it."

Joan was right; Vesper circled her sniffing like crazy, then skittered over to Sayer's side rather than begging for a petting.

Sayer and Joan grabbed coffee and settled around the kitchen table. Vik realized there were no more coffee mugs.

"Uh . . ." Sayer plucked a wineglass from the kitchen and handed it to Vik with a Cheshire-cat grin. "Welcome to chez Sayer. Nothing but the best for our guests."

Vik grumbled while he poured coffee into the wineglass.

While Sayer explained the fake DNA and the note about Adi, she evaluated their small team.

Vik, undertaker-handsome, unfazed by anything the world threw at him, whip-smart and kind.

Joan, proper, tenacious, willing to work day and night to bring justice to the dead.

Ezra, in the hospital, driven now by his own demons.

A motley crew, but they would all work as hard as they could as long as they had to in order to bring Adi Stephanopolous home and catch a killer while doing it.

"So," Sayer said, wrapping up, "looks like we're forming our own band of Irregulars for a little while. Let's find Adi and catch this bastard."

"Speak for yourself, I'm never irregular." Vik waggled his eyebrows.

Joan groaned. "You do know that Sayer was making a Sherlock Holmes reference, right? The Irregulars were his off-the-books investigators."

Vik rolled his eyes. "Of course I do. I was trying to bring a little levity to this borked situation."

They all took a deep breath and dove back into the case.

"If Winters was framed, then we've been on the wrong path for days." Joan shuffled through the files Sayer laid out on the table. Her blue-gray eyes squinted with obvious stress. "Planted fingerprints and DNA is a serious frame job."

"Exactly," Sayer said. "So, did someone hate Franklin Winters enough to do this? Maybe some kind of transphobic killer? Someone who wanted him dead because of his gender identity? Or was this something else? The cages, the experiments, the photographs all make this feel like someone killing for a reason far greater than just to frame someone. If you wanted to frame Franklin Winters, you might shoot someone and plant his fingerprints on the gun. What we've got here is way more complicated. I think these killings had a purpose all of their own. If that's true, one key question is, was Winters just a convenient scapegoat or is he still part of this somehow?"

"We need to reassess everything. Let's pull apart what's for show and what's the true heart of this case," Vik said, sipping coffee from his wineglass.

Sayer got up and began re-creating the whiteboards they had back in Quantico.

"Let's start at the beginning. We know that almost a year ago the unsub kidnapped Gwen Van Hurst. Then, about six months ago, he kidnapped Leila Farouk. As of yesterday, we know that he has kidnapped Adi Stephanopolous. We also know that he held Gwen and Leila in separate locations in cages, forced them to inhale DMT, and showed them images of ancient mythology.

"We know this is some kind of experiment. I looked up the story of the gods Leila was shown, Osiris and Set. I've sent the images to the guy at the Smithsonian so I'll get more detail soon, but based on the mythology I read, I think it's safe to assume that twins and the afterlife play an important part in whatever pathology he's playing out."

Sayer paced in a tight arc back and forth across her small kitchen, stepping over Vesper, who lay in the center of the room.

"Also, based on everything I learned about Adi Stephanopolous, death is important. Apparently Adi was found dead, without a pulse, along with her mother and twin sister. The Coast Guard fished them out of the ocean and revived Adi but weren't able to save her family."

Sayer stopped pacing. "We're stuck with a riddle to untangle. We don't know how much of what we're seeing is a real reflection of the unsub and how much of this is show for us. Considering the forged transfer notice for Leila, the amount of effort and time put into framing Winters, and the booby traps at the scenes, I'd say that the only thing we absolutely know for certain is that we're dealing with the most organized killer I've ever heard of."

Joan spoke up. "With the specter of the frame-up, I don't think we can trust any of the physical evidence we've found. It could all be planted."

Vik nodded in agreement. "That also means the locations don't mean anything. The catacombs, the basement bomb shelters, they were all chosen to help frame Winters. So they can't tell us anything about our unsub."

Sayer kept pacing, her hands fidgeting with each other. "But the cages weren't necessary to frame Winters. The videos and the use of DMT. Plus, the victimology isn't inherently related to Winters. The importance of twins and the underworld. I think it's safe to assume those things are related to the real scenario our unsub is acting out here."

Vik drained his coffee. "So we've got a profile of a killer that's incredibly smart and organized, a pathology relating to twins and the afterlife, and . . . ?"

"And, that's about it. The things we usually use to track down a killer, triangulating where he might be based on murder locations, physical evidence, straightforward profile, are all out the window." Sayer paused her pacing, trying to figure out how to divide up the work.

"All right, we know that there's a very good chance our killer is somehow connected to the Sanctuary House shelter. All three young women spent decent amounts of time there, so I think that should be our first focus. That might even be where he found Franklin Winters to frame. The director, Mrs. Calavera, gave me her employee and volunteer list," Sayer said as she handed out the list. "Joan, would you be willing to talk to everyone on that list and see what you can shake free?"

"Certainly," Joan said as she looked down at the list. She made a soft "Hmmm."

"Something wrong?" Sayer asked, sitting down.

"Yeah, this list is definitely incomplete."

"Oh yeah?" Sayer's attention perked up.

"Yes, because I should be on here. So should Andy Wagner and a dozen other FBI agents."

"What?"

"Last December a whole group of us went over to Sanctuary House to help wrap gifts for the kids there. I know some agents went back once or twice to work at the kitchen. But none of us are on this list."

Sayer sighed. "Okay, can you also follow up with the director and make sure she just left those names off because she assumed we aren't suspects?"

"Very good." Joan nodded curtly.

"Vik, since I probably shouldn't deal with Senator Van Hurst again, can you go back to the original Gwendolyn Van Hurst case and pull it apart? See what we missed. See if you can find any other links between our three victims. Talk to the good senator and see if you can actually get anything useful out of him."

"Aw, Sayer, you sure you don't want to come with me to interview Van Hurst? You two get along so well." Vik chuckled.

"Shocking as it may sound, I think I'll let you take care of that." Sayer picked up the profile folder Andy created before they arrested Winters. "I'll pick up the profiling and victimology work since I've got some psychology background. I'll also follow up at the Smithsonian on the imagery that Leila Farouk was being shown and see if I can find anything that makes sense in terms of links between those myths."

"You heard anything from Ezra?" Vik asked. "He's an Irregular, right?"

"Yeah," Sayer said. "I called him this morning to let him know the latest with the DNA and the possible frame job. I have him looking back over Van Hurst and Winters. He'll let us know if he finds anything we missed."

She rubbed her eyes. "Man, sometimes it's hard for me to even remember why I decided hunting serial killers was a good career choice." She sat back and looked at Joan and Vik. "I mean, I remember the first case I was part of, didn't even have my Ph.D. I felt like what I was doing was somehow dark but also noble. Hunting monsters."

Vik grunted.

"Thing is," Sayer continued, "I remember I felt a thrill at it all. It was . . . thrilling."

"You think?" Joan seemed vaguely disgusted at the thought.

"Yeah, I think I enjoyed facing my fear of the worst that could happen. But I took it a step further. I told myself that by putting these bastards away, I was taking complete control." Sayer sighed. "Why'd you get into this job, Joan?"

Joan tilted her head slightly. "When I was ten, a little girl was killed at my school. I saw the whole process up close, the investigation, the court case. I think seeing the peace it brought her family when the boy who did it was put away . . . it was satisfying. Like a way to really help people."

Sayer and Vik nodded with understanding.

"What about you, Vik?" Sayer asked.

Vik glanced over at Sayer with a squint. "Is this seriously the conversation we're having right now? You want to know why I do this job? It's to stop evil assholes from hurting anyone else. I put them away. It feels good. Ta-da!"

Sayer held up her hands in surrender. "But I want to plumb the depths of our reason for doing this profoundly messed-up job."

Smiling, the trio broke up, each heading in a separate direction. Sayer couldn't stop imagining Adi's eyes as she drove north.

EZRA'S ROOM, GEORGETOWN HOSPITAL, WASHINGTON, D.C.

Ezra stared at the pale gray hospital walls to avoid looking down at the bandages on his knees. They ached to the core of the bones that were no longer there. The pain was so deep he wanted to take the sharpened metal corer that he used to collect soil samples and jam it up into the stumps. Real pain would be a welcome break from the phantom burn.

His finger hovered over the morphine drip. It would cut the pain, but it would also dull his mind. And he needed to be sharp because he was going to nail the bastard who did this to him. Who did this to Sayer and Gwendolyn . . . to Cindy.

Rather than push the button, he lifted the next file from the towering stack—crime scene reports, the autopsy, interview notes, the whole enchilada.

And he would read every last word to make sure no one missed anything. At least his confidence had returned after finding out he was right about the messed-up dates. For a little while there he had been convinced he would never be able to do anything again, stuck in a bed with a messed-up brain for the rest of his life.

"Fake DNA, eh?" Ezra said out loud to himself to shake off the thought. "Cool. Fucked up, but cool. All right, you bastard, let's see what you left for me."

Ezra flipped to the first pile of documents gathered by the data team just after they found Gwendolyn Van Hurst. After they arrested Winters, no one had bothered to go back through the original info gathered about the senator. But after the phone call from Sayer about the frame-up, all bets were off.

He scanned the names of Van Hurst's personal staff. All three pages.

"Geez, dude, why does one guy need twenty-seven personal staffers?"

He ran his finger along the list. Gardener. Maid. Butler. Personal assistant. Masseuse. Chef. Damn, this guy lived the high life. Ezra had to remind himself that the dude's entire family was dead. He probably didn't enjoy the chef-cooked meals. Though it probably didn't hurt either.

Nothing jumped out at him.

He shuffled to the next stack of pages. A printout of Senator Van Hurst's personal phone records. With vague interest, Ezra flipped through until he came to the day that Gwen made the first 911 call to the DCPD. He noticed that a strange number made an incoming call that connected with the senator for thirty-three seconds. Something deep in his brain rang a bell. Curious, he gathered the rest of the phone records from that day, including the 911 call to DCPD.

As his eyes roved back and forth between the two lists, Ezra let out a low whistle.

"Oh my God!" Ezra said as he fumbled wildly for the phone to call Sayer to report what he found.

"Agent Altair." The art history expert held out his hand and they shook.

"Dr. Batra."

"I insist you call me James! Sit, please."

For the second time, Sayer sank into his comfy leather chair and pulled out a folder.

"Thank you so much for seeing me, James."

The ancient-art expert waved his hand in dismissal. "How often is it that I get to work on something that actually matters. Usually I drone on about things made by people who died thousands of years ago." His brown eyes crinkled with a well-used smile. Something about his smile reminded her of Jake, and it made Sayer's stomach flip-flop. The faint scent of sandalwood filled her senses and she looked quickly away, focusing intently on the file in her hand.

"Could you take a look at these three images? We rescued a second girl and, though we believe the other aspects of her experience were similar to Gwendolyn Van Hurst's, this victim was shown Egyptian imagery instead of Maya. I suspect they show twins as well, but I'm not certain if they refer to a specific mythology."

James took the glossy printouts. "Ohhh, this one is twenty-second dynasty. Clearly Egyptian. And you said on the phone that this second girl is actually Egyptian?"

"That's right."

"Interesting. Using her own cultural heritage . . . Let me take a look." He intensely studied the photos. "Fascinating!" He jumped up and pulled a few books off his towering bookshelves. He flipped through the pages until he found what he was looking for. "Aha! Let me show you."

He thumped the heavy book down on Sayer's bruised legs. She managed not to gasp in pain.

"Osiris and Set. Twin brothers and mortal enemies." He tapped the book. "This is what the girl was being shown. These are all scenes from the legend of Set murdering his twin brother, Osiris."

He gestured to an image of two Egyptian gods standing facing each other, holding a rope between them, each with a foot up on what looked like a large heart.

"See the one on the left with the jackal head; that's Set, sometimes called Seth. On the right with the flail is Osiris."

"Could you give me the short version of the legend?"

"Of course." James leaped up again and pulled down another book. He flipped until he found the right page. "Osiris and Set were twin brothers, both sons of the god Geb. Osiris married their sister, Isis, and the two ruled over a golden era of prosperity. Set, jealous of his brother's success, plotted his murder."

"So these brothers were enemies, not a team?" Sayer asked.

"Yes, exactly right. Set hated Osiris and . . . well, it's a long story about trapping Osiris in a tree, then eventually killing him. But the important part of the myth is that Set eventually hacked Osiris's body into pieces and scattered his body across Egypt."

"Okay." Sayer stared down at the ancient carving. "So this is very different from the Maya Hero Twins."

"Indeed. Though there are some similarities. After Osiris was chopped up and scattered, Isis, his beloved wife, scoured the kingdom and reassembled his corpse. She tricked the sun god, Ra, into bringing him back to life. But in the end, it didn't work and Osiris descended into the underworld, where he ruled for the remainder of time."

"So there is travel to the afterlife, reincarnation."

James nodded excitedly. "Exactly. Some similarities. We've got twin siblings and a descent into the realm of the dead. Though obviously some differences. These twins were at war, not partners like the Maya twins. But still, definite links."

The art expert held up a finger. "Hang on, I just had a thought."

He flipped through the book to another image. "You said the poor girl was in a cage with a kitten?"

"That's right."

"In Egyptian mythology, cats were often seen as psychopomps!"

"Psychopomps?"

"Yes, yes, spirit guides for the recently departed. A psychopomp is a creature that safely guides a soul into the afterlife. Most cultures have them. In ours it's the Grim Reaper."

"Okay?" Sayer wasn't entirely sure where James was going.

"And the first girl had a dog, right?"

"That's right."

"In ancient Maya mythology, the primary psychopomp was a dog named Peek. The dog was able to guide the dead through the trials of Xibalba."

"Whoa, so maybe the animals are there in the cages to help . . . guide them into the afterlife or something?"

James practically bounced with excitement. "Exactly. It fits with the mythologies here. The girls are given a drug that encourages hallucinations of portaling to other realities and such. They are fed mythologies about travels into the underworld. Then they are provided a psychopomp, a companion to help them get to the afterlife success-fully."

Sayer excitedly tapped out her notes as James finished up. "That's great information, thank you." When she tried to e-mail her notes she realized her phone had no bars. "No reception here?"

"No, sorry. Something about the walls. When you get to the door it picks back up," James said.

"Well, thank you so much, Dr. . . . James." Sayer stood up. "I think I've got everything I need. If I have any questions, can I call you?"

They both stood and James looked like he wanted to say more. "Yes, of course. Call me anytime. Actually . . ." He paused.

Sayer's finger hovered over her phone, ready to type more notes on any additional insight he had.

"I was actually wondering if . . . Would you like to go out for dinner sometime?"

"What?" Sayer looked up from her phone.

"I'm wondering if you are interested in going out to dinner some-time." He blanched at the flabbergasted look on her face. "I'm so sorry if that's inappropriate." He stumbled over his words. "Oh goodness, I just asked you for a date in the middle of a murder investigation—"

"No!" Sayer said. "I mean, it's not inappropriate. I . . . just don't . . . I mean. I haven't." She took a deep breath. "What I mean is, I really appreciate the offer. My . . . I was engaged to be married and my fi-ancé . . ."

"Oh dear Lord, I'm so sorry. I apologize to you and your fiancé. I saw no ring, so I assumed . . ."

"No, he's dead."

James visibly paled and stared at her in horror for a long moment, and then his face broke into a rueful grimace. "Well, I feel that this has gone well. The first time I ask a beautiful woman on a date in a decade and I'm no better at it now than I was in junior high." He grew serious. "I am so sorry, Sayer. I understand. The offer stands if you'd ever like to have dinner, just as friends or, well, whatever you'd like."

"Thank you. I'll . . . let me think about it?"

"Of course!"

They both stood in awkward silence. "I should go . . . thank you again." She hurried away, stomach roiling with a wild mix of longing for Jake but also confusion about the fact that she was actually very interested in going on a date with this man.

As she stepped out the side door into the gray afternoon, her phone buzzed with a voice mail from Ezra.

"She called her father!" Ezra shouted into the phone.

"What? Slow down," Sayer said.

"The day that Gwendolyn Van Hurst called 911."

"Yeah?"

"Before she called 911, she called Senator Van Hurst!"

"What?" Sayer hurried to her bike.

"Exactly! I saw the call on the day she made the 911 call, and the number rang a bell for some reason but I didn't think anything of it until I checked it against the 911 call. Both came from the same number! And, get this, the call connected. There was a thirty-three-second conversation."

"And if Van Hurst spoke with his daughter on that day, why didn't he report her location? Why didn't he move heaven and earth to save her?"

"Unless . . ."

"Unless he had something to do with her abduction in the first place!"

"Exactly!"

"To quote Vik, holeeee shit."

Ezra and Sayer both let the importance of what they'd just uncovered sink in.

"Thanks, Ezra. You might have blown this one wide open. Can you follow up with the data team and find out if Van Hurst has any kind of science background that would allow him to make DNA?"

"Will do, Sayer. You know, he's got over twenty people on staff. I'll check their backgrounds as well."

"Great idea. Van Hurst definitely seems like the type to outsource. Vik's there now interviewing Van Hurst's staff," Sayer said. "I think I might just go join him. Have a little chat with Van Hurst myself."

"Go git him, Sayer!"

They clicked off and Sayer let her mind spool upward.

The senator spent time at Sanctuary House. Why on earth wouldn't he tell them that he'd gotten a call from his daughter? Why not say something unless he had something to hide? Was Van Hurst the unsub all along?

Sayer texted Vik. *I'm on my way. Gwen called Van Hurst day she dialed 911! Don't tip him off. BRT.*

VAN HURST ESTATE,
NW WASHINGTON, D.C.

The frizzy-haired maid, Maxine, opened the door for Sayer.

"Special Agent Altair, so nice to see you again. Your partner is still interviewing the staff in the kitchen." She gestured for Sayer to follow.

Sayer tried a smile but mostly managed a teeth-baring. She knew her predatory anger was showing, but she didn't bother to hide it. "Actually, I would like to speak with the senator, please."

"Oh, uh . . ." Maxine looked around, hoping for someone to save her from Sayer's dangerous eyes.

"He is here, correct?"

"Yes, ma'am, but—"

"Good, get him, please."

"Would you . . . like to join your partner in the kitchen?"

"Yes."

Maxine wrung her apron through her fingers. "Of course. The kitchen is just through there. I'll, uh, let the senator know you'd like to speak with him."

Sayer strode off toward the kitchen and said back over her shoulder, "Tell him it's not optional."

She wound her way through a series of hallways and was almost convinced she was lost in the labyrinthine mansion when she finally pushed through a double swinging door into a cavernous kitchen.

The scent of fresh-baked bread filled her nose, making her stomach grumble and her mouth involuntarily water. Vik sat at a small table surrounded by a phalanx of industrial ovens, three long stainless steel counters, and a wall of cabinets. He scrawled notes in his notebook and didn't notice Sayer's arrival.

"Wow," Sayer said, staring at the huge space.

Vik looked up. "I know. I think this kitchen's bigger than my house."

Sayer sat down and shared what Ezra told her.

He groaned. "You're telling me that he might've been right under our noses this entire time."

"Maybe; it at least means the good senator has something to hide. Considering the press conferences and leaks and . . . well, I don't know what his game is."

Vik considered this. "You think this is some kind of political stunt? Garner sympathy and win the presidency?"

"That seems . . . extreme," Sayer acknowledged. She wiped a line of sweat from her forehead in the overwarm room. "But we know he spent time at Sanctuary House, so he had a connection to all three girls. Plus, who hears from their kidnapped daughter and then doesn't immediately notify the FBI? Even if the phone was answered by his staff, surely they would have told him. Let me take the lead here; I want to ask him about this without letting him know that we know Winters was framed."

"Agent Altair." Van Hurst's baritone voice echoed along the cavernous kitchen. "Maxine tells me that you need to speak to me. Do you have an update?"

Sayer stood and gestured across the small table. "Please have a seat, Senator."

The politician came to a stop next to the table but remained standing. "If you don't have an update, I'm afraid I don't have time—"

"Sit." Sayer interrupted him, her voice firm.

Van Hurst crossed his arms and tilted his head, assessing Sayer. "I don't believe I will until you tell me what this is about. I've opened my home, offered my help. I've thrown every bit of political juice I can to get your team everything they need. I don't appreciate the way you're looking at me right now. Tell me what is going on or I'm leaving."

Sayer stood across the table from Van Hurst and forced herself to take a deep breath. "Fine. We have reason to believe that Winters was not acting alone. We also happen to know that you spent time at Sanctuary House in D.C., the place that connects all three missing girls."

Van Hurst squinted at Sayer. "Of course I've spent time there. So has half of Washington, D.C."

"Did you ever come into contact with Leila Farouk or Adi Stephanopolous?"

Van Hurst stared at her in disbelief for a brief moment. He jabbed a finger toward her. "You come in here, even after you have the bastard that killed my daughter, and you throw suspicion at me?" He straightened up to his full height, shoulders back. Formidable rage radiated off him like a bear about to attack. "You walk into my house and accuse me of killing my own child? That's it, Agent Altair. I let Janice Holt talk me into keeping you on this case, but this will officially be the last case you work for the FBI." His face flushed red. "Now get out of my house."

He spun to storm away.

Sayer said almost at a whisper, "We know she called you."

Van Hurst froze, his back to Sayer.

"We know you spoke to her. The call connected. Why didn't you tell us?"

"I have no clue what you're talking about," Van Hurst growled, and began to walk away again.

"Don't make me come back with a warrant," Sayer called after him. "You know something"—her voice rose—"and if you killed

Gwendolyn, I'll make sure you pay for it." Sayer's heart roared in her ears. This man, so powerful, so able to pull the puppet strings of D.C., would be a hard man to convict. But if she could prove he killed Gwen, Sayer would do whatever it took to bring him down.

As Van Hurst continued to leave, Maxine ran into the room. The maid caught his arm and shouted directly into his face, "I'm sick of the lies. Just tell them what happened so they can stop thinking you did this!" Her shrill voice echoed through the cavernous room.

Sayer and Vik watched as the senator turned on Maxine as though he was about to scream right back. Sayer took a step forward, ready to intervene if Van Hurst got physical.

Instead, his shoulders fell. His entire body collapsed inward, his head falling forward into his hands. Maxine put a gentle hand on his shoulder.

"Please, just tell them what happened," she said softly.

Van Hurst nodded, and Sayer realized he was crying. Head still hung low, he turned back to Sayer and Vik. His face reflected pain so deep he could barely breathe. "She called me." He took a shuddering breath in. "I answered because the only people who have that number are family." His body shook with the effort of speaking. "I . . . I, oh God, forgive me."

He turned away.

"The senator thought it was a cruel joke." Maxine wrapped her arms around Van Hurst. "He thought it was a crank call from some nutcase trying to rile him up, and so he . . . hung up."

Van Hurst looked up into Sayer's eyes, and the wellspring of pain flowing from him almost made her turn away.

Through his tears he said, "I may be a bastard . . . I know I am. I'm a politician, for chrissake. Just like your grandfather." He spoke to Sayer. "He was one of us." Van Hurst sniffed, tried to straighten up. "When I picked up the phone, it was . . . She just sounded incoherent. It didn't sound like Gwen at all. I thought . . . oh God." He swallowed hard. "I might be a bastard, but I loved my daughter, Agent

Altair. And I have to live knowing that she called her daddy for help, and I hung up on my baby. I hung up on her and she died knowing I did that."

He turned away and a sob racked his body.

Sayer and Vik looked at each other, eyebrows up.

Maxine continued to soothe Van Hurst. "You have to believe him, Agent Altair. I was here when it happened."

Sayer stared at the senator and had to admit that he was extremely convincing. She pinched the bridge of her nose and let out a long breath. "All right. I'm going to follow up on this, check your records back into the Stone Age. I'm going to see if there is any other evidence connecting you to these murders and, if there is, I won't hesitate to arrest you."

Head down, Van Hurst nodded. "Fine, Agent Altair. Do whatever you have to do. But please believe me that I did not kill my baby."

Sayer and Vik let themselves out and stood together on the driveway.

"This fucking case," Sayer said.

"I know," Vik said.

"Well, that explains why he's been such a jerk during this whole investigation." Sayer looked back up at the mansion. All the trappings of success but nothing but sorrow resided inside.

"Yeah." Vik looked back as well. "Guilt's a terrible motivator. He was flailing around, trying to do anything he could to make up for failing his daughter."

"But if he's not the unsub, then who the hell is?" Sayer reached in her pocket for her worry beads and cursed their absence for the hundredth time. "Someone connected to him and Winters? Or is Van Hurst just an asshole with nothing more to do with this than the bad luck of having his child murdered? What the hell is going on?"

ROAD TO
ALEXANDRIA, VA

Sayer waved good-bye to Vik and took off on her motorcycle. Dusk fell as she rode from the upscale D.C. neighborhood toward Alexandria. Rather than getting off at her exit, she decided to drive out into the mountains to let her mind wander.

Most cases had some kind of internal logic, some thread that could be unraveled, but this case felt like the clues were running off in a thousand directions. Nothing tied the pieces together. She needed some time to think, let everything roll around in her head.

Just a few miles into the Virginia mountains, the scent of honeysuckle replaced the gritty exhaust of the city. The cool evening air and the empty country road gave her the space to unclench her shoulders, let her mind expand. Though the bruises along her body ached, they also made her feel alive, aware of every inch of her body.

Sayer could tell that the frame job was the key. But why?

The question bounced around until Sayer stopped consciously thinking about it and just let the road rumble beneath her. After almost an hour of riding, she knew there was something there, some connection she was missing, but she needed more to connect the dots.

She turned her bike toward home, realizing that she was looking forward to seeing Vesper.

When she pulled up, Tino sat in his customary place out in the garden. A string of cheerful lanterns blew in the gentle breeze, casting a soft glow across the brick patio. Vesper leaped up to greet her.

"Vesper, good boy!" Sayer let him leap up to lick her, knowing she should stop him but enjoying his unbridled joy too much to care.

"A fine evening to you, Agent Altair."

"Hey, Tino, glad you're home. Vesper and I missed you."

"The feeling was mutual, indeed."

Sayer began her way up the stairs to her apartment.

"You look like hell in a handbasket," he called out.

"Feel like it too," she grumbled.

"Care to join me for a bit?" Tino asked, holding up a half-empty glass. "I was just about to make myself another caipirinha. I could whip you up a glass as well."

"Caipirinha?"

"Brazilian drink; cachaça, sugar, and lime."

"Cachaça?"

Tino chuckled. "It's like rum. Come, sit back down. I think Vesper's parents should at least know each other beyond hello."

Sayer paused. Her entire body buzzed with exhaustion, but the last thing she wanted to do was go into her apartment, where she would just end up staring at Gwen's murder file, or maybe she would spend some time looking at her disastrous research, trying to figure out where she'd gone wrong. With a shrug, she said, "All right, as long as this isn't a come-on."

Tino laughed with a deep belly rumble. "Oh, calida, I can promise you that you aren't my type."

He strolled in to make fresh drinks while Sayer sat under the paper lanterns, Vesper at her feet. Jasmine and bougainvillea vines twisted along the wooden fence, creating an arc of pink and white flowers around the garden. Beyond a small patch of lush grass, hundreds of flowers and herbs bloomed. How had she never noticed what a lovely spot this was? Tino must work tirelessly to keep it so nice.

The roar of a plane rumbled far above and Sayer looked up. A few stars managed to shine through the light pollution like lighthouses on lonely shores. For a moment she remembered the last camping trip she went on with Jake. The Milky Way had been so bright it was like a cosmic white road cutting across the sky. Jake and Sayer had made love under a riot of stars on the slick rock that still radiated heat from the day.

Vesper seemed to notice her mood turn toward sorrow and he got up to nudge her hand, a gesture asking for a pet but also offering comfort. Sayer took him up on his offer and was letting her stress and sorrow bleed into Vesper's soft fur when Tino returned.

"Cheers, to co-parenting the best dog in the world." Tino raised his glass and they drank in silence for a few minutes.

Drink half gone, Sayer let out a long sigh. Tino did as well. Sayer looked over at him. His wire-rim glasses and short cropped hair made him look like an elderly Spanish gentleman, but she realized he wasn't as old as he seemed, maybe early forties. Sayer knew that he had children but she knew nothing more about him.

"Want to talk about it?" she asked.

Tino chuckled. "I was about to ask you the same thing."

"You first. Why the heavy sigh?"

"Just life, calida. Just life."

"Oh yeah?"

Tino looked over at Sayer. "You really want to hear my problems?"

"Sure. It might distract me from mine."

Tino laughed again. "Well, ten years after achieving the perfect life, successful career as head chef in a Michelin-starred restaurant, two beautiful children, adoring wife, I'm still figuring out who I am."

"What happened?" Sayer pointed back to his small downstairs apartment.

"I realized it was all a sham."

"Oh yeah?"

"More specifically, I realized that I'm gay. Let me tell you, that's a bomb to drop on your loving wife."

"Oof, I bet." Sayer drained her drink. "Did she kick you out?"

"No, we're friends now after a few rocky months. She asked to keep the kids full-time until I figure out exactly what I want to do next, but we still love each other. And I stay involved with their lives."

He took a long draw off his drink. "Which is all wonderful. But now I live in some random apartment in Alexandria. I share custody of a goofy dog with my upstairs neighbor who I don't know at all. And I spend my days reading, gardening, and sipping coffee, wondering what to do with my life."

"Doesn't sound so bad to me right now. What do you want to do with your life?" Sayer asked.

Tino chuckled, bristling his salt-and-pepper mustache. "Well, I'd like to find a nice man to date. I think I want to go back to school, though I don't know what I would study."

"Well, post on dating sites and sign up for some classes then."

"You make it sound so easy." Tino stood up and reached for her empty glass. Vesper jumped up as well, tail wagging. "You're probably right. I sit here ruminating and reading and petting this creature when I should probably be doing something about this new life I'm supposed to be building. But right now I can't seem to plan beyond getting us another drink. I shall return."

While Tino retreated, Vesper on his heels, Sayer glanced at her phone. No messages. No texts. Nothing but silence. The case had hit a wall and with Van Hurst out of the picture, Sayer was out of suspects.

"So," Tino said as he settled back down and handed her another caipirinha, "what's your problem?"

Sayer barked a laugh at his blunt question. "I don't even know where to begin."

"Well, begin at the beginning."

Sayer ran through her own history in her mind. Watching her parents die in a car crash when she was nine. Growing up with her high-powered grandparents. Her uneventful college and grad school days. Meeting Jake, the dashing FBI special agent, during her first major research project on serial killers. Jake convincing her to join the FBI rather than going into academia. Jake proposing. The call from Holt about Jake . . . killed in the line of duty. The blur since then of work and more work, nothing but work.

"Well, it's been a rough few years. . . ."

"I surmised as much after breaking into your apartment."

"Yeah," Sayer said, "about that—"

Tino waved his hand. "No, no, you're not going to change the subject that easily. What I meant was, you've got nothing but half-unpacked boxes, a bare futon in the living room. Beer and hot dogs in the fridge."

"Yeah, living like a poor college student, I suppose."

Tino pressed his lips together. "Hmm. More living like an emotionally damaged woman who doesn't want to commit to anything or anyone, even something as mild as her own apartment."

"Ouch."

"Sorry," Tino said with a shrug. "I'm no good at platitudes these days."

"No, no, you're right. As I said, it's been a rough few years." Sayer reached down and rubbed Vesper's ears. "Maybe I need to start rebuilding my life too." Sayer let her mind wander briefly to Dr. James Batra, the handsome art historian who'd asked her out. She shook the thought away. "But right now most of my angst is about the case I'm working on."

"A murder, I assume?"

"You must not watch much TV. It's the biggest case out there." Sayer pinched the bridge of her nose.

Tino held up his book. "I prefer to edify my mind rather than fill it with tripe and horror."

Sayer laughed. "Tripe and horror basically describes my life right now."

"Want to talk about it?"

Sayer pondered. Talking about a case with civilians was frowned upon if it was just information sharing, but agents consulted with people all the time. Maybe talking about it with a non-agent would help her see the big picture.

"Well, I can't tell you much—confidentiality—but the gist is that there is a missing girl being tortured or possibly starved to death and I can't find her."

"Oh good Lord. That's terrible!" Tino leaned over and placed a large, gentle hand on her shoulder. "Though you know that it's not your fault."

"No, it actually is my fault. We were . . . misled, and I fell for it. And we went way down the wrong road."

"Sayer, you aren't God. You aren't magic. You are human and can only do your best."

Sayer sighed. "You know the hardest part about cases like this one? This right here." She gestured to the garden.

"You sitting out here having a drink?"

"Exactly." On cue, Sayer took a long gulp. "That girl, I know she's out there somewhere in a cage. She could very well be being tortured this minute. And I feel like I should be tearing down the sky looking for her with every breath. With every second of my life. But, after a day or two, things drag on and I have to eat. Then eventually, I have to sleep. Eventually I have to let go of that obsessive need to knock down every door in the world until I find her."

Sayer held up her drink. "But what right do I have to be sitting here in this beautiful place, enjoying drinks, petting my dog, and sharing a conversation with you? I feel like the world's worst person, but I don't know what else to do."

"Oh, calida, that's no way to look at it. Right now, you are her only hope. You're that girl's possible salvation, and to save her will require a marathon, not a sprint. You need to take care of yourself so you can keep going until you find her. You know the airplane mask metaphor . . ."

"Yeah, yeah, you put the oxygen mask on yourself before you can help anyone else. I get it logically. It's just, in my gut, it tears me up."

Tino reached out and gently squeezed her hand.

"The heart of what I can't figure out right now is . . ." Sayer sought a way to frame the thought without revealing too much. She turned to Tino, assessing. "Here's a question for you, definitely not related to this case. You understand?"

Tino nodded. "I understand, calida. What you're about to ask has nothing to do with this case of yours."

"Exactly. So, say you are a murderer."

Tino snorted. "Okay, me who carries spiders from his home rather than crush them."

"Yes, you're a killer. Why would you frame someone for murder?"

"Aren't you just a font of rainbows and sunshine."

Sayer scowled at him, and he raised his hands in mock surrender. "I kid, I kid. Let me think about that. . . ." Tino rubbed his mustache. "I believe I can think of only two reasons." He held up one finger. "Revenge." And then a second finger. "Or to get away with murder."

"That's all I can come up with," Sayer said. "Revenge seems unlikely. So, to get away with it. You really want to kill, have to kill. You're a smart serial killer, so you kill someone, then pin it on someone else. That makes sense. But once that guy was framed, then what?"

"Then you do it again. And again," Tino said.

His comment hung in the air, penetrating Sayer's slightly drunk brain. "You frame someone again, and again," she muttered to herself. "Again and again."

Dugald Tarlington appeared in her mind. His orange prison garb, their conversation with him asking if the fMRI could prove his innocence, his tears over the JCPenney catalog because he missed his family.

The stack of research that sat on her kitchen counter. Wendy's comments about Dugald Tarlington's perfect brain. Brain scans of three separate men arrested for serial murder that insisted on their innocence. Their brain scans all normal.

"Oh my God," Sayer practically shouted. She jumped up. Vesper joined her, tail wagging at her excitement.

"Tino, I think you might be a genius." She gave him a solid smooch on the cheek. "I have to go!"

Without waiting for a response, she bounded up the stairs to her apartment, Vesper hot on her heels.

Sayer stumbled inside to her stack of files and pulled out the three normal fMRIs. With shallow breath, she flipped open the three case files in a line on the kitchen table and moved back and forth between them, reading one, then the next, then the next. Then back to the first, the second, the third.

The loose threads of the case began to connect until a woven mosaic appeared in her mind. An image that explained it all.

Sayer didn't even bother to look at the time before she dialed an FBI psychologist. For every serial killer the FBI arrested, the Behavioral Analysis Unit conducted an in-depth psychological interview to help with profiling and to create a comprehensive database.

"What the hell, Sayer," the psychologist answered, his voice thick with sleep.

"When Dugald Tarlington was arrested, you were the psychologist who worked with the task force. Did you do the intake interview with him?"

"What the hell? It's three in the morning. Are you drunk?"

"No . . . maybe a little. Listen, I'm sorry but this is important! What did you think?" she demanded.

"What did I . . . Sayer, what the hell is going on?"

"I just need to hear what you thought about Tarlington. I've read your official report but I'm reading between the lines and just want to hear the truth from you. Please."

"Fine." Sayer could hear sheets shifting as the psychologist sat up in bed. "Dugald Tarlington didn't score at all on the Psychopathy Checklist. Either that man is not a psychopath, or he is the most intelligent one I've met."

"Do you think he did it?"

"You know I can't make that assessment."

"Off the record, as my friend. Do you think he did it?" Sayer pressed.

The psychologist remained silent for a very long time.

Finally he said, "No, I don't. If you asked me to make a call on his innocence without all the evidence against him, I would've said that there was no way. To be honest, that case has really messed with me because clearly Tarlington murdered those women. DNA doesn't lie."

Sayer let out her held breath and mumbled a vague thanks, heart pounding against her chest as she hung up.

After another hour poring over the files, she took a brief moment to make sure she was sober enough to drive before jumping on her bike and roaring north toward the city.

Fifteen minutes later she double-checked the address on Vik's file. To be honest, she'd expected a bachelor pad in an impersonal high-rise or something. Instead, she stood in front of a robin's-egg-blue Victorian cottage, complete with a cluster of worn wooden rocking chairs on the wide veranda.

With a shrug, Sayer pounded on the door.

"Vik?" she called loudly.

Moments later the door flew open. Vik stood, feet planted, gun at his side.

His hair stood up into a massive dark cowlick, and his pale-blue pajama pants glowed in the faint moonlight. He blinked rapidly.

"Sayer. What's wrong?" He lowered his gun and stepped aside, gesturing for her to come in. "Get in here before you wake the whole neighborhood."

He gently shut the door behind her. "What's happened?" His eyes held wide with concern.

"I have something to show you. Need fresh eyes that I can trust," she mumbled, the rum drinks souring her stomach.

Vik stared incredulously at Sayer for what felt like an eternity. "Something so urgent it warrants a visit in the middle of the night . . . without a warning phone call?" He squinted at Sayer before making up his mind. "Fine, of course. When's the last time you ate something?"

Sayer shrugged. "So long ago I can't remember."

"Okay, food and coffee first, then we talk." He led Sayer into his kitchen and pointed to a carved mahogany table. Vik got fresh coffee going in his espresso machine and reheated leftover Thai curry atop a pile of coconut rice.

He placed the food and coffee in front of her and she inhaled it without a word.

"Okay, belly full of food and one cuppa caffeinated elixir of life . . . now, what's so important that it couldn't wait?"

"Before I say anything else"—Sayer looked around at the lovely, fully stocked kitchen—"I officially declare we should be meeting here instead of at my apartment."

"No joke," said Vik. "Now, talk."

Sayer pulled out her stack of files and placed them open, one at a time, in front of Vik.

"Four separate cases. Four serial killers including our buddy, the Cage Killer, or whatever you want to call the bastard."

Vik looked down at the case files in front of him. "Okay. Go on."

"I need you to listen to me and then tell me if I've gone round the bend, all right? If you're on board with the idea, then we bring in the rest of the team."

"All right," Vik said, looking like he wanted to check to make sure

Sayer wasn't feverish or something. Instead, he got up and poured himself a coffee.

"Okay, the Cage Killer case, we've got a frame-up that feels way too complicated to be a simple frame job. Normally when you frame someone, it's to hurt that specific person somehow. You frame someone to get them sent to jail or whatever."

"I'm with you." Vik encouraged her to go on.

"All right, so this frame job doesn't feel like that. It feels like a way to get away with murder. The cage murders have all the marks of a genuine serial killer—the cages, the ancient imagery, the experimental aspects. Whoever is doing this has his own pathology." Sayer got up and paced as she spoke.

"Right," Vik said. "The frame job was most likely to divert our attention from the real killer. Frame Winters, the killer gets away with murder."

"Exactly. So . . . if you're a serial killer, do you start off your first kills with an elaborate frame job?"

Vik leaned back in his chair. "Well, no. From what I understand, killers like this usually start out small, work their way up to more and more elaborate scenarios."

"Right, and we've been going on the reasonable assumption that these aren't his first kills. But we assumed that any earlier kills would have been less organized and therefore might have flown under the radar because they weren't quite so planned. Maybe his modus operandi wasn't as formalized."

"Sure, but we plugged the info into ViCAP and nothing matched well enough to get our attention," Vik said.

Sayer tapped the files in front of Vik. "ViCAP doesn't include closed cases."

She let that sink in for a minute. Vik's eyes widened.

"Holy shit. How could we have missed that?"

"Exactly. What if this isn't his first frame job? This is just his first failure?"

Vik ran his hands through his wild hair, the implications of Sayer's idea sinking in. "Say this killer has been killing people for years and years; he could have framed a hundred people by now and that's why we had no clue he even existed."

"Exactly!" Sayer felt triumphant and a bit relieved that Vik was seeing what she had.

Still wide-eyed, Vik looked at the glossy murder scene photos spread in front of him. "Holy shit," he repeated. "You think these three old cases are frame jobs by our unsub?"

"I do. At least, I think it's possible." Sayer sat down hard in a chair. "I just can't decide if my idea is based on one too many rum drinks and an overactive imagination, or if there's really something here."

"Well, why would you think these guys are innocent? What would make you pick these three cases?"

Sayer took a deep breath. "So we talked about my research before."
Vik nodded.

"I'm scanning the brains of these bastards, looking for the markers that will help us understand what's going on with their neurology."

"Right, you mentioned the little dongles in the human brain that determine how mean someone is."

"Heh, yeah, the amygdalae. Big ones mean a person is probably a super altruist, and small ones mean a person tends toward being a sociopath. But it's not so simple. There are many different parts of the human brain that contribute to things like violent behavior. For example, the prefrontal cortex governs things like executive function."

"Yep, ya lost me. Executive function?"

"That just means things like impulse control and how well you respond to other people's emotions."

"Gotcha."

"So, I'm looking at a whole mess of different aspects of these men's brains, trying to find some commonalities. Sort of serial killers' brain templates."

"And all the other brains you scanned fit your theory." Vik pointed to the files.

"Exactly. I don't have a huge sample size, but all nine other brains I've scanned had clear issues, often multiple problems. But these three men all have perfectly normal brains."

Vik looked hard at Sayer. "I've got to ask. This isn't just some way to support your research, is it? I mean, if this is true, it would basically prove your theory."

"I honestly have no idea. I don't think so but, if I'm right about these men being framed, it sure does prove that my research is right."

Vik rubbed his chin, nodding. "Well, I think you might be on to something. I'm on board."

Sayer slapped the table with excitement and began to gather her files. "That's all I needed to hear. I'm going to Holt at first light. We've got to follow up on this ASAP!"

Vik grimaced and patted Sayer on the back as she headed out the front door. "Good luck with that. . . ."

UNKNOWN LOCATION

Adi Stephanopolous ground her teeth. The grinding sound kept her alert, cleared her head from the massive dose of drugs from the night before. Her body ached with the tension of imagining her escape over and over. Adi rifled through the chip bags and prewrapped sandwiches the monster left for her in the corner of the cage. In the darkness, she ran her hands along the bars. She felt around for anything that would help her pry open the enormous padlock on the cage door.

The bird fluttered to the top of the cage and cooed a few times before Adi could hear its shit plopping on the crinkly chip bags.

The acrid stench of urine singed her nose and she felt a moment of embarrassment at what she was reduced to. Like an animal, Adi had to squat and relieve herself through the cage floor.

The lavender scent of the cleaning fluid the monster sloshed beneath her mixed with the stench of urine. If Adi survived this, she would never be able to smell lavender again without gagging.

Adi reached through the cool iron bars and let her fingers curl around the padlock. If she could just get some leverage, she could pop the lock open. Though, rather than escape, Adi was slowly forming a different plan. If she got out of this cage, she would find a weapon and wait for the monster to return. He would suffer, die at her hands. Unlike Clem, named for forgiveness, Adi's name meant vengeance, and she was ready to live up to her name.

As her hands roved across the edge of the cage, a slender metal bar wiggled beneath her fingers. She played at it and it gave even more.

Heart pounding, she began to work the metal bar back and forth, determined to break it off.

Adi worked the bar for what felt like hours. Eventually her fingers began to bleed so she took off her T-shirt and wrapped it over her hand. The bar moved one inch up and down, then two, then five, until she could feel the joint about to break. Finally, with shaking hands, she felt the last snap of metal and the bar came loose.

With a cry of triumph, she slid the bar down along the leg of her jeans.

Exhausted, Adi drifted off to sleep.

ASSISTANT DIRECTOR HOLT'S OFFICE, FBI HEADQUARTERS, QUANTICO, VA

Sayer sat outside Holt's office writing notes to distract herself while she waited. Her knee bounced to an internal rhythm that only her jangled nerves could hear.

Holt showed up around six thirty, silver mug in hand.

"No wonder everyone thinks you sleep here," Sayer said as Holt unlocked her office without offering a greeting. Sayer immediately rethought the wisdom of joking with Holt, especially before she finished her morning coffee.

"Can I come in and talk to you about something?" Sayer asked as politely as possible.

Holt grunted an affirmative and flicked on the lights. "Talk," she said as she unpacked her bag onto the desk and turned on her computer.

Sayer took a deep breath and explained her theory to Holt. As she spoke, Holt sat down and sipped her coffee, turning her high-backed office chair so she could stare out the window to watch the first hint of dawn skim the ocean of trees.

"So," Sayer continued, "I strongly suspect that there are at least three other frame jobs out there. . . ." She wound down the spiel and waited to see Holt's reaction.

"You're telling me that you think that at least three cases that the FBI closed over the past few years are actually frame-ups."

"Yes," Sayer said.

"Or, to rephrase that, you think that we have wrongfully convicted at least three men for serial murders that they did not commit?" Holt's voice got ever so slightly louder and Sayer swallowed hard.

"Yes."

"No," Holt said.

"No?"

"That's right. No."

"Uuuuh." Sayer wasn't sure how to respond.

"You will not follow this train of thought anywhere."

"What? If this is true, the Cage Killer investigation is far bigger than we imagined!"

Holt put her travel coffee mug down gently on her desk and took a deep breath in and out. When she opened her eyes, they radiated murder.

"I'm only going to say this once. The level of scandal this would bring down on our heads at this moment will prevent us from functioning. You will drop this. Focus on the Cage Killer case. Solve that one. When this case is done, I promise you I will open an investigation into these allegations."

"But—"

Holt held up a hand, but Sayer couldn't stop herself.

"But if these cases are connected, how can we solve the Cage Killer case without all the information available to us? This unsub is . . . way beyond any kind of evil we've hunted before."

"I said no and meant it. If you want to ask someone in the medical examiner's lab to reevaluate the evidence in the old cases, that's fine. But until I have someone confirm for me that the DNA in those cases was man-made, I will not have you running off on a wild-goose chase." Though Holt's voice was soft, she slammed a fist down onto her desk, making her files jump.

Sayer's heart hammered against her chest.

"A wild-goose chase that will leak," Holt said. "I've spent the past two days hunting the weasel feeding the public information to no avail. This kind of scandal would go from Van Hurst to the media to Congress in no time flat."

"But—" Sayer tried again.

"No. This is a fine theory, but there is nothing to support it beyond your own research. I'm sorry, Sayer, but you get this damn investigation wrapped up or I'll put someone else on the case."

Sayer stood still, unable to decide how to react. Holt didn't fuck around, and no one survived directly challenging her. And up until this case, Sayer had always respected Holt, but this was too far. Sayer couldn't let something this big go. But she also knew better than to unleash the rage building in her chest toward Holt.

"Fine," she managed to say.

"Good. I mean it, Sayer. I know you want to dive into this challenging puzzle, but let it go. I know you want to be the avenging angel of justice, but you are an FBI agent and you work for me. Now you'll have to excuse me, I have a meeting."

With hands shaking from the effort of restraining her emotions, Sayer calmly opened the door to find Andy Wagner waiting outside.

"Morning, Sayer, how's the Cage Killer case going?" The profiler flashed a smug grin.

Sayer managed not to punch him as she walked away without saying a word.

VIK'S HOUSE,

NW WASHINGTON, D.C.

Sayer spent half the day fielding calls, typing reports, and following up dead-end leads.

By 3 P.M., Joan and Sayer sat around Vik's gleaming kitchen table. Joan looked exhausted, dark smudges beneath her eyes, hair pulled back into a messy bun.

The emotional wear was seriously affecting Joan. Sayer found her disheveled appearance strangely comforting—if Joan, she of eternal calm, was thrown by this case, then Sayer's own jangled nerves weren't something to worry about. She looked down at her own wrist, ringed with a purple bruise where Vik had pulled her out of the basement before the bomb went off.

"You've already talked to Holt?" Joan asked.

Sayer nodded, cringing. "Yeah, and it wasn't pretty. So this is . . . way off the books. Everyone all right with that?"

They all nodded.

"Good. So, let me review the three cases I've got, most recent first, and then let's bounce these around with the Cage Killer case to see if there are any clear connections." Sayer's fingers worked the pen she held, an ineffective substitute for her worry beads. "Is this a total whack job of an idea? Let's tear it apart."

She tacked a series of murder scene photos to the whiteboard.

"Okay, case number one, Dugald Tarlington, also known as the Baltimore Strangler. Tarlington was convicted two years ago of four murders. Joan would probably remember the details since she was the ME on the case, but each victim was strangled to death over a period of hours, sometimes days."

"That's right," Joan said. "I remember that case clearly. Tarlington would bring his victims to the edge of death but not actually kill them, over and over. The women had multiple ligature marks in various stages of bruising. He used a thick leather belt or something similar. I suspect that the goal was to not kill them for as long as possible, especially considering that he got better at it over time."

"Better at killing?" Vik asked.

"No, better at keeping them alive. His first victim only had three distinct ligature marks on her neck and was probably strangled a few times over a few hours. His last victim, let me see." Joan flipped through the summary file. "Yes, she had too many marks to count. Based on the extent of petechial hemorrhaging in her eyes and the damage done to the tissue in her neck, I estimated that she might have survived up to a week being strangled again and again."

"A sexual sadist, then?" Vik asked.

Sayer nodded. "That's what the agents on this case assumed, but there was no other evidence of torture. Usually a sexual sadist doesn't limit his cruelty to one form of torture. Plus, the way the bodies were treated after death, there seemed to be none of the disgust most sadists feel for their victims."

"So there were questions about his motive," Vik said.

"Yeah, but with a DNA match, no one really cared," Sayer said. "In fact, I remember Andy was thrilled to get to write such an unusual profile. The constellation of characteristics Tarlington displayed were so unusual that he came up with a new type of sadistic killer for the profiling textbook he's writing."

Joan shook her head. "Andy did seem unduly thrilled about that case, didn't he?"

"So there's a similarity to our current unsub. The way he's killing is so unusual our goddamned profiler is thrilled to have the case." Sayer couldn't keep the anger out of her voice. Andy just always seemed a little too thrilled about the unsubs they hunted.

Sayer began tacking up the second file.

"Okay, possible frame job number two." Sayer tapped the photo of a handsome, graying man wearing blue medical scrubs. "This is Tom Middleton, an anesthesiologist at Holy Cross Hospital just north of D.C. This charming specimen experimented with his anesthesia and murdered six women by basically putting them to sleep."

"That's it?" Vik asked.

"Yes." Joan opened the Middleton file. "I didn't work this case, but it came through our lab. I remember discussing the details with the other medical examiners. There was some disagreement about the goal of the murders. They initially felt like mercy killings."

"Mercy killings?" Vik asked. "Like he thought he was performing an act of mercy, saving his victims from something terrible?"

"Exactly. But Tom Middleton didn't quite fit," Joan said. "He brought the women to a U-STOR storage unit, where he set up a mini medical suite. He strapped women to a table and injected them with different mixtures of various anesthesias, like cocktails of medications. Almost like he was conducting his own experiments."

"So you didn't think he was a mercy killer?" Sayer asked.

"No, I never bought that theory." Joan shut the folder. "Based on the kinds of drugs he injected into his victims, the murders felt more like experiments. Like he was trying out various drugs to see what they did."

"So another experiment," Vik said.

"And another case where the motive just never felt totally right. Andy and the Behavioral Analysis Unit could never fully agree on Middleton's motive. But, just like Dugald Tarlington's conviction, no one ultimately cared because the DNA evidence was unequivocal."

Sayer tacked up the third file. "Okay. Last but not least, we've got John Kent, beloved park ranger convicted of killing nine women."

Vik whistled. "Nine. I remember this guy, like five or six years ago? Kept the women in a cabin hidden way out in the Blue Ridge Mountains."

"Exactly. When the FBI finally tracked him down, he claimed he'd never even heard of the cabin, but they linked him to the crime scene through DNA and fingerprints that proved he'd been there."

Vik groaned. "Evidence we now know could've been planted."

"Is that true, Joan?" Sayer asked. "That's one of the questions I had about my grand theory here. Was it even possible to manufacture DNA six years ago, or is this fairly new?"

Joan closed her eyes, thinking. "I'm not sure about the exact time-line, but I remember hearing about the possibility five or six years ago. If I heard about it back then, that probably means that the tech-nology existed for a year or two before that. I'll look it up to confirm, but my guess is that, yes, it would have been possible then. Though it suggests someone on top of the latest research."

"Okay, so let's assume it was technically possible to manufacture DNA back then. John Kent's cabin had six holding cells in the dirt-floor basement. Women were kept there for one or two days. The un-sub primarily targeted real estate agents."

"Why real estate agents?" Vik asked.

"We never did figure that out, but the theory was that it was just expedient," Sayer said. "Being a female real estate agent is actually one of the most dangerous jobs for a woman. Part of your job is going out to houses to meet clients. . . ."

"Ah, just an easy way to get a woman alone in an isolated place."

"Exactly. There was even some question about the size of the unsub. He apparently lured real estate agents to houses and then drugged them, a behavior Andy thought suggested that he was infirm or physically weak."

"That's a similarity," Joan pointed out. "The Cage Killer also drugged the women when he abducted them."

"Right. When the FBI raided the cabin, we found evidence that the women were transported in a wheelbarrow, so the investigative agent proposed that he was a small man, that maybe he couldn't carry the women on his own."

"And how did he kill his victims?" Vik asked.

"He basically bled them out. There was some suggestion of a medical background because of the precision with which he sliced the victims along their arms and legs."

Joan nodded. "That's right, like a hunter bleeds a deer."

Sayer paced around Vik's roomy kitchen. "Right, which is a relatively slow way to die. It would have taken the women at least a few hours to die."

"Any reason why?" Vik finished off another cup of coffee.

"No clue. And no one bothered to figure that out because—"

Vik groaned. "Because the DNA match to Kent was incontrovertible, so they didn't need to know his motive for a conviction."

"Exactly."

"So, let's talk about similarities and differences between these three cases and the Cage Killer. I've got my own thoughts, but I'd like to hear from you all. Do you see clear similarities between these cases?"

"Sure," Joan said, shuffling through all four files. "There's no direct evidence of sexual assault beyond a single sample of DNA on all the victims' bodies. In fact, there's no real evidence against any of these men beyond the forensics. No witnesses. No other physical evidence."

"Plus no clear motive." Vik looked back over his copy of the case summaries. "All these men had clean records, no criminal activity, were seen as reliable and upstanding by those around them. They had none of the warning signs of psychopathy. In fact, without the

DNA evidence, I'd bet none of these cases ever would have gone to trial."

"The kicker"—Sayer tapped their photos—"is that all of these men continue to insist that they are innocent despite the clear physical evidence against them. Unusual considering that once these bastards are caught, they usually can't wait to gloat about their kills."

The trio stared at the four glossy photos on the whiteboard. Franklin Winters, Dugald Tarlington, Tom Middleton, and John Kent. If Sayer was right, they were looking at four more victims of the same unsub.

"So there are definitely links in terms of the evidence." Vik held open his broad hands. "But what about motive and MO? Far as I can tell, these are all very different kinds of murder."

Sayer ran her finger along the long line of victim photos. Counting Gwen, twenty women, all dead. "Let me tell you what I think. I think these murders all reflect an obsession with death." She paced faster.

"Um, don't most serial killers have a thing for death?" Vik asked.

"Not like this. If you look at all four cases, they're all about walking that line. It's not the killing he likes, it's when they teeter on the edge. Hell, in the cage killings he even provided the victims with their own psychopomps, maybe hoping they would be able to move back and forth more easily."

She pointed to each photo. "The John Kent case feels like it was about sheer bulk. The unsub just killed and killed and killed. He let the women bleed out so he could watch them cross over. Then you've got the Tom Middleton case. There, the unsub is trying to move the victims to the very edge of death and then bring them back. Or maybe just a slow descent into death somehow. In the Dugald Tarlington case, he's also bringing them to the edge of death, seeing how close to the line he can get. And finally, the Franklin Winters case. Obviously the victims are being nearly overdosed on DMT, but this is far more elaborate. It feels like maybe this is a new phase in the killer's MO."

Sayer stopped pacing. "I think our unsub is obsessed with crossing that line and coming back. Think about the video he left us of Gwen dying. For some reason he wants to know what happens at that exact moment of death. Maybe see if a person can move beyond that line and return."

"The Death Walker," Joan said softly.

"What?" Vik leaned forward.

"Making victims walk the line between life and death, the Death Walker," Joan said.

"Usually you hate naming these guys." Sayer was shocked.

Joan nodded. "This one just feels different."

This case was hitting them all hard.

"Sounds like a modus operandi." Vik contemplated his empty coffee mug.

"So, let's say his MO is experimentation with crossing the line between life and death. So, now what? Can we use that somehow?" Joan asked.

"Well, it gives us a real profile. We know his pathology. The question is why? Why is he so obsessed with this question? We figure that out and we'll find our guy."

Joan's voice returned to normal. "Did you know that scientists have studied near-death experiences and found that death is far more complex than we once thought? We think of death as a specific moment, but that's not accurate."

"What's not to get? Your heart stops beating, you're dead." Vik's coffee jitters were making him edgy.

Sayer shook her head. "No, Joan's right. Human consciousness is a lot more complex than that. I've seen the research on near-death experiences. Though most people who die and come back have only vague memories of what they experienced, some have really clear recall. Including details that they could only know by being there. These are people who were declared dead. No brain activity, no pupil dilation, no heartbeat. Yet they remember specific things that EMTs or doctors have said over their presumably dead bodies."

"Seriously?" Vik said. "We're not talking woo-woo science?"

"No," Joan said, "these are real scientific studies."

"Okay, so maybe there's something about that gray line between alive and dead that interests our unsub. What else?" Sayer asked them. She could see them flagging and wanted to wrap up.

"I'm willing to bet that twins are key. Maybe our unsub has a dead twin and he wants to go see his twin in the afterlife but be able to return?" Vik suggested.

"Interesting."

"An unsub with a twin . . ." Joan rubbed her chin.

"Not sure it helps us, but yeah. Something to keep in mind." They sat in silence.

"So now what?" Vik finally asked.

Sayer flopped into a chair. "First things first. Do we all agree, these are linked?"

Joan raised a finger. "I can think of a potential problem with this theory. Let's say you're right and this guy has been killing for a very long time. What are the chances that you somehow chose those exact cases for your research? I mean, there are hundreds of killers arrested every year. Doesn't it seem a little bit far-fetched that they all got your attention?"

Sayer grunted agreement. "I thought about that. And yeah, it seems . . . unusual, but these cases all exhibit extreme violence. I think our killer is seriously messed up and his kills all reflect that. The fact that I picked these at all suggests that there is an underlying pathology. Plus, there's a decent chance there are more cases out there we haven't found."

"I'm willing to bet there are exactly five others," Vik said.

Sayer nodded. "I agree."

"Uh, did I miss something?" Joan asked.

"The unsub called Leila Farouk 9.2—"

Joan groaned. "She was part of his ninth experiment, subject two."

"Exactly," Sayer said. "So we have four cases; that would mean there are five more out there we're unaware of."

They sat in silence for a moment contemplating.

"Okay, so back to the question. We agree these cases are linked?"

"Yes," said Joan.

"I do," Vik agreed.

"I do too. For all of these cases, we keep following the trail of physical evidence and it keeps leading us in the wrong direction."

"Instead of the Death Walker, which is kind of cool, we should totally be calling this unsub the Red Herring." Vik waggled his eyebrows, trying to bring some levity to the room.

Joan rolled her eyes at him.

"Can we focus?" Sayer rapped her knuckles on the table, frustrated. "We keep following the evidence and it's biting us in the ass. So let's stop. Let's take a step back and investigate from the ground up."

Joan pulled out her laptop. "Before we go any further, let me see if I can go into the lab and check the DNA samples from the three earlier cases. The evidence might already be in the warehouse, so I'll need to have it sent to the lab ASAP."

She typed with expert speed. As her eyes scanned the screen, her face got increasingly grim until she finally said, "Well, I've got bad news."

"Bad news?" Sayer came over to the computer to see what Joan pointed at.

Three files were open, and each of them said in red letters, *Evidence Destroyed During Processing.*

"What does that mean?" Sayer asked.

"It means the DNA samples were so small that to do the analysis, we had to destroy the last remnants of the sample."

"So there's nothing left," Vik groaned.

"Nothing left, so no way for us to determine if they were real or not." Joan stood up and put a hand on Sayer's shoulder. "Sorry."

"Goddammit. This case . . . I swear." Sayer pondered their next move.

"Can we get the original investigation files?" Vik asked.

Sayer held up the thin stack in her hand. "These *are* the original investigation files."

"What?"

"The DNA evidence was found quickly. The evidence was a slam dunk in all three cases—"

"So they had no need to go further." Vik flipped open the top file. "Unbelievable. They didn't even look at the logs of people who came and went from the park where Kent's cabin was located."

"Exactly," said Sayer, "so who knows what they missed."

"I've already sent the files from the three other cases over to Ezra. I'll ask him to comb closed cases for any others that might fit our new MO."

"And we can go check out the previous murder scenes," Vik suggested.

"Good idea. We can't go to the Tarlington murder site; it's in his workshop outside his family's house."

"Tarlington's family still lives there?" Vik seemed horrified.

Sayer nodded. "His family doesn't believe he killed those women. Despite the physical evidence in the workshop, they insist no one died there."

"Well, might turn out they're right," Vik said. "Won't they be vindicated."

"Vik and I will go up into the mountains and check out the cabin where Kent bled out the women. Joan, can you go to the U-STOR storage unit where Middleton killed the women in his little mini medical suite? I know they still haven't rented that unit. The owner wants to preserve the spot, like a memorial or something."

"Sounds good." Joan slid the files into her bag.

"Let's get on it. If we're right about this, not only is there an innocent girl missing, there are at least three innocent men rotting in jail for horrific murders they didn't commit."

EZRA'S ROOM, GEORGETOWN HOSPITAL, WASHINGTON, D.C.

Ezra watched the harried nurse just outside his door bobble the metal tray. He saw it falling but still let out an involuntary shout when it hit, the bang reverberating with his scream down the hard tile hall.

Hands shaking wildly, Ezra tried to calm himself, but the sound kept booming in his head, an echo of the bomb. He pressed his hands over his ears and squeezed his eyes shut.

Big mistake.

Every time Ezra closed his eyes he saw Cindy. The look on her face at the exact moment she realized what she'd done. Her mouth made a small O of surprise as the conflagration exploded around her. Then she was gone.

The worst part was that Ezra couldn't remember anything else from that moment, not even the pain or his own fear. Nothing but that image of Cindy.

And now he felt nothing but pain, agony radiating from his stumps.

"Focus, you idiot. Don't let the bastard win," Ezra mumbled to himself.

With hands still shaking, he picked up the three cases Sayer had sent him. If these were all frame jobs, Ezra knew there had to be some link hidden in these files.

He started with the Gwendolyn Van Hurst file. He wanted to review it before he dove into the other three.

Ezra opened the autopsy report the crime scene techs had printed for him that first day.

His gaze fell on the photo of Gwendolyn Van Hurst. Unable to look away, Ezra took it all in. Her dusky lips. Her sunken body like bird bones held together with loose skin. Her slack face where there once was so much life. Ezra went to clack his tongue stud against his teeth, but of course it had been removed for surgery. His fidget gone, he resorted to tapping his fingers while he read Joan's report.

Tacked to the back of the autopsy was the original DNA result.

He blinked rapidly. *Two Matches,* it said across the top.

Two? Ezra didn't remember anything about a second DNA match in the report.

He scanned down. Match one, Gwendolyn Van Hurst. Match two, Joan Warren.

"What the hell?" Ezra muttered.

He pulled the notes from the task force meeting where Joan got the results. No mention of FBI Chief Medical Examiner Joan Warren's DNA. Why weren't Joan and Sayer all over this? This suggested a major DNA contamination problem.

Curious, he opened his laptop to confirm what he was seeing in the report.

Online and paper copy of the DNA result next to each other, Ezra's gaze traveled back and forth between the two. Back and forth again.

Hands shaking again, he pulled up the three other cases. He tapped the keyboard, scanning documents and online records for almost thirty minutes before he reached for his phone to dial Sayer's number.

Sayer's phone buzzed on Vik's table.

"It's Ezra." She clicked her phone to speaker.

"Ezra, you're on speaker. Vik and Joan are here too. You got something for us?"

"I've sure as hell got something." His voice sounded shaky.

"Uh-oh," Vik said. "That doesn't sound pretty."

"It's really not."

They could hear Ezra's thick breathing.

"You okay?" Sayer asked.

"Yeah, I've just got a killer headache from looking at my computer."

"Thought you're on a computer ban."

"I am, but I had to make sure I wasn't seeing things."

"Seeing things?" Sayer's stomach flip-flopped at the tone in Ezra's voice.

"Yeah. No other way to say it . . . someone is altering files inside the FBI system."

"What do you mean?" Sayer asked; her stomach went from flip-flopping to full-on plummeting. This damned case.

"Our files. The ones actually in the computer system. Someone is changing them."

"Changing them?" Sayer's voice rose.

"Yeah, I first noticed with Van Hurst's DNA report."

Sayer and Vik groaned at the same time. "More trouble with the DNA?" Sayer said.

"A hell of a lot more trouble. The initial report came back with two DNA matches."

"Two?" Joan asked. "But I read the report and there was nothing about two matches."

"You probably opened the electronic version. By total accident, I happened to have the original report from the lab. The one that came directly from the tech."

"Wait, two matches. Who was the other match?" Joan leaned forward in her chair, eyes wide.

"Joan," Ezra said bluntly.

"Joan, like sitting-right-here Joan?" Sayer said.

"Exactly," Ezra wheezed.

Joan flushed bright red, blinking with confusion. "My DNA was on the report? But . . . oh my God."

"Joan . . ." Sayer reached out and put a gentle hand on her shoulder. "You know there's always the possibility of contamination from the person who collected the samples. It happens. It's not a big deal."

"It really is. . . ." Her eyes watered. "That's some serious contamination. I must have . . . messed up somewhere." She put her head down into her hands.

Sayer shook her head. "It's not unheard of for some cross-contamination to happen in the lab."

"It's unheard of in *my* lab." Joan's voice cracked slightly.

"Does this negate Winters's claim?" Vik asked. "I mean, if there's contamination—"

Joan firmly shook her head, wiping away tears and taking a deep breath. "No, if that DNA sample came back as manufactured, then it was man-made. No getting around that."

"So, it was just some kind of contamination?" Sayer cast about for a possible explanation.

"Or something," Ezra confirmed. "Because this case isn't the only one that's been altered."

"What?"

"Yeah . . . Joan's DNA showing up on the Van Hurst report is certainly a problem, but the much bigger issue is about our files in general."

"Explain, please." Sayer felt slightly nauseated.

"I traced the DNA report back through the system."

"You can do that?" Sayer was surprised. Most crime scene techs weren't exactly computer savvy.

"I'm like a freaking Renaissance man." Ezra let out a breathy laugh. "But yeah, I was originally recruited for the tech team, been hacking computers since I was twelve. When I got to the academy, found out I preferred working crime scenes."

"Been hacking since you were twelve; aren't you like thirteen now?" Sayer gently kidded.

"Har har."

"Okay, so you traced the file . . ."

"And whoever entered it the first time probably entered it correctly. But then, like forty minutes later, someone went into the system and altered the file."

"What on earth?" Vik asked. "Who would care about lab contamination enough to change an internal file?"

"Oh, it gets worse," Ezra said. "All three of the other cases you sent me, they've been altered as well."

Sayer's mouth fell open and she plopped down in the nearest chair. "Can you say that again?"

Ezra took a long, raspy breath in. "I went back through the three other cases. All three have been altered after the fact."

"Can you tell what they originally said?"

"Nope. I can only tell when they were altered, but no clue what the original files said. But those files show tampering all over the place. Autopsy reports, field notes, hell, even the task force meeting notes were changed."

"Did you check any files other than the four we're focusing on? Maybe it's just a system glitch that looks like someone altering things?" Sayer asked hopefully.

"I thought of that, so I checked ten other cases. None of them had anything like this."

"So all four possible frame-ups have been altered inside the FBI system."

"And no others."

"Is it possible someone hacked our system?" Vik asked.

Ezra let out a short laugh. "I guess it's possible, but that would be one hell of a feat."

"Ezra, to get into the system we all have our own login ID. Can you trace the alterations and figure out whose login is being used?"

"I think so. It might take me a while to figure out how to access that kind of metadata, but it's here somewhere."

"Great, get on it. We need to figure out what the hell is going on here."

"I'm on it." Ezra hung up.

Sayer rubbed her aching shoulder and winced at the tender bruising. "Well," she said with a heavy sigh, "I know of at least one person who has illegal access to our files."

Vik nodded. "Senator Van Hurst."

"Exactly." Sayer held up her phone. "Let's call Van Hurst and make sure he isn't somehow involved."

She dialed, temples throbbing with stress. She spoke briefly with Maxine until the senator got on the phone.

"Agent Altair. To what do I owe the pleasure? Please tell me you have a break in Gwen's case."

"Of sorts. I'm actually calling to ask how you've been accessing our internal files."

Van Hurst sucked a breath in through his teeth. "I'm sorry . . . revealing a source . . . that doesn't seem right."

"Senator Van Hurst, we're concerned that the person leaking our task force files to you has hacked the FBI system and is illegally accessing data. You aren't the press; you have no legal protection. We could charge you with accessory to felony, because that's what tampering with FBI files is."

Van Hurst sighed. "Oh, fine. I don't even know who the source is anyway."

"What?" Sayer said.

"I've just been getting files anonymously via e-mail."

"I need you to send those to us right away."

"Sure, sure. Why not. But I'm sure they're coming from someone there. I wouldn't have used them if I weren't confident they were really your . . . internal files."

"How could you know that?"

"Before the first e-mail, I got a phone call. Just an electronic voice telling me to check my e-mail. It was a direct line from your building in Quantico. Came up on my caller ID."

"All right, thanks for cooperating." Sayer hung up and looked around the room.

"Okay, if it's coming from inside the building, that means it's likely not an external hack. Which means—" Vik began.

"—that someone actually inside the FBI is altering these files," Sayer finished.

"But why?" Joan asked. "What do they gain messing with our case files? Why take my name off the DNA match? I mean, it saved me some embarrassment, but I need to know there's a problem so I can fix it. And why is this person only messing with the Death Walker files?"

"Because . . . they're the killer?" Sayer said tentatively, the idea too horrific to contemplate.

"Holy shit," Vik whispered. "You think the Death Walker works at the FBI?"

Sayer, Vik, and Joan sat around the table, horror washing over them.

"Let's play this out and see if we're jumping to the wrong conclusion. What are some alternative scenarios?" Sayer got up and started pacing.

Eventually Vik shook his head. "I can't come up with an alternative. Assuming Ezra got it right, we know three things." Vik counted on his fingers. "One, someone in the FBI is altering files. Two, that person is only altering the Death Walker files. Therefore, three, that individual knows that these cases are somehow connected."

"And who else could've made that connection between the cases?" Joan said. "I mean, who else other than the killer."

"Okay, so let's say the Death Walker is an FBI agent; how does that play out?" Sayer clenched her empty hands, desperate for something to fidget with.

"Well, if you were going to try to frame people, it's a brilliant place to be," Joan offered. "The killer could manipulate the investigations from the inside. Keep an eye on evidence. They could make sure we weren't on the right path."

"It would explain the DNA evidence," Vik said. "He didn't need to worry about us going back and checking old DNA evidence; he could just destroy it and alter the files."

Sayer stopped pacing. "We need to tell Holt." She began to gather her things, dread percolating in her gut like sour acid.

"No." Joan put a gentle hand on Sayer's, stopping her.

"No?" Vik asked. "Why on earth would we keep something like this from the assistant director?"

"Because I know for a fact that she has altered autopsy data before," Joan said. "Until we know for sure who the killer is, we don't know who to trust."

"Uhhhh. What are you talking about? You think Assistant Director Holt is the Death Walker?" Vik let out an incredulous laugh.

Joan closed her bloodshot eyes and seemed to be bracing herself for something. "Sayer, I've thought about telling you many times. But I could never quite justify it."

"Tell me what?"

"It's about Jake."

"Jake? As in Sayer's fiancé?" Vik asked, eyes sliding back and forth between Joan and Sayer. "As in, was killed in the line of duty three years ago, Jake?"

"You're saying that Holt went into the FBI file system and changed something about Jake's autopsy?"

Joan, eyes still closed, nodded slowly. "That is exactly what I'm saying."

"And how do you know that?" Sayer demanded.

"Because I did his original autopsy, and I know that the information they put into the official report was . . . significantly altered."

"Significantly . . ." Sayer's voice trailed off. "But why would Holt do that?"

Joan finally opened her eyes. "I have no idea, Sayer. I wouldn't have even noticed the discrepancies except that I had to write my annual review at the end of that year. I wanted to put a specific note about Jake in my review, and so I went back to the autopsy report to get the details correct."

"And what was different?"

"Everything. Including the cause of death."

"Jake was shot."

Joan closed her eyes again. "No, he wasn't. He drowned."

"Drowned?" Sayer's vision blurred. "But that makes no sense."

Vik asked, "How do you know it's Holt that made the changes?"

"Because I went to her about the discrepancy and she told me that she was the one who did it. That it was for internal security." Joan looked over at Sayer, apology in her eyes. "She asked me to keep it quiet. So I did."

Sayer's world began to tilt. She leaned forward, head between her knees, trying to keep from passing out.

Vik jumped up and got her a glass of ice water. "Hey, sit up and drink this."

"I'm so sorry, Sayer. I know I should've told you before now, but I just didn't know why Holt changed it. I assumed there was a good reason."

Sayer leaned back in the chair and chugged the cold water, trying to clear the tempest of emotion knocking her off-kilter. "Do you know anything else?"

Joan shook her head. "That's all I know. But in this context it seems . . . suspicious."

"What could Jake's death have to do with the Death Walker?"

"No idea. But if we don't know who the killer is, well, then we don't know who to trust."

Sayer gave Vik a weak smile of thanks for the water and stood up on shaky legs. "Okay, then I guess it's just us for now. Let's stick with the plan. It's late and we all need some dinner and sleep and I need some time to process this. I see two big holes in the earlier Death Walker investigations. I'll ask the park ranger at Shenandoah to send Ezra the logs for the park. Everyone coming and going has to sign in. I'll also ask the storage unit where Middleton killed the women to send us their customer logs."

Vik looked shocked. "Those records aren't in the original files?"

"Nope, they never bothered to gather them. Had the DNA match, remember." Sayer tapped the line of photos on the whiteboard. "Let's get these balls rolling and tomorrow we can split up, go to the original murder scenes. See if there's anything there."

UNKNOWN LOCATION

Adi woke to the *click click click* of the projector. The whirring of the smoke machine. The monster's footsteps shuffling around in the dark.

She watched the masked man shuffle around the small room.

"They've realized you are missing." The creature chuckled. "But you are my pinnacle. I knew it would happen like this. A flash of brilliance, a breakthrough!"

Adi felt beyond any emotion she could recognize. Where she had been filled with murderous rage earlier, she felt fear now. "Please, not again."

The weight of the last year of her life crashed down upon her. Adi felt the loss of her family. In that moment she wanted to go back to the glorious calm she felt seeing Clem. She missed her so much. The numbness she had cultivated for so long was stripped away by those few moments holding Clem's hand.

Adi wanted to be with her family once again. "Let me go or just let me die, please."

"Not yet, 9.3. I need to reproduce my results one more time. The hallmark of any good experiment is a reproducible result. After that, I'm happy to fulfill your wish for death."

"No," Adi croaked, grasping for any last remnants of power she had.

"No?" The monster seemed genuinely curious.

"I won't come back this time."

The monster chuckled. "We'll just see about that, won't we?"

The images appeared and the smoke began to fill the room. Adi curled into a ball, clamped her hands over her ears, and squeezed her eyes shut. Then she opened her mouth and took a deep breath, inhaling as much smoke as she could. The oblivion couldn't come quickly enough.

"Yes, that's right. Breathe deep, 9.3. Go see your sister once again."

ROAD TO
ALEXANDRIA, VA

After arranging to have the Shenandoah National Park and U-STOR customer records sent over to Ezra at the hospital, Sayer rode home.

Down in the garden, Tino sat in his usual spot, Vesper dozing at his feet. When Sayer approached, his eyebrows shot up.

"Whoa, calida, you look terrible."

"No joke." Sayer gave him a rueful smile. "Hey, thanks for talking last night."

"Anytime. I enjoyed your company. Did it help?"

"It really did. It helped me, and it helped my case. So . . . thank you." She started up the stairs.

"Hey, I made lime soup if you want some," he called up to her.

Sayer could smell the subtle citrus tang wafting from Tino's apartment.

"I'd love some."

Tino shooed her upstairs and arrived a minute later with a deep bowl of hot soup that Sayer inhaled. While she ate, Tino fed Vesper and directed her to the shower with a good-night kiss on the cheek.

"You need to rest, calida. Sleep well." He let himself out.

On autopilot, Sayer rinsed off in the shower and then collapsed into bed next to Vesper, her brain spinning a million miles an hour. Curled around the already snoring dog, she stared at the photo of Jake next to the bed. If he wasn't shot, then how in the hell did he die? Jake was one of the strongest swimmers Sayer had ever known. Drowning made no sense at all.

"Can't figure this out right now. Need to focus on one crisis at a time," Sayer mumbled as she clicked off the light. Vesper's tail wagged in response to her voice. Sayer buried her face in his warm fur and fell into a deep sleep.

She crashed down into a vivid dream. Jake stood at the edge of the ocean, waves buffeting his bare feet. He wore slacks rolled up to his knees and the thick green sweater knitted by his Irish grandmother. He had salt-and-pepper stubble on his chin, hazel eyes crinkling into a smile.

He spoke, but Sayer couldn't hear what he said. Every time his mouth opened, cold breath left his body. He seemed desperate, still trying to talk even though no sound came out. Jake's life escaped, little by little, until his body began to sag. His lively face and strong eyes began to flicker. Faded into fear.

Sayer tried to run toward him across the wet sand, but her feet sank deeper and deeper until she was buried up to her waist. Unable to move forward, she flung herself back and forth, wailing with sorrow at being unable to reach Jake.

He fell to one knee, head bowed, weakening.

Before he toppled forward into the water, he looked up into her eyes.

Sayer saw no love, no sorrow, only accusation.

"How could you not know?" Jake gurgled as the waves reached his mouth.

He slipped beneath the frothy surface, and Sayer screamed and screamed until she woke up.

The phone buzzed on the bed next to her.

Still lost in her nightmare, Sayer fumbled for the phone.

The screen said, *Nana*.

"Hello? Nana, are you okay?" she slurred.

"Sayer?"

Nana's voice sounded so small and frightened that adrenaline spiked Sayer wide awake.

"Nana? What happened?"

"Someone left blood on my doorstep. Along with a package."

"What?" Sayer was already up, pulling on clothes. Vesper danced around her legs in groggy confusion.

"Sayer, I think the package is for you."

After Sayer's frantic calls, half the FBI descended upon Sophia McDuff's doorstep.

Sayer arrived just before the bomb squad, who immediately evacuated the entire block. Groggy, frightened families in robes and pajamas huddled behind the cordon at the end of the block. Sayer sat next to Nana, wrapping an arm over the woman's thin shoulders. Without a word, they watched the bomb squad robot seal a lid over the large cardboard box soaking in a pool of blood still crimson under the yellowish streetlights.

"Whose blood is it?" Nana's voice was finally back to normal after the initial scare. "Not the last missing girl . . ."

"Dear God, I hope not," Sayer said, not trusting her own voice. It was so much blood. "Want to tell me what happened?" Sayer tried to distract Nana from the chaotic scene.

Nana shrugged. "Someone knocked. I opened the door."

"Without looking through the peephole? It's after midnight!"

Nana dismissed Sayer with a wave. "Oh, what does an old lady have to worry about these days?"

"Nana, there's something called a home invasion robbery—"

"Oh please, I have my pepper spray inside. Plus I have a mean right hook. They can try to push past me."

Sayer let out a short laugh and wrapped her arm tighter around Nana's shoulders. Though she sounded tough, and Sayer wouldn't want to mess with her, Nana was getting on in years and Sayer felt a wave of protectiveness she'd never felt before. For a brief moment the fear of losing her last parental figure paralyzed Sayer's heart. Fatigue made it hard for her to shake off the feeling.

"All right, so you opened the door . . . ," Sayer prompted.

"And I saw that box. It had your name scrawled on it, as though it was written by a preschooler." Nana tsked. "But then I smelled the blood. It . . . made me gag, it was so strong. Like iron. I should've stepped outside and chased the bastard down; imagine trying to scare an old lady."

"Nana, please do not go chasing after people leaving bloodied boxes on your front steps."

"Oh, fine. I just hope there's not a chopped-up dead body in that box or something."

"Nana!"

"What, don't tell me you hadn't thought of that already."

Sayer just sighed. "You're right, the thought occurred to me, but the blood doesn't look like it's leaking from the box." She straightened the blanket on Nana's shoulders, but the old woman shook her off.

"You okay?" Nana glanced over at Sayer.

"Yeah." Sayer's eyes scanned the FBI agents bustling around, photographers, bomb squad, crime scene techs; was the Death Walker one of them? Was he here pretending to help but actually reveling in the fear and chaos he created?

While she tried not to focus on the possibility that their unsub could be one of her own, Vik screeched up in his old Nissan.

He rushed over. "You both okay?"

Nana piped up. "Just some bastard trying to scare me."

Sayer laughed. "Some bastard that clearly doesn't know Sophia McDuff."

Vik gave them a lopsided smile. "I know, right?" He trotted off to help coordinate the scene while Sayer stayed with Nana.

"I asked if you're okay because I'm worried about you." Nana took Sayer's hand.

"What?"

"You used to be full of fire. Lately you seem kind of absent from life. I mean, look at your apartment."

"Nana, I appreciate your concern, but now really isn't the time to discuss my private life."

Nana nodded. "Of course. I just wonder if this shell you've put yourself in isn't interfering with your ability to do your job too."

Sayer gritted her teeth and didn't respond, focusing on the hazmat removal team instead.

Seeing her stress, Nana said, "Sorry. You're right. Now's not the time."

Once the package was safely removed and the house thoroughly searched, Nana's neighbors huddled back into their homes, whispering to each other with concern.

As the last neighbors disappeared behind closed doors, Sayer said, "I'm sorry too, Nana. I never want my work to affect you, especially not like this."

"Oh, stop fussing. For God's sake, I was married to a senator." Nana stood up and stretched. "We had bomb threats. Once, a man tried to stab Charles at dinner one night. When you do something important, people get in your business. Now, let's see if we can go inside and get some tea."

After throwing back a scalding Earl Grey and making sure Nana was secure with a cop stationed outside, Sayer rushed to the lab to see what the killer had left for her.

FBI HEADQUARTERS, QUANTICO, VA

"Files." The evidence tech seemed vaguely disappointed. "Files and a single CD."

A cardboard box sitting in a puddle of blood . . . Sayer had half expected human body parts, maybe even parts of Adi Stephanopolous. Intense relief flooded her entire body.

"Have you had a chance to look at any of it?" Sayer asked.

"No, ma'am. The bomb guys had to make sure there wasn't a bomb so we just got it up here. We've just finished processing the outside; nothing inside has been checked. Assistant Director Holt figured you might want to be here to help sort through it."

Sayer grunted approval. She snapped on gloves and approached the box sitting on a long stainless steel table.

"No blood inside?" she asked.

"None. The box was lined with plastic to protect everything."

"Hmm," Sayer said to herself. "So why all the blood at the scene . . . ?" She circled the table, taking in the folders and the CD in a clear jewel case next to the box.

The windowless lab and fluorescent lights made it possible to ignore the fact that it was the middle of the night. Still, exhaustion and stress gnawed at her shoulders, her bruised body aching with the desire to stop moving, maybe lie down in a soft clean bed.

Pushing away the longing for rest, Sayer contemplated where to dive in. As she continued to circle the table, Vik whooshed through the door, pale as a ghost. He carried two coffees.

"I bring gifts."

"You are clearly a fucking genius," Sayer said, and took the offered coffee. She held it to her nose and breathed in the aroma, eyes closed. The familiar scent awoke her body, chasing away some of the fatigue. "Hey, thanks for showing up so fast and taking over the scene for me. Sorry I dragged you out there in the middle of the night."

"Pssh, yeah, 'cause you're the one that poured a few gallons of blood on your grandmother's doorstep. I blame you."

Sayer flashed a half smile and pointed to the box of gloves. "Want to glove up and help me sort through these files?"

"Boy, do I!" Vik said with false enthusiasm.

The crime scene tech stepped out for a moment and Sayer looked Vik in the eye. "Hey, one of us needs to stay with the files at all times. If someone here is the Death Walker . . ."

"Then we need to make sure he doesn't tamper with anything." Vik finished her sentence. "Bet he wouldn't mind seeing our reactions to these files either. We should take note of anyone who comes in here scoping out the scene."

"Exactly. And I think we should keep most of the analysis to our little band of Irregulars until we know more."

"Though you realize, if this is what we think it is . . . the cat's outta the bag on the older frame jobs."

Sayer took a deep breath. The fact that they kept information from the task force wasn't going to go over well, even if it was only for a day. She couldn't worry about that now.

"So . . . there's almost thirty file folders, divided into nine colors," Sayer said.

"Nine, huh."

"Yeah. How much you want to bet one color for each experiment this bastard conducted? I think he just sent us his research files."

"But why?" Vik asked out loud.

Sayer shrugged. "Who knows? Let's get started and maybe we can figure that out. Let's catalog the files first, then see what's on the disk together?"

Vik grunted agreement, and they sorted the files by color.

Sayer began with the olive-green file folders. The first one she opened had nothing but a date and title: *The Sleep*.

She flipped through the pages, reading little bits here and there.

"These are his experiment notes from the Middleton murders. I mean, the women who were killed with anesthesia in that storage unit."

Vik looked up from his red file. "These are notes from a case I don't think we have yet. These are older, maybe ten years back."

"Good God," Sayer said softly.

"Yeah, it's bad. So far I've read about three victims, all starved to death."

They both took a deep breath, then went back to reading, taking notes for further investigation.

After Sayer finished all seven olive-green files, she sat back, overwhelmed.

"You okay?" Vik asked.

"Well, I've just finished reading detailed notes taken while this monster watched women slowly die. He recorded everything, their vitals and their reactions. Some of these women were conscious for a very long time. The things they said . . ." Her voice broke.

"Damn." Vik put a gentle hand on her shoulder.

"Yeah, but that's not even the worst part."

"It's not?" Vik scrunched his face like he didn't really want to know what was worse than women begging for their lives.

"The worst part is . . . the experiment he conducted here, it's fascinating."

"What do you mean?"

"This is one of the most important studies I've ever read on the neurology of death. As scientists, it's not like we can set up experiments to study what happens at the exact moment of death. Emergency deaths are too sudden, and even when we know death is coming, it's impossible to predict the specific moment. Even if we could predict the right time, who wants to die strapped into an fMRI machine? And medical professionals are obligated to focus on either saving the person or making them as comfortable as possible. So we have an endless supply of anecdotal evidence about death, but virtually no data."

"And our unsub is gathering that data?"

"Exactly." Sayer pointed to a chart in the file. "So, as he slowly administered different cocktails of anesthesia, he had the women hooked up to an EEG machine as they died. He measured their brain waves as he tinkered with their levels of consciousness. The data he gathered is . . . unbelievable. Just one example, there are stories about patients about to die having a few moments or even a few hours of incredible lucidity. Patients who haven't been able to speak for years suddenly interact with their families, tell stories, share memories. Some patients who have been bedridden for months can suddenly get up, walk around, even dance. Then, after that brief burst of activity, they pass away."

"Yeah," Vik said, "I remember my grandma getting up and playing the piano about an hour before she died."

"Exactly. For a long time stories like that were dismissed as wishful thinking on the part of families, but more recently there's been some speculation that brain activity spikes shortly before death. Neurologists think the sudden lucidity could be a result of the brain being flooded with chemicals in a last-ditch effort to remain alive."

"Whoa."

"Even more whoa, this data basically proves it. This is the first evidence I've seen. It's . . . groundbreaking research."

"So our serial killer also just happens to be a brilliant scientist?"

"I'd say so." Sayer nodded.

"Fantastic, brilliant, but evil . . . the best kind of killer. And we still don't know why. Why the obsession with the dying moment?"

Sayer shrugged and drained her coffee.

Joan staggered in, bleary eyed, clothes rumpled.

"Huzzah, reinforcements," Vik called out.

Joan shot him a scowl. "Sorry, was over in the ME lab helping set up the blood for DNA analysis."

"Was the DNA manufactured?"

"No. That's the first thing we checked. The blood and DNA are completely real. We sent most of it off for full analysis but put ten samples into the three-hour machine. We should have the results by sunup."

Sayer pulled out a stool next to her. "Well, glove up and dive in. We have a lot of work to do. Anyway, Joan, you might actually appreciate this stuff."

"Appreciate? I find that difficult to imagine." She sniffed.

"Yeah, he sent us his research files. It's some of the worst things I've ever read, and the results he got were . . . amazing."

Joan looked skeptical as she pulled on gloves.

Sayer, Joan, and Vik read through all the files, sharing insights, taking notes, and comforting each other.

After they finished, Sayer got up, pulled off her gloves, and stretched her back. "All right, so what do we know?"

Joan remained seated, propped against the table for support. "We have five more cases to track down to connect to the Death Walker. And we know that the unsub is incredibly smart, probably has a science background, and, as we already knew, is obsessed with the moment of death."

Vik tilted up his empty coffee cup, hoping for a few more drops. Disappointed, he got up to toss the empty cup into the trash. "Add that to the twins stuff, right?"

"Yeah," Sayer said, "that stuff has to be important somehow. All these cases are looking at the various aspects of that moment when a person literally dies. But why? No way this is idle scientific curiosity. There's a reason, even if it's only in his twisted mind."

"Well, the unsub's evolving, getting more specific . . . ," Joan offered.

"Right, so the progression, we've got the first five cases, all older. It's possible that no one was framed for those murders since they don't seem to be in the system. Is it possible that he killed"—Sayer consulted her notes—"that many without anyone noticing?"

"It seems possible," Joan said. "We just said the Death Walker's smart. Maybe the first experiments were less well planned. Maybe the unsub counted on no one connecting the murders but, over time, realized that the body count was too high. If the Death Walker got worried about being caught, it would make sense for him to switch over to the frame-ups we see in the three cases you identified."

"That makes a lot of sense." Sayer reached for her worry beads to help her think and once again cursed her empty pocket. "Okay, we need to fill in the entire task force on what we've found. Our unsub has officially connected the cases for us, so no need to keep the task force in the dark about the fact that these cases are all frame jobs."

"People are going to be angry," Joan said.

"They sure are, but we're not going to let anyone dwell on that. The important question, now what? Do we tell them about our suspicion that the Death Walker might be one of our own? How do we investigate these cases if the unsub is possibly in the room?"

"I think we have to keep that quiet. If the unsub is an FBI agent . . . we can't tip him off that we know."

"Uh, Sayer?" Vik held up a finger. "You forgot the CD. We haven't seen what's on it."

Sayer froze. How could she forget something so obviously important? Her lack of sleep was beginning to affect her ability to do her job. Any worse and she was going to have to step aside.

After the crime scene tech set up the DVD player, Sayer, Joan, and Vik gathered around the small screen.

The video was high quality, much better than the grainy black-and-white video of Gwen's death.

In full color, Adi Stephanopolous sat in a cage, DMT smoke billowing around her. Ancient Greek images projected onto the uneven walls.

The girl curled into a ball, shuddering with emotion.

"No, please, not again," she whispered. "I've done what you wanted. Please, let me go."

Sayer squeezed her hands together to counteract the feelings of rage and impotence that threatened to burst from her chest. She wanted to pull that girl from the cage and wrap her arms around her. Protect her from the horrors about to come.

They all held their breaths, terrified that they were about to watch Adi's death.

"Not yet, 9.3," a raspy voice off camera said. "I need to reproduce my results one more time. The hallmark of any good experiment is a reproducible result. After that, I'm happy to fulfill your wish for death."

"No." Adi looked up, her eyes resolute.

"No?" the voice offscreen asked.

"I won't come back this time." Though her words were said with conviction, the girl's face contorted into a sorrowful mask. Her lips trembled as she spoke.

The offscreen voice chuckled. "We'll just see about that, won't we?"

Smoke began to obscure the camera. Adi curled into a ball, clamped her hands over her ears, and squeezed her eyes shut.

"Yes, that's right," the voice said. "Breathe deep, 9.3. Go see your sister once again."

The video jumped in time. The room, still lit only by the projected images, was free of smoke. Adi was clearly visible. She didn't move.

No signs of breath. Two IV lines ran from her arms to drip bags. One of the IV bags hung empty. Across the top the empty bag said DIGOXIN.

Sayer let out a soft "No."

"Witness her death, or what should be her death," the voice said. "But now, watch what I can do."

A hand reached out and turned the valve on the second IV line into Adi's arm.

"Watch as I bring her back. As you will see, subject 9.3 will be fully coherent, entirely undamaged by her journey beyond the veil."

The girl suddenly jolted, her arms leaping up like she had received an electric shock. Gasping for breath, Adi rolled to her side. "Nooooo." She let out a sorrowful moan.

"Did you see your sister? Did you touch her?" the voice demanded.

"Please," Adi sobbed. "Please, let me go back. I'll do anything, just let me be with Clem again."

The video cut to black.

Over the dark image, the voice continued. "Finally, my work is complete. Finally I have the answers I need. I'm so happy I could share my research with you. No one else there will appreciate it. Of course, this means I don't need 9.3 any longer. I wonder if you can find her before she dies, Sayer."

The video ended.

Sayer blinked back the wall of emotion that threatened to completely tear apart the shredded curtain in her brain. She could no longer pull tight the wall between her emotions and this case. She couldn't pretend that she didn't care.

Sayer was going to find that girl alive, or die trying.

"Sayer?" Joan said loudly, her calling Sayer's name like an echo of the unsub saying her name in the video. "You still with us?"

Sayer snapped out of her emotional tempest. "Yeah, I'm here. Screw the rules. Screw taking this slow. I want everyone in the building down to the fucking janitor poring over these files looking for any clue. We need a way to find out where he's keeping Adi Stephanopolous, and I don't care if the entire universe knows it."

Sayer was slightly surprised to find late-morning sunlight shining through the windows of the conference room. She managed to explain everything to the task force without breaking down, though what she wanted to do was fall to her knees and pull her hair out with frustration.

Andy Wagner was particularly angry when he found out about the three other frame jobs, all closed FBI cases.

He leaned back in his chair and groaned loudly. "You thought keeping this a secret was the way to go? Plus, this bullshit is going to come back and bite us in the ass."

Sayer was completely done with his nonsense. "Yes, thank you for your productive and erudite analysis of the situation."

A few chuckles around the room made Andy flush, and he looked ready to say something snide but thought better of it. "All I mean is, we're already looking like morons in the public eye. This is going to kill us."

Sayer's last small semblance of calm snapped. "Yes, and imagine how bad it will look when everyone realizes that your profiles, which were instrumental in supporting the DNA evidence, were all completely wrong!" Sayer shouted the word *wrong,* all inhibition gone. "Your profiles that seemed so fucking perfect, they helped convict at least three innocent men!"

Andy stood up and faced off with Sayer. "You think so? Well, let's wait and see who our unsub is." He stormed out of the room.

Sayer stood at the head of the table, heart pounding, hands shaking. The entire task force sat in uncomfortable silence.

Vik cleared his throat. "So, does anyone else have anything to add? Any questions?"

Silence.

"No? Okay then, I'd say we're done here." He gestured for people to leave.

As everyone began to stand, Joan's phone pinged. The whole room froze, holding their breath as she read the message.

"It's the DNA result from the blood puddle."

"And?" Sayer asked.

"And it's a complete mess. There are dozens of DNA samples mixed together."

Joan stared at her phone, silent for a moment.

"Joan?"

"We haven't compiled a complete DNA profile, because of the numerous sources. But the techs compared a few of the partial strands against the DNA from the older case files."

"And?" Sayer grew impatient.

"And they found a few reasonable matches. At least three were a match for the victims bled out up in the mountain cabin. One matched the DNA of a victim in the Dugald Tarlington strangulation case. And one matched Gwendolyn Van Hurst."

"Whoa," Vik said.

"If I had to guess," Joan continued, "I would guess that the blood you found was the blood of all the victims of Death Walker cases. Twenty-eight women's blood, mixed together."

"Why the hell would he do that?" Sayer wondered out loud.

"To prove without a doubt that the cases are all connected," Vik said.

"Now he's just playing with us." Sayer's eyes scanned the room. Was he there with her, reveling in their infighting? Enjoying their horror? She fought to keep her face calm. No need to feed the bastard's sick ego.

As they filed out of the conference room, Sayer's phone buzzed with a text from Ezra.

Found a match on the Shenandoah Park and U-STOR logs. Call me asap!

Sayer, Vik, and Joan quickly retreated to a private room.

"Hey, Ezra, you're on speaker. We're all here. What've you got?"

"Andy freakin' Wagner is what I've got!" Ezra's voice barely rose beyond a whisper.

Sayer's brain shut down and could form no words.

"Uh, I thought you just said Andy Wagner?" Vik said.

Papers shuffled on the speaker. "Yeah, Andy Wagner, like FBI lead profiler. He apparently rented a storage unit at U-STOR six years ago. Way before the murders. And then he camped at Shenandoah National Park just four months before the murders there began."

Sayer's brain finally kicked into gear. "Why would he sign his real name? He's an asshole but not a moron."

"I don't know, but I checked the handwriting against the signature we've got on file. Sure as hell looks to me like Andy Wagner's signature. I'll send it to the experts to make sure."

"Well, Andy is rather . . . overconfident," Joan said. "Perhaps he thought he could get away with it, maybe even reveled in the risk?"

Sayer barely heard Joan speak. She felt an emotion she couldn't even identify. Pulsing red light drifted in from the edges of her vision. Her entire body tingled like it was about to be electrocuted.

Without any conscious thought, she moved toward the door, her only plan to destroy Andy Wagner. Her hand fell to her gun.

"Hey!" Vik grabbed at Sayer.

Sayer swung around and violently shoved him off.

She continued to storm toward the door when Joan called, "Sayer. Sayer, no!"

Joan wrapped a surprisingly strong hand around Sayer's arm and held tight.

"Sayer, listen to me." She spoke with a smooth but firm voice. "If it's Andy, we need to prove it's him. To do that, we need to make sure he doesn't know we're on to him. We want him to think he's in the clear. Maybe he'll lead us to the girl. We can still save her."

Sayer tried to pull away one more time, but Joan's words filtered in through the roaring chaos in her head.

She looked around, her vision clearing.

Sayer blinked and sagged against the nearest wall.

"Everyone okay there?" Ezra asked from the phone Sayer hadn't even remembered dropping on the ground. She picked up the phone, hands shaking. "Yeah. Yeah, we're okay. Sorry. Joan's right. Let's go nail that bastard."

The trio sat around the small conference table.

"How could it possibly be Andy?" Joan asked. "It just doesn't make any sense."

"Well"—Vik rubbed a hand through his hair—"we did ask ourselves who benefited from these murders."

"But how did Andy benefit?" Joan asked.

"Oh my God, of course." Sayer got up to pace. "His career. In every one of those cases, he offered the perfect profile. These cases were all unusual in their own way. He's gotten fame and fortune from his groundbreaking new serial killer profiles. Hell, he got a book deal out of it."

"So he's an attention hound?"

Sayer stopped pacing and leaned on the table. "Who knows?"

"But could he have done it? I mean, he's a psychologist, not a doctor or anything," Vik said. "Could he even make DNA?"

"Well, let's find out. Let's also find out if that bastard has a twin. . . ."

Sayer called Ezra back.

"Ezra, two quick questions. One, does Andy have any science background? And two, does he have a twin?"

"On it. Give me five minutes." Ezra clicked off.

Joan shifted uncomfortably. "You really want Ezra to open that file? Our personnel files are confidential—"

Sayer dismissed her with a wave. "One thing I know we can look at, lab access logs." Because everyone had their own personal code, they could check to see when Andy had entered the medical labs.

They all stood up.

Joan nodded. "I've got those logs on my computer."

They followed Joan down to the ME lab. She typed quickly and let out a small sound of triumph.

"Here it is." Joan scanned the screen and then grimaced. "Look at this." She turned the screen so Sayer and Vik could see.

"Andy's code was entered into the main lab door here; here's another one. And here. All of these entries are in the middle of the night."

"So Andy's been sneaking into the lab at night and using our own equipment to make DNA to frame people?" Sayer just couldn't believe it. "That's . . . insane. Way too risky. Don't we have cameras on everything?"

Joan shook her head. "There are cameras on the exterior doors of each building, but we have none in the hall and none here in the lab. Too many sensitive images . . . no one wants video of an autopsy leaked."

"And that bastard just figured no one would notice," Sayer said.

"To be fair, he was right," Vik pointed out. "I mean, if Winters hadn't happened, we never would've known there was anything going on."

"You're right, of course." Sayer paced the entire length of the lab. "So where's the stuff he used to manufacture the DNA? He couldn't store it here."

"Hey, remember when we ran into Andy in the hall last week? I remember thinking that it looked like he came out of the storage closet looking guilty as hell. . . ."

They grabbed gloves and hurried out into the hall. Gloves on, Sayer pulled open the storage closet and flicked on the light. The scent of lavender cleaning fluid filled her nose and she remembered Leila.

"Hey, Leila mentioned the cleaner that the Death Walker used. Said it smelled like lavender . . ."

"Jesus," Vik muttered. "He was stealing cleaner from the FBI and using it to clean up murder sites?"

"Unbelievable," Joan said.

Sayer gingerly began rifling through the shelves, shifting massive packages of paper towels, stacks of sponges, bottles of industrial cleaning fluid. In a back corner, she found an old plastic bin with a lid.

"Hey." She called over Vik and Joan.

"Vik, can you take a few photos before we open this? Just in case."

Vik's camera flashed, making spots dance before Sayer's eyes.

As she blinked rapidly, her phone buzzed.

"Ezra?" She tapped speaker.

"Yeah, I took a look at Andy's file."

"And?"

"And, he was a biology major in college."

Vik sucked air in between his teeth. Joan groaned.

"All right, thanks, Ezra. What about a twin?"

"I'm not seeing anything in his file. I'll keep digging." Ezra clicked off.

The three agents exchanged a look and Sayer stepped up to the plastic bin. She gently lifted the lid. Inside, rubber tubes, glass vials, and sealed jars of liquid sloshed in the dim light.

"Joan, does this look like stuff you could use to make DNA?"

She leaned over to closely inspect the contents. "It sure does."

"All right, time to call in the crime scene team," Vik said firmly.

"And time to talk to Holt."

Holt sat at her desk with a perfectly flat expression while Sayer explained everything that had happened during the last fifteen hours. The meeting at Vik's house. The discovery that someone within the FBI was tampering with files. The package on Nana's doorstep. The files about experiments. The video of Adi Stephanopolous. And, last but not least, the information implicating Andy Wagner.

After spewing everything out as quickly as possible, Sayer fell quiet and waited for Holt's reaction.

Holt closed her eyes and sat stone still for almost five minutes.

Sayer's throat tightened, anxious for Holt to react. She'd never seen Holt like this, wearing a gargoyle mask of silence.

Finally, Holt let out a long breath.

"Well, to be fair, I should have known better than to ask you to let something go."

The assistant director took another deep breath, face still blank.

Sayer stood stock-still, waiting for the explosion.

Strangely, inexplicably, Holt half smiled. "You're telling me that you think my lead profiler, a senior agent in the Behavioral Analysis Unit, is a serial killer and has been framing innocent men for murder for a decade . . . innocent men who are now rotting in jail? Hell, one of those guys is on death row. It would appear that I've now presided over the largest screw-up in the history of FBI screw-ups."

"I'm sorry," Sayer said softly.

"No, I'm sorry." Holt put her head down into her hands. "I don't have any rage for this one. I've spent the last nine years trying to right this ship. Trying to steer this office toward something good, helpful, right." She looked up, face grim. "I tried to repair the previous scandal with the lab. Agents stepping out of line. And now this." She looked up at Sayer. "I was wrong. I shouldn't have told you to leave this alone. I thought I was doing damage control, but now I think maybe it's time to burn it all down."

"Uh . . ." Sayer wasn't sure what to say.

"Well, no choice but to clean house. I can see that now." She pulled out a piece of paper and a pen. She paused, pen aloft over the paper. "I've been hunting leaks, propping up our labs turning out questionable forensics, shoring up the walls around this office, but I'm just done. If the foundations are weak, we need to tear everything down and hope that they can build something new."

She began to write something.

Sayer shifted from one foot to the other, trying to be patient. Holt wrote and wrote until Sayer couldn't wait any longer. "Or, you know, we could just investigate and then arrest whoever is doing these terrible things. Let the public know that we don't hide our mistakes, that we aren't afraid to root out internal problems."

Holt let out a cynical laugh. "You make it sound easy. That's not how this all works. You know that."

Sayer shrugged. "Well maybe that's how it should work. Maybe that's what needs to change."

Holt looked up at Sayer as if seeing her for the first time. "You know, maybe you're right." She contemplated for a long moment and then gave a curt nod. "You are right. I'm done playing all these damned political games. Let's actually just do what's right for a change. Pursue this all the way. If Andy Wagner is a serial killer, find evidence and we will take him down."

Sayer let out a hard breath and nodded. "I'm on it."

As she pulled open the door, Sayer turned back to Holt. "I have a question for you."

"Okay."

"It's about Jake."

"What about him?" Holt spun her chair to face Sayer, something unidentifiable in her eyes.

"I want to know how Jake actually died. And I want to know why you altered his autopsy." Sayer wasn't totally sure it was true, but she trusted Joan and she had to find out for sure.

"Dammit." Holt turned away to look out the window.

Sayer's stomach fell. "So it *is* true."

"How?" Holt asked.

Sayer realized she couldn't throw Joan under the bus. "We were looking over the files for discrepancies and found the changes you made. Ezra couldn't access the original, but it looks like you changed almost the entire file."

Holt's nostrils flared. Eyes reflecting no anger, only pain. "Sayer, I'm trying to protect you and your career. And this unit."

"You know I don't want your protection. I want the truth."

Holt bowed her head slightly in acquiescence. "When this case is done, okay? Let me put out one inferno at a time."

"You know I won't let it go, right? I won't let myself focus on that right now, but I can't let it go."

"I know."

Without another word, Sayer left.

MOUNTAIN ROADS, VA

As dusk approached, Sayer and Vik followed Andy Wagner.

Andy left Quantico in his old white Suburban and headed south into the mountains. A ceiling of low gray clouds rolled in as they wound along country roads. In the rain-heavy light, white flowers exploded along honeysuckle vines. A breeze blew through the window, cooling the damp sweat on the back of Sayer's neck.

It was almost possible to forget that they were hunting a murderer.

They rode in silence, both contemplating the fact that they were tailing one of their own.

Sayer's phone buzzed and she broke the silence. "It's Joan. They found Andy's fingerprints on the equipment we found in the closet. She'll test the other material to see if they can match it to the chemicals he'd need. But holy hell, man, I can't quite believe this. Andy Wagner . . ."

"What's his deal? I mean, he's clearly a troglodyte, but where's he even from?" Vik asked.

Sayer chuckled. "He's from Westchester, Virginia, what we called 'horse country' growing up. The people there live in mansions and go on foxhunts, do cotillion, debutantes and all that. Basically rich country folk who think they're British aristocracy."

Vik nodded. "Makes sense, he's got the entitled-jerk thing down pat."

"Yeah, he mostly just annoys me, but man he sure pushes Joan's buttons. You see her face when he got all pushy during that task force meeting?" Sayer let her mind drift to the medical examiner. "Joan's pretty messed up about this one."

"She and Andy weren't close, were they?"

"No way. No one's close to Andy. I just think she feels responsible. Her lab might have missed something that ended up getting who knows how many people wrongfully convicted."

"Yeah. Plus I think knowing Adi's still out there is really freaking her out," Vik said.

"Freaking us all out. Though right now I sure as hell hope Adi's still out there."

"I could say the same to you, though," Vik added. "I mean, you look like total hell." He flashed a Cheshire-cat grin at her.

Sayer snorted but then grew serious. "It is, though. Messing me up, I mean."

Vik nodded with understanding. "Sorry, I'm feeling pretty pissed off right now. I just can't believe Andy did this."

"Yeah, me too." Sayer pondered. "Hey, in the video he used the phrase 'beyond the veil' twice. That some kind of religious reference or something?"

"Not that I'm familiar with."

They returned to silence, trailing far behind, following the dot on Sayer's phone pinging from the tracker they put on his car.

After another thirty minutes, Andy turned onto a gravel driveway and Vik pulled to the side of the road. A trail of gray dust rose to meet the low sky as Andy wound up the long driveway. Through a thick copse of oak trees, Sayer and Vik could barely see Andy come to a stop in front of a small log cabin.

He got out of his car and hurried inside.

"This his home address?" Vik asked.

Sayer shook her head. "Nope, this address isn't on his file at all."

"We go in or wait him out?"

"I think we've got to go in. What if Adi is in there? We've got the fingerprints on the equipment as probable cause. . . ."

"Call SWAT?"

Sayer hesitated. She wanted to bring Andy in herself, but he was an FBI agent, highly trained, and obviously willing to kill. "Yeah, let's call them in."

"While we wait, let's get close, see what we can see?" Vik adjusted his belt.

"Perfect," Sayer said.

They radioed for the SWAT team and then slipped from the car, hands on their guns, rage in their hearts.

Sayer and Vik made their way up the hillside. Oak trees creaked and groaned around them as the wind picked up, bowing majestic branches to and fro. Storm clouds towered far above, blocking out the setting sun, blanketing the mountains in a darkening gray.

Andy Wagner's cabin sat in a small clearing. A thin layer of moss grew on the northern side of the old cabin. Its front porch leaned precariously to the side, suggesting a rotting foundation. Sayer gestured around back, and Vik nodded.

Gravel crunched under their feet as they crossed the driveway. Crouching low, they made it to the cabin and pressed themselves against the worn logs. Sayer pointed to the window and then, slowly, cautiously, peeked above the sill.

Inside, deer heads adorned the walls. A fully loaded gun rack sat above a collapsing sofa. Faded kelly-green carpet looked so thin it was almost possible to see the floor underneath. A dusty copy of *Dogs Playing Poker* hung above the stone fireplace.

In the dim light, Andy sat in the kitchen packing a small back-pack. Sayer gestured for Vik to come look as well. Together they watched Andy shove tools, a cloth tarp, and a length of rope into his bag. He stood and strapped a long knife to his belt.

Finally Andy pulled on a headlamp and lifted a shotgun from the rack.

Realizing he was heading for the door, Sayer and Vik dove behind a woodpile, flattening themselves onto the cool dirt.

Sayer leaned into the wood remembering all the creatures that liked to nest in woodpiles. Snakes, brown recluse spiders. Also snakes.

Vik pressed next to her and she could practically hear his heart pounding.

Andy tromped down the back stairs in heavy boots and strode off into the dense woods. They waited a long moment and then cautiously followed, guns drawn.

Though they could easily see Andy's headlamp, Sayer didn't dare turn on her own flashlight and so they fumbled along, trying to re-main silent without getting too far behind.

Dusk descended into total darkness as the first drops of rain began to fall.

Sayer's foot caught on a slender root and she stumbled forward. Vik reached out with his free hand to steady her.

Where was Andy heading? Some kind of underground chamber? Was this his lair? Would he have Adi there?

Andy slowly pulled farther and farther away from them until Sayer felt like she had to rush. She hoped the light rain and gusting wind would cover any sounds they made.

Then Andy's light went dark.

Sayer and Vik froze, backs pressed together. A shiver raised the hair on Sayer's arms. The cold rain began to soak her clothes. Night sounds of animals shuffled in the trees overhead. This was why she hated nature.

The rustling darkness extended into a full minute of vigilance. Sayer started to wonder if they had just missed Andy going below-ground.

Less than a few feet away, a large animal rushed them from behind. As Sayer spun, a spotlight burst on, blinding her.

She blinked rapidly, gun pointing at the headlamp.

"Sayer? Vik? What in the ever-loving hell are you doing out here with your guns drawn?"

The light lowered and Andy's face appeared.

"Andy." Sayer acknowledged him. "You want to get the light out of our faces and put down that gun?"

"My gun . . . what the hell is going on here?"

"Gun down, Andy," Sayer said firmly.

"You first. You and Vik look like you're about to shoot me. What the hell?"

"Not a chance. We know what you've done. We're here to bring you in. SWAT will be here any minute."

"What I've done . . . ? What the hell d'you think I've done? I'm just out here checking my rabbit snares."

Sayer didn't respond.

Andy shined the light back and forth between Sayer and Vik and then threw back his head with a gut-shaking laugh. "Are you trying to pin some shit on me? That's rich."

"If you haven't done anything, then just come in with us and clear everything up."

"You're serious?" Andy turned to Vik. "Is she serious?"

"For sure," Vik said.

His laughter transformed into rage as he refocused on Sayer. "You bitch. Are you setting me up for something?" His eyes widened. "I know you hate me, but are you actually setting me up for this Van Hurst mess?"

She tightened her grip on her gun, relaxing her trigger finger in case she had to fire.

"You coming with us or should we wait for SWAT to arrive?"

"Holy shit, you really are serious." His eyes wandered to the woods.

"Don't even think about it, Andy."

He let out a harsh laugh. "You know, I could live out here for months." He held up his hands and slowly lowered the shotgun. "But you know what? I'm going with you. And when this is over, I'm going to destroy your career. You are going to crash and burn, Altair. You're done."

Sayer moved in and roughly cuffed him. "You know what?" she asked as she pulled his hunting knife from its sheath. "You aren't even the first person to threaten me with career destruction this week. Maybe work on a more original threat next time." She yanked him to start moving.

They made it back to the cabin just as the SWAT team arrived. They took over the scene, transporting Andy back to Quantico. As he climbed into the van, he silently stared at Sayer with burning hatred.

The search team arrived with dogs and began a sweep of the surrounding mountains.

Sayer watched them range up into the mountains, hounds baying with excitement.

Vik came out of the house and stood next to her. "We'll get a full search going in the morning."

"Anything in the house?"

"Nah. It's clean as a whistle. Nothing to tie him to the Death Walker cases."

Sayer let out a long breath. She'd been hoping this was it. They would find Adi and be done with this goddamned case. "We know whose cabin this is?"

"His uncle's. But it sounds like Andy's been living here for about a month."

"Why?"

"Just got off the phone with the team at Andy's house. They talked to the wife. Apparently she kicked him out."

Sayer grunted. "Can't blame her. She willing to say why?"

"Just because he's an asshole, sounds like."

"Amen." Sayer paused by Andy's car, prying the small tracker off his bumper and dropping it into her pocket. "Okay, so he's living up there. There's no sign of any underground structures, but we'll have the infrared cameras up at first light. Crime scene is at Andy's house tearing it apart." She turned to Vik. "Shall we go see what Andy has to say for himself now?"

"Let's do it," Vik said with a fake British accent.

"He's lawyered up." Holt stood outside the interrogation room looking royally pissed. Her full Valkyrie fury burned in her eyes. Sayer felt a moment of relief; defeated Holt was not something she ever wanted to see again.

"What else?" Holt barked.

"We're looking for any other properties he had access to. Search teams are ready to go at dawn around the cabin. Warrant's being served at his house right now. Crime scene is there and, well, you know."

"They still all working overtime?"

Sayer nodded. "For sure. Anything's there, they'll find it."

"Good." Holt stared through the one-way window. "You really think Andy Wagner killed all those people? I mean, I knew he was an asshole, but this is beyond the pale."

Sayer stared as well. Andy had lost some of his bluster, but he still looked angry. He held his hands in a ball. His bloodshot eyes slid around the room slowly. Sayer let a moment of pure schadenfreude wash over her. "Couldn't happen to a better guy . . ."

"It's not funny, Sayer. I need you to be sure. This unsub is a master of manipulation, so you'd better double-check everything. I want his lawyer talking about pleading out before we step into a courtroom. We might have to admit we royally cocked this one up, but we don't need our dirty laundry aired in court."

Holt gave Sayer a hard pat on the back and walked away.

Her phone buzzed and Sayer read the text as Vik arrived.

"News?" he asked.

"Yeah." She looked up, a grin on her face. "They found more equipment in Andy's garage. Plus, they found a stack of ancient-religion books and a stash of powder that they think might be DMT."

Vik looked a little stricken. "Man, you think he really did it?"

"We'll see, I guess."

"I still can't wrap my head around it. I've worked with Andy for years and he's smart, like verging on creepy smart."

"Well, our profile did say this unsub would be unusually intelligent."

"Yeah." Vik ran a hand through his hair. "Holt said he's lawyered up so he won't be saying anything tonight. I'm gonna go home and get some sleep so we can hit the ground running tomorrow morning." He tilted his chin up in a farewell and headed off.

Sayer remained, staring at Andy. She simply couldn't believe that she'd worked alongside a killer for so long, but then she was always surprised when she finally caught a killer. They were always more mundane, less frightening than she expected. People like to imagine serial killers as avatars of pure evil, but the reality was far more terrifying—true evil is nothing more than some guy with a tweaked brain. The real monsters are just human beings cut loose from the thin moral bonds that hold us.

However much she hated Andy Wagner, he was nothing more than a man, and she would relish watching him pay for what he'd done, but she also wanted to understand why. Had he been abused as a child? Was he a sociopath from birth? Was there something she could have done to stop him before he even began? Plus, some part of her still wasn't fully convinced.

The overwhelming urge to find out compelled her into the room. Andy's nostrils flared with rage as she sat across from him.

"Your lawyer probably won't make it till morning," Sayer said.

They sat across from each other for a long while, Sayer examining his expressions. His anger, his desire to hurt her.

"We found the stuff in your garage," she poked at him.

"I want my lawyer," he replied.

"I'm not asking you anything, just updating you."

"You know I wrote the fucking FBI handbook on interrogation, right?" Andy pushed his balled fists into the table, causing his knuckles to go white.

"I do, thanks for that." Sayer flashed a smile just to annoy him further. "Did you know they say that psychopaths are particularly skilled at manipulation? A study last year showed that psychopaths were far better than average people at picking victims. They had 'em watch videos of people walking, and from their body language, the psychopaths could tell who had recently been a victim of a violent crime."

Sayer leaned a little closer.

"People like you can read other people. You know what someone's gut is telling them and you play with that. You know who you can victimize. Who better to write the book on interviewing other psychopaths?" Sayer blinked innocently.

Andy looked away, struggling not to respond.

"The best part, all those profiles . . . now everyone will see how you made them so perfect. You wrote the profile, and then just framed some poor guy who fit it to a T."

Andy exploded, lunging at Sayer. The handcuffs snapped and the table scooted ever so slightly, but Sayer sat calmly just out of reach.

"I'm the best profiler in the world, you bitch. Just because your research isn't worth a crap doesn't mean mine isn't."

Sayer rolled her hand. "Yeah, yeah. We also found out that your code was used to access the lab suite at night. Over and over again you snuck down there. I wonder how long it took you to get the DNA right."

She stood up to go. "You know, the real kicker was your name on the logs at the park and storage unit. That was how we finally figured out it was you."

Sayer watched a flicker of fear cross Andy's face as she left. The genuine depth of the look broke something loose in Sayer's mind.

VIRGINIA MOUNTAINS

Sayer roared away, troubled. Something on Andy's face triggered a gut feeling that Sayer couldn't ignore. The evidence against him was lining up perfectly. Too perfectly. Andy was certainly the perfect patsy; everyone hated him. He was belligerent and bigoted. Even Sayer was enjoying watching him squirm.

The rumbling bike woke up her bruises so that her entire body ached. Her eyes burned in the cold air but she left her visor up, wanting the shock to her face. She flew along the back roads, forcing herself to free her mind, let whatever was bubbling to the surface flow.

She thought back to Dugald Tarlington. His tears over the JCPenney catalog had made her gut twinge. She'd felt deep down that he wasn't the kind of man to strangle four women. But then she'd dismissed it as nothing more than the work of a brilliant killer. She'd had the same gut feeling about Winters and had ignored it then too. When had she lost faith in her own instincts?

When Jake died, that's when. She knew she needed a curtain in her own mind to do this job, but what walls had she put up to deal with his death? Her own need to cordon off parts of herself meant that she cut off the things that had once made her a good investigator—her passion, her instincts, the wild connections she could make. She was shutting down the very parts of herself that made her the best at what she did.

Sayer pulled over to the side of the road and turned off her motorcycle. The night sounds of the forest replaced the sudden silence. The smell of damp soil and fresh leaves filled her nose. High clouds rushed across the moon.

For a few minutes, Sayer let herself think about Jake. About the sound of his laugh. The burn of his stubble on her lips. The sense of so much loss welled in her chest. She missed him. She longed for just one more moment to feel his warm arms around her. A tear leaked from the corner of her eye. She struggled to keep the emotion in, but the floodgates burst and a sob racked her entire body. Still looking up at the moon, she shuddered and cried for everything that could have been and never would.

She had never let herself mourn, and it was destroying her from the inside out. So she let the sorrow consume her until tears could no longer fall.

In the empty space left behind, Sayer felt something new. A release of something she'd held locked inside. Balling up her feelings about Jake had allowed her own beliefs and values to become twisted as well. She knew the answer to Adi's question about justice versus vengeance. She might hate Andy, she might want him to pay for all the jabs and smug insinuations that Sayer couldn't do her job, but her desire for vengeance was clouding her ability to seek justice.

Buried deep under her intense dislike of Andy, her gut was telling her he was innocent. She was letting her own anger and hurt get in the way of what she knew was right. Finding the real killer, catching him, and putting him behind bars would strip away the dark hand of anger clenching her heart.

"I keep following the trail of evidence and it keeps leading me to a clear conclusion. But we know our unsub manipulates evidence. Why would this case be any different? Stop considering evidence, Sayer," she said to herself. "Start considering the bigger picture. Start listening to your goddamned gut."

An owl hooted as if in response, and Sayer smiled. A real smile.

She drove back to Quantico knowing what she had to do. She didn't like it, but it was the right thing.

Andy sat half dozing, still handcuffed to the table. He opened his eyes and frowned. "You come back to gloat some more?"

"No." Sayer sat down. "I just spent the last hour thinking about this case and you're right."

Andy rolled his eyes. "Yeah, I remember this part of the book I wrote. Try to get the subject to feel like you're on their side."

"No, listen. I went and looked at the lab equipment we found in the closet."

"Is that what you're using to frame me?" Andy seemed angry but also deflated. Tired.

"I'm not framing you; just shut up and listen because I think someone else is."

Andy raised his eyebrows. "Okay."

"Know what I found?"

"Let me guess, you found my fingerprints."

"No," Sayer said.

"No? Then why the hell am I locked in here?"

"I found your fingerprint. Singular. I found bottles wiped clean except for a single, perfect fingerprint."

Andy's eyebrows went even higher.

"Exactly what I'd expect if the fingerprint was planted," Sayer continued. "But there's a hell of a lot of evidence, Andy. Like a mountain of evidence that I need convincing isn't real."

"I don't even know what you think you've got on me."

Sayer paused, hoping she wasn't just about to make a colossal mistake. If Andy really was the killer, the worst thing she could do would be to tip him off to all the evidence against him. She searched his bloodshot eyes and knew she was right.

"The lab stuff we found in your garage?"

"Easy to plant." Andy shrugged. "You see that place? My wife's practically a hoarder. It's like a five-and-dime store piled to the rafters with junk."

"So someone sneaks in and plants it . . ."

Andy sat up straighter. "Yeah, did you find anything at my uncle's cabin?"

"No."

"Right, so whoever framed me didn't know I got the boot from my wife. Didn't know they should've planted the stuff up there instead."

Sayer sat up more as well. "Okay. And if you really were the Death Walker, you'd certainly need your equipment wherever you were." She leaned back, thinking. "You know anything about computers?"

Andy snorted. "I use my index fingers to type my reports."

"So, no way you hacked the files. What about your name on the visitor logs at Shenandoah National Park and the storage unit?"

Andy shrugged. "I've never been to that park. You saw my cabin; I like my nature with a dash of dead animal. Also never heard of the storage unit. Handwriting isn't all that hard to fake. It's why courts hardly ever admit it into evidence."

Sayer nodded, agreeing. "Okay, that's fair. What about that day we bumped into each other? You looked guilty as hell."

Andy shifted uncomfortably in his seat. "Yeah . . . that's why Janey kicked me out."

"What?"

"I was on the phone with . . . my girlfriend."

Sayer groaned. "God, you're a piece of work. Okay, so you go into the closet to talk to your mistress? Who knows that?"

"No one, far as I know. Maybe someone in the ME's lab since it's right next to the door?"

"Fine. How about your PIN code? Someone entered it to go into the lab suite at night."

Again Andy shrugged. "No clue. Sorry to say. You really think it's someone inside? One of us?"

Sayer nodded, thinking.

"Well, anyone could just watch me enter my code. That's not exactly rocket science."

"Whoever did this has pretty extensive computer knowledge. They probably just hacked your file and looked up your code." She watched Andy regaining some of his swagger. "Why are you such an asshole, anyway?"

"Because people like you come in and get everything handed to you on a silver platter while old guys like me have to work our asses off."

Sayer rolled her eyes. "Which part of my life was handed to me? When I watched my parents die in a car accident when I was nine? The murder of my fiancé? The fact that you and everyone else here seems to think my research is worthless? Or the fact that I'm lead on a case that will go down in the history of the FBI as the biggest failure in the history of failures, including at least two false arrests, a lab scandal of epic proportion, and a grieving senator who will make sure this all comes out in the end—"

Andy actually laughed. "Well, when you put it that way, I'm a little bit glad to be on this side of the table."

Sayer let out a long sigh. "You're a dying breed, Andy Wagner. And thank God for that. But that doesn't mean you're a serial killer." She put her head down into her hands and her entire body screamed for rest. She felt her eyes flutter closed and her body relax, demanding sleep.

She jolted herself up. "All right, Andy. I'm convinced. Nothing I can do tonight."

"Know what you can do?" Andy pulled his face into an angry grimace. "You can bring me a copy of the case files. All of 'em. Kent,

Middleton, Tarlington, and Winters. I want to look at them together and come up with a new profile. This bastard tried to frame me and I'm going to help you stop him."

Sayer pondered for a very long time. If Andy turned out to be the killer, this would be a huge breach of ethics, but Sayer was done ignoring her instincts. "All right, Andy. I'll have the files sent down to you before I head out. I'll tell the guard you have permission to call me if you find something."

"Thanks, Altair. You might not be as bad an agent as I thought." Andy pressed his lips together with vague disgust.

"High praise, indeed," she said as she let herself out.

Sayer barely remembered driving home and crawling into bed with Vesper with her clothes still on. The last thing she thought was, *If it isn't Andy, then who?*

Unable to answer her question, Sayer fell into a dreamless sleep.

The doorbell jolted Sayer awake. She fumbled for her phone.

Dammit, not even midnight. She'd just fallen asleep.

Sayer stumbled down the hall. Vesper barely lifted his head from the pillow as she left.

She looked through the peephole and saw Joan, so she pulled open the door.

"Oh no! I've woken you." Joan cringed at Sayer, hair a massive pouf atop her head, clothes rumpled. "I didn't expect you to be asleep already." The exhaustion pulled Joan's face into new worry lines that Sayer had never seen before. Her eyes looked rheumy and skittered around.

"No worries, I just fell asleep. Is everything okay?" Sayer gently took her arm and pulled her inside. Something about Joan's demeanor was seriously concerning. Was she about to have a nervous breakdown?

"I heard you went to talk to Andy twice this evening." Joan wore sneakers and a baggy navy-blue tracksuit, her hair pulled back into a slick bun.

Sayer had never seen Joan without her signature knee-length skirt and Mary Janes.

"Yeah, I went to talk to him."

"You don't think he did it," Joan said matter-of-factly.

"I don't. Do you?"

"I've got access to the same data you do. I'm sure it's occurred to all of us, but I dismissed it. Too much evidence against him, and it just feels right to me."

Something about her attempt to convince Sayer of Andy's guilt sent up a small red flag. "Yeah, I'm not saying that I'm sure Andy's innocent, but it'll take a lot to convince me that this isn't just another frame job. Everything feels a little bit too much like all the other cases, you know? Forensics make him look guilty as hell, but the motive just doesn't add up for me." Sayer gestured for Joan to follow her into the kitchen. "Let me put on some coffee; I'd love to bounce thoughts off you. You can be my reality check."

"What do you mean?" Joan asked as she followed Sayer.

"We've been looking at Andy's profiles and assuming that he was using these murders to advance his career. But that's just a little far-fetched. We even said it ourselves: this murder is about walking the line between life and death. That's the obsession, so how do Andy's career goals fit into that? You think I'm crazy?"

"No, but I think maybe you're . . . overthinking perhaps." Joan perched on the edge of a seat, hands folded in her lap. "You know how it is with these types of unsubs; sometimes you never figure it out. We may never know why Andy is so obsessed with what's beyond the veil."

The comment sent up a huge red flag in Sayer's gut. Something wasn't right.

"Fair enough," Sayer said. "Hell, I might be hallucinating all of this. I can't even tell which way's up right now and I'm pretty sure I haven't slept in six months according to the way my body feels."

Sayer's phone buzzed in the bedroom and she held up an apologetic finger to Joan while she shuffled to get it.

"Hey, hope I didn't wake you." Ezra's voice sounded hoarse.

"Nah, just sitting here talking to Joan about Andy."

"Yeah, well, I just finished combing the medical files from Quantico and found a few twins. I know we've got Andy but wanted to fill you in anyway."

"You went through every single person's file one at a time?"

Vesper curled around Sayer's feet and groaned as he immediately fell back asleep.

"Yep, took me all day," Ezra said.

"Nothing more in Andy's file?"

"Nada, zip, zilch, zero on the twin front. Three people that work at Quantico have twins."

Sayer sighed. "Okay, e-mail me the info and I'll double-check tomorrow."

"I also found one other twin-related thing, but it's kind of crazy."

"Oh yeah?" Sayer said as the phone buzzed. She looked at the screen, someone calling from the FBI. "Hey, Ezra, can you hang on a sec, I've got another call coming in."

"Yep, I'm not going anywhere. Har har."

Sayer let out a laugh and clicked over.

"It's a woman." Andy's voice was loud with excitement.

"Whoa, what?"

"I missed it just looking at each case alone, but the pattern's there when I look at all the cases together."

"What're you talking about, Andy?" Sayer's heartbeat sped up a notch.

"It's not any one thing, but the unsub in each case is described as small. They used a wheelbarrow to move bodies. They seem sickly or weak. That, combined with the complete lack of sexual assault in all the cases, I can feel it in my bones that we're looking for a woman."

"Okay, Andy . . . I've got Ezra on the other line. Let me think about that and I'll follow up in the morning."

Andy just grunted agreement and hung up.

Sayer let Andy's idea sink in as she clicked back over to Ezra. "Sorry about that. What's the crazy twin thing you found?"

"Well, it seems kind of ridiculous, but whatever, in for a penny and all that." He paused. "So, Joan's got some medical problem from a twin that died in utero."

"Oh yeah?" Sayer glanced out into the kitchen, where Joan sat, hands still folded in her lap.

"Yeah, I had to look it up, it's a rare disorder called fetus in fetu or vanishing twin syndrome. It happens when there are twins in utero but then one twin's body basically absorbs the other. It can cause serious medical problems, but most of the time all it does is creep people out."

"How so?" Sayer kept her voice even.

"Apparently, one twin absorbs the other, so, depending on how far along the second fetus is, it can have, like, a fully formed body that gets sucked into the other twin's body. Sometimes the twin can emerge later. Like some kid in Kazakhstan who went to the hospital with a distended belly. Doctors operated expecting to remove a big ole cyst. Instead, they found his twin inside his body like a parasitic growth. The fetus was basically complete with hair, eyes, teeth, even a face."

"Whoa."

"Yeah, it's crazy, like some people have whole body parts sticking out of their own. But apparently Joan's isn't messing with her physically so it's just an addendum in her file."

"Okay, thanks, Ezra." Once again Sayer felt faint twinges of concern in her gut.

"One more thing. So I cross-checked the dates from the photo album. Andy was in town in March when the photos skipped a week. But . . . uh, after this twin thing I checked Joan . . ."

"And?"

"And, Joan went to some forensics conference in March. Sayer, Joan was out of town that week. That's pretty weird, right?" he asked. "Is she there with you? Should we be freaked out?"

"Thanks, Ezra. I'll get back to you in a few minutes, okay?" Sayer needed a moment to think.

"Uh, Sayer—"

She hung up on him midsentence and stood in the dark, letting the sickly tingle of fear creep up her spine. When it reached her head, it turned into an electric buzz.

Images flashed like a strobe light.

Joan typing away at the computer like a pro, clearly knowledgeable about the FBI file systems, maybe even able to hack the system.

Joan talking about the unsub, never using the word *he* to describe the killer, always *the unsub*. Naming the killer the Death Walker and then using the name over and over as if it pleased her.

Joan coming in to help her and Vik with the research files when she had no reason to.

Joan's DNA found at the murder scene, dismissed as contamination.

Joan who did the autopsy on Mrs. Van Hurst and would have known about the dead twin from her medical records.

Joan out of town the same week as the killer.

Joan using the term *beyond the veil* just moments ago. The very same term used in the videos.

Beyond the veil. The unusual phrase echoed inside Sayer's head until she couldn't hear anything but the roar of certainty.

Add Andy's conviction that the Death Walker was a woman and the final piece dropped into place.

Joan was the Death Walker.

She ran through mental gymnastics, denying that it could be true. How ridiculous it was to think that the tiny little medical examiner, Joan Warren, could be a serial killer.

But every fiber of Sayer's instinct screamed that she was right.

"Sayer, you okay? Was that Ezra?" Joan called from the kitchen.

Sayer managed to croak out a "Yeah," as she tried to control her breathing. "Hang on."

Her gun sat out on the table next to Joan.

Hell, she could be totally wrong; maybe lack of sleep really was messing with her brain. How could Joan possibly be the Death Walker? Sayer needed some time to think.

She felt the small tracker still in her pocket. New plan. Plant the tracker; get Joan out of here, making sure she didn't know that Sayer suspected her; and then follow to see where Joan went. That was the answer.

With a deep breath, she shuffled back out.

"Sorry about that. Ezra just letting me know that he didn't find anything more on Andy."

"He found something, though?" Joan smoothed her hair back primly.

"Nah, just looking for more people with twins." Sayer's throat felt tight with the effort of relaxing her entire body despite the fact that it vibrated with the certainty that she was staring into the face of the most accomplished serial killer she'd ever met. Instead of lunging across the table to throttle the truth out of Joan, Sayer gave a half shrug. "He found a few, so he's sending me over a list, but it sounds like a dead end. I'm going to call him back in a few minutes after I take a look."

Joan tilted her head, skittering eyes on Sayer. She stared for just a half second too long and Sayer swallowed. Her throat was so tight it made an almost comical gulping sound. Her fingers closed over the tracker.

"So . . ." Sayer tried to smile warmly. "Was there something else you wanted to talk about tonight? 'Cause if not, I think I could actually use some sleep."

"Not tonight. I just couldn't sleep and heard that you talked to Andy, so . . . I just wanted to see if you'd learned anything new."

Joan pointed the gun at the dog and pulled the trigger.

Vesper yelped, releasing her. He fell to the floor, whimpering, and Joan kicked him, spinning his body into the corner.

Sayer lunged with a cry.

Her body slammed into Joan's, but the small woman managed to remain on her feet. She sprang back and turned the gun back on Sayer.

The two women froze, panting. Sayer realized she was looking into a well of true madness.

"You are a terrible liar." Joan chuckled, her face burning with manic triumph. She didn't even seem to notice the dog bite on her arm.

Sayer stared at Vesper's still body, then up at Joan, her mind reeling. "You killed Cindy. One of us. How could you?"

"One of . . . us." Joan threw her head back and laughed. "One of you, you mean. You think I'm one of you? You saw my work, Sayer. You know what I am."

"You're a murderer." Sayer's left arm spasmed, muscles clenching in pain. She pressed her palm to her shoulder and tried to focus.

"I'm a scientist," Joan spat. "Doing important research."

"Those traps weren't part of your research."

"Yes, yes, that's true." Joan cocked her head at an odd angle. "Though it was part of the fun. I only wish I'd figured out just how much fun before now." The wild grin spread back across her face. "Everyone just cared so damn much this time. Those pathetic evidence techs practically stopped eating and sleeping."

"You enjoyed watching that?" Sayer couldn't keep the disgust out of her voice.

"Oh, I enjoyed watching it all. I knew I needed to be inside the FBI when I started my research, but I had no idea how much fun it would be to pull the strings of the investigations." She cackled.

Sayer sought an opening. A moment of distraction she could use to attack.

"Feeding you all clues, watching you jump, watching you put the

"Sorry, Joan. Maybe tomorrow everything will seem mor— The two women stood up and paused for another slightly-to moment. The hair stood up on Sayer's arms as she struggled shudder. She glanced at her gun sitting on the table and almost rea for it, but she wondered if she could actually use it against Joan. rule of guns: don't pull it if you aren't willing to use it. Could she sh the woman she had considered a friend for so long?

Sayer decided she just wanted to get Joan out of there. She began t move toward the door, prompting Joan to follow. As she walked to the door, her body felt jerky as she tried to look natural. The back of her neck prickled as Joan walked directly behind her. She turned to flash what she hoped was a normal smile and opened the door. She reached out and gave Joan's shoulder a pat, releasing the tracker into the loose pocket of her jacket.

Joan paused and then smiled as well. "Sleep well." She stepped outside.

"Good night, Joan." Sayer began to shut the door.

In a flash of movement, Joan slammed her body backward. The door flew into Sayer, sending her stumbling into the wall.

Before she could right herself, Joan yanked out a small gun and pulled the trigger. Sayer heard the small *pft* of the silenced gun. She gasped as her left shoulder exploded with pain. The intensity blinded her, her vision collapsing into white static.

She sagged back into the wall, hand pressed to the small hole in her shoulder. Blood oozed between her fingers, sticky and warm. The sharp iron tang filled the room.

The sound of Vesper growling snapped Sayer back. As her fight instinct kicked into gear, adrenaline flooded Sayer's body. The entire world became high contrast, sharp and clear.

Vesper flew at Joan from the bedroom, growling with guttural rage.

Joan spun toward the dog as the silver streak collided with her. She threw up her arm and he clamped down. The wet sound of puncturing flesh accompanied Joan's scream.

puzzle together. Leaking everything to the media. It was like writing a mystery novel: throw in a few red herrings, a few exciting break-throughs . . . honestly, it's better than any of those crime drama TV shows."

Joan took a satisfied deep breath. "And you, Sayer, oh, you were the most fun of all. This case really got to you, and I had a front-row seat to watch all your little defense mechanisms crumble. I'm just happy to see that my Joan persona worked so well. You had no clue, did you?"

"No, I didn't," Sayer said, determined to keep her talking.

"Good. Good. Joan was meant to be the opposite of a killer. Sweet, thoughtful, a little prude. Really, Joan was meant to be the last person you'd ever suspect. A well-timed voice crack here, a tear there. Lots of stiff upper lip barely concealing how much she cared. God, what a horribly boring person Joan was. So, what gave me away at the end? Ezra find out about my . . . sister?"

Sayer shook her head. "Deep down I knew. Once I realized it wasn't Andy, I put the pieces together. So, why frame Andy?" Sayer swayed, trying to think of a way to get away from Joan.

Again Joan laughed, waving the gun languidly. Her physicality was so different Sayer would never have even recognized the woman she'd known for so many years. Joan's shoulders sat back and down, her limbs fluid, lips open in a relaxed pout.

"I needed a backup plan. Kind of a meta-frame, if you will." Joan chuckled. "I'll admit, by this point, I didn't expect to even need it. I got away with framing those men for so long, I thought the FBI would never figure it out. I was a little disappointed, but then . . . finally, you landed one of my cases."

She looked wistfully away and Sayer tensed to attack.

Joan noticed. "Eh, eh, not a chance. I'm just trying to figure out how to get out of here without killing you."

Sayer glanced down at her shoulder, blood soaking the front of her shirt.

"Oh, don't worry, it's a clean shot. I plan to keep you alive."

Sayer looked back up at Joan. "Why?"

"Because, after I complete the final step, I have to disappear forever. I want someone here to know what I've done. It's why I sent you my files." Joan's eyes gleamed. "You're going to be my biographer. Tell the world about my research!"

"Final step?" Sayer asked.

Joan ignored her. "I knew you would appreciate my files."

"I could never appreciate what you did to those women," Sayer spat.

Joan tilted her head with bemusement. "Now, Sayer, I believe that you called my work . . . what was it? Groundbreaking. Brilliant. The pinnacle of a lifetime of work!"

"The pinnacle . . ." Sayer desperately sought some kind of weapon. Her gun in the kitchen was too far away. She needed something to throw at Joan, but her concentration blurred with pain.

Joan paused and a faint smile passed her thin lips. "Do you know what brain death is?"

"The irreversible cessation of all functions of the entire brain, including the brain stem." Sayer recited the official definition.

"But you know it's more complicated than that."

"I do."

"Back in the old days, when someone's heart or breathing stopped, they were dead—"

Sayer tried to inch forward but her vision swam, the room tilting slightly. "But now we have machines that can keep us breathing and our lungs working forever." She huffed with pain.

"Yes, yes, exactly right!" Joan did a little hop back and forth with glee. "So, without the heart and lungs, determination of death comes down to the brain," she said, shuffling with pleasure. "But the brain is intensely complex."

"You do remember that I'm a neuroscientist, right?" Sayer tried to keep the anger from leaking into her voice.

"I do. It's why I chose you for my files. And yes, brain death is certainly associated with the brain stem. Without a functioning brain stem, everything breaks down. But what about that gray area in between, when only a small portion of the brain stem functions? What about when the brain stem is undamaged but everything else is destroyed? It's a conundrum."

"And that's what you were . . . researching?"

"Oh no!" Joan giggled a little with manic glee. "I was only looking for one thing . . . safe passage beyond the veil. We might not know exactly what death is, but we do know it's often a reversible process."

"Near-death experiences—" Sayer said.

"Exactly! I knew you'd understand." Joan's body quivered with emotion. "You said it yourself, there's good science proving that life isn't binary, there is something more than just life and death."

Joan's eyes glossed over with feverish excitement. "People who are technically dead, their hearts stopped, brains quiet, who still see and hear things. They float out of their bodies and travel along a tunnel, into a light." Her voice fell to a whisper. "Beyond the veil."

She poked the gun toward Sayer. "You know I'm right. And I finally realized that all I needed to do was find a way to open the gates in our minds. The DMT." She reveled in her own cleverness. "After my first eight experiments, I finally realized that I was approaching death all wrong. There's just something about the human mind that craves explanation."

Sayer forced her body to move slowly. Muscles quivering, she kept a blank face, hoping the ranting woman would be too caught up in her self-importance to notice.

"I conducted all those experiments on random subjects before I realized that all those earlier subjects had nothing to prime their minds for the journey. No one to cross over and find."

"They were human beings, not subjects," Sayer said.

"Yes, yes, humans . . . and humans need meaning. I added the animals to guide them, the ancient religious imagery, the DMT to simulate death, but most important, a twin to seek out! This was my pinnacle. The DMT–digoxin combination worked! Now I can take the final step. You'll find all of this in my notes."

"The final step for your twin?"

Joan's whole body went rigid. "It's my turn to travel beyond the veil and finish what I started so long ago. You want to see what that bitch does to me every day?" Joan yanked up her shirt. Puckered scars and suture lines mottled her stomach. Joan turned sideways, lifting her arm while still pointing the gun at Sayer. Just below her waist, a row of human teeth emerged from her flesh. Above them, almost at her armpit, long human hair sprouted above the outline of a partial ear just visible beneath the surface of her skin.

Sayer let out an involuntary gasp.

"That's her hair and bone and teeth pushing out from inside me. Once, I coughed up a distal phalanx. When I was twelve, fetal foot bones fell out of my stomach, one by one. I killed her in utero, and since that day, she's been trying to murder me back."

Sayer rocked back, unable to respond.

Joan dropped her shirt, refocusing on Sayer. "I was a murderer before I was even born. Now I'm just fulfilling the last piece of my destiny."

"And so you want to go into the . . . afterlife to find your twin?" Sayer asked, confused.

"To find her and kill her once and for all," Joan spat. "I absorbed my sister in the womb and she dissolved into a thousand fragments. Now she wants me dead. This is the only way to stop her." Joan's eyes flickered with madness.

Her small body shook; her hands trembled. Her eyes rolled erratically.

Sayer prepared to attack.

"Sayer? You okay?"

Both women jumped at the sudden sound of Tino's voice booming from below.

Sayer couldn't let Tino come in! She had no doubt Joan would shoot him.

"I'm good, Tino. Sorry to wake you." Sayer tried to sound calm, but her voice rasped with pain.

Both women waited, Joan's gun steady on Sayer. Silence.

The half-open door swung inward. "You sure?" Tino asked as he stepped in.

"Tino, no!"

Joan swung the gun around and Sayer dove. Seeing the attack, Joan lashed out, punching Sayer in the shoulder.

Sayer collapsed in agony as Joan trained her gun on Tino.

"Hands up. Don't move," Joan barked.

Tino took in the scene, eyes darting from Sayer to Vesper to Joan. He nodded ever so slightly but was far calmer than Sayer would have expected. He smoothly lifted his hands into the air.

Sayer staggered to her knee, desperately pressing her hand to her shoulder to stop the steady trickle of blood. "Don't shoot him, Joan. He's just my neighbor."

Joan's hand shook slightly. Eyes darted around the room looking for an out. She focused on Tino with a grin. "I think your neighbor's going to come with me." She gestured for him to move.

Eyes narrowing, Tino refused to move.

"Move or I will kill you," Joan said.

Sayer nodded for him to go.

Tino understood, and he shuffled slowly out the door. Joan followed close behind.

In the doorway, gun still on Tino, Joan turned. "You know, you weren't supposed to figure it out so quickly. But you're too late. After all these years, I'm finally going to complete my final step." Spittle flew from her mouth as she spoke. "If you follow me, your neighbor and the girl will both die."

Joan forced Tino down the stairs.

Sayer pulled herself up, her vision narrowing at the effort.

She shuddered against the wall for a long moment. She looked over at Vesper, blood staining his silvery fur. She pulled herself over and touched his limp body. "Help's on the way. Come on, Vesper, you're a fighter," she whispered.

Something about the dog's warm fur beneath her hand shattered the last wall inside Sayer's heart. With her self-doubt gone, anger flamed into an inferno raging in her chest. Without any more hesitation, she grabbed a belt, her cuffs, her gun, keys, and phone.

As she stumbled toward her motorcycle, she wrapped the belt around her shoulder and let out an involuntary groan as she pulled it tight over the wound.

The bike roared to life as she dialed Vik.

She frantically explained everything as she brought up the tracking app on her phone.

"Rally SWAT, I'm on her tail. I'll update my location. She's planning to kill them both. Send someone to help Vesper."

She clicked off and throttled the bike so hard the back wheel jittered sideways. She flew after Joan, praying to whatever gods might exist that Tino and Adi would be okay.

UNKNOWN LOCATION

The metal door clanged open.

Adi's eyes peeled open, sparking a cascade of flashing lights. The veins at her temples throbbed like a vise compressing her skull.

She sat up, blinking at the two figures silhouetted by the doorway. Her heart beat faster.

Two people? The police? Someone here to save her?

"Help," she called across the room, unable to fully focus in the bright light.

As they approached, she realized it was a petite woman pointing a gun at a rotund man. The man paled at the sight of her in the cage.

"You okay?" He moved toward her.

"Don't move," the woman barked. He froze.

"You?" Adi stood up in the cage. The woman looked so harmless. Mussed dirty-blond hair, narrow features. But Adi recognized her body language. "You did this to me," she growled.

The woman flashed a manic grin. "Aw, you seem shocked. So glad you'll get to meet the real me. Now you can die knowing what a great contribution you made to the world."

Adi ignored the woman. "I'm Adi," she said to the man.

"Tino." He bowed his head slightly.

"Shut up or I'll shoot one of you," the woman said too loudly. Her head ranged back and forth unnaturally. "I'm keeping you alive because I might need leverage later. But I only need one of you."

"Whatever you want, Joan," Tino said softly to the woman.

The monster gestured Tino toward a pipe. "Sit down. Hands around the pipe."

He complied, but as he looked back at Adi, he winked. Something about the gesture filled her with hope.

The woman cuffed his wrists around the thick pipe. She assessed Tino and Adi, nodding, confident that they weren't going anywhere.

She bustled away from the cage and out the door. A few minutes later she returned, pushing a pallet stacked high with medical equipment. She disappeared behind a wall of boxes and Adi could hear her unloading and assembling something.

Tino gave her a reassuring smile and mouthed, *Don't worry.*

Adi nodded sharply.

"Now, security. Just in case," the woman muttered to herself. She moved around the massive basement with a roll of wire and strange metal boxes.

Finally, she wheeled the smoke machine around the boxes and disappeared from view.

Adi heard the plastic *click-click* of electronics being turned on. Then the raving woman's voice muttering so low Adi couldn't make out the words. It sounded like some kind of prayer, lilting, repetitive, pleading. The woman must have connected a heart rate monitor because a loud *beep-beep, beep-beep* filled the room.

The whirring smoke machine turned on.

Moments later, smoke began to drift above the boxes. Though the woman would get the full effect of the drugged smoke, Adi knew it would eventually fill the room, sending her into another hallucinatory nightmare.

Adi wanted to warn Tino what was about to happen, but she was too afraid to make any noise. Instead, she curled into a ball and waited.

MOUNTAIN ROADS, VA

The motorcycle vibrated over the rough country road, sending bolts of pain like lightning from Sayer's shoulder. Her grip on the handlebar felt weak. Her vision fuzzy.

Despite feeling faint, Sayer rode hard for almost twenty minutes. She called Vik with an update as she pulled up in front of a dilapidated iron gate.

"All right," she said into her mic, "I'm at some kind of old estate." She read off the address.

"Okay, hang tight, Sayer. We're on our way." Vik's voice sounded calm, confident.

Sayer slung her leg off the bike and moaned at the pressure on her shoulder. Blood seeped from beneath the belt. Her shirt stuck to her skin, rubbing the edges of the gunshot wound like sandpaper.

"You know I can't wait. I have no idea how long her plan'll take, but I know she'll kill Adi and Tino when she's done."

"Come on, you can't go in alone."

"Vik, you know I've got to."

Vik sighed. "Be careful, Sayer."

Sayer grunted and clicked off. Gun out, she crouched through the gate toward the looming house.

Moving in the shadows as quickly as she could, Sayer made her way up the massive staircase to the front door. Her eyes flicked from window to window, making sure Joan wasn't watching her approach, about to take a shot.

Marble lions flanked the top of the stairs and she touched one on the head as she crept by. The wet blood on her hand left a red streak across the white stone.

The front door stood ajar and Sayer leaned against the wall just outside. Her body melted against the cool brick, begging her not to move. Would it really be so bad to just rest here awhile? Only a few minutes. As her eyes fluttered shut, the world began to spiral downward.

Her eyes flew open. A jolt of fear that she'd almost passed out brought her back to full attention.

Riding a wave of adrenaline, Sayer moved smoothly into the house, gun up.

Faint moonlight shone through the two-story windows illuminating a grand foyer. Dual marble staircases curved upward. A series of large rooms opened up to the left and center of the first floor. To the right, a single hallway led into darkness.

What next? Tino and Adi had to be here somewhere, but where? The Maya viewed caves as entrances to the underworld. Gwen and Leila had been kept belowground.

If Joan wanted to open the gates of hell, she would do it in the basement.

Sayer moved toward the dark hallway, but her legs wobbled. She fell to one knee, barely catching herself before she toppled over completely. Breathing felt like so much work, almost too much. How could she stand back up if she could barely breathe?

The photo of Leila screaming floated before Sayer's eyes. The blood on her chin. Her eyes lost in terror. Sayer couldn't let that happen to Adi. Or worse.

Trying not to moan, she pushed herself up. A small cry of effort escaped her lips but she got herself upright. Giving up on caution, Sayer strode into the hallway. She knew she didn't have much time before she lost consciousness.

In the kitchen she found a wide, industrial staircase leading down. Stumbling forward, Sayer careened into a large metal door at the bottom.

The door gave easily under her gentle push and she slid inside. A maze of old furniture and boxes wound through a long, cluttered basement. A few bare bulbs hung from the ceiling. In the stark light, she could see a cage hanging halfway across the room.

Thin eddies of yellowish smoke drifted in the air.

Over the roaring of her own heart, Sayer could hear the steady beeping of a heart monitor.

Joan's last experiment had begun.

Sayer's eyes watered at the acrid scent in the room: urine, lavender cleaner, and musty smoke. She hurried toward the cage, head swiveling back and forth, watching for Joan.

The cage hung in a small clearing among the clutter. Inside, Adi lay curled in a ball. A pile of old wrappers and empty water bottles filled one corner of the cage. A bird fluttered in the other corner.

Against the far wall, Tino sat handcuffed to a pipe.

He raised his chin in a greeting. Sayer returned the nod, then limped to the cage.

"Adi?" Sayer slurred.

The girl looked up, frightened.

"Agent Altair?" The girl's eyes darted around with fear. "Are you really here?"

Sayer began to speak.

"Shhhh, she'll kill us if she hears you." Adi pulled herself over until she and Sayer were face-to-face. Both women leaned forward until their foreheads touched through the bars. Sayer wrapped her fingers over Adi's.

"Is she here?" Sayer whispered.

"Behind those boxes. I think she's hooked herself up to the machines."

Sayer squinted into the smoke, torn between the need to get Adi out of the cage and the desire to stop Joan's sick experiment. She should secure Joan, but she just couldn't bring herself to leave Adi behind. If Sayer didn't make it, the least she could do was make sure Adi got away.

"Hang on, I've got an idea." Sayer let go of Adi and roved her hands along the edges of the cage until she felt a bolt just inside the corner.

"I can pry off these bolts." Sayer looked around for some sort of tool. "I just need something metal to get you out of here."

Adi blinked a few times as if confused, but then she set her mouth in a determined line. She slid her hand along the side of her pant leg and pulled out a short metal bar.

Sayer nodded appreciatively and took the bar. She forced the slender edge under the side of the bolt, bowing the thick metal back and forth with effort.

As she pushed, Sayer glanced over her shoulder. Was Joan crouching nearby, camouflaged by the swirling smoke? The back of her neck tingled, anticipating a thrusting knife or a gunshot at any moment.

The bar dug into Sayer's palms as she strained to lean her entire weight onto the bolt. The effort pushed her wound against the belt and she let out a grunt of pain.

The bolt snapped.

The sharp crack triggered a spike of terror and Sayer spun around, heart fluttering with the conviction that Joan was closing in. Nothing but smoke moved in the dim light. Sayer's hands and feet burned with pins and needles. Was this blood loss or was the smoke already taking effect? Sayer tried to clear her head. The first side effects of DMT were paranoia and tingling extremities.

Sayer took a calming breath and turned back to Adi. The corner of the cage had shifted slightly downward, groaning under the girl's weight.

Sayer moved over to the second bolt. Her hands felt swollen and sluggish. Thin rivulets of blood ran down her arm and dripped onto the bar. Sayer fumbled, her fingers slippery with blood against the cold metal. She let out another grunt, this one of frustration.

Adi put her hand over Sayer's. "I can do this. You go stop her."

Sayer was about to protest, but she looked up into Adi's eyes. Despite all she'd been through, Adi looked determined, strong.

Sayer huffed in agreement and passed the bar back to the girl. She needed to stop this before they were all too far gone.

"There are traps on the floor, be careful," Adi whispered, and set to work on the second bolt.

Wasting no time, Sayer stumbled toward Tino. She looked for a way to free him, but he was cuffed to a solid network of pipes.

He gestured for her to leave him and go after Joan. She didn't dare lean over to talk to him, so she simply nodded with understanding.

Smoke grew thicker as she neared the sound of the machines. Sayer came around the corner of the boxes to see Joan on an antique four-poster bed surrounded by medical equipment. The DMT machine churned out smoke near her head. Spots of blood rose from the dog bite on her arm.

The beeping of the heart rate monitor slightly increased as Joan clearly began to hallucinate. She shook her head back and forth on the bed.

Sayer took a shaky breath in and scanned the small clearing around the bed. Traps, Adi had warned her.

Through the increasingly thick smoke she could just make out a network of clear wire in a crisscross pattern inches above the floor. She followed one to a small metal box. Directional explosives of some kind?

Sayer scanned the floor directly in front of her and saw nothing. She took a stuttering step into the clearing, moving slowly across the open space, trying to hold her breath. The smoke tickled her skin, tendrils wrapping themselves around her ankles and wrists, around her neck, and sliding into her nose and mouth. The hallucinogen slowly took effect.

Another step and a wire appeared in front of her leg. Sayer tried to gingerly step over it but her balance wobbled. She fell forward, managing to barely miss the wire. A wave of nausea swept up from her stomach and she doubled forward.

Intensity of light, visual trails, moderate confusion, a buzzing sound, nausea, auditory hallucinations . . .

Sayer reviewed the symptoms of DMT exposure in her head. She stood and moved forward again even more slowly, terrified of missing a trip wire.

The beeping of the heart monitor slowly expanded around her until its pulsing replaced the air. The bare bulb hanging above Joan throbbed with the heartbeat, burning Sayer's eyes. She struggled to breathe, convinced the oxygen was gone. The only way to breathe was to match the rhythmic heartbeat: in, out, in, out. Her shoulder began to throb in unison with the sound. Her entire left arm hung useless. Blood seeped faster, pushing out as she could feel her own heart beat like a drum against her ribs. A hallucination or was she finally bleeding out?

Intense realistic hallucinations, heart palpitations . . .

Sayer listed the next stage of DMT exposure.

She cautiously moved forward but the room shifted, tangles of shadows writhing like a nest of snakes. Still she took step after step, willing herself to put one foot down in front of the other. Her legs shook, threatened to collapse again, but Sayer drove forward like a juggernaut focused only on reaching Joan.

Something caught against the front of her shin. A snake?

Sayer instinctively dove forward just as the small explosive went off behind her. Metal shards slammed into the backs of her legs. They seared her flesh, flaying open a thousand tiny cuts through her thick pants. Still stumbling forward, she crashed into the smoke machine.

The burning cuts on her legs felt distant. Like someone else's pain.

Bodily disassociation, increasing visual disturbance until complete visual collapse, unconsciousness . . .

Some small part of her brain screamed to turn off the smoke machine. Her fingers sought something, anything to make it stop. They closed around a cord and she pulled. The whirring sound ceased.

Gulping for fresh air, Sayer pulled herself up next to Joan's bed. Vision swirling, hands shaking, she tried to understand what she was seeing. An IV line ran into each of Joan's arms, and both IV lines had a timer. One counted down from five minutes. The other counted down twenty-nine, twenty-eight . . . Trigger timers for the IVs. The first IV bag said DIGOXIN; the other said ATROPINE. Sayer's brain screamed that she had to hurry. That the first IV was about to trigger, but she couldn't seem to figure out what to do next. How to turn it off.

A metallic crack echoed like thunder across the room. Adi breaking the bottom from the cage?

The sound of metal slamming onto concrete thrust Sayer into the car accident when she was nine.

She turned her head side to side; a twisted car appeared smoking around her. Her sister, Macey, reached for her. Sayer tried to grab the toddler's hand, but their hands passed through each other. Macey's pleading joined the thumping heartbeat. *Sayer, please. Sayer, please.*

Sayer turned toward the front of the car, where her parents' bodies were trapped among the wreckage. Fragments of blood, a blur of white bone, singed flesh.

A sob escaped her lips as she frantically tried to get to them.

"Mommy! Daddy!" she cried out.

Her father turned his head slowly. He opened his mouth and the sound of hell emerged. The deep groaning pulsed with the heartbeat that animated Sayer's entire body. She began to scream.

But then Jake appeared and held out his hand. His eyes calmed her.

"Jake?" Sayer could make no sound. He took her hand and Sayer felt warmth. He helped her stand.

"Do your job." He brushed her lips with his thumb, then turned and walked away.

Sayer turned back to the car accident but found Joan in the bed.

The digoxin timer on five . . . four . . . three . . . With a cry, Sayer yanked all the wires and tubes from Joan's body. The heart monitor stopped. The silence was like a scream of relief.

As the air cleared, so did Sayer's head. She wiped away a small trickle of blood running down her front and let her head tilt forward against the old mattress. She needed to secure Joan but would rest for just a moment. Just shut her eyes. Both of her legs gave way and she fell to her knees. Sayer's gun slipped from her hand onto the bed.

She felt Joan begin to stir, her body shifting in the old bed.

Sayer lifted her head as Joan's eyes rolled open. She had to secure Joan, but she couldn't force her muscles to move.

"No, no, no, no," Joan moaned. "You have to let me finish."

"You're not getting a damn thing you want," Sayer whispered.

In response, Joan slowly pushed herself up like a leviathan awakening, back arched, head bowed, hands curved into claws against the bed. "Nooooo!" Joan stood to her full height, lifting her arms above her head with a howl of animal rage.

Savage eyes on Sayer, Joan reached out and grasped Sayer's shirt. She pulled Sayer up with inhuman strength.

Sayer desperately reached for her gun, but Joan jerked her body forward. With her other hand, Joan punched Sayer in the cheek.

Sayer's head snapped back.

The detonation of pain broke Sayer's inertia. With her own roar, she flung her right arm up, breaking Joan's grip.

The effort made Sayer lurch backward and she fell. Joan saw Sayer's gun tumble to the floor and she dove, hands curling around the black metal.

She looked down at Sayer.

A blur of motion slammed into Joan, toppling her off the bed.

Adi and Joan crashed to the floor, gun skittering away.

The two women grappled, Adi clawing wildly at Joan.

Joan punched Adi in the gut so hard the girl doubled over. Joan rolled on top of her, straddled her chest, and wrapped her fingers around the girl's throat.

Adi gurgled for breath as Joan squeezed so hard her knuckles turned white.

The world pitched and rolled as Sayer struggled upright. Her entire horizon began to collapse, but she flung herself onto Joan. A final burst of rage fueled the punch she landed on the side of Joan's head. Joan lost her grip on Adi.

Using the last of her strength, Sayer rounded for a second punch, landing squarely on Joan's jaw.

The woman's body flew backward and crumpled against the wall. Sayer crawled over to her. With trembling hands, she pushed Joan's arms around a thick pipe and pulled cuffs onto her wrists.

With Joan finally secure, Sayer slumped forward, her consciousness flickering.

Joan muttered through her swollen jaw, "Just let me die. Let me go and end this, please. All my research . . ."

Sayer watched as Adi pushed herself off the floor and approached Joan. Towering over her captor, Adi cocked her head. Sayer realized too late what she was about to do.

"No, Adi!"

Adi cried, "For Gwen and Leila!" She raised the metal bar above her head to strike Joan.

Sayer tried to reach for Adi's wrist but couldn't move, only croak, "Justice isn't the same as vengeance."

"What?" Adi turned her wild eyes on Sayer.

"You asked me about the difference between justice and vengeance." Sayer gasped for breath. "Vengeance is just your own pain. Killing Joan will mar your heart forever with that pain."

Sayer held up a shaking hand toward Adi. "Would Gwen and Leila want that? Let justice be done, for all three of you."

The girl stood for a long moment, panting, eyes darting back and forth between Sayer and Joan.

With a sob, Adi's face collapsed. She dropped the bar.

Sayer reached for Adi's hand and their fingers folded together as she faded into unconsciousness.

Sayer woke in the hospital. She vaguely remembered the door bursting open, Vik there with gun drawn, SWAT teams pulling Joan away, helping Adi into the ambulance, Adi refusing to let go of Sayer's hand.

Vik realized Sayer was awake and hurried over.

"Hey there." He smiled his lopsided grin. "How come you get to have all the fun?"

Sayer laughed, her entire body protesting. Her shoulder ached but the sharp pain was gone.

She turned her head to see Adi in the bed next to hers.

"She okay?" Sayer whispered.

"You don't need to whisper, she's knocked out right now while they finish up their tests. Good news is doc says she should make a full recovery with the wonders of modern medicine. Doc says you'll probably have a spotty memory for a few days and some seriously awesome scars, but the shot went right through your shoulder. Your legs . . . well, they'll probably never be bikini ready again. . . ."

Sayer snorted.

"Otherwise, you'll be fit as a fiddle in no time," Vik said.

"Tino?"

Vik chuckled. "I'm guessing you didn't know about Tino's job before he became a chef?"

Sayer shook her head and immediately regretted it.

"Army interrogator."

Sayer's mouth fell open and she grunted a laugh. "Well, that explains why he was so calm. He's okay?"

Vik nodded. "Seems totally fine."

Then she asked the question she was most afraid to ask.

"Is Vesper . . . ?"

"He's gonna be okay." Vik pulled up a chair and plopped down. "He's got some seriously bruised ribs and they had to amputate a leg, but he'll be fine. He took a chunk outta her arm before he went down. Pretty sure that dog's gotten more praise in the past ten hours than I've gotten my entire career." He waggled his eyebrows.

Sayer sat back with relief.

"You feeling okay?" Vik made full eye contact, not letting Sayer get away with anything.

"Yeah. I think so." Sayer closed her eyes. "I still can't believe what Joan did. Man, Vik, you should've seen her. It was like she was possessed, a totally different person. Guess it'll take me a while to wrap my mind around what just happened. Plus, let me tell you, do not do a ton of DMT."

Vik let loose a full belly laugh. "I know! Hey, I've got something for you."

He pulled a string of worry beads from his pocket.

Sayer took them, tears welling.

"Eh, I keep seeing you reach in your pocket. It's driving me crazy." He paused. "I ordered 'em all the way from Greece. They aren't from your dad, but I figured—"

"Thank you," Sayer whispered as she rolled them through her fingers. The sensation soothed her tense shoulders. She could feel her entire body relaxing as she fidgeted with the beads.

"So . . ." Sayer looked away for a moment. "We missed it."

"I know," Vik said much more softly.

"After she finished her little experiment, she was going to kill Adi and Tino."

"Yeah."

Sayer shuddered slightly. "What I can't understand is, how did she sustain her act for so long?"

"Remember how we were talking about your research and I told you that you're forgetting something?"

"I can barely remember my name right now," she joked.

"I said you forgot that evil exists. There's just pure evil out there, and Joan was it. We're digging into her past. Remember that kid she said got murdered in the neighborhood where she grew up?"

"Vaguely," Sayer said. "Some girl killed at her school."

"Well, we tracked down the case. Girl got her head bashed in behind the elementary school. Teenage boy went to jail for it after a witness placed him at the scene."

"Oh my God."

"You guessed it. Little Joan Warren in the flesh. She even testified against the kid in court. The prosecutor said she was so convincing, the kid got tried as an adult, life in prison."

"Holy shit!" Sayer leaned back, slightly overwhelmed.

"I know! Holt's got an agent digging back into the case right now. Digging into everywhere Joan lived. She'll be rotting in a cell for the rest of her days."

"Whose house was that? Where Joan . . ."

"Some old lady. They found her body upstairs. Looks like Joan killed her over a year ago, kept paying the bills and e-mailing the old lady's family so no one noticed."

Sayer groaned.

"Thought you'd want to know that Winters is already out. Probably going to sue us to kingdom come." Vik shrugged. "So, you up for visitors? You've got a menagerie out there waiting to see you."

"I do?"

Vik laughed at her surprise.

"Sayer, the people out there love you. Maybe it's time you start noticing how much."

He left Sayer to contemplate what he'd said. Maybe it was time to remember that she was still alive.

A few minutes later the door opened.

Jackson flew into the room and leaped onto the hospital bed. Macey ran in behind him. "Jackson, get down!"

"No, he's good." Sayer wrapped her good arm around him. "Am I glad to see you!"

"Me too, Aunt Sayer! Did you catch another bad guy?"

Sayer laughed. "I sure did."

Macey came and squeezed her hand, looking like she was about to cry. "Don't ever do something like that to me again. I need my big sister, okay?"

Sayer's mouth opened but she wasn't sure what to say.

Nana hobbled through the door on crutches, a full smile on her face.

"Oh, Sayer, thank God you're okay."

"Nana, what the hell happened?"

The spry woman glanced down at her ankle in a cast with annoyance. "Well, I decided I wanted to try skydiving before I die—"

"Nana!" Sayer let out another laugh.

Tino backed into the room rolling a bassinet behind him.

In the clear plastic hospital bassinet, Vesper lay on his side, head up, tongue out, tail thumping with excitement.

"Vesper!" Sayer reached out her hand as Tino pushed the dog next to her.

"This beast, I swear. Your dog misses you." He winked. "He's still recovering from surgery, but the vet said he would recover faster with his family. I had to pay your nurse a handsome bribe to bring him in with me."

After making sure Vesper was comfortable, Tino gave Sayer a kiss on the cheek and eyed the thick bandages on her shoulder. "You going to be all right, calida?"

"I will. I hear that you neglected to tell me about your time with the army. I thought you seemed a little too mellow during that whole thing."

Tino shrugged. "Eh, that was a long time ago. I knew you would find us."

Something about his confidence in her brought tears to her eyes. To avoid crying, she turned to Vesper. A long row of staples sealed the gruesome scar along his chest where his leg once was. She rubbed his silky ears and he pressed his head into her hand.

Nana saw Sayer's emotional shift. "Can you handle all of us here right now?"

Sayer nodded. "I might need to rest, but it's nice having you all here. Please don't go."

Jackson bounced around the room, exclaiming how cool all the hospital machines were. Nana sat on the edge of the bed asking Macey how things were at home. Tino and Vik chatted about a new restaurant opening up in downtown D.C. Adi slept peacefully, her child's face at rest. Sayer decided in that moment she would ask Mrs. Calavera about taking Adi in. She had an extra bedroom and the girl was almost eighteen. Adi needed a safe place to be with someone who truly understood what she'd gone through. Adi, Vesper, and Sayer could all recover together.

Smiling at the idea, her hand buried in Vesper's warm fur, Sayer leaned back and let the murmur of her loved ones' voices rumble in her chest as she drifted off to sleep.

Sayer woke in the dark hospital room. A figure sat in a chair against the wall.

Seeing Sayer stir, Assistant Director Holt stood up and straightened her cobalt-blue pantsuit.

"Came to check on you," she said gruffly.

She stepped into the faint light of Sayer's bed.

"Glad to see you're going to be fine."

"Thanks," Sayer said.

"I've put in the paperwork to get Dugald Tarlington, Tom Middleton, and Jack Kent released. Thought you'd want to know."

Sayer nodded thanks.

"I might not be assistant director much longer as the level of clusterfuck I presided over becomes clear to the public."

"Wasn't your fault. We all missed it."

Holt took a deep breath. "You know that doesn't matter one bit. I'm a goner, so before I go, I wanted to give you this."

She pulled a file from her briefcase and handed it to Sayer.

On the tab it said JAKE PENDLETON.

Holt snapped her briefcase shut and squeezed Sayer's hand.

"You didn't get it from me. Now, get some rest."

As the clacking of Holt's shoes echoed away down the hall, Sayer opened the file and began to read.

Acknowledgments

I'm not even sure how to thank everyone involved in making *Caged* happen.

I'll start at the beginning and thank my parents, Bob and Judy, for being endlessly supportive of all my harebrained ideas, including moving to the jungles of Belize, getting a Ph.D., and writing a book. Thanks also to my sister, Shelley, for her support and encouragement.

This book wouldn't exist without my son, Grayson, who is an endless source of joy in my life, and my husband, Sean, the best beta reader a person could possibly have.

A million thanks to my amazing agent, Amy Tannenbaum, and to my editor extraordinaire, Leslie Gelbman. Amy and Leslie are the kind of publishing team every author dreams of working with! Also, many thanks to everyone at St. Martin's for all their hard work.

Special thanks to Megan Coen; our brainstorming lunches helped me work through some of the most sticky problems and confounding twists in *Caged*.

Thanks also to Tiffany Nelson, everyone at Codex, and the entire Curbside Crew (especially Theresa and Judy), who read earlier versions of *Caged* and encouraged me while I was writing.

Finally, thanks to Richard Leventhal, my graduate school advisor, who hasn't disowned me despite the fact that I left academia.

If you'd like to learn more about the science behind *Caged*, visit ellisoncooper.com and join in the conversation!